Joan O'Neill's Novels

'Take three generations of women given to impulse-mating ... colourfully entertaining.' Terry Prone, *Irish Independent*

'Great dialogue and terrific set pieces, all the hallmarks of Joan O'Neill's writing.' Julie Parsons, *Sunday Irish Independent*

'O'Neill has a strong sense of place and wonderful descriptive powers – so lively that one can almost smell the rashers sizzling or feel the heat of the lush Wicklow meadows.' Maureen Cairnduff, *Irish Independent*

'A dramatic plot, very believable human characters. Their emotions and reactions are so true, irrepressible and natural.' Katie Donovan

'Joan O'Neill takes the most ordinary, everyday, trivial details of life and by ordering them in a certain way elevates them to the level of art. This is life as we know it.' Robert Dunbar, *The Gay Byrne Show*

'A compelling sense of storytelling.' *Woman's Way*

D1350627

By the same author in Hodder and Stoughton paperbacks

Leaving Home
Turn of the Tide
A House Full of Women
Something Borrowed, Something Blue

for children
Daisy Chain War
Bread and Sugar

About the author

Joan O'Neill began her writing career in 1987 with short stories and serials. Her first novel, *Daisy Chain War*, published in 1990, won the Reading Association of Ireland Special Merit Award and was short-listed for the Bisto Award. She lives in County Wicklow with her family.

Perfectly Impossible

JOAN O'NEILL

CORONET BOOKS
Hodder & Stoughton

First published in Great Britain in 2002 by Hodder and Stoughton
First published in this edition in paperback in Great Britain in 2003 by
Hodder and Stoughton
A division of Hodder Headline
A Coronet paperback

1 3 5 7 9 10 8 6 4 2

A CIP catalogue record for this title is available from the British Library

ISBN 0 340 81843 3

Typeset in Plantin Light by Palimpsest Book Production Limited,
Polmont, Stirlingshire
Printed and bound in Great Britain by
Mackays of Chatham plc, Chatham, Kent

Hodder and Stoughton
A division of Hodder Headline
338 Euston Road
London NW1 3BH

To my family

ACKNOWLEDGEMENTS

Thanks to my editor Carolyn Caughey for her belief and encouragement throughout, and to Julie Crisp and all at Hodder and Stoughton for their hard work on my behalf.

Thanks to Jonathan Lloyd, Tara Wynn, Carole Jackson, and all at Curtis Brown.

Thanks to John, Gerard, Jonathan, and Robert, for their endurance, to Elizabeth and Laura for their comments and inspirational ideas – and to all my family, and the O'Neill family for their support.

Thanks to Justin MacCarthy for his detailed legal advice.

Thanks to Elaine Jerrard for sharing her knowledge of the world of Estate Agents so generously with me.

Thanks to Carmel Crawford for her insightful information on Letting Agenting.

Thanks to Christine Barnes for giving me the idea for the heroine's career in the first place!

Thanks to my writing group for their patient and honest advice at the first-draft stage for which I am deeply grateful: Sheila Barrett, Julie Parsons, Alison Dye, Phil MacCarthy, Cecilia McGovern, Renata Ahrens-Kramer.

Thanks to Norma Dagg for her helpful information last time.

Thanks to my loyal readers who drive me on.

I

Suddenly, into the silence screeched the train, racing over the bridge, its noise shattering the peace, its metal gleaming in the glare of the river that ran along beside it. Out poured business men and women in dark suits onto the platform, all hurrying towards the ticket barrier and the waiting cars, where partners sat impatiently with fraught children, their minds on dinners and homework. That's what life should be like for me, Cara Thompson thought. It seemed so little to want, yet so difficult to achieve it.

Here was her husband Andy, now, jumping onto the narrow platform, his hair gold in the sun, his brown eyes deep and troubled. Cara caught her breath as she watched him stop and look up and down the station, uncertainly before coming to greet her, his downcast appearance like a warning. The meeting with Mr Morgan, his boss, about his promotion obviously hadn't gone well.

'Hello,' she said, cheerfully, going to meet him.

'Have you been waiting long?' he asked sulkily.

'Hours,' Cara said, giving him a kiss on the cheek.

'God, how you exaggerate. The train is only ten minutes late.'

'It felt like hours.'

The whistle blew, startling in the air, the stationmaster's voice staccato as he announced the train's departure.

'Come on, let's get out of here.' He steered her towards the car, still a little nervy, his face pale under his sallow skin,

Cara beside him a tall, slender woman with long black hair, delicate features and a graceful walk.

As soon as they were alone in the car Cara, bursting with curiosity, asked, 'How did your meeting go?'

'Later,' was all Andy would say.

They drove towards home, past the railway cottages, and the Imperial Hotel, whose dull façade seemed to suggest customers sipping drinks in dark corners. Andy, lost in his own little world, made no effort to talk. A man in a vest was trimming his privet hedge while his wife held a conversation with her neighbour. Further along an old woman sat on a chair outside her door while two men leaned against the wall chatting. A boy kicked a ball against the wall of the village pub. Cara didn't try to force a conversation out of him. Instead, keeping her voice light, she described the happy afternoon she'd had dividing her time enthusiastically between pruning and weeding. He listened edgily.

Turning away from the town, they swept under the brick arch, and took the country road where wide fields sloped up towards the hills, the blossoms on blackthorn bushes hanging like wreathes. Primroses clustered in the ditches. The summer was on its way.

Over the shoulder of the hill the sky stretched out, a great yawning space, the sea below it encircling the valley in darkness. This landmark was Cara's favourite view. It marked the descent for home. She knew every field, who owned each of them, and which piece of land was next to be sold for building. She knew the names of the farm houses that lay dotted among the patchwork of fields, out of the way farms that had been auctioned by Bradley and Thompson, her father's firm of estate agents, where she was a junior partner. There was the farm that they'd auctioned the previous week for just over a million pounds, no sign of life anywhere, except for cows moving deep in the grass.

Their own house at the end of a lane was a solid, edge-of-the-country, Victorian cottage. It had been a wedding present from Cara's father which Andy had expected as part of the wedding ritual. A tangle of honeysuckle edged its way prettily round the windows. Its front garden was already blooming with forsythia and plum-coloured lilac.

'I tied up the rose bushes too,' Cara said brightly, parking outside it.

'So I see,' Andy said, scuffing the gravel as he went to open the door.

His only concession to gardening was mowing the lawn on Saturdays at a fast pace so he could spend the afternoon watching sport. Cara followed him inside.

'I'm going to take a shower,' he said. Pushing past her, he went straight upstairs. She heard him moving around as she set the table, and the rumble of water through the pipes. Back downstairs, casual now in sweat shirt and jeans, still tight-lipped, he poured himself a glass of red wine, drank it quickly and was back refilling his glass without saying a word.

'So, what did Mr Morgan say?' Cara's hopes of a reply diminished as Andy stood over the stereo, a CD in his hand. As the voice of Phil Collins flooded the room Cara clapped her hands over her ears in protest, hoping he'd turn it down – which he had no intention of doing.

'Do we have to talk over this row?'

'It's not a row,' he protested, flopping down on the sofa, making himself comfortable and unfolding his newspaper, a screen against her.

With a heavy sigh she went into the kitchen to check the oven.

Returning with his favourite lamb casserole she asked, 'Do you think you could bestir yourself and come to the table or would you like me to serve you there?'

'I'd hate you to put yourself out,' he said, throwing down his newspaper and coming to join her at the table.

'Andy, what's up?' Cara was beginning to wonder if he was ever going to tell her.

'I've lost my job.' His voice was full of anxiety.

'What!' Shocked, she looked at him.

'You heard me. I'm not going to repeat what I just said.' He was waiting for her to speak and, judging by the way he was looking at her, anticipating words that he would much rather not to have to listen to. 'Well, aren't you going to say anything?' He prompted with a look that said the sooner she spoke the better.

So, another of Andy's precarious jobs had come to a sudden end, just as Cara thought that he was doing well at last, getting somewhere in the corporate world. Her first reaction was to make light of the matter. 'Don't be upset. It's not worth worrying about.'

'That's a weird thing to say.'

'What I mean is that we can manage for the moment. My salary can support both of us until you find something else.'

'So my job is of no importance? The money I earn isn't worth bothering about?'

Cara flushed. 'No, no. That's not what I meant,' she denied hastily, breaking off, searching for the right words, realising how tactfully she must put things, knowing that she wasn't skilled enough to stem his rising anger.

'I suppose compared to the precious inflated salary you get from your father, it isn't.'

Cara found herself counting to ten.

'That's not what I meant, and you know it.' She took a deep breath. 'Listen, darling, what I meant was that we'll manage until you get something else. And you will. There are plenty of other jobs out there.'

'That's not the point. I was just beginning to find my feet, get stuck in.' He stopped, cast around desperately.

Cara looked at him quickly, wondering what to say next, pausing to think what his world felt like at that moment. In age, he was almost two years older than her, but in outlook, much younger.

After supper he sat on the sofa in the sitting room, tense and silent, a glass of red wine beside him, another Phil Collins CD playing at full blast. Cara tidied up automatically, then sat down shakily at the kitchen table with a cup of tea, her eyes shut tight, trying to think of what to say next to him.

As the evening went on the tension mounted, Andy with an impenetrable look in his eyes, Cara knowing that she must be careful to the point of seeming indifferent or she would be accused of patronising. No matter what she said her words would only spark off a blazing row.

Shades of doom loomed in the look on his face as he said, 'I need a drink. I'm going to the pub.'

'I'll come with you.'

'There's no need. I won't stay there long.'

She persisted, knowing that sooner or later they'd have to talk and a few drinks might loosen him up.

The Crowing Cock was packed. Andy propelled Cara into the dim nook where two of his friends were gathered with their respective partners, women she met occasionally at parties or at occasional functions at Andy's golf club. Cara smiled and tried to seem interested as they talked about golf and argued about politics, wondering how she could have been so foolish to think that they would be left alone. When the conversation turned to asylum-seekers, a new political hot potato, Andy, with a couple of drinks in him took a strong line on the matter. Emptying his glass, he gave his views with confidence, denouncing the government for its inability to deal with them.

This caused an argument with Bob, a solicitor, who muddled him with laws and quotations.

The argument took a turn for the worse with Andy complaining about overpaid corporate bosses who sat on their fat arses all day behind huge desks doing nothing more strenuous than scratching themselves and firing people. Ken Little, a bank manager, retaliated, accusing Andy of exaggeration.

Suddenly Andy slammed his drink down and said, 'I should know. I've just been fired by one of them.'

Everyone felt awkward in the silence that followed. Ken broke it by saying how sorry he was. Andy brightened, saying that he wasn't beaten yet, that he'd plans for setting up in business on his own.

'Oh, yea!' Bob said.

Cara caught him wink at Ken in an understanding way and wished they could withdraw from the conversation and the pub. Andy was getting quite drunk.

On the way home she said furiously, 'Who does Bob think he is, turning on you like that? He's supposed to be your friend. With friends like that who needs enemies!'

Andy stayed silent.

'How you put up with them I don't know. I find them hard going.'

That remark only served to fuel Andy's indignation. 'It was you who wanted to come to the pub with me. You didn't have to.'

'I didn't know they were going to be there.'

'Well, they were and you made no effort with the conversation. You looked bored to death.'

'You were all talking at once. I couldn't get a word in edgeways.'

'Oh, forget it. God, you're difficult.'

Cara leaned back and closed her eyes, letting him rant on

alone, fearing she would explode and say something from which his self-respect wouldn't recover.

She was tired and not looking forward to having to tell her father this latest news, dreading the thought of what he'd have to say on the matter. She'd avoid telling him by postponing her visit to Rockmount for as long as possible.

Andy's drinking bouts usually ended in aggressiveness followed by self-reproach, and attempts at reconciliation next morning. This time was different. Next morning he didn't say a word. Returning from the bathroom, she caught him unawares, gazing by the window in the process of getting dressed, a scared look on his handsome preoccupied face. Did she imagine it; or was his body less defined and was his thick hair receding?

He was changing into a different person, she reflected, and she didn't know if she could cope with him. If only he could get out of this wretched bad patch, she was sure they both could look forward to a better future.

Home from work a few days later, Cara dumped her briefcase in the hall and made straight for the kitchen where she got a beer out of the fridge. She drank it from the bottle, letting the cold liquid slide down her throat, then headed for the bathroom, peeling her clothes off as she went. She stayed in the shower for ages, thinking of the rows with Andy.

She was the sole breadwinner again; Andy seemed pleased to let her get on with it. Released from the anguish of the daily grind, he continued to let her run the household while he lounged around the house, his domain during the day. Each morning she got ready for work in a few minutes, downing a cup of coffee, tiptoeing around the house, so as not to wake him from his hungover sleep. Often she got home late, sometimes shopping on the way. When she did finally get home Andy would usually be stretched out on the couch, playing his stereo or watching television; evasive, unprepared to hold a discussion of any kind with her, newspapers, dirty coffee mugs and overflowing ashtrays scattered everywhere. She tried to be patient, cooked him tasty meals, did everything possible to keep things smooth, reasoning that after all it wasn't his fault he'd lost his job. Nothing worked. He was always in bad form. It seemed to be one thing after another. Still, she was tough enough to cope, she told herself. Walking back to the bedroom she saw Vanessa's Mercedes coupé was parked outside, wealth in every line of it.

In the sitting room Andy and Vanessa were having a drink, Andy sprawled on the sofa in his old ripped denim jeans and vest, Vanessa sitting opposite him.

'Great to see you.' Cara gave her friend a hug. 'How was Morocco?' she asked, standing back to admire Vanessa's tan.

'Terrific.'

'Did Edward go?'

'No, he had to cancel at the last minute, so I went on my own. It was great.'

Andy said, 'I've invited Vanessa to stay for supper. What are we having?'

'I'll get something in a few minutes.'

'Andy, get off your fat arse, and get Cara a drink. She looks as if she could do with one,' Vanessa said to him.

Vanessa had always talked to him like that, in a kind of play-acting way, the faintest touch of flirting in her teasing tone. Her toughness suited him. It sharpened his interest in her, and gave him a licence to say what he felt like to her. This freedom between them cemented their odd relationship. It suited Cara too. She valued Vanessa's friendship and she admired her. Vanessa had balls and style. Cara considered her appearance. There was an air of authority and precision in her manner. Her black designer suit was well cut and subdued, without a hint of jewellery, just her tanned cleavage through her white shirt. Vanessa carried herself with distinction, from her black hair drawn back into a severe knot to her Marco Moreo shoes.

Behind Vanessa's mask of dignity was a tough woman, with a cruel streak that gave her a brutal edge, especially in the way she treated men. She would spar with them, using her spark of cruelty to get them into bed, kick them down afterwards. She knew no different. Tears and tantrums or grief of any kind were alien to her. During their college years Cara and Vanessa had often shared adventures of one kind or another, often going off with other girls on daring expeditions that left them little energy for their studies. The bank and nights spent working as a barmaid when she should have been sleeping financed Vanessa's education.

Andy slunk out.

'Andy's just told me the bad news,' Vanessa said.

'Isn't it awful,' Cara said, collapsing into the nearest chair. 'Did you know it was coming?'

'I hadn't a clue. It was a complete shock. Andy seemed to be getting on well. He thought he was up for promotion. The irony of it.' A shudder of sorrow for their predicament ran up her spine.

'He's taken it badly this time,' Vanessa said.

'Don't I know,' Cara muttered. 'When I said not to panic, that my job could tide us over until he found something that really suited him, he hit the roof, accusing me of having no regard for his contribution to the household.'

'He's down. He'll bounce back. He always does.'

Cara was unconvinced, thinking of the now penniless Andy and how much he hated living from hand to mouth and how he'd felt he'd been on the brink of making something of himself this time. She wished she had Vanessa's confidence. Vanessa never seemed to worry about the future and never felt she had to prove anything.

'It's you I'm concerned about. You have a lot to cope with,' Vanessa said, casting a critical eye over Cara.

'I'm all right,' Cara said bravely.

'Your Da'll help you out, won't he?'

Cara shook her head. 'Keeping Pamela in the style and elegance she's become accustomed to is draining him. You can't imagine how he has let himself go with his cash since he married her. She's spending for Ireland.'

'Preposterous bitch,' Vanessa exclaimed. 'In a way he deserves it. I just think it's criminal that you should have to be so worried about everything.'

Cara stood up. 'I'll survive. I'm making spaghetti bolognaise for dinner. Stay if you like.' She didn't really want to be on her own with Andy.

'Why not. Well, no actually. I'd better get home. I've got things to do.'

'Oh, come on. Stay.'

'No, you two have things to sort out. And tomorrow I'm in the Four Courts early.'

'Lucky you.' The self-sacrifice in Andy's voice was pathetic as he returned with Cara's drink. 'Here,' he said solicitously, handing Cara her drink, 'have the last decent glass of wine in the house. I won't be buying that brand any more.' His voice was filled with pain at the thought of the economies the loss of his job would inflict on him.

The contrast in their lives couldn't be more different, Vanessa's job exactly what Andy would like for himself. Anger flared in Cara at his self-pity. Preparing supper was the opportunity she took to retrieve herself, leaving Vanessa to try and jolly him along.

2

Rockmount was an early Victorian house in Sandymount. Its dark flint walls were brightened by wisteria, the rest of the garden was in shadow. The sound of the piano came clearly across the lawn, someone striking the last chord, hanging on to it for dear life before slamming down the piano lid. Upstairs, the curtains were drawn across her father and stepmother's bedroom window. Cara turned her key in the lock with a sudden impulse of dread at having to make excuses for Andy's absence. She knew that there was no hope of getting Andy to go with her to Rockmount, no matter how much persuasion she used. Pride would prevent him. She couldn't help reflecting on the hazards of having married a man her father overshadowed and undermined. When they were newly married Andy had been more amenable, had tried to appear not to take any notice, and he'd seemed to be doing all right. But lately time spent at Rockmount seemed to encroach on his precious isolation.

John Bradley and his long-time friend Jack Ray were crossing the hall.

'Cara!' said Jack, coming towards her, smiling, taking her hand in his heavy ringed one, his breath reeking of tobacco and whiskey.

'Jolly nice to see you. Do you know you're growing prettier with each passing day?' he said.

'Thank you,' said Cara, bowing her head a little.

Her father, an immense man, his adventurous spirit shining

out of his blue twinkling eyes, kissed her cheek, his blue-grey moustache scratchy against her soft skin.

'Where's that husband of yours?'

'He couldn't make it, sorry,' she said.

'Hmm. Something going on between you two?'

Sometimes Cara found it difficult to take his enquiries, several meanings to be interpreted in their concern.

Turning a bright smile on him to hide her irritation, sick of being treated as if she were still a child, she said, 'I hope I'm not late,' too polite to tell him that it felt better when Andy kept away from him.

'You look blooming,' Jack said, bridging the gulf yawning between father and daughter with surprising tact, his eyes narrowing on her face as he patted her arm in a fatherly way.

Cara looked at him quickly, thinking what a good sport he was.

'Probably because I'm eating like a horse,' she said.

'Speaking of horses, will you be joining us for the hunt on Saturday, John? What a cracking trail we've planned.' His roar of laughter crinkled his rugged face with the prospect of a good day's hunting.

'Love to,' said John who'd been planning on spending a happy day off in his greenhouse growing rare specimens of plants.

They all moved into the drawing room. Maura, Jack's wife was already ensconced there, sitting at the closed piano, her head inclined, listening to their conversation. She was wearing her best blue frock; the diamond brooch pinned on her maternal bosom especially for this occasion, which she considered to be of some importance.

'Cara!' She pressed her lips against Cara's cheek, and stood back to take in Cara's appearance. 'How are you?' She was looking at her as if she were trying to remember what the world was like when she was young.

'I'm fine, thanks. How are you?' Cara asked.

'Oh, the usual aches and pains, nothing to worry about.'

'Where's Pamela?' Jack asked John.

'She'll be down shortly. Not feeling very well.'

'I hope she hasn't been overdoing things,' Jack said.

'Nothing more strenuous than a bit of shopping, I'm sure,' Cara replied.

'Cara!' Jack said, disappointed that Cara never showed any tenderness towards her stepmother.

Lowering her voice so that only Cara could hear, Maura said disapprovingly, 'Your stepmother is always late.'

'Drink? John asked Maura.

'Just a drop,' she said. 'I don't touch the stuff as a rule. Not too much,' she protested as John poured. 'I might get tipsy and ruin the evening.'

Out on the terrace Jack was looking at the view, his eyes on Howth in the distance, the setting sun striking the lighthouse.

John said to Cara, 'What's up with Andy this time?'

'He's upset. He lost his job,' she blurted out.

John said, 'He's not suited to software. I did warn you.'

'Perhaps not.' Cara backed away.

Rich aromas emanated from the kitchen as Cara went down the stairs to the basement. Elsie, Cara's aunt, was neat in a white apron, her movements quick and efficient. Her grey thinning hair was caught up in a neat bun, a touch of rouge coloured her cheeks. She was a wonderful cook of the traditional method and had a tremendous amount of energy for the enormous size of her.

Cara loved the kitchen. It had always been somewhere to drop into at any time when she needed to air her anxieties about school, or even her father, or to tell some gossip to Elsie. As a child she'd followed Elsie around while she did her chores. She'd learned how to cook, listening to stories of cruelty and eviction while Elsie stirred mouth-watering sauces and jams, or rolled out the finest delicate pastry, presided over the making of cowslip wine or blackberry jam, or taught Cara the value of herbs and spices.

Elsie was a great amateur of medicine too. When Cara showed any sign of sickness, unless it was serious, she did the doctoring. She didn't hold with prescription drugs but relied on her remedies, her miraculous medal, her scapulars and holy water, her safeguard against all known ills. She had remedies and potions and pills in every disguise: Friars' Balsam, Zambuk for cuts, horehound and honey for sore throats, bread poultices for boils and swellings, quinine for colds, syrup of squills and senna tea for constipation, Epsom salts, beef tea and calf's foot jelly for pains in the bones.

'There you are, and how are things in Wicklow?' Elsie asked, as if she were enquiring after an acquaintance.

'Quiet,' said Cara, noncommittally. 'What's for dinner?' she said with a sense of anticipation, realising she was hungry, lifting the lid off the bubbling saucepans to check their contents.

'Stuffed loin of pork and all the trimmings.'

'Jack and Maura are here,' she said, inspecting the oven.

Elsie, vigorously whipping cream, said, 'I know. I heard the car. I didn't know until this morning that they were coming. I just wish Pamela had informed me sooner.'

Cara knew what it was like in the kitchen nowadays. Sometimes Pamela invited people home to dinner without warning and poor Elsie had to stretch the food like elastic.

'Be an angel and decorate the dessert,' she said, pointing to the tub of glazed cherries.

'Oh, but you do like Jack,' Cara said, popping a cherry into her mouth, licking her fingers.

'A proper gentleman,' said Elsie, prodding the potatoes with a fork. 'Always asks after my health. Not like some I could mention,' she added, throwing her eyes ceilingwards. 'Couldn't care less if I dropped down dead at their feet.'

'Dad says she's not well.'

'Cooling her heels after the barney they had when she got back from her shopping spree I shouldn't wonder,' said Elsie knowingly.

Cara sighed. 'Nothing unusual about that.'

'I'll take something up on a tray if she doesn't appear.' Elsie went to the oven to baste the roast.

Cara loved Elsie, who'd come to live at Rockmount after her mother's death when her father had done everything to console her and his cumulative efforts had failed. Cara couldn't articulate her loss or talk about her loneliness, but she knew there was no cure for it now that her mother was buried in the graveyard. The very thought was abhorrent to her, but she couldn't talk about it. More certainly, she couldn't accept it.

Wandering around the empty house and the gloomy garden, she felt miserable, enclosed in darkness. Her father took her to Gino's Fast Food Corner, an indulgence for him, because he hated the 'ruinous' fast food they served. While he sipped his coffee she ate her sausage and chips. Cara, observing him up close for the first time since her mother's death saw the change in him. He smiled at the waitress while he ordered, teased Cara about the grease that went into making her meal but, though he did his best, his heart wasn't in it either. His natural exuberance had deserted him, his eyes were dead in his head, and his winter coat seemed to weigh him down like a burden that was too heavy for his lighter frame. Confused, he felt inadequate, incapable of amusing or entertaining her, and was apologetic because of it.

When he couldn't provide a remedy for her depression he found a way round it. After a consultation with his sister Elsie, who lived in England and who'd been recently widowed, he wisely took the practical action of inviting her to live with them. It could have ended in disaster. Instead, it ended Cara's loneliness and made her happy again.

Cara never forgot the day Elsie arrived with all her luggage. Bright and jaunty in a bright red suit, her hat tilted to one side of her grey-blonde hair; there was an excitement in her.

'What a darling you are,' Elsie had said, brushing her unruly curls out of her eyes, taking her by the hand and walking with her into the house. Light followed the darkness that had all but eaten her up. Cara began to recover, thanks to her observant and loving aunt who did everything to cajole her out of her misery. Although Cara couldn't pour out her troubled heart, nor make any mention of her mother, she felt close to Elsie. Elsie's care and devotion brought joy to her lonely days. She would take her on nature walks, teaching her about trees and shrubs. Often she took her away to a great world of adventure, through forests and mountains in the stories she read of the escapades of Fionn, and his companions Oisín, Diarmuid, Caoilte, Conan Maol and all their hounds.

The cumulative effects of Elsie's efforts paid off. Cara accepted the change of direction in the household, even Elsie's occasional assaults on her personal hygiene. She realised that her chastising and simple house rules were for her own good and safety. Cara was happy through her childhood, the years flying by, and the bond so strong between them that nothing could break it.

John was happy too with the changes. He was making money, buying houses cheaply, doing them up to show them to their best advantage before selling them for a profit. Time passed. Thanks to his sister, his tragedy was eased. Comfort was back in his life and that was important to him.

John and Elsie had a good relationship, their mutual dependence being the main one. While she kept house for him with great style, never bothering him with domestic trivia, he met all the household expenses without question, his love of good living dictating their lifestyle.

John was exuberantly generous with Cara. The extravagant purchase of a Volkswagen cabriolet when she got a place in college, and which she drove too fast, dismayed Elsie. His absurd generosity was his way of compensating for the loss of her mother in some practical way. Elsie felt he should be investing money for Cara rather than lavishing it on her. Distressed as she was about it, and worried as to whether Cara would ever get to her destination and home in the dangerous vehicle without a disaster, she kept her mouth securely shut.

Cara grew into a beautiful woman with lots of friends. Suzanne, her other close friend, lived in a big house nearby. Because her father, a stockbroker, was often away from home, her mother was indulgent to Suzanne's whims. Her closest friend was Vanessa, whom she met in the college debating society.

Vanessa was the eldest child of a ne'er-do-well docker and a sweet-natured quiet mother who eked out her wages working in a local bar to help educate her eldest daughter. A scholarship law student, her manner was tough, insolent even, sometimes. Deep down she was as soft as butter. Vanessa's kind heart she got from her mother. Her devotion to Cara had a quality of gentleness that she didn't reveal to many people. Even though they were the same age, Vanessa treated Cara like a younger sister to her to be shielded from the big bad world. She got pleasure out of watching over her, the sad circumstances of her own family never quelling her zest for life. Cara was the link between the three friends. They danced at discos, shared their experiences with boys and even shared their dates sometimes.

When Andy was introduced to the family Elsie was the only one who accepted him. She liked his laughing ways and proper manners. She enjoyed his company and respected his importance in Cara's life. It was Elsie who swept John's doubts about Andy aside and encouraged him to fork out for the cottage for them. It was Elsie's delight at Cara's pregnancy and her generosity in her readiness to help out that gave Cara back her rapture when Andy was unwilling to accept it. It was Elsie Cara had gone to when she lost her baby.

The events of Cara's sad years reared their shadowy presence only occasionally, when something uncomfortable happened to her. Pamela Beaumont, a social columnist for a trendy magazine in Jersey, began coming to Rockmount the year before Cara got married. Occasionally she stayed overnight, then weekends, but always in the spare bedroom that her father had redecorated. The following spring he had the whole house repainted and redecorated to Pamela's taste.

They started entertaining, small informal dinner parties with close friends. Then Pamela's friends from abroad began to appear, a trickle, then a flood of them, taking up all the space, partying, carousing. Pamela got into the habit of snapping orders at Elsie and bossing her around, causing rows with the angry Elsie. Elsie ranted about Pamela's lack of decency and self-respect, her sleeping under the same roof as a man she wasn't married to for everyone to see. According to Elsie Pamela should have stayed in the background, not flaunt herself. 'Nothing but an overdressed tart,' she was fond of saying.

The marriage of John Bradley to Pamela Beaumont was a decidedly uncomfortable event. It had involved Cara in all sorts of difficulties and compromises. Now Pamela accompanied John wherever he went. The quiet, dignified life of the family changed dramatically. Pamela had a frivolous quality that unsettled the household routine and shattered the peace. The happy times Cara had enjoyed with her father were over for good. Their precious times together, staying in grand hotels, dining at the best restaurants, visiting famous buildings, museums, her father explaining the unfamiliar food, strange customs of an area, were just a memory.

While John was enjoying this injection of life his new wife had brought to his home, Cara clearly wasn't happy. What irked her most was the fact that Pamela dominated the household. She did what she wanted to do, pleasing herself, consulting no one, not caring what anyone thought.

Elsie, suspicious of the new wife she felt her brother had 'bought with his money and position', also resented the changes. 'One swallow never made a summer,' she declared.

'I'd better run upstairs, let Pamela know I'm here,' Cara said, escaping.

She found Pamela, wrapped in a bathrobe, sitting at her dressing-table, the breeze from the open window ruffling her blonde hair that hung loose around her shoulders, making her look younger than her forty-five years.

'Oh, there you are, darling,' she greeted her. 'I'm afraid you'll have to hold the fort until I come down.'

'OK!' Cara said, perfectly aware that her conversational skills weren't enough to enthral Jack the way Pamela's did.

'I feel a bit off. It's this unusual weather, hot one minute, cold the next,' she said in her actressy voice, sniffing slightly. 'I'm taking care of myself.'

Pamela did little else except take care of herself, Cara thought unkindly, taking a good look at her, wondering what her secret weapon with men was because she was not pretty. Her eyes were too close together, and she had a habit of looking down her long nose. Yet she had the reputation of being a beauty when she appeared out of the blue and snapped up John Bradley. A lot of women of his acquaintance were jealous it was said. Could it have been her life long experience with men that had made her so irresistible to him?

'Do remind Elsie to chill the wine,' Pamela said, leaning towards the mirror, doing up her hair with painstaking slowness.

'Right,' said Cara, glad to go from this room Pamela shared with her father. It was no place for her.

In the dining room John sat carving, his back to the wall, Maura beside him, very upright in her chair, her hands clasped in her lap, Jack on his left, Elsie next to him.

Eventually, Pamela, bare-shouldered in a black dress, glided into the room.

'Lovely to see you,' Jack said, going to her, kissing her.

She stretched out her hands to him. 'I'm sorry I wasn't here to welcome you. I wasn't feeling very well,' she said, languishing towards him, her neat, flaxen head bowed, her perfect complexion intact, despite her day's shopping with her friends.

'You look wonderful, as always,' said Jack. 'Doesn't she, John?'

Bracing himself, John said, 'Perfect,' turning his attention to his wife, hoping she had nothing worse than a chill.

During the meal the talk turned to parties and gatherings and the scores of invitations Pamela felt they should attend but would have to turn down. Entertaining did not come as naturally to John as it did to her and he was pleased.

'I'm thinking of whisking her off on a Caribbean cruise to cheer her up. You can hold the fort now that Andy's free to look after your office, can't you, darling?'

'Yes, of course,' Cara said warming to the idea.

'So how are the folks?' Andy asked when Cara got home.

'Pamela's not so well. Dad's thinking of taking her on a Caribbean cruise. He wants me to look after his office.'

'That's a bit of a tall order. The way the traffic is at the moment it'll take you all day to get there.'

'He suggested I stay at Rockmount and I thought, well, why not?'

Andy turned from the window, an interested look in his eyes.

'So, you want me to manage on my own?' he said, following her.

'Why not? It'll give us a break from each other. Just what we need.'

'You know I can't boil an egg.'

For Andy to cook was a debasement of his status, the household duties Cara's domain and an outlet for her boundless energy.

'You could try learning.'

'Oh, don't worry about me,' he said sarcastically, not at all pleased.

The knot in her stomach was causing pain. 'Dad needs my support.'

'Next you'll be carrying him around on your shoulders.'

'I'm dedicated to my work and, despite of what you think, I've worked hard to earn my living.'

Andy looked at her, the pupils of his eyes almost black in the dim light. 'You're spoiled by your own success. And I'm sick of it. Sick to death of the way you talk about your work. It's a job that's all. I mean, a way to earn a living.' Suppressing his anger he turned away to end the conversation.

The contempt in his voice angered her. 'Are you objecting to my work?'

'No. I just can't stand the way you think about it, and your father. It's as if that's your whole life and nothing else in the world matters. It should be a way of putting food on the table, paying the mortgage, that's all. Your commitment should be to me.'

'You're saying I should devote myself entirely to you, be an extension of you. Well, I tried that. Tried to have a family, and failed.' Tears were in her eyes. 'So I buried myself in work, and I hate to be told there's no merit in it. Especially at a time like this when we need my job so badly.' She could have bitten off her tongue.

'All I'm saying is that you shouldn't be so wrapped up in your father. Who's going to look after your office while you're away?'

'Daddy thought you'd do it, seeing as you're . . .' Her voice trailed away.

'You told him I lost my job.'

Warily she looked at him, afraid of his anger.

'How dare you discuss me with your father when I'm not there. I'm perfectly capable of making my own decisions. I don't need him to make them for me.'

'You're thirty-three years old, squandering your brains away in the pub. You haven't got a clue what you want to do.'

'I just need a lucky break, that's all,' he argued.

'In a funny sort of way it's what we both need,' Cara retorted.

'Funny? Am I missing the joke here?'

'Can't you understand? How do you think we can possibly go on with this sort of bickering? The magic's gone out of our relationship. There's no intimacy, no warmth, no conversation, for God's sake.' Cara was in pain now.

'It wasn't always like that.' He threw her a look of disgust.

'I know.' She was remembering the years of carelessness and lack of forethought with regret. Glorious, happy days, her care of him giving her a secret warmth, the delicious meals she provided for him, and the way she starved herself so she could fit into her clothes, going to expensive hairdressers to have her hair expertly cut in the latest style. She had been happy to be at his beck and call; she was up early for work, coming home late, just in time to make supper. Often she slept in front of the television until Andy shook her awake, telling her it was time for bed. That was the way she loved him.

'So running off is the answer, is it?'

Hurt by this rebuke she sprang back. 'I'm not running off. Just taking a time out.'

'Go on then, go,' he shouted at her.

That night she packed her bag. Her hands were shaking. At least she wouldn't have to cook his meals, and she could stop being solicitous to him. At the moment she didn't want to be anywhere in the vicinity of him.

3

———◆◆———

Cara arrived early at Bradley and Thompson Limited in Merrion Row on Monday morning. The big airy open-plan office on the ground floor was a hive of activity, young men and women with preoccupied faces huddled over computers, attached to telephones. This was thanks to the booming economy Ireland was enjoying. At the reception desk, behind the exotic flowers and brochures illustrating the impressive houses on the Bradley and Thompson list, was Isabella, the dazzling Spanish receptionist. Tall, with lustrous hair and twinkling eyes, she was oohing and awing with her luscious lips at a man at the entrance, who was obviously having difficulty understanding her.

'So, what are you trying to say?' he said, staring at her with alarm.

'We are not heer,' she said.

'What do you mean you're not here? Aren't you standing in front of me, for Christ sake?'

'We are not heer yet,' she repeated slowly, trying to gloss it over as best she could.

'I think she means we're not open yet,' Cara said.

'Seems to me anyone can get a job in this bloody country these days. You don't even have to be able to speak English,' the frustrated man said, staring at Isabella insultingly.

She averted her eyes, murmuring and gesturing incoherently.

'Who did you want to see?' Cara enquired.

'George Flatley.'

'He won't be long,' Cara said calmly.

At that moment George Flatley, the tall balding accountant, entered, looking frazzled before the day had even begun. He shook hands, gestured to the lift.

'Impossible to get staff,' he said, shunting the man before him down the corridor to his office.

John Bradley's glass-fronted office took up a huge corner at the end of the corridor. A stickler for punctuality, her father was there, large as life behind his huge desk, waiting for her. His eyes lit up when he saw her.

'Cara, good to have you here,' he said, rising courteously and smiling down at her, looking gratified. 'Come, sit down. It's only right that you should have my desk while I brief you about what's going on in the office.'

He told her about his plans: the new markets he was exploring, the foreign competition he was bent on beating off with new technology he planned to have implemented by the end of the year.

'George is hoping to be made a director of the board at the Annual General Meeting.' John looked doubtful.

'Why not? He's trustworthy, dedicated to the business.'

'The trouble with him is that he lacks vision. But he's certainly someone you can trust when I retire.'

'Dad!' Cara said, shocked. 'You're not thinking of retiring?'

John laughed. 'I'm sixty-four, remember.'

It was hard to believe, Cara thought, as her eyes slid over the elegant moustachioed confident man who stood before her, full of austere assertiveness, back ramrod straight, shoulders powerful, his appearance immaculate in his pin-striped suit. Here, surrounded by everything that symbolised his success, she found it impossible to imagine this place without his commanding presence.

'You're my only child. I'll want you to take over at some stage.'

'Take over!' Cara repeated, the oppressive weight of running the family business too much to think about.

John Bradley's expression relaxed into a grin. 'Don't worry, it's not going to happen just yet, but when the day comes I want you to be able to stand on your own two feet so there's no harm setting the wheels in motion. After all, it's what I've been grooming you for. You have all the appropriate skills.' He was taking the easier, circuitous route to make his point, smiling to ease the fear that must have showed in her face.

Swallowing back her panic, she said, 'Well, maybe some day, but you're too active a man to even think about it yet.'

Her career had taken off from the start. Under her father's tutelage she developed a keen sense of property. John Bradley, one of the most successful estate agents in the country, had an unfailing eye for seeing potential in the most obscure property, especially if it could be bought reasonably and sold when renovated and redecorated. Together with Cara he would spend long days scouring the countryside for possible purchases.

The mention of a derelict house that was for sale was enough to send them off for a closer look. If he saw something worthwhile he would deem it worthy of further investigation by Joe Murphy, his builder, and send him to spy out its potential. Discussing their discovery together with the excitement of children discovering a new toy was half the fun to John and Cara.

Cara had worked hard, made sacrifices that neither she nor Andy had ever envisaged, often working all weekend. Her reward had been a gift of her own office in Arklow, a branch of Bradley and Thompson which she was building up into a very good business.

When he'd finished taking her through the business of the day John checked the calendar on his desk.

'It's now the tenth of April. We'll be back May twenty sixth, in time for the start of the building on the Quays apartment block.'

'Good.'

'By the way, how did Andy take to being left on his own?'

'Not well, but he'll cope.'

'Won't do him any harm.'

Though John totally disapproved of Andy he knew the lad was brainy and thought that it was time that the lazy shiftless arrogant sod got off his backside and made something of himself. He'd done nothing but give Cara grief from the day they'd got married. Still, John supposed 'things' would settle down between Andy and her again. They usually did. Meantime, he hated seeing her unhappy, and knew that she was making the best of a bad situation. Although he had anxiety about this present plight, with Andy out of work yet again, he understood the need to keep out of things. You made your bed; you lay on it that was his motto. He just hoped that the right job for Andy would present itself soon, for Cara's sake, because nothing less would suit him. Meantime, he'd sent Mark Downes, his most promising young estate agent, to run the Arklow office while Cara was in head office.

'I hope you both have a wonderful time,' Cara said as he got up to leave.

'We intend to,' John said, full of beans, his face wreathed in smiles. He looked like a child going to a party, waving to everyone as he left.

Alone, Cara sat down at his big desk and looked around, the responsibility of having to run his office on her own hitting her. It was a challenge and she liked challenges. She checked her father's diary. He was an organised man, had a regulated day with timetables to keep him in check, so he could have the weekends off to be with Pamela. Cara was the opposite. She didn't mind if she had to show people houses at weekends, especially if there was no one else available. She'd rather do it than lose a possible sale. She took phone calls, pencilled in relevant appointments,

Through the glass partition she could see Debbie, the newest recruit, straight from college, clueless, but ready to take the world by storm in her own lights. The long-suffering Mrs Moody in her statutory navy blue suit, John's personal assistant, was instructing her, digging her acrylic nails into the agitated girl.

George, in his plate-glass compartment, was absorbed in a sheet of figures, his head bent over his desk, the lines of his skull through his thinning hair, his calculator beside him. Cara turned back to her desk. She had plenty to do. There was a report to be written for a meeting with the city planners during the week, figures from George to accompany it, the staff to supervise, all crises to be averted until her father's return.

Within an hour what she'd written looked acceptable to her. When she'd finished it she sat staring at her wedding photograph on her father's desk, her laughing up at Andy, Andy laughing too, so handsome, his hair flopping forward, his eyes proud as he looked at her. That was five years ago, when they were madly in love. It was Suzanne who'd introduced them, telling Cara that Andy was a great person. She was twenty-two at the time, and trying to pretend that the raucous discos with the girls were still the fun they had always been. From fleeting romances she'd rapidly recovered, thinking herself lucky to have a resilient heart, never suffering grief and anxiety like her friends did.

Until she met Andy.

She hadn't seen him until the night of the end of term ball. He was the sexiest student there, with blond hair and moody chocolate brown eyes and an unattainable attitude. The most gorgeous man there, she'd fallen helplessly and hopelessly in love with him. Determined to have him, she deliberately plucked him from the arms of a tall dark girl and flirted madly with him.

'So, you're an only child. Spoilt rotten by a doting Daddy,' he'd said leading her to her open topped car parked in the college car park.

She didn't deny that her father's life revolved around her.

'Believe me, it's a burden,' she said, feeling herself blush as he shot her a look of sympathy.

'I am sorry,' Andy had said in a mock-serious tone, kissing her slowly.

Desperate with desire, she broke all her own rules, and lost her virginity to him on their second date. From then on they'd spent every minute of their free time together, drinking lager and lime on the terrace, giving parties when her father was away on business and having sex at every opportunity. Andy failed his degree and, broke, moved back home to his mother while he studied for the repeats in the autumn.

When he did finally qualify he asked her to marry him. She was ecstatic. When he said the words 'love, honour and cherish 'til death do us part,' her happiness was complete.

As soon as he qualified he got a job in telesales for a large computer company. It was a start. They got married, her father protesting that she was too young, Cara insisting that Andy was the only man for her, her love for him her great pride. She was a rock to build his strength on. She was good for him, calming him when he became too emotional and keeping him balanced.

Andy was promoted to sales representative in his company and was given a brand new Toyota Corolla. Three months later, just as he was beginning to make his mark, he lost the job. Cara had no idea why. This was the pattern that followed in the next two jobs. It was always the same, always when he was settling in, getting somewhere, and Cara could never fathom why it kept happening.

Where was that young man she'd married, leaning over bars telling jokes, laughing with his friends, their extraordinary affection bordering on near-worship of him? Everything had been a joke to him then. He had laughed at every solemn ritual, had even laughed through the imprisoning wedding vows. Now, full of resentment and bitter jealousy, he was the reverse of those things, with flash tempers and mercurial moods, jumping up and flouncing off as soon as supper was over, at other times grilling her about her day, demanding to know the details of some innocuous function she'd attended.

Cara was sorry for him, but not enough to rush back home and into his arms. Work was too enjoyable. It was the only place where she didn't have to concentrate on Andy and his needs and problems. She gave it her personal best and it gave her time to herself. She'd ring him during the day. She'd ask him what he was up to, jolly him along. Not at the moment, of course, she was far too busy, and she didn't really want to speak to him.

Printing out a copy, she took it into George's office. George, the knot of his tie loosened, his face shiny with perspiration, said, 'You'd want to get cracking if you're to be on time for Murphy,' a hint of criticism in his voice.

'I'm off right now.'

'See you in the morning.' Here she was scurrying out of the building, clutching her briefcase, a thrilling escape.

By the end of the week Cara's only desire was to crawl home, and calm down in front of the telly. George had been hassled and bad-tempered, going on and on to the point of boredom about the troubled planning permission for the new apartment block on the Quays that John Bradley was hoping to start building soon.

Over a sandwich at lunchtime she'd had to coax Debbie

out of the doldrums, listening to her complaints about Adam, her boyfriend, who refused to go on holiday with her. Isabella had ended the week in floods of tears, managing to explain eventually to Cara that she was stuck with the impossible 'Eeenglish' language, Cara trying to steer her in the right direction by assuring her that she'd help her all she could, getting her to trust her.

Driving in the heavy traffic each evening, she dreaded the quiet nights ahead, watching telly, assuring Elsie that she was all right. All Elsie's concentration went into the care of her, so determined was she to keep her there as long as possible. Cara was thinking of Pamela and her father somewhere in the Caribbean, preoccupied with one another while the office was in turmoil.

She phoned Vanessa most nights to discuss the stressful challenges of working in the city. They would arrange to meet for lunch but more often than not Vanessa got held up in court, or with clients and had to cancel.

Cara began to establish a pattern to her day. She went to work early and took her lunch break at midday, often going for a walk through the city, observing new shops and restaurants, sometime browsing in Stephen's Green shopping centre.

Dublin city had changed into a throbbing mass of traffic; the streets crowded, long queues for buses and taxis everywhere since Cara last worked in it. Grafton Street had a festival atmosphere. Buskers sang and played guitars alongside accordionists, accompanying the shoppers. An orchestra struck an unmusical note outside Bewley's, the violin screeching above the heads of New Age travellers and beggars squatting in doorways, jugglers juggling their coloured balls to its rhythm. Ethnic minorities in vivid flowing colours sold copies of *The Big Issue* at traffic lights to commuters in fogged up cars. The smell of coffee and fast food was mixed with the tar and dirt in the air. Cara hated it all.

She missed the quiet of the countryside. She missed her home.

Most afternoons she headed for the new estates at the city margin or out into the open countryside to windy fields marked out for development by rutted tracks. Andy phoned her several times to find out how she was. On each occasion she purposely kept the conversation light-hearted, pretending that she was too busy to have time to think. A sense of failure swept over her at the thought of their lives apart.

The truth was that she missed him. She thought of him during the day and last thing at night, thought of the baby they should be having by now. She'd built up her life with him, good times and bad, and now it was crumbling before her very eyes with one humiliation after another. Living with him had become a nightmare. He felt that it was all her fault and she blamed him. She wondered if things were ever going to be right between them.

The idea of spending the rest of her life alone was her great fear, but the thought of starting the whole process all over again was a living nightmare.

4

Vanessa, full of beans, phoned Cara to arrange a night out together. They used to love going out on the town for relaxation, all three of them, before Cara and Suzanne were married, cruising around the city bars, all night at their disposal, lying on in bed late on Sunday morning in Vanessa's, followed by a leisurely brunch, no one to dictate to them. Now that Cara was temporarily 'free', Vanessa thought they'd do the same.

In The Clarence they bumped into Edward Cockrell, Vanessa's on/off boyfriend, that Vanessa was trying to avoid these days.

'Vanessa!'

'Edward! What are you doing here?'

'Hoping to find you.'

'Something wrong?' Vanessa asked, glancing at her watch.

'You haven't returned any of my calls.'

'I've been busy,' Vanessa said, lamely.

'Dinner?' he persisted.

'OK.'

'When?'

'Soon.'

'Promise.'

Vanessa nodded.

'I'll phone you.'

Vanessa would have agreed to anything to get rid of him.

'He's very keen on you,' Cara said, taking up the menu.

Vanessa sighed. 'Edward's all right, in his own way, but he's not interested in a casual relationship. He had to go and spoil the good time we were having by suggesting marriage.'

Cara looked at his retreating back. Edward, a barrister, was a tall, dark and confidant.

'Would that be such a bad thing?'

Vanessa shrugged. 'Terrible. Being married to a man with an ego the size of Ireland would be embarrassing if you're any way intelligent at all. I want to still be me when I wake up every morning. But no, he's hell bent on getting engaged. One minute we were sailing along happily together, the next he was bullying me into marriage, for God's sake! The lengths some men will go to get their hands on a woman. It was a shock, I can tell you.'

'I'm sure it was. What did you say?'

'I was speechless with horror at the idea. Then, when I recovered, I more or less told him to feck off, that I'd got other plans. It took a lot out of me.'

Cara smiled and sat back. 'What must it have taken out of Edward to be turned down flat?'

'He didn't appreciate it, I can tell you. He thinks I'm behaving childishly. He should have known better.

'He got overconfident. You can't be single these days without some predatory male asking for your hand in marriage, thinking they're doing you a favour into the bargain.'

Cara giggled.

'Life's only beginning to get good for me. I got myself through college on a shoestring, and the last thing I want to do is bugger it up with commitments. I've got a job and a life that I like, with all the fringe benefits, and Edward wants to rob me of it all. He won't be happy until he turns me into a doormat, with loads of screaming brats, while he's off pontificating in some court or other, leaving me endless lists.'

'You could do worse. He's well connected, parents who are practically Irish nobility.'

Vanessa turned up her nose.

'Pretentious snobs.'

'He has money and good prospects.'

Vanessa gave her a filthy look. Cara swallowed a quick pang of regret. 'Next you'll have me making announcements and wedding lists.'

'So,' Cara said, straightening herself up, 'did you tell him you didn't love him enough?'

'Love doesn't come into the equation. I want to be single, free, and Edward's desperate to whisk me up the aisle and start a family.'

'Because he's in love with you.'

'Because he wants to settle down with someone who looks good on his arm, is intellectually challenging, who can help him get to the top of the ladder, while at the same time taking care of his kids, and I fit the bill. As for me, I want to have some fun. Is that selfish?'

'No, not at all. When Andy proposed to me I never thought it through. Marriage was a foregone conclusion. It seemed to be the right thing to do at the time.'

'We all make mistakes.'

'Nessa!'

'Sorry. I wasn't thinking. I'm just so anti-marriage at the moment.'

'We have our ups and downs, I'll grant you, but we'll work things out. Will you be seeing Edward again?'

'Oh, I suppose we'll sort it out. He won't stick it out for long. He'll throw in the towel in a week or two, bounce back optimistic as ever.'

'What'll he do next to woo you?' Cara wondered.

'Who cares. I don't want to belong to anyone until I've worked out where I belong for myself. After a hectic day I need to be quiet, on my own, at home, hiding from the rest of the world. It's my place, with my own things. Nothing bad can happen to me there. I've been a long time on my own in a job I love, making plenty of money that I've no intention of sharing with anyone. I'm not ready for that kind of commitment. Maybe I never will be.'

'You're supposed to want marriage and babies and all that goes with it. Most of our friends from college are hitched.'

'Ugh!' Vanessa pulled a face.

'If you don't hurry up you'll be past it.'

Angrily, Vanessa bit down hard on a roll. 'Do I look worried?'

Strong, articulate and argumentative, she battled for her clients day in day out. Passionately believing in justice for all, she ran a free legal advice clinic where she fought like a tiger for people who were being unjustly treated and couldn't afford to do anything about it. Vanessa loved the law. The law was what she knew and understood. She had always wanted to be a solicitor. Forty per cent of Vanessa's work was in family law and she worked extremely hard. Honest and courageous, she believed in the truth, and would fight to the death for her clients. Her apartment in the Merrion complex had cost her a fortune, but it was worth it. There she could prostrate herself in front of the television with a curry from Bindi's on the corner, and take a long soak in the bath with a fashion magazine before going to bed.

'By the way, Suzanne's home from Scotland. Isn't it great?' Vanessa said.

'Already!'

'She phoned to say she'd arrived and that she's up to her eyes settling into the new house with the baby and everything.'

'Lucky her,' Cara said enviously.

'She phoned your office too, left a message there.'

'I'm looking forward to us all being together again soon. We'll have a laugh.'

The following week Cara went to visit Suzanne. Her friend's house was set in a quiet cul-de-sac of new houses at the back of the tree-lined square where her original home was. Cara looked with interest at the big houses, a tone of prosperity about them; nothing changed since they were children.

Suzanne appeared at the door almost as soon as Cara rang the bell. Slim and beautifully tanned in shorts and a T-shirt, her long hair slashed into the latest style bob, she looked like a young girl. Her years away from home had done her good.

'Oh, my God, it's really you,' she cried.

They hugged each other. Suzanne drew back to gaze at Cara as if she might disappear again as quick as she came.

'It's so lovely to see you. I missed you so much,' Suzanne said. 'I heard from Vanessa about you and Andy,' she added, surprised at her friend's waif-like appearance. 'How are you feeling?' She held Cara at arm's length.

'Terrible.'

'I'm so sorry. Come on in,' she said, leading her down a corridor to the kitchen.

Through the French door Cara saw the pram, and tiny brown arms moving in the sunshine. She felt an ache in her gut. 'How is the baby?' she asked, swallowing to stop the tremor in her voice.

'Oh, just a baby. Sleeps, eats, shits like any other baby.'

Cara knew that Suzanne was being purposely dismissive so as not to make her feel bad.

'Come and see for yourself. I think she's awake.'

Suzanne went down the garden, Cara following, her eyes on the tiny garments on the washing line above the bushes, an unwillingness to see this baby she'd heard so much about. A beautiful baby with wisps of corn-coloured hair and clear blue eyes smiled up at Suzanne, arched her back, and stretched her arms towards her.

'There you are, Lucy darling.' Suzanne lifted her out of the pram. 'This is Cara, my oldest friend.'

Tentatively Cara extended her finger. The baby latched onto it and tried to stuff it into her mouth.

'You are nice,' Cara said, not knowing what else to say.

'Here, take her.' Suzanne held Lucy out like a parcel.

Cara felt a chill of fear. To have to try and get used to the idea of Suzanne as a mother was one thing, but to have to hold and admire this baby was really difficult. The baby took one look at her, crumpled her face and began to cry, flailing her arms towards her mother.

'There, now,' Suzanne said, taking her back, Lucy's sobs subsiding as she said, 'She's teething, poor lamb,' leading the way back indoors.

In the kitchen Suzanne sat down and settled her position to give Lucy more comfort, her face drawn down gently towards her, her body sheltering her, not permitting anything to disturb her feeding. Placidity in her demeanour, Suzanne looked as if motherhood had overtaken her completely. Cara's eyes blurred at the tableau before her. A dreadful loneliness overcame her, as she stood there almost forgotten. She felt so alienated from Suzanne, as she cradled Lucy, sad that she couldn't even offer to take the baby to give Suzanne a break when she'd finished feeding her. Awkwardness and a feeling of jealousy prevented her. She'd have to do it sooner or later she realised, but not now. Going to the sink she filled the kettle, striking this busy attitude to protect herself, knowing that it was all wrong and that she couldn't keep herself closed to her emotions.

Lucy brought to life the idea of her own baby, and the memories of that awful Sunday three months into her pregnancy when the pain had struck, twisting into her stomach like a knife, forcing her to take a deep breath, pause and wait. A cry came involuntarily with the next stab of pain, more of a scream that tore from her, convulsing her whole body, bringing Andy tearing into the room to enquire what was the matter. 'I think I'm losing the baby,' she'd gasped. When the pain had struck again he'd carried her up to bed and phoned the doctor. She'd lain there, waiting, shaking, blinded by tears, alienated from her real self, her thought only on her baby, a feeling of dread weighing down on her pain.

By the time the doctor had arrived she'd lost it. Sometime later Vanessa had called to see her. She'd taken over, making her tea, full of proprietorial concern, denying Andy the right to fuss over her. All Cara could think of at the time was that she'd let her baby down by failing to hold on to it, and there was nothing anyone could do to help her. The doctor had assured her that she'd have more babies, but her resistance was low, her will to carry on shaky. The days merged into one another. She was tired all the time, so she rested. A shadow of her former self her father, concerned at the change in her, had insisted she return home to be nursed by Elsie.

She tried to stay calm, and womanly, show restraint and not cry all the time, but she failed. Her heartbreak lasted a long time; her crying held Andy at a distance. It was obvious that he too was upset, yet at the time Cara couldn't help thinking that something within him was breaking free from her, something else that they might have shared. She denied to herself that it was her marriage, convinced that their love for one another, which would inevitably last until death, would see them through every crisis like a safety net.

In hindsight Cara realised that her marriage had begun to break down at that time. It was nothing to do with outside influences. Her frightening alienation from Andy had been the greatest hazard. Her lost baby, the only important thing in her life at the time, caused lasting damage.

Suzanne, seeing her expression, said, 'You'll have children of your own one day, Cara.'

Cara flinched. 'Children! I wouldn't mind if I could have just one, before it's too late,' she added, falling into an uncomfortable silence.

'God knows how many I'll have,' said Suzanne carelessly. 'Dick thinks there's nothing to it. It's all right for him, he doesn't have to walk around swollen to monolithic proportions for the best part of nine months, sick as a dog, permanently exhausted and incontinent.'

Cara's eyes filled with tears. 'It's what I dream of.'

Suzanne laughed to lighten the atmosphere. 'I know, and I suppose I'm making light of it but, believe me, it's worth it,' she said. 'Lucy's not much of a nuisance as long as she's fed. Are you, my darling?' She kissed the top of Lucy's downy head and put her back in her pram.

'Now we can have a cup of tea and a chance to catch up,' Suzanne said, Tell me, how's Andy?'

'He's finding life difficult. He can't wait for me to get back home but just now I feel that I can't cope with him. I seem to do nothing but bolster him up.'

'Losing one's job can put a strain on any relationship. Perhaps it's no harm to let him go his own way for a while.'

Cara nodded. 'I was glad of the chance to get away from him for a while.'

They sipped their tea in the shade of the apple tree while the baby slept, Suzanne recounting the birth of Lucy, the move home. Cara, her hands locked in her lap, told of the tiffs with Andy, usually about his future, not amounting to much at first, but threatening greater rows with each downward spiral his career had taken. She threaded the strands of her life with him; lifting fold after fold of the web of gaffes he'd made, and described briefly their changed circumstances since the loss of his job.

'Andy feels that he doesn't even have to contribute to our lives now. I think that he's very depressed.'

'What makes you think that?'

'Nothing specific. Isolated incidents. For the first time he isn't bothering to look for work. He just sits at home doing nothing, condescending to do the shopping occasionally. The days go by. He doesn't even bother to read the newspaper anymore. No one calls to the house except an occasional friend to take him to the pub.' This last sentence was declared vehemently.

'How awful.'

'He can't think of anyone else's misfortunes, just his own situation, and his particular feelings. He phones me to try and patch things up, but we only end up shouting at each other.'

Cara leaned back in her deck chair, her eyes closed to stop the tears.

'Tell him to stop phoning. If you spend your time apart fighting on the phone then it's no good. You have to give yourselves a proper break from each other. Don't take his calls. Get out and socialise more. That'll keep your mind off things. I've got a babysitter organised so we can get out a bit, have a good gossip and giggle like old times. We'll go anywhere you want as long as it's not too far or too late.'

'But that's my problem. I haven't got much interest in anything outside of work. It's my whole life just now.' Cara's lip trembled.

'Well, you'll just have to find yourself something to do after work,' said Suzanne, the eternal optimist. 'We'll go to the pub. That'll be a start. I can't drink while I'm feeding Lucy, but you can get rat-assed. By the way, we're having a housewarming party on Saturday. You'll come, won't you? It'll give you a chance to catch up with old friends and gossip, and meet our neighbours.'

'I really don't think I'm up to a party at the moment.'

'Don't be such a misery guts. This is me, Suzanne, you're talking to. I know you. You're just making excuses, and they're not acceptable.'

A tear dropped on Cara's hand. Suddenly, she bawled, noisily. Suzanne took her in her arms, cradling her, saying 'There, there', the way she'd said it to Lucy, realising that Cara, who wouldn't harm a fly, had been through the mill. Who would have thought that the well spoken trendy Andy, with his easy-going attitude, his good manners, his expensive taste in everything, would have transformed into this immature selfish loser that Cara had described, who treated her so carelessly.

'You just have no confidence at the moment. It'll do you good to get out a bit. It'll be like old times, all three of us together again,' she murmured consolingly.

5

<hr />

When it came to the evening of the party Cara wasn't looking forward to dressing up. Rummaging through her wardrobe she picked out a black Prada dress, a birthday present from Andy. A critical eye over her slim reflection in the mirror made her heart leap into her throat at memories of the last time she wore it, Andy, telling her she looked ravishing, pulling her towards the bed . . . No, she couldn't wear it. What about the red Karen Millen slip of a dress she'd treated herself to after a blazing row with him over something stupid, which she couldn't recall? No, it was too short. Her black leather trousers with her new black halter-neck top, and plenty of jewellery. Too tarty. Back to the safe black dress. She turned her attention to her make-up, lavish with the mascara and lip-gloss, wondering what she was doing putting herself through this unnecessary torture.

Lights blazed in the windows of Suzanne's house. The sound of loud music and the babble of voices floated towards her through the open front door. Taking her courage by the scruff of the neck she marched up the steps. Suzanne came to greet her in a long cool summer dress with slits up the sides and matching beads.

'Hi, Cara! You look lovely. I'm so glad you made it,' she said. 'I've got some interesting people for you to meet.'

Cara followed her down the hallway into the noisy drawing room. 'This is Cara Thompson everyone.'

There was lots of hand-shaking and lots of smiling, lots of unfamiliar faces. A glass of champagne was put into her hand while she stood amid the chattering rowdy group, mostly neighbours who all knew one other. Cara wished she could turn and run. She gulped down her drink and helped herself to another one from the nearby table in the mood to get drunk. No, maybe that wouldn't be such a good idea, not at Suzanne's housewarming party.

Rachael Short, a college friend, greeted her.

'Cara, it's great to see you again. You're looking fantastic. You remember Tom, my other half, don't you?'

'Yes, of course,' said Cara. 'Hello, Tom.' She shook hands with him.

Dick, Suzanne's dapper husband, came barging out of the kitchen, arguing loudly with the most devastatingly attractive man Cara had ever laid eyes on. A hush fell when they saw Cara.

'Cara!' Dick exclaimed. 'Great to see you again. May I introduce you to my boss, Guy McIntosh? Guy, this is Cara Thompson, Suzanne's best friend.'

Their eyes met, his dark, assertive, taking possession of her, his presence negating everyone else in the room. They were staring at one another, an invisible line drawn between them and the onlookers. She noted the intensity of his sea-green eyes glowing from beneath their thick dark lashes, his jet black hair, his square tanned face over the white collar of his shirt, his strong shoulders straining in his suit, a suit that depicted a man of importance.

'You're Dick's boss?' she said finally.

'That's right. I came over from Scotland with Dick on Friday. Just had time to see what a fabulous place it is.'

She'd never seen such a beautiful man in her life. She knew he was from Scotland by the soft lilt of his voice. His skin smooth as a baby's, and his head was tilted in an arrogant way, his smile bold, as he gazed at her. With those extraordinary looks and the confidence and strength he radiated, he was used to smiling at women, she thought. She wondered what a hot-blooded male like him with so much passion in his eyes would be like in bed. Nothing like Andy, that was for sure. Ashamed of her thought she blushed.

'And you? Have you always lived in Dublin?' he asked.

Briefly she explained that she was from the locality but that she lived in County Wicklow since her marriage.

'And your partner? Is he here?' he asked, looking past her.

Suddenly the room felt horribly oppressive. 'She shifted from one foot to another. 'No . . . he's . . . eh . . . we've separated for a while.' What made her say that?

'Oh!'

She felt herself beginning to panic in the expectant pause that followed, knowing she must say something to fill the gap in the conversation. His eyes were fixed on her, the best looking male in the room, and she couldn't think of anything to say. Her mouth was dry. She took a slurp of champagne and found herself saying, suddenly, 'And you? Are you married?'

'I was. My wife died.'

'I'm so sorry,' she said.

'Thank you,' he smiled, acknowledging her sympathy.

Suzanne came to the rescue introducing them to other people in the room.

There was more hand-shaking. Trays of canapés were passed around.

Dick called, 'Food's served.'

Everyone filed into the dining room. There Cara was launched into several conversations ranging from the Olympic Games in Sydney to a recent drug's scandal at the local school.

'They should have sniffer dogs outside the school gates,' Dick said.

'Do you play golf?' she heard one of the male guests ask Guy in a condescending way.

'Yes, I do.'

'What about a round tomorrow while this good weather holds?'

'Unfortunately I can't. I'm going house-hunting tomorrow.'

The music started up, pounding and intrusive. Two women started the dancing, jiggling their hips. Cara watched them. Guy McIntosh stood remote and imperious, deliberately letting his eyes circle the room, observing the dancers, probably considering this party to be dull compared to what he was normally used to.

'Come on, let's dance,' said a Jennifer Lopez lookalike to him, dragging him out into the middle of the room, swooning erotically.

Cara watched her flinging herself around with a lot of drunken lurching.

Suzanne cornered her. 'Gorgeous bit of stuff, isn't he?' she giggled, dying for Cara's opinion.

'Not bad.' Cara was non-committal.

'What did you say his name is?' Vanessa asked, leaning back against the wall, surveying him.

'Guy McIntosh.' Suzanne said slowly, her eyes on Cara. 'I feel so sorry for him. He's terribly lost and lonely since his wife's death.'

'Doesn't look it to me,' said Vanessa.

'He's been living like a hermit. It's such a shame. He's so lovely. We're hoping the change of scenery might do him good. The thing is he doesn't know a soul here, apart from us.'

Vanessa said, 'I guarantee you with looks like that he won't be living like a hermit for long. He's a real catch. Looks like Russell Crowe.'

'My favourite film star,' said Cara dreamily, feeling a blush rising in her cheeks.

People were talking around her, convivial, the party in full swing. Just as she was hoping to leave quietly without insulting anyone Guy caught her eye briefly and approached her.

'You're not going are you?' he asked, slipping past a knot of people to get to her.

'I have an early start in the morning.'

'Just one dance?'

Everyone was crowding onto the floor, stamping their feet, singing to the music. Cara felt herself being almost lifted into the tangle of dancers. She was surprised at her feeling of pure pleasure as she danced, and didn't mind at all that her hips met his to the rhythm of the music. She let herself get absorbed in the music and this man she knew nothing about.

The loud ringing of the doorbell interrupted them.

'I'll go.' Suzanne disappeared.

Andy strode into the room brandishing a bottle, a puzzled Suzanne behind him.

'Where's my wife?' he called out, swerving past the dancers, to stand menacingly between Cara and Guy.

'I want a word with you,' he said to Cara.

Cara only smiled and said, 'Please, Andy, not now.'

Dick placed a restraining hand on his arm. 'Easy, Andy. You're drunk.'

Andy shook it off. 'I am not drunk. I drove all the way over here to be with my wife.'

'Come on, I'll get you a cup of coffee.'

'No!'

Stunned, Cara watched Andy as he elbowed through.

'See, I knew it,' he said, grabbing hold of her. 'Snogging everything in sight the minute my back's turned.'

'How dare you,' Cara retaliated, breaking free of him.

Andy wheeled around, colliding into the arms of Guy McIntosh who seized him by the shoulders.

'You're drunk, mate.'

Andy shook him off. 'If I am it's her fault.'

Cara was rooted to the spot.

'Andy! Stop.' Dick shouted.

'No, I won't. It's time I told her a thing or two,' he said to Cara, pushing his mouth against her ear.

She faced him.

His voice was a tortured wail as he said, 'You left me.' Turning to everyone he said, 'She's a clever girl, my wife. Looks like she got what she wanted. Isn't that right, darl . . . ing?'

Cara drew in her breath as expectant faces gazed at her. 'I'm going.' She turned and walked away.

Andy followed her and barred her way.

'You say I never go anywhere with you, now I'm here, and you storm off with your nose in the air, acting as if I was a piece of dog dirt stuck to the sole of your shoe.'

Guy sauntered up to him.

'That's what you're acting like.'

Andy said to Cara, 'You make me fucking sick, so you do.'

Cara said, 'Get out of my way.'

'You heard the lady,' Guy said.

Andy swung at him wildly, stumbling backwards. Guy seized his arms. Andy howled.

'That's enough,' Guy cautioned.

Struggling to free himself, Andy wailed.

Vanessa shouted, 'Stop, Andy! You're behaving like a spoilt child. Go home and grow up, for God's sake,' escorting him to the door.

'Don't let him drive,' Guy said to Dick.

'I'll look after him,' Dick said, steering Andy out the door.

Suzanne, the perfect hostess, put the music on to fill the gap in the conversation. Vanessa grabbed the nearest man and led the dancing.

Cara left quietly. Guy followed her down the dark street in his car.

'Wait! I'll see you home.'

She got in.

'I'm sorry about that. It was the last thing I expected.'

'Forget it. What you need is a good night's sleep. It won't seem so bad in the morning,' he consoled her.

'Well, this is it,' she said outside Rockmount, looking straight at him, telling him without words that this was it, that she liked him but that she didn't want anyone invading her space.

'I enjoyed meeting you. I hope we'll meet again.' He was looking back at her; nothing embarrassed in his gaze.

'Maybe, sometime.'

'Soon,' he smiled, as if too much insistence might put her off. She was opening the door of the car, giving him one last look that said I fancy you too but there's nothing I can do about it. His dark expressive eyes possessed her, not letting go, so full of such longing that she couldn't resist him when he put an arm around her shoulders, and gathered her to him. Something inside her sank like a stone as she leaned against his shoulder, just for a second, promising nothing because she had nothing to give, and saying goodbye. She drew in her breath, knowing she had to gain control, end it fast. She was getting out of the car, saying goodbye, walking away. It was over before it had begun.

Once in bed she reflected on the party and what a disaster it had been. Andy had behaved monstrously. She cringed thinking about it. What was he thinking of to do such a thing? He'd done it because he was desperate to sort things out, desperate to get her back. She flopped back into her pillows thinking about him at home, all alone. She should go back, beg his forgiveness, listen quietly while he lectured her sternly before throwing her bodily from the house. But why would she want to go back to things the way they were, rows all the time, none of the intimate loving familiarity that they once shared.

Her thoughts turned to Guy McIntosh. Nothing had happened between them, yet she felt that he'd invaded her life. With a jolt she realised that she knew very little about him apart from the fact that he was Scottish, and the new managing director of the Irish branch of Dick's firm, oh, and that he was house-hunting. It hadn't even occurred to her to ask him where he was staying in the meantime. Probably one of the plush hotels in the city centre.

6

━━━━◆◆◆━━━━

Cara was still reeling from the emotional shock of the incident at Suzanne's party when she called to Suzanne's the next evening.

'I'm so sorry. What must you think of us? I do apologise.'

'No need.'

'I can't believe Andy did that. I hope it didn't wreck your party,' she said awkwardly, flushing to the roots of her hair, recalling the awful scene Andy had made. 'I do know one thing. He'll be embarrassed at meeting you and Dick again after last night. That's why I called in. I didn't want to leave it too long in case you thought I was embarrassed too.'

'Don't be silly, Cara. It wasn't that outrageous. We know Andy. He was trying to assert his authority. It was embarrassing for you, I know, but we didn't mind at all.'

'It was pretty horrifying just the same.'

The shame, the humiliation of everybody knowing that they were separated stung her. He'd left them standing openmouthed. Andy, of all people, acting like that. Andy, who'd always been so circumspect, so careful not to offend had seemed unable to stop himself.

Cara felt a stab of pain as she spoke. 'It's terrible and I don't know what to do. I mean what am I supposed to do after the performance he gave?'

'Avoid him.'

'How can I?' Cara gulped. 'I'll want to know how he is.'

'Oh, Cara.' She flung her arms around Cara and hugged her hard. 'You're in worse trouble than I thought.'

'I know.'

Suzanne glanced sideways at her. 'Maybe you both need a session with a marriage guidance counsellor.'

'Counsellor!' Cara groaned, trying to imagine Andy having his marriage analysed by a complete stranger and failing. 'Andy wouldn't talk to a stranger about the intimate details of our marriage. He'd find the very idea appalling. 'He won't even talk to me, for God's sake.'

'But it might help him to cope better.'

Cara shook her head. 'He won't. I know him.'

'By the way, what did you think of Guy McIntosh?' Suzanne asked.

'I haven't really given him a lot of thought,' Cara lied, keeping her voice deliberately casual, wanting Suzanne to think he hadn't affected her.

On Monday morning Isabella was late for work. When she finally arrived she was in a foul mood. She'd been standing for the past hour waiting for a bus, exposed to men and their rude remarks.

'It's that skirt,' Mrs Moody said scornfully, pointing to the minuscule skirt peeping out from under her red jacket.

'What's whrong wit it?' asked the frustrated Isabella.

'It's too short and too tight.'

Scorned, Isabella began to list her grievances, starting with the climate, to Cara who wasn't in the mood to listen to her. Her father and Pamela were due home soon and she had so much to sort out before their arrival.

Andy phoned her to apologise for his bad behaviour at the party and to find out how she was. She purposely kept the conversation to a minimum, pretending that she was too busy to have time to talk. They agreed to meet at the cottage for a 'chat' as Cara put it, determined to keep things as casual as possible, the following Sunday evening. Filled with dread at the thought of it, she wondered how she should behave. Should she remain formal, or should she casually sit down with him and discuss their lives over a cup of tea as if they weren't all that important. The truth was that she was devastated. How she would feel about returning to the house she could only guess.

When she did arrive and parked outside the cottage she felt torn between the sanity of ownership and anxiety at what might have happened to her home in her absence. She glanced nervously at the front door. Should she knock, or should she open it with her key?

In the end she let herself in, nervous about seeing him again. The scene that met her was so unfamiliar that she hardly recognised the place. The dining room table was littered with beer bottles, overflowing ashtrays and empty take-away cartons. There was Andy, sitting amid the chaos playing poker with his friends, tipsy. He was barefoot, his hair a mess, a cigarette dangling from his lips as he shuffled the cards. Ken was counting chips, Don and another man, a stranger to Cara, sat poised, eyebrows raised inquisitively. Cara stood absorbing the sight before her.

'Sorry if I'm interrupting,' she said, embarrassed, feeling like a stranger.

Andy grinned openly at her. Tapping his beer bottle, he said, 'Want a drink? There's some wine left.'

'Want to play?' the stranger asked.

Andy threw him a filthy look.

Cara was mortified.

'No thanks.'

'Right,' said Ken.

She went into the kitchen, their laughter ringing in her

ears. Everything was a mess, dirty dishes in the sink, crumbs everywhere.

Upstairs she roamed restlessly from room to room, taking a secret check to re-acquaint herself, straightening the towel on the towel rail. The bedroom was the same as when she left, the bed unmade. She went around fidgeting with ornaments, straightening pictures, a photograph of Andy and her leaving for their honeymoon in Los Angeles, Elsie caught in the frame, chin lifted. Cara remembered Elsie coming to her, amid all the goodbyes, saying, 'Oh, I'm going to miss you.'

Andy burst into the room.

'It's great to see you,' he said. 'Listen, I'm sorry about the lads. I wanted everything to be nice for you. I'll get rid of them as soon as I can.'

Cara exploded. 'Look at the state of the place,' she said. 'You're living in squalor, there was no other word for it.'

'I was going to do a big clean up when they've gone.'

'You were leaving it a bit late.'

'No, you're early, that's all. Anyway, I'm too busy with other things,' he said shiftily.

'Like what?'

'I've told you already on the phone. I've got a loan of a computer. I'm organising a business of my own,' he said.

Crap, thought Cara, looking him in the eye, wondering what to say to him, how to pose the questions she really wanted answers to, how to begin to get back to where they had been before he lost his job. She could tell that Andy wanted this from his quick smile and from the tone of his voice. But, with the amount he'd had to drink, he wasn't in any condition for a heart to heart discussion.

'You've been drinking, and you're not eating properly. You look terrible.'

'Then come back home and look after me.' His voice was plaintive.

'Being your domestic companion is not enough for me. Anyway, we agreed that we'd give each other some space. Didn't we?'

'How much longer do you need to sort yourself out? A month? Six months? A year?' He reached his hand out to her in appeasement. She backed away, uncertain of herself, uncertain of their relationship.

'Tell me what you want,' he said.

Mustering up her courage she said, 'I think we should separate for a while.'

Andy grabbed her arm. 'You really mean it, don't you?' His eyebrows were raised, his face a mask of pain.

'If you don't mind I'll get some of my stuff and get out of your way.'

He looked at her, shaken. 'Don't be ridiculous. You can't mean that. Remember our marriage vows. Love, honour and cherish, for better or worse.' Andy's voice was breaking. 'Just because I had a few friends in for a game of poker.'

'No! It's not that. It's everything, your drinking, your lack of motivation, and your lack of interest in me.'

'And what about your lack of interest in me? You're wedded to your job and your precious Daddy. I don't count. I never did.'

'I . . . I . . .' She felt terrible.

'You haven't bothered about me for ages. You never loved me properly,' he shouted.

'Keep your voice down,' Cara hissed. 'Your precious poker buddies will hear you. I'm sure they'll be wondering what's keeping you.'

'To hell with them. Cara, listen, tell me what you want, exactly.'

'I want you to get off your arse and do something useful

with your life. Until then there's no point in continuing this discussion. I'm going to pack some of my stuff to take back to Rockmount.'

Swiftly she swept stockings and underwear into a hold-all, tipped bottles and make-up in after them.

'You're making a big mistake, walking out like this.'

'Sorry, but you won't twist my arm this time.' She turned away, distancing herself from him with her silence.

He slammed out the door.

She packed some of her clothes, dropped in a few of her favourite books and a few CDs. The bedroom looked bare as she left, sneaking downstairs, hoping to get out the front door without more scenes of embarrassment.

Andy was waiting for her in the hall, the poker players gone.

'Got everything you need?' he said nastily, standing guard with his arms folded.

'Yes.' She gave a quick glance round.

Walking away, knowing she was doing what millions of women want to do but can only dream about, getting out of a bad marriage, she felt awful.

He followed her.

'This is a serious error of judgement, Cara.'

She didn't answer.

His voice rose as he said, 'I hope you're satisfied, breaking us up like this. Don't go,' he pleaded as she got into her car.

She held herself aloof. 'I thought we'd weather this particular storm, but we haven't. Not this time.'

He put a finger to his temple. 'Why don't you blow my brains out and be done with it?'

She drove off leaving him standing there, looking after her, a bewildered expression on his face.

Back in Rockmount she phoned Vanessa for an emergency

meeting to discuss this latest development. They agreed to meet that night in the local pub in Sandymount.

'So? greeted Vanessa. 'You finally told him you didn't love him?'

'No, of course not. I do love him. It's just that I can't stand him at the moment.'

'Men!' She sniffed, her eyes full of sympathy for Cara.

'Blames me for everything. Says I didn't give him any support. Didn't love him enough!'

'Did you ever hear anything so ridiculous in your life?' Vanessa threw her eyes to heaven.

'He complained that I was too involved in my work, and not committed to him.'

Vanessa laughed at the good of that.

'Be honest, Nessa. Where did I go wrong?'

Vanessa, eager to side with Cara in her sad tale, said, 'You did *too much* for him. That's where you went wrong. When I think of what you put up with over the years. All that waiting around for the phone call that was going to catapult him into the success zone, the various jobs you had to take an interest in. You went through all his different phases with him like a dutiful wife, and all he did was mess things up for you.'

'I feel cowardly, walking out like that.'

'You did him a favour. Giving him a chance to get back on his feet. As things are he doesn't stand a chance with you around. He's too scared of you.'

'What's scary about me, for heaven's sake?'

'You're beautiful, clever, successful, and he sees himself as the bum who gate-crashed your life, stole you from your adoring father and landed you with nothing but a pile of problems.'

'But . . .'

'And, to add insult to injury, you've refused to make any more compromises and have taken charge of your own life at last. Now, tell me that's not scary to a weak man like him.'

Stunned by Vanessa's homespun psychoanalysis, Cara sat back in her seat to think.

'And why should you feel bad? It's time you thought about yourself for a change.'

'I'm thinking that maybe I'm not marriage material after all. Marriage is such a difficult business.'

Vanessa gave her friend's hand a squeeze. 'Maybe you don't want to be married,' she countered. 'Maybe the last thing you want is a husband at the moment. All they want is total commitment, loyalty and looking after with no responsibility on their part.'

'Maybe you're right.'

Vanessa sipped her pint, straightened up as she said, 'You could have a perfectly good life as a single woman. You have a good job, enough money to live quite comfortably on. What more do you want?'

Cara tried to imagine herself single, free, and couldn't. 'It felt weird at Suzanne's party, not having a partner.'

'You don't need one. You can always phone a dating agency if you want an escort for the night. That's what I do when I'm stuck.'

Shocked, Cara looked at her. 'Are you saying I should get rid of Andy altogether? That he's totally dispensable?'

'No, nothing as drastic as that. But honestly, Cara, you don't need him at the moment. The important thing is that you don't rush back to him, panic-stricken. Not until you find your inner self. Otherwise he'll only start fucking you around again. Take time to prove to yourself that you're not dependent on him and that you don't love him too much.'

'How do I do that?'

'Don't get in touch with him. At least not until you've expanded a little.'

'You're making me feel like a rubber band.'

Vanessa shook her head. 'You've led a very sheltered life, and moving back to it isn't the answer.'

'I don't know how long I can stick Rockmount. Elsie means well but it's positively claustrophobic.'

'If it gets too much for you, you're welcome to come and share my place for a while. Or rent a place of your own. You can afford it.'

Cara was thoughtful. Maybe Vanessa was right. Maybe she didn't need an irritating husband. But did she want to be single? Somehow she couldn't imagine sitting at a boring desk for the rest of her life, dating boring businessmen in boring suits.

'There's a lot to be said for the single life. No household to run, no one else's dirty washing to do and, best of all, you can keep your salary for yourself. Apart from anything else, dating is much more exciting, much more fun, believe me.'

'I did think that Andy had something more to him, though, than just the run of the mill stuff,' Cara said.

'Like what?'

'Oh, I don't know. It was all so exciting when we met. When he came into a room, I just swooned. And then he was so interested in everything. Now he's not interested in anything. At least he never discusses anything with me.'

'Take a complete break from him. Don't even talk about him. Not a word about Andy for the whole month, nothing. Concentrate on what you want as a woman. What do you think of that?'

'I'll try.'

7

On Tuesday George Flatley invited Cara to lunch. He wanted to have a chat with her about the business. He knew a quiet place. At one o'clock sharp he escorted her to Keogh's in South Anne Street and led her to a dark booth where he ordered a pint and a steak pie for himself, and a mineral water and salad roll for her. They chatted about trivial office matters until the food arrived.

'You couldn't have come to us at a better time,' he said. 'We're up to our eyes and short-staffed.'

'Get in a book-keeper,' Cara advised.

Work, work, work, that was all George ever thought about. He'd started his career with John Bradley and, as the business grew, had taken on the increasing workload in the accounts department single-handed, starting at eight most mornings, working late into the evening. He kept the entire place running smoothly, coming to work at the weekend sometimes.

Cara sat listening to his trivial complaints, knowing he wasn't saying what was on his mind by the heaviness in his face, and the blankness of his gaze intimating that he was simmering over something.

When the food arrived she watched him eat ravenously, cramming the food into his mouth, thinking that it was no wonder he was a martyr to indigestion.

'So, what's really on your mind?' she said. 'You might as well spit it out.'

'It's not just the staff shortage. It's much worse than that.

It's that site on the Quays. It's costing a fortune, and they won't grant the permission.'

'Is that what they've said?'

'Not in so many words. But it's sectioned land. They'll turn your father down.'

'He'll get around them. He usually does.'

'Not this time.' George threw up his hands helplessly, not really trusting her, the situation desperate enough for him to confide in her. 'He stands to lose everything,' he said, sitting back, watching for her reaction.

'I'm sure that's not the case. He knows what he's doing, knows all the right people.'

'I don't share your optimism.'

'What do you want me to do about it?'

'Try and talk him out of buying it. He won't listen to me.'

'Surely it's too late?'

'The final papers aren't signed.'

'If you can't get through to him, he'll hardly listen to me.'

'He might. It's the only chance we've got.'

'I'll have a word with him.'

The surly stubborn expression that George usually kept hidden from her father was there, no blankness now to camouflage it. He was stashing ammunition against her father, waiting for the right time to say 'I told you so'.

Right! So, get on with it. She mustn't flap, no matter what, she told herself.

'You do that.'

'I'd better get a move on,' Cara said.

There was a house she had to see with Joe Murphy, the builder who'd worked for them for donkey's years, at three o'clock and she'd promised Suzanne she'd call in on her way home.

Three hours later, Cara walked into Suzanne's kitchen. There was Guy McIntosh at the kitchen table with Dick

poring over sheaves of papers. He greeted her, barely looking at her.

'Make the boys a cup of tea, Cara, like a good girl,' said
Suzanne, busy with the baby.

Without a word Cara did so. Guy took the tea she handed
him with just a thank you. While he drank it she watched him
closely, listened to his deep husky voice as he talked to Dick.
I wouldn't blame myself for falling in love with him, she
thought, scandalised at the idea of it, at the same time wishing
she were more beautiful, more talented, more interesting.

When he finally turned his startling eyes on her she had
an overpowering desire to rush into his arms. Suzanne,
catching sight of Cara's flushed cheeks, recognised the signs.
Embarrassed, Cara left the kitchen and went out into the back
garden. Guy followed her. They seemed alone in the world as
they gazed at one another with fascination, his intimate glance
making a violent impact on her.

He said, 'What are you doing this weekend?'

She would be relaxing, reading the Sunday newspapers,
taking the dog for a walk.

'The usual uneventful stuff.'

'Don't worry. I'm not asking you out on a date. Suzanne
tells me you're an estate agent. I thought you might find me
a house in County Wicklow.'

'Oh! I'll check if there's anything suitable.'

Next day Cara checked her list of houses in the Wicklow
area. What about that big house outside Arklow that she'd
seen recently? She got on the phone to Murphy telling him
that she wanted him to look over a property with her again,
urgently. Murphy agreed to accompany her there. She trusted
his opinion and realised that this foray into the countryside,
though time-consuming, was essential.

Murphy spent ages talking about the possibilities and
probabilities of the property. Cara was too busy thinking of

its potential to worry about trivialities such as blocked water supply, leaking roof and gates off their hinges that Murphy had pointed out. All those matters could be discussed later. The most important thing was that it was an ideal location for Guy McIntosh.

She phoned Guy to invite him to view it on Friday. They agreed to meet in Jury's. To her surprise he was already there, talking to the barman about the district, quite at home in a place to which he was so much a stranger. Cara stood there, waiting. When the barman turned to her, so did Guy.

Suddenly he saw her. Her heart leaped as he came towards her as if he'd been led towards her all of his life.

He smiled. 'Hello, Cara. How nice to see you again.'

Recovering her composure she said with a cool smile. 'Hello, Guy,' trying to hide her uneasiness because she was nervous.

Cara drove them through miles of green fields stretching to the horizon, Guy looking around him with interest. Once off the dual carriageway the roads narrowed through villages with their scattering of houses and shops and brightly painted pubs in yellow and orange, in total contrast with the stark colours of the landscape. Nearer to Arklow new estates sprouted up in the surrounding fields. Caravan sites and holiday homes overlooked the sea. At the far side of a shop selling ice cream and buckets and spades, Cara turned into a lane flanked on either side by rusted iron gates and screened by trees, their overhanging branches casting dark shadows across their path and obscuring the view.

There, at the end of the lane, facing them, was an elegant stone house, high and square, with an unused air, its long sash windows fogged up, its shallow steps up to the hall door washed by a reluctant May sun. A pile of rubble no one had bothered to shift leaned against the gable wall. There was an uncomfortable pause as Guy looked at it with curiosity. He stepped out of the car, walked past brambles and scutch grass up the path, thick with weeds, and looked with appraising eyes past the rubble, the outbuilding, the stacks of bricks, randomly placed in the courtyard, to the fields across the valley and the peaks of dunes that edged them. Cara kept her distance. Somewhere in a nearby hedge a robin sang. When he finally turned back to her the look of delight in his eyes enchanted her.

'Interesting,' he said. 'Let's go inside.'

She led the way up the shallow steps, turned the key in the reluctant lock, and opened the door, waiting for Guy, who was gazing up at the house for structural defects. The hall was strangely soundless; the remnants of flock wallpaper the only sign that life had been lived there. The late sun poured in on the four closed dusty doors that waited to be opened.

They went from one sumptuously large room to another, mounted the wide shallow staircase and went along a panelled corridor of mahogany doors opening into bedrooms with immensely high windows facing south-west. Guy cranked up a window in one of them.

'This is a beautiful place,' he said.

Cara joined him, gazing at the belt of beech and oak trees that screened the house, and the dark fields beyond it where sheep grazed. Their attention focused on the long wide stretch of sand and the sea in the distance cloaked in a bluish haze.

Breathing in salt air Guy said, 'I love it.'

Murphy arrived.

Cara introduced Guy to him saying, 'I'd like you to meet Joe Murphy, our builder. Joe, meet Guy McIntosh.'

Guy gave a formal bow in his direction.

'Nice to meet you,' Murphy said, entering the house with authority.

He was at the peak of his performance, darting here and

there, sighing over the neglect of the stripped pine floors, the fungal patches on the cut stone around the windows, the damp plaster on the fretwork ceilings. He poked about investigating every nook and cranny, turning up his disapproving nose, and clicking his tongue at the terrible neglect, showing off his knowledge in front of Guy.

'Damn carelessness is responsible for a lot of this,' he said, rubbing off the bluish mould with his hand.

'An Englishman bought it several years ago and began restoring it. He left midway, so it's now derelict again,' she said apologetically, as if the fault lay with her.

'Shame on him. He should have stayed here and kept an eye on the place.'

To Murphy he said, 'I like it. How long will it take to make it habitable?'

Murphy scratched his bald head. 'Let's see, joinery, plastering. There's a helluva lot to be done. Mind you, it wouldn't take much more than a few months, given the good weather. We'll need more labour.'

'Give us an exact date?' Guy said to him, arching an eyebrow enquiringly.

'That's a tricky one,' Murphy wasn't giving a direct answer. 'Let's see, June, July, August. That's the summer gone. We'll be buried in rubble for the first while,' he said gloomily. He was shaking his head, gazing up at the blank spaces in the roof, his bald head gleaming in the sun. 'Don't know what the wife'll say. No holidays for us again this year.'

'August the . . . ?' Guy was pushing for a deadline.

'It'll be hard going to finish it by the end of August, but we'll try.'

Cara didn't question Murphy. She knew the way he worked. Murphy's time was never skimped when it came to duties and responsibilities to a project. A dedicated worker, he would stay there until midnight, wet to the bone in the icy cold weather sometimes, tripping back and forth giving his men hell for any little mistakes.

His son Dave arrived to give his opinion on the roof.

'I won't venture up there,' said Murphy, wisely.

For all his enormous size and power Dave was as light as a feather on his feet, nimbly climbing up scaffolding, wonderfully agile as he walked along the roof.

'It'll be treacherous hard work to get it right,' Dave sighed, when he'd climbed back down the ladder.

'We'll get started as soon as you give the word,' said Murphy.

'Now, the thing is how long can you wait?' Murphy asked Guy.

Guy said, 'As long as it takes. I don't seem to have a choice in the matter because I like the place. But if you get it done sooner I'll make it worth your while.'

Murphy and Guy shook hands and exchanged complicit grins. With a wave he clambered into his car and speeded away to a myriad other tasks to be done. Dave took off in his.

Chilled, Cara locked the door of the house. Guy, waited for her. They stood there for a moment or two, Guy staring at the house, Cara shivering from the coldness of the empty building.

Guy took off his jacket and wrapped his coat around her. He caught a whiff of her delicious perfume as he did so. On the journey back the car felt warm after the deserted house.

'Let's have dinner,' Guy said.

Cara looked at him.

'Tonight?'

'Why not? You've made a sale. That's worth celebrating, isn't it?'

'Yes, but . . .'

Meet in an expensive restaurant. Eat and drink publicly? A cold desolation crept over her as she thought about it. Why not? He was a client, wasn't he? Surely they could wine and dine expensively if they wanted to, couldn't they? Indeed, it might be graceless to refuse.

She decided on The Peacock Alley in the new Fitzwilliam Hotel.

8

The Peacock Alley Restaurant had been Cara's choice, yet, arriving at it, she shrank into the upturned collar of her jacket, nervous of meeting a friend or acquaintance.

'Let's have a drink first,' Guy said, taking her jacket.

Their joint entrance to the chic restaurant caused a stir, two beautiful people having a celebration dinner, enjoying each other's company. Cara, in the lavender backless Marc O'Neill dress she'd bought on a whim one rainy Saturday afternoon, felt the admiration ripple around her. Imagined disapproving eyes melted magically.

As she watched Guy order their drinks a curious sensation surged through her, a feeling of confidence, and an exciting power of freedom. It was like a dream being here with this man who was so handsome and assured. He made her feel totally removed from the daily demands of her role as Andy's wife. In fact she felt so alienated from Andy that she couldn't think why she'd ever want to go back to that life again.

The barman brought a bottle of champagne and two glasses.

'Here's to us,' Guy said.

They touched glasses, toasting their new friendship, gazing at one another with steady fascination.

'You've changed your hair.'

'I put it up, that's all,' she said, touching the coils with her fingertips.

His look was flattering. 'You look wonderful.'

She blushed.

Under the cover of people taking their seats at a nearby table he leaned towards her and said, 'Let yourself go, forget everything and concentrate on enjoying yourself.'

He was reading her like a book, making her feel conscious of being a woman. Perhaps the understanding of women was the result of a lifetime's study. She had no way of knowing. She sipped her drink, making it last, like a child at a party, glancing at him from time to time, wondering what sort of man was this to have taken over her mind so completely.

'Are you hungry?'

'Starving.'

'Good.'

Guy ordered lavishly and with total assurance. While they waited for their meal they drank perfectly chilled Chablis, and Guy, his eyes shining in the candlelight, told her about himself. He lived in Edinburgh, he said, and he took his career very very seriously.

They talked and talked. He told her about his job as managing director of IPS Software Company. That he was here to open a factory to develop equipment for mobile telephones. He explained the stresses of this particular assignment and his ambitions for the company which made his work so demanding, which was why he had to keep himself at the peak of his physical fitness, playing squash and golf.

'And how long will you be here for?'

'That depends on a lot of things.' The blatant intent in his eyes made her swallow hard. 'I've kept my home in Edinburgh, though I'm hardly ever there. It's home to my son in the holidays. But I'm considering moving here permanently to get my son away from the sadness of the house without his mum. Give him a fresh start.'

'You have a son?'

He nodded, smiling. 'Ian. He's fourteen, away at boarding school most of the time. I try to spend the holidays with him.'

'Are you from Edinburgh originally?'

'I was born in the roughest area in Glasgow. I come from a working-class background. My father was a docker. He was a tough high-spirited man, drank a lot and got into fights. He fell off a girder when I was seven, died as a result. My mother worked in a factory. I was the only one, always on my own. No one sheltered me. I had to rough it with the other children on the street. I fought my own battles and there were always battles going on. Every day there was something to fight about. We were thieving, robbing food and cigarettes from shops. Anything to survive. Someone would bolt with the spoils. Whenever a fight broke out I fought the bullies. I was bigger than they were. When they ran home screaming and blubbering, their mothers would come running down the road to defend their brats. I stopped getting invited to their homes by way of punishment. So I was left out of things. Got blamed because I was big for my age and tougher than the rest of them. I could beat any one of them to a pulp. I became a hero as I grew up because I was always fighting over something, defeat the forces of law and order, desperate to shock someone of importance.'

'Far from humble,' Cara laughed, knowing he was probably more clever and superior to anyone else in the neighbourhood.

'There was no point in being humble if you valued your life,' he said.

She pictured him on street corners, fighting with older boys, his fists flailing as he beat them to a pulp, teaching a lesson to anyone who tampered with him, nothing cowardly or vulnerable about him. He was still strong, well able to defend himself against anyone who provoked him. Apart from his obvious strength, he had the added advantage of a sharp ready tongue. He let no one pierce his armour, she guessed, his subtle mind being his main weapon.

'I did the unusual thing of studying hard and graduating at the top of my class. Then I joined the RAF. They sent me to college where I got my training in electronics and learned to drink, of course.'

'Of course.'

He laughed recalling that time. 'It was brilliant. I was one of the lads. After I qualified I got offered a job in Edinburgh, got married, the usual stuff. My life was sorted, or so I thought. Then fate played a cruel trick. Hazel, my wife . . .' he stopped, looked away as he took a long sip of his drink. 'She died suddenly having our second child. The doctors had warned us that she shouldn't have another, and she'd accepted that, or so I thought.' He looked sad as he said, 'She must have wanted a child so desperately that she was prepared to take the risk. I wouldn't have let her if I'd known.' His voice trailed away.

'She didn't tell you?'

'Not until she was four months pregnant when it was too late to do anything about it. She must have realised that I would be against it.'

'I'm so sorry,' Cara said, seeing the pain in his eyes.

'And you? Have you got children?' he asked, smiling at her once more.

She tried to keep the regret out of her voice as she said no, she hadn't, not elaborating. When it was time to leave Guy paid the bill, leaving a generous tip, and ordered a taxi.

Cara leaned back, relaxed, as the taxi floated towards Sandymount. Guy brushed his arm against hers in a steadying gesture as she alighted from it. They walked up the path together his hand loosely on her arm.

At the hall door she said, 'I'm going to make myself some coffee. Would you like some?'

'Why not.'

She unlocked the door and led the way into the drawing room where she left him while she made the coffee. As she carried it back the drawing room from upstairs came the familiar voice of Elsie calling out, 'Everything all right, Cara?'

'Fine,' Cara called back, gently shutting the drawing room door.

They looked at each other and giggled like naughty children. As she went to pull the curtains Guy followed her.

'Don't shut out the beautiful night,' he said his hand on her arm, as he looked out at the lawn, silver in the moonlight.

She swung round to face him. He reached out a hand and touched the curve of her mouth with his lips. It was a soft, tentative touch that thrilled her like a first kiss. She didn't feel strange with him as his arms went round her as he smiled down at her.

Then he kissed her properly.

'I've wanted to do that all evening,' he said in a low voice, full of longing.

He kissed her again, deep and hard this time, drawing her into his arms. His body against hers, the touch of his fingers on her bare back, made her catch her breath. His lips moved to her throat and it was as though she was drifting, breathing in his clean smell that was like leaves after rain.

Warning bells sounded in her head, her inner voice that asked herself, what am I doing here? What do I want with this man? Her mind shied away from the fact that she was a married woman, the pull of desire too strong to stop her. He was taking down the straps of her dress. This wasn't right! This man was a stranger, nothing to do with her. He shouldn't be here. She was married to Andy. She'd get hurt. The tightness in her chest turned to panic.

Her eyelids snapped opened. Trembling, she pushed him away.

'That's enough,' she pleaded, her heart not in it. 'We shouldn't be doing this.'

'Of course we should,' he said gruffly, reaching for her, his face intent with desire. 'We're consenting adults. We both want it.'

It was true. Pitched into a battle of desire, they clung together, their pulses racing, Guy bombarding her with kisses like someone starving, escalating her desire for him, his weight pressing her back against the wall, She was burning up, her body aching to be taken, her mind protesting at the wrongfulness of it, wrenching her in two.

Her mind won. With superhuman effort she pulled away.

'Sorry, Guy,' she said, steadying herself, straightening her dress.

'What's the matter? Did I come on too strong? I'm sorry. It's been so long.'

'It's not that. It's Andy. I can't do this to him.'

Surprised, Guy said, 'But it's over between you two.' He was taking her in his arms again, dismissing as irrelevant what she'd said.

She shook her head, loosening herself from his arms. 'Obviously, it's not. I can't see you again.'

He was quiet, observing her with half-closed eyes.

'You mean it.'

Her hands were trembling as she moved away.

His face changed as he glared at her.

'I'm sorry.'

In the charged silence that followed he said, 'I'd better go before I make a complete fool of myself.'

They stared at each other, the air cold between them as he backed away angrily, straightening his shirt, brushing back his hair with his hand. He was gone, striding out of the room.

Turning at the hall door he said, 'I still want the house,' looking at her as if from a distance, silently reprimanding her for leading him on then driving him away. She heard his footsteps in the hall and the bang of the front door.

From the window she watched him stride off, hurt in every line of his body. Cara drew in her breath to stop herself from crying. Wretched and trembling she turned from the window. She'd had a little too much to drink and had got a little carried away. She felt her cheeks flame at the shame of it.

So what! It was a casual acquaintance and that's all it could ever be. They were doing business together. He was randy, she was available. Maybe he was the kind to take advantage and rub his hands with satisfaction afterwards. She wondered as she stood there if he had been using her as it suited him. Who did Guy McIntosh think he was? Did he expect to bed every female he encountered just because he was attractive?

In bed she couldn't sleep. Every sound, every sigh of the wind made her jump. Her head was sore. She thought of Guy McIntosh and how furious he'd been. So, he'd made a blatant pass at her. Why was it such a big deal? What did she want? A sensual encounter with a charming stranger that could lead to a romantic involvement? Quiet nights on her own watching telly, eating pizza in her woolly jumper and bed socks? Or did she want Andy and her marriage? She thought of Andy in his lonely bed. Even though they were apart, she was hardly going to bed the first attractive man that crossed her path. She was old-fashioned enough to still believe in the ritual of marriage and to try and resolve her differences with Andy.

Still, she would have liked to stay friends with Guy. How could she possibly do that now? It would be embarrassing.

Men! Who needed them? They only hurt you she thought, pounding her pillows in frustration.

9

'Time to get up,' said Elsie, carrying a cup of tea in one hand, a letter in the other.

Cara sat bolt upright in bed. 'I'll be up and dressed in a minute.'

'There's no rush, it's Saturday. This card came for you,' she said.

'Having fun. Weather wonderfully hot,' Cara read it, wishing she were there too.

'What a view,' said Elsie, gazing at the long white beach in Barbados. 'It's paradise. I can just picture me there. It makes me think of holidays and where I'd like to go this year.'

For years she spent her holidays in Bundoran or Kilkea, though John would have sent her anywhere in the world. Now that her friend Betty Nutgrove had saved enough to accompany her on a cruise she was obliged to hold the fort here.

Elsie said, 'So who was that attractive man who was here last night?'

'A business acquaintance. Dick's boss, in fact. He's interested in a house we have in Arklow,' said Cara taking the easy way out. 'Sorry if we kept you awake.'

'Don't worry, I wasn't asleep.'

'All the same, I shouldn't have invited him in,' Cara said, thinking that having him under the same roof as Elsie had been too much of a responsibility.

In the old days Elsie would have guessed what was going

on. She'd always been one step ahead, ready to prevent disaster, soothe agonies, smooth out embarrassments. Now she looked at Cara with an indifferent expression, not putting her thoughts into words, accepting of any situation presented to her, for which Cara was grateful though she was loathe to admit that Elsie was getting old.

'No word from Andy?' Elsie asked pointedly.

Cara shook her head. 'Nothing.'

'He's not himself,' Elsie said suddenly letting caution slip by making a comment.

'Maybe not. But you know me, smiling through my tears. I must go and get dressed. Where are my beige slacks?'

'They're in your wardrobe. I ironed them for you. I wonder what you'd do without me. Where's this? Where's that? What'll happen when I take a holiday? How will you manage?' Elsie was dusting the dressing table with her sleeve while she was talking, pushing around all Cara's jars and bottles. Poor woman, ready to do anything to make Cara happy.

'You're a saint. Why do you bother with me?' asked a perplexed Cara.

'I take pride in you,' Elsie said, picking up from the floor the dress Cara wore the previous night. 'Look at this lovely dress,' she said, turning her attention to Cara, her eyes reprimanding. 'Thrown there.'

She hung it in the wardrobe and left the room.

After breakfast Cara said, 'Look at the time, I'll be late.'

'Where are you off to?' Elsie said, glancing suspiciously at her.

Cara said casually, 'I'm taking Bouncer for a walk. It'll do him good.'

'Take your jacket, I know you think I'm a fussy old thing but do be careful of that east wind.'

Cara set off along the seafront, glad to escape and avoid the boredom of a long gossipy lunch with Elsie and her friend

Betty Nutgrove. She walked with restlessness, hurrying along, Bouncer dragging behind, sniffing the ground.

In the park she spotted Suzanne wheeling her pram as she'd hoped she would.

'Come on, Bouncer,' she called impatiently, tightening his chain round her hand, increasing her pace.

He ignored her, stopping to lift his leg at a tree stump.

Finally she caught up with Suzanne.

'Dick said you had dinner with Guy,' Suzanne said accusingly.

'Yes.'

'You didn't you tell me you were meeting him.'

'It was a last minute decision, after we viewed a house.'

'So, how did it go?'

'Dinner was fine, the rest awful.'

'Oh!' Suzanne said, eyeing her curiously.

They sat on a park bench. Cara told Suzanne about it, making it all vividly clear again; the meal, bringing Guy back to Rockmount, the late hour, her struggle to keep her virtue.

'He read the signals all wrong.'

'Did he? Maybe you were giving the wrong impression.'

Ashamed, Cara said, 'I'd had a bit too much to drink. I suppose I wanted to get my own back on Andy. But I couldn't do it to him, and Guy wasn't impressed.'

'Cara, Guy's vulnerable. He's doesn't need someone to mess around with his feelings. He needs to have a bit of fun in his life.'

'Well, that's that then. No harm done,' Cara said, making light of it.

'He such a romantic person, don't you think?' Suzanne said, glancing at Cara girlishly. 'I'm hoping he'll settle down here, become adjusted. He's got a home in Edinburgh, you know, and a son there.'

'Maybe a woman?' Cara was probing.

'There was someone for a while. Nothing serious, I don't think. But the thing is he's not getting any younger. He's thirty-nine. Soon he'll be forty and he needs a proper base.'

'Probably has had lots of women,' Cara mused.

'No. He's had some adventures in his travels, I think, but according to Dick Guy can be shy. He's not half the flirt Dick is. God, he's such a flirt. It's maddening.'

'In the nicest way, I'm sure. Harmless.'

'Hmm, I'm not so sure. I often wonder if he's thinking about other women when we're making love.'

'Of course he isn't,' Cara consoled.

Suzanne refused to be reassured. She said restlessly, 'I'm not so sure. He's home so little. Still, at least when he's away I don't have to watch him doing it. I'm shielded by my ignorance.' She gave a brittle laugh.

Lucy cried. Suzanne rocked the pram until Lucy, eyes half-hooded, thumb in her mouth, fell asleep again.

Suzanne looked at her watch. 'I'd better get home. It's nearly lunchtime. Dick's playing golf this afternoon.' With a sigh she got up.

'I'll walk with you.' Cara dragged a reluctant Bouncer to his feet.

Suzanne said, as they walked along, 'Will you be seeing Guy again, do you think?'

'It's unlikely.'

'You never know. He's an unlikely sort of man. Only next time, make sure you're over Andy because there'll be no making excuses.'

'I don't think there will be one. I can't see how we can face each other again.'

'Stranger things have happened.'

'It's so peaceful,' Cara said, evading the issue, looking up at the gold reflecting clouds as they walked into the empty square. The sun shining on the façades of the houses burnished the windows gold. Bouncer loitered at a lamp post. Suzanne and Cara stood chatting outside Suzanne's house, the sun warming their bare arms. Suddenly the door of her house burst open without warning. Dick came tearing out, his golf bag slung over his arm.

'Where were you?' he called to Suzanne, his face ugly with annoyance.

Shocked, Suzanne recoiled. Cara caught the quick look of fear in her eyes and felt the sensation of it as her friend said, 'I went for a walk.'

'All that time? I waited to have lunch with you.'

'It's only lunchtime now.'

'You knew I had a golf match at one fifteen.' To Cara he said as he came nearer, 'She's at it again. Taking off for hours on end.'

Dick flung his golf bag into the boot of his car, got in, slammed the door, started the engine and tore off, waking Lucy as he went and frightening her. She bawled.

'What the hell's eating him?' Cara asked.

'He's jealous of the time I spend with Lucy,' said a red-faced Suzanne. 'It's a sore point at the moment. He's getting fierce with all the stress of late.' Hastening up the path, she called over her shoulder, 'Don't worry, I'll calm him down later on,' to make light of the situation.

Cara walked home fast, breathing deeply, her heart hammering. She'd always known Dick to be an impatient man, but she'd never seen him wound up like that before. She felt sorry for Suzanne and wondered if she could be biting off more than she could chew in her effort to keep Dick happy.

On Monday Cara slumped back against her pillows. She felt so tired that she considered taking a day off but she couldn't miss a day while her father was away.

She heard the phone beside her bed ring while she showered. It stopped, rang again, stopped. Whoever it was would catch up with her at work. She did her make-up, pulled her hair back into a tight knot, touched her cheeks with blusher and sprayed perfume on her neck and wrists, took her briefcase and left, giving Elsie a peck on the cheek.

Once she was in the car her spirits lifted. The sun came out as she drove to the office. It was a promising day, a day to get on with her life, and forget about everything, even Guy McIntosh. She met Vanessa and Suzanne for lunch.

Vanessa was just back from a visit home and wanted to talk. Usually full of chat, she spoke sporadically, as if she were talking to herself.

'Something the matter?' Cara asked.

'It's Zoe,' said the distressed Vanessa, squinting through the smoke of the pub.

'What is it this time?'

'She's up the spout again.' Vanessa stopped to inspect her polished nails, her head stiffly to one side.

'What!' Suzanne said.

They were all aware of Zoe's escapades and Vanessa's concern for her, which she never tried to conceal.

'Who's the father?' Cara asked.

Vanessa shook her head. 'She thinks it could be one of the gardeners in the Botanical Gardens.'

'She thinks!' said a shocked Cara.

'Well, it could be him,' protested Vanessa. 'She's been seeing him on a casual basis. On the other hand it could be her previous fella.' Her voice was cool, and her detachment a pretence as she said, 'It'd be better if it was him, but getting hold of him might be difficult. He went to Australia a couple of months ago and God knows if he'll want to come back.'

'How far gone is she?' Cara asked.

'That's the thing. She's not sure, but one way or another she can't afford to hang around. If Dad finds out he'll kill her,' Vanessa said. 'Mum wants to get her married off to save the heartache.'

'What do you think? Will this gardener do the decent thing if need be?'

Vanessa glanced sharply at the clock. 'That's the question. She was to tell him last week only it was raining all week and he wasn't in, so that's put the kibosh on things. Dad won't stand for it, though.' Vanessa's voice rose. 'He is so touchy about things like that. Not that he's any example with what he gets up to.'

Cara didn't doubt that for a moment. Her knowledge of the situation was based on past melodramas in Vanessa's household.

'He'll probably turn her out onto the streets,' Vanessa sighed gloomily. 'I had an awful job persuading him to let her back in the last time, after she was nicked for shoplifting. This is much worse. What'll she do? Where'll she go? She's never been anywhere.'

Cara always admired Vanessa for making something of herself. She came from a tough background – too much drinking in the family and too much interference in other people's business, which could be summed up as a real Dublin city trait.

'Too right,' Suzanne said.

'Life,' she said. 'There's always something to worry about.'

Vanessa was concerned about having to share her home with her sister, even temporarily. She didn't want to be tied down with anyone. 'Footloose and fancy-free' she described herself and went about as if she had all the time in the world in which to find a husband and bear children, if she ever decided to do so.

'The work's waiting,' she said, rising. 'Say nothing,' she cautioned Cara. 'People being so narrow-minded still, and all that.'

The drama of this exposé quickened her steps. Cara was left alone with her thoughts.

As soon as she got back Isabella rang from Reception.

'There's ha man here to see you,' she confided in a husky voice.

'Who is he?' Cara asked

'A Meester Ghuy something. He say that it's hurgent.'

Cara swiftly ran a comb through her hair, and went downstairs. Her heart gave a lurch as she saw him standing waiting for her, in his perfectly pressed suit, his manner poised and cool almost to the point of insolence. She felt crumpled, ungainly, as she went to him.

'Hello. What can I do for you?' There was annoyance in her eyes as she looked at him.

He held out the brochure. 'It's about my house,' he said, seeing it already as his property, forgetting that he hadn't yet bought it.

'Your house?' She looked at him warily as if he were up to something.

'The house in Arklow,' he corrected. 'There are one or two things I want to look at again. It won't take long.'

'I've instructed Mark Downes to deal with it,' she said, her detachment a pretence.

His eyes opened wide in surprise. 'So you're telling me that you're going to abandon me? Leave me with someone else?' he asked with a smile to cover his annoyance.

She looked at her watch thinking of her appointments for that day, the e-mails she hadn't answered, furious at any doubt being cast on Mr Downes' excellence as an estate agent.

'Wouldn't your father think it odd that you should leave me just now, with all the trouble about the damp walls and everything. Wouldn't he think that you were failing in your duty?' He stood there, dark, attractive, vibrant, and wronged, watching her, expecting trouble.

Cara burst out laughing at the idea of it.

'Duty! How old-fashioned,' she said, thinking how dare he assume that because he chose to buy that house that she'd be there, thrilled to see him. Surely her duty was to herself, to keep away from him.

'I'm not asking anything difficult or unsuitable, only for you to do your job. After all I'm not a run-of-the-mill client buying a two-up-two-down in Crumlin. I am buying a top market house.'

'Mr Downes is perfectly capable of looking after you. He deals with top market properties all the time.'

Guy McIntosh wasn't listening to her. 'Mind you, I wouldn't want you to do anything you were dead against.' He was taunting her.

'Of course not.'

Why was he talking as if it mattered, they mattered, saying things to make her feel that there was something more than the usual client relationship, making her feel guilty because he was hurt at being rejected.

'Right,' she said, agreeing too quickly, her face expression-less. 'I'll meet you there in an hour,' giving him no choice but to agree.

She'd been prepared to fight him, but he'd beaten her before she could begin. He glanced at her in a measuring way, blaming her for everything that had gone wrong between them. Wasn't it perfectly understandable that she, a married woman, wouldn't want to get too close to a man she found attractive, and who obviously found her attractive too? They should have had dinner and left it at that.

Her annoyance diminished as she left the city and drove south early to check the house before he arrived. Discon-solately she walked around, opening shutters and windows, letting the light into the stuffy rooms. In the archaic bathroom she turned off a dripping tap.

At last he arrived. She came downstairs slowly and let him in. He stood outside resentful that she hadn't been on the look out for him, hadn't flung the door open as he approached.

'That creeper will have to go before it pulls the wall down with it,' he said, walking past her, not seeing himself as a potential buyer but already the owner.

'I would have thought it enhanced the house,' she said obstinately.

'It chokes the gutters, pushes its way through the windows, not to mention the structural damage it covers up.'

His hand behind his back broodingly, the house already a burden, he stood in the damp, sooty drawing room.

'I'll restore these old creaky floor boards, and those wonderful ceilings,' he said triumphantly. 'And I'll have plenty of wood surfaces, ranch-style, and get some decent furniture. That's what it needs. I'll buy some nice things. After all I'm going to be here for a while.'

She was imagining him searching for the right furniture, fabrics, bedspreads and rugs. He could afford it.

'I'll make it beautiful.' He was chatting away in a friendlier manner, giving no hint of what was really going on in his mind, as though their earlier contretemps had been perfectly normal.

She followed him from room to room with cold courtesy, unable to imagine him living there. He might be making plans but she doubted that this house could ever be revived to its former glory. He would put it up for sale in no time.

The truth was the businessman side of him had taken over and he wasn't thinking of her. She might have been a piece of furniture. Give him a chance, she thought, be friends so as to reassure him that you have no feelings for him at all.

'I'll get a surveyor to look over it,' he said.

'I look forward to hearing from you,' Cara said politely.

His leave-taking was brusque. Well, she wouldn't have

many more dealings with him. What an unknown quantity he was too. He'd charmed her. She knew that she too had charmed him. And it wasn't to punish Andy, though that might have been part of it. Would she hear from him after he'd bought the house? Would he phone late some night, ask her out for a drink, not because he was desperate to see her again, but because he was lonely? Men hated being on their own.

Perhaps he would resurface. Perhaps he would go for good. Who could tell? Did she want to be involved with him? The answer to that was a very definite no.

IO

❖

John and Pamela returned the following Friday afternoon. Cara, waiting for them, ran down the steps to throw her arms around her father.

'Good to be back.' He held her tight for a second before releasing her to be kissed on the cheek by a gloriously tanned Pamela, cool in jeans and a white top, looking more like a sister than a stepmother. There was the bustle of getting themselves and their luggage into the house, Pamela rapturous about the holiday to Cara, how thrilling they'd found it, what an opportunity it had been.

John was eager to hear Cara's news.

'First things first,' Pamela said, distracting him with a drink.

Elsie appeared, putting her head round the door first as if testing the waters, smiling briskly at Pamela, hugging John with restrained delight. Pamela took out a folder of photographs from her handbag, famous landmarks, bridges, fountains, all taken from various angles. It had all been splendid – the ship spectacular. Nights had been spent drinking champagne, days sunbathing on deck, sightseeing, making quick purchases on their various stop-offs. She pointed to her bulging bags; the evidence of her zeal in buying presents for everyone.

'The ship was loveliest at night when it was floodlit, a floating palace, isn't that right, John?' she said, replacing the photographs carefully that Elsie'd swooned over, claiming

John's sole attention with her secret looks, love turning her hostile to everyone but him. Cara felt like a child, excluded by her parents in their private memories, driven from them with their possessiveness. Elsie looked with distaste at the clutter all around, and left saying dinner would be in an hour.

Finally, Pamela went upstairs to take a shower, saying she felt hot and sticky after the journey.

'I'm taking Bouncer for a stroll, Cara. Coming?' John said.

Cara hastened to get her jacket, John already setting off, a delighted Bouncer scrambling for the door.

They walked along, Cara filling him in on new office news, John giving Bouncer's lead a yank every time he tried to stop. His face intensified with surprise when Cara told him of George's fear of the planning permission for the Quays site falling through.

'That's George for you, panicking the minute my back's turned. It won't happen. I'll swing it with the city chaps.'

'How'll you do that?'

'By giving them enough zeros to make their eyes water. That'll do the trick. Mark my words that apartment block'll be built, and soon too, before builders hike up their fees again. I'll have it sorted out in no time. The important thing is that we market it in such a way as to get the adrenaline flowing. Tell the rich clients it's what they want because they sure as hell don't know.' He laughed enthusiastically.

Cara was used to her father's methods of doing business. An avid networker, he knew everyone and everyone knew him. 'There'ya are, John,' friends and colleagues would say in bars and restaurants, ordering him a drink as soon as he walked in the door. He used his popularity to woo the politicians and people in power to get what he wanted. Maybe his approach was unconventional, but what harm was that? There was no denying his success. When he homed in on something new he made it pay. He had the Midas touch. Glancing at him, Cara saw the excitement in his eyes, his plump cheeks and his swelled chest, and relaxed.

They turned into the sunshine, walked along the front. They sat down on a bench overlooking the sea. White yachts were moving slowly towards the haze on the horizon.

'It's good to be home,' John said, smiling up at the sky, inhaling the smell of the sea. 'And how have you been, darling? I don't want to interfere but how are things between you and Andy?' he asked, giving her a worrying look.

The thought of Andy troubled Cara enough to make her want to forget about him. John, noting her reticence, said, 'You don't have to discuss him if you don't want to.'

'We've separated for a while,' she said, hesitantly.

'Any particular reason?' he asked.

Cara told him about the afternoon of the poker game, taking herself by surprise by admitting that she'd been enraged at the time, and was now ashamed of her bad temper. The barriers Pamela had thrown up earlier with her possessiveness were gone now that they were out of doors and away from her. His interest in every detail was a source of comfort to her. Nothing was really altered in this father-daughter relationship.

'It seems so trivial now,' she concluded.

'It's strange how sympathetic we can be from a distance, yet so irritated at close range.'

'Andy was furious with me for leaving him like that. Things have gone from bad to worse.'

Being with her father again, feeling his gentle reassurance as she filled in the picture of the last month, searching her memory for the most trivial recollections, her need to share them with him, cleared the air. Cara pressed her wet face against her father's jacket. He put his arm around her.

She wiped her eyes saying, 'I'm sorry. I didn't mean to cry.'

'I'm sorry you had cause to. 'Best to let him cool down.'

'Andy seems to be making an effort. He's got a computer installed and he's very enthusiastic about getting his ideas off the ground.'

'That's good.'

'He's desperate for me to go back and I certainly don't want to do anything to antagonise him while he's in this frame of mind.'

'It's a delicate situation,' John said. 'What you do next is your prerogative in the circumstances. I'm sure you'll sort it out and be back together again soon.' He put his hand over hers.

They sat like that, their eyes on the view.

'Talk to me about Pamela,' she said. 'Are you happy, Dad?'

'Very happy,' he replied.

'Good. I'm glad.'

'That's all I want for you too, my darling, your happiness. Now, we'd better get back or they'll will be wondering where we've got to.'

He let go of her hand and stood up; leading the way along the path, Bouncer following obediently, his lead tightly wound around John's fingers.

Cara called to see Suzanne the next evening. Suzanne was feeding Lucy who smiled and cooed at Cara.

'I see she's finally making herself at home with you,' Suzanne said, wiping the baby's mouth, and putting her in Cara's arms while she cleared up.

With Lucy's head propped awkwardly against her shoulder Cara patted her back. Lucy belched softly.

'I was so jealous of you having this adorable baby,' Cara said, the idea of it making her laugh.

Suzanne said, 'You and Andy'll have one of your own.'

Cara said, 'I had a talk with Dad about Andy and me. He assumes I'm going back to him.'

'Aren't you?'

Cara said, 'Andy's doing his best. He's making all sorts of promises to get me to go back.'

'And you're prepared to give him another chance?'

'Yes. I've told him I'll give it another go, not that I expect him to change that much. He never will. He goes through life with such certainty that his is the right way that he doesn't see the pitfalls. He's so superior sometimes.'

'Everybody has to feel superior to somebody sometime,' Suzanne said wisely.

'I want things to be different. I want him to earn some money for a start.'

'You'll have to take him down a peg or two. Say to him, "You'd better start making money, you have expensive tastes."'

Cara said, 'He has, and he's been set in his ways too long. That mother of his spoilt him.'

'So when will you go home?'

'I'll be seeing Andy on Sunday. I'll decide then. To tell you the truth I can't wait to be back in my own home again.'

'I'll bet.'

'How's Dick?'

Suzanne sighed. 'He's in Scotland with Guy. They're busy with appointments and arrangements and who they'll be meeting next.'

'When will they be back?'

'I haven't the faintest idea.' Suzanne was annoyed. 'Do you know, Cara, we planned this move so far ahead, talked of it in so much detail, that I thought it would be bliss. Everything we dreamed of.'

'And isn't it?'

'No, because now that we're back home, and things are at

last coming round the way we wants them to, Dick's on to the next thing. He's on the go all the time. I don't know when we sat down to a meal together last.' She looked wounded and rightly so, Cara thought.

'He'll settle down when the business gets more established,' she consoled her.

Suzanne shook her head.

'He loves going off with Guy. They're meeting some titled people for dinner tonight. Dick loves titled people, especially women,' she said suddenly.

Cara didn't know the answer to that remark.

11

When Cara arrived at the cottage the following Sunday Andy wasn't there. Walking around, inspecting everything, she could see that he had gone to some pains, the furniture polished, everything spick and span, for her visit. When she heard the sound of a car, footsteps hurrying across the gravel, she went to the front door to greet him. He handed her a bunch of red roses.

'I went to get you these.'

'Thank you. They're lovely.'

'How are you?'

'All right, thanks. Having a look around.'

He nodded. 'How's Elsie?'

'Fine.'

'And Bouncer?' he asked, adding a note of enthusiasm to his voice that Cara didn't miss.

'His usual lazy self.' She glanced up and smiled at him for the first time since he'd entered the house, appreciating the effort he was making to take an interest in life at Rockmount.

'And how have you been?'

'OK.'

'How are the friends?'

'I haven't seen much of them. I've put them out of my mind.'

Cara didn't ask why and he didn't volunteer. She went into the kitchen. Andy followed her, stood guard over the kettle.

'I'll make you a cup of tea,' he said.

They sat down at the table; Andy poured out the tea. Cara watched him. To her observant eyes he appeared the same. He looked up and met her gaze, his eyebrows raised.

'How about coming home. I miss you.'

'On one condition.'

Andy looked at her sharply. 'Which is?'

'That you join Alcoholics Anonymous.'

'Why should I do that? I'm not an alcoholic,' Andy protested.

'You have a drink problem that needs to be dealt with, Andy.'

Cara, not wishing to provoke him further waited silently.

'All right, I like a few drinks, but I can control my drinking.'

Cara lowered her eyes, kept her head down as she considered the grain of the tabletop, waiting nervously for his next comment.

'Right,' he said, finally, when he saw no sign of her backing down. 'If that's what you want, I'll give it a go.'

'That's a promise?'

'I said I would. Now will you come home?'

'Yes.'

So Cara returned home that night. They were back to their old routine. At first they were like strangers, Andy meeting her at the station in the evenings, always glad to see her, always polite, ready to listen to her news, saying little until they were on the slope for home.

She went through her days in a haze of understanding, everything glossed over, or at least trying to understand the difficulties Andy was facing. Cara indulged him once more with her cooking and cajoling, but making love was awkward, Andy kissing her deferentially, fearful almost, as if it was a duty, no trace of the passionate young man who'd swept her off her feet. Despite everything, Andy seemed to be coping better. They would go to the cinema once a week, together, never to the pub. He was attending AA, battling with the booze, but only to please her. Apart from the occasional slip he was managing, and he was spending a lot of time at his computer.

Gradually in this calmer atmosphere the pattern of their lives together resumed and improved. What Andy had accomplished so far, with his computer, Cara had no idea. As usual he was uninformative. Once or twice he came near to achieving something. This she'd guessed, because he'd got all fired up, going to meet people, working up his enthusiasm with endless telephone conversations. He said there was no point in counting his chickens before they were hatched. She knew that it had all come to nothing by his slamming down of the phone, calling whoever was at the other end 'a shit' or worse. His abrupt answers when she spoke to him indicated that he was upset, but still he remained tight-lipped, not knowing how to behave when things went wrong. He would retreat from his mistakes into baffled silence, humbled, deliberately not being his real self to hide the faults he'd displayed when challenged. Defeated, he would be on the brink of collapse, but his natural optimism would eventually exceed his incapacity. Courageously he would bounce back, resume his efforts in good spirits, not put off for long, and not holding a grudge, never doubting his own ability.

Cara treated him carefully when she saw a 'mood' coming on, determined to keep her side of the bargain. At times like that she would take herself off to the city for a shopping spree, sometimes with Vanessa or Suzanne, or both if they were available. Occasionally, she went alone. She would have coffee in the quiet atmosphere of a department store and read a newspaper or magazine. Often she called in to see Elsie on the way home. 'Earn gold and wear it,' Elsie would say approvingly, and Cara did that, building up an extensive wardrobe with each of Andy's moods.

Sometimes she would walk for miles along the secluded beach near home, feeling unconstrained, examining her life. Where were they going? What were they doing? What was Andy doing? Would he get his project off the ground? She had no idea. What she did know was that they weren't like any of the young couples she encountered on her way, happily holding hands, laughing together. That part of their lives was over.

The fact was that Andy was making an effort and that was enough proof for her that he was doing his best. While some people were watching for the marriage to disintegrate, her father was watching for signs of improvement with the surveillance of a concerned parent. Conscious of this, Andy became even more self-conscious in his presence. He would bring her flowers to save face, and she would accept them and the fact that she was the one who must help him, and she would, for as long as she could. Money was only money after all. She would spend it to provide him with time and to bolster him up in his project, now that he was fully occupied with it and keeping off the booze. That was the most important thing for the moment.

At the office a couple of weeks later Isabella was airing her grievances to anyone who would listen. She was earning less than the basic wage.

'You're here to learn English.' George was taking advantage of her scant knowledge of the English language.

Scornful, she felt she had much to put up with in this country. 'And it is always raining,' she said, 'and crowded. In Spain it ees hot now.'

'The rain in Spain falls mainly on the plain,' Debbie joked.

Cara would like a holiday in Spain at that very minute. If she could persuade her father to get involved in
Spanish property there would be constant trips to Spain.
She might even consider staying out there for a while. It
might do Andy good to get out of the rut he was in. He
might even be persuaded to work with her there. There
was a distant relative in Madrid that she'd heard her father
speak about.

Cara left them to argue among themselves. She had an
appointment, walking quickly and purposefully through the
streets to show a couple, who were both in business one of
the newly built apartments in Temple Bar. Women loitered,
children tugging at their skirts to look in shop windows
at sweets and chocolates piled in pyramids. The smell of
pizza from Milano's was sickly sweet in the air. People
spilled into street from shops, others stood in shop doorways.

Then she saw him crossing the Halfpenny Bridge. He came
out of the crowd. Cara's heart lurched. She wanted to keep
going, disappear into the crowd before his very eyes, like a
conjuring trick. He barred her way. She couldn't turn back,
people were surging forward and she was stuck. There wasn't
a corner where she could escape from him.

As he walked towards her she was conscious of that air of
excitement that she'd felt when she'd first met him. They
stood there, a sense of awe about their meeting like that.
He's so handsome she thought, looking at him, wondering
what monstrous authority in him made him stand so tall and
upright. His eyes were tawny against the light, his black hair
trailed over the sharp white collar of his shirt. People's faces
blurred, their voices faded.

'I'm glad I bumped into you,' he began. 'I've been meaning
to get in touch.'

Steering her by the elbow out of the crowd he said lightly,

'I had the survey back. There's a problem with the extension to the kitchen. There was no planning permission for it.'

'Oh.'

'I've been advised to withdraw my offer until it can be sorted out.'

'I'll get Dad to get in touch with the solicitors. See what can be done.'

'How about having dinner with me?'

Cara held her breath. Her mind was racing. Her letting him down would be difficult, though a matter of principle.

'I'll phone you.'

All three of them were working out in the gym.

'How are things with Andy?' Vanessa asked.

Cara looked around seeing nothing but a dull, dreary void. 'I thought it was going to be better.'

'And it isn't?' Vanessa prompted.

'He seems to be acting a part. Going through the motions, his words belying the look in his eyes. He hints at all these plans he has, but no one takes him seriously. It's this attitude he has. This air of indifference.'

'I admire you for going back to him. It must have taken a lot of bottle.'

Pedalling furiously on an exercise bike, Cara remained silent.

'He has his problems, I grant you,' said Suzanne. 'But once they're sorted out and he gets a job that he likes, it should be plain sailing. He'll be perfect.'

'Perfect!' scoffed Vanessa. 'There's no such species as a perfect male.'

Vanessa's expectations from men were too high. Every love affair she embarked on seemed to backfire. She had turned into a complete sceptic.

'And you, Mother Teresa,' she said to Cara, 'you'll have

to leave him eventually before he turns you into a nut case like himself.'

'He isn't that bad,' Suzanne protested.

'He's a freeloading bum. He sees you as a meal ticket. I did warn you against Andy, Cara, but you went ahead and married him.'

'Vanessa!' Suzanne was horror-stricken. 'That's going a bit too far.'

'Sorry, but that's my opinion.'

'Cara didn't ask you for it.'

Vanessa shrugged. 'I'm paid large sums of money to give it.'

'When it's requested.'

'You don't have to worry about my feelings, Suzanne,' Cara said. 'I'm well acquainted with Vanessa's opinion.'

Suzanne turned on Vanessa. 'No man stands a chance against you. You make fun of them. And your expectations are too high.'

'Not true,' Vanessa said, pedalling industriously on her motionless bike.

'Then why don't you go off and marry that Edward Foxtrot or whatever his name is who's so desperate to get his claws into you? We could all do with a day out.'

'His mother wouldn't like it.' Vanessa stretched her arms. 'Bloody marriage? Who wants it?' she sighed.

'Everyone should get married. It's the natural thing to do.' Suzanne was defensive, trying to hide the fact that she felt like a neglected loveless wife.

'If there's one thing that's convinced me that marriage is a no-go area it's the amount of divorce cases that land on my desk.'

'Marriage can be claustrophobic,' Suzanne conceded. 'Dick and I don't have much fun anymore.' It took all Suzanne's courage to admit this to Vanessa.

'That's the understatement,' said Vanessa derisively, glancing out the window. 'It's going to be a long hot day and I'm going to make the most of it.'

'What about love?' Suzanne asked.

'You don't need marriage for that,' guffawed Vanessa. Unless, of course, it's a good career move.'

'Like a judge or something?'

'Exactly,' said Vanessa.

'You're obsessed with the law, Vanessa,' Suzanne said.

'What about kids? Don't you want any?' Cara asked Vanessa

'Never.'

'You're out of touch with your feminine side,' Suzanne said.

Vanessa shrugged. 'Maybe I am. Who cares?'

Fears welled up in Cara's mind when she was on her way home about the true situation between Andy and herself, her uncertainties increased by Vanessa's chilling words. Absurd questions that were unanswerable raised their ugly heads. What is the point of it all? Where is it leading? She would never make Andy into the man she wanted him to be, and she would never escape him either; her way out was blocked.

She delved into the past, thinking of the chances she'd given him over the years. To stay with him, in the cottage, year in year out, seeing nothing but the same places and faces, the same view, was unthinkable. Yet despite everything she'd have to give Andy one more chance, if only to prove to herself that she'd done her best.

As she put her key in the lock, the sound of the television from behind the drawn curtains irritating before she ever got inside the front door.

12

Out of the blue the following Friday evening Dick called to the cottage, accompanied by Guy. It was the end of a hot June. Cara was watering the flowers, dragging the hose from one place to another, her jeans wet and muddy, grass stuck to her shoes.

'Andy's not around?'

'He went into Arklow. I'm not quite sure how long he'll be though,' she said.

'He asked me to come and look at something he thinks I might be interested in.'

'I'm sure he'll be back shortly if he's expecting you.'

In contrast to his hand-made Savile Row suit, Guy was wearing faded Levis, a T-shirt that exposed bronzed muscular arms and Adidas trainers.

'You're soaked.' Guy said, giving her that heart-melting look of his, watching her trailing the hose over the grass.

'It's too good an evening to waste indoors and the garden is parched.'

'Come to think of it, so am I.'

'Would you like a beer?'

'I thought you'd never ask,' Dick said. 'I'll get them.'

Dick disappeared into the cottage. Guy took the hose from her, hunkering down to wind it up.

The scent of flowers and soil were heavy in the heat. Cara wiped a trickle of perspiration from her brow.

Heart hammering, blood tingling, she said, 'You have a nerve turning up here.'

'How else was I going to get to see you? You haven't returned my calls.' Straightening up, he smiled his warm smile. 'How come you're so uptight?'

'It's dangerous.'

'I like danger.'

'Well, I don't.'

'Look, Dick asked me to drop by with him after work to check out what Andy's working on.'

'How are you getting on with the house?'

'We had to track down the previous owners. Search the records for planning permission. There definitely wasn't any so we have to go about getting it, or the council would have wanted it torn down. I'm making so many changes. You won't recognise it.'

'I have other plans,' she said, looking at him, seeing his dissatisfaction in her excuse. 'I'll get Dad to go down. He'd love to see it.'

Dick reappeared with three cans of Budweiser. He and Guy followed her across the lawn to sit under the mulberry tree. Gnats danced in the shaft of light, the scent of jasmine hung in the air around them.

Andy arrived. Dick went to meet him.

'Good of you to call,' he said, delighted to see Dick.

'You remember Guy McIntosh?' Dick asked.

Andy stared at him. For one heart-stopping moment Cara thought that Andy was going to be rude to him. He stayed polite.

'Hello, there,' he said, coming quickly across the lawn to shake hands with Guy, shading his eyes against the sun.

'Good evening.' Guy greeted him genially, Andy begging him not to stir himself.

Cara joined in the trivial comments about the weather.

'So,' Andy said. 'How do you like Ireland?'

'Enormously. You people know how to enjoy yourselves. Pubs everywhere.'

'All in the pursuit of happiness,' Andy said, smiling.

Their eyes met. Guy looked away first.

'Right, let's have a look at what you've got, Andy,' Dick said.

They walked back to the house. Cara went into the kitchen to get more drinks, an excuse to get away from there. She put her hands to her head, exasperated, wishing Guy hadn't turned up like that out of the blue.

'Guy was telling me that he was in the RAF,' Andy said to her when she brought fresh drinks into the sitting room.

'Oh.' Cara was wishing she were miles away.

'The happiest days of my life,' Guy said.

'I'll leave you to it,' she said, going back out into the garden.

Her calmness lasted until she was alone. She sat on the garden seat, dejected, her eyes on the valley beyond the garden lying in a tranquil haze, the first of the houses in the new housing estate already occupied, washing on the clothes line.

Before they left Guy came to her.

'Goodbye, Cara. Thanks for the drinks.' Lowering his voice he said, 'Say you'll come to see the house. I don't want it all to have been for nothing.' He was gazing down at her, frowning a little as if waiting for a rejection.

She kept her eyes on her drink.

'When will I hear from you?' he asked, grasping her wrist like a handcuff, looking at her with his intense gaze.

'I'll ring you.'

'I've got big plans for that house, you know.'

She darted a nervous glance at Andy. He was gone, walking briskly with Dick to his car to see him off. Guy joined them. Cara watched with a pang as they stood for a few minutes,

Andy ardently talking, Guy interjecting occasionally, his face averted, a sardonic expression on it. She couldn't catch what they were saying. Andy returned.

'Well, what a surprise that was,' he said, sitting down, stretched his arm across her shoulders.

'What was?'

'Dick turning up like that, bringing Guy with him. You never know what might come out of it. He might fix me up with a job in his company,' he added.

She wondered if Andy had asked him for a job. It couldn't possibly have come up unless Andy had dragged it into the conversation. This was too embarrassing.

'I told him I was available,' Andy said, as if reading her thoughts.

'Was that wise?'

'Why not? It's not a crime, is it, to be looking for work?' he asked with a wry smile.

Cara was thinking of Andy, possessive, interfering, always wanting to find out everything he could about other people, his interest surprisingly nosy.

'Guy's company always seems to be so pressured, so very busy.'

'I've almost forgotten what that's like,' said Andy.

You never knew, Cara thought unkindly. Guy and Dick are so different to you. They come from a completely different world.

'I could begin work straight away. After a trial period I'd be in charge of a department.' Andy began pacing up and down, restlessly considering his options.

'What exactly would you be doing?'

Lost in thought, he didn't seem to hear.

'The job might not be here. I might be sent away.'

'Where?'

'To Scotland or the States. Anywhere. They've got branches

all over the world.' Smugly, he smiled, looking into the distance as if seeing a rosy future, mistakenly assuming that Cara shared his enthusiasm.

Cara, watching him surreptitiously, wondered if Guy would uproot him, send him off to get rid of him. She doubted it.

'I didn't think much of Guy to begin with, but he has good points,' Andy continued. 'He knows the job. Don't you think it would be a great idea, me working for him? Think of what I might learn.'

There was a ring of doom to these words.

'Don't bank on him too much,' was all Cara could manage to say. 'Look at those roses. Haven't they come on really well?'

Her attempt to change the subject implied awkwardness, a cover up. Andy noticed. His irritation flared into sudden anger.

'Why do you say don't bank on Guy? Has he said something to you?'

'No, of course not.'

'Has Dick?'

'No, he hasn't.'

'Well then, there's hope. I must have some plans for myself,' he said defensively.

'All I'm saying is don't be too hopeful.'

His self-esteem was lowered by what he took to be her indifference, but really was her fear.

'I can't win with you, can I?' The intensity of his scorn made her cringe.

'I'm too tired to argue,' she said, not wishing to go down that well worn path with him. 'Let's wait and see.'

He stood up strode back to the house.

She sat there for a long time, her wrist still tingling where Guy had held it. Thinking of him, she wished he were still there with her.

13

---◆---

The days passed by with Cara going around in a daze, seeing Guy's face everywhere, wondering when, if ever, she would ever see him again, at the same time not wanting to bump in to him. She avoided Suzanne's house so that he wouldn't think she was hoping to meet him there. The less that was said to anyone about her feelings for him the better.

She couldn't stop thinking about him dancing with her at Suzanne's party, the look of love in his eyes, the feel of his arms around her waist. Those first tender kisses that barely touched her lips and drove her crazy with desire. She spent her evenings imagining where their next meeting would take place, what it would be like. Sometimes she thought she'd die if she didn't see him again soon. She knew she was falling in love with him and never imagining for a moment that her love would be reciprocated now that she had rejected him. He had charmed her and because of this she felt that her life had changed, everything hanging in the air.

That Guy had more to him than was obvious Cara knew, and she was willing to concede that there was a touch of the forbidden fruits about him. At night she thought about him and felt forlorn and vulnerable, the world a cruel place. If only to see him for a little while, talk to him, let him take her in his arms. This had to be done now or it would never be done, and she would truly die. But obstinacy prevented her from talking to Suzanne about him, begging her help, so she adopted an attitude of not caring to protect her and tried to forget him.

Things got bad again with Andy. Some man he'd pestered with his ideas had sent him an e-mail calling him a time waster and an exhibitionist, and saying he didn't want to hear from him again. He started having liquid lunches at his local, often inviting a couple of reprobates back to watch a soccer match and to partake of a few cans of lager. Cara came home one evening to find him with his pals singing their heads off, screeching with laughter, drunk as skunks. Maurice, the landlord, had called Andy's behaviour 'objectionable' and accused him of perpetrating the late-night gatherings that threatened the good name of The Crowing Cock, evicting him on the spot.

It was as if Andy was acting like this because he couldn't live up to his own brilliant expectations of himself, as if he couldn't make up to her, no matter how hard he tried, for failing to be what she expected him to be. His behaviour was met with rows, then silent acceptance, and unspoken blame. But Cara's resentment of her time and devotion to him, and the helplessness of the situation, was growing.

By now Guy had phoned several times to invite her to see his house. Finally she succumbed and went to visit him in Arklow. A large skip was in the driveway, full of rubble and shattered glass. Stripped of its creeper, and sleek with its new double-glazed windows, the house looked different, completely unconnected to the photograph in the For Sale brochure.

The hall smelt of new paint and varnish, the pale coloured walls giving it a great feeling of space and light. The wooden floors were freshly stained and polished to a burnt umber. New curtains matched the new cream-coloured suite of furniture in the drawing room. On a desk in one of the corners there were photographs in silver frames. Cara knew one of them would be of his wife. She would have liked to take a closer look, so as she could imagine her as a real person. Not wishing to violate his privacy she desisted.

Guy caught up with her at the door of the drawing room.

'Of course it's not finished,' he was saying, taking her hand, gently leading her around.

'It's wonderful,' she said. 'It must have cost an absolute fortune.'

'Yes, but I'm having great fun splashing out on it. And it's so worthwhile, don't you think?' You see, I like beautiful things. he said, showing her his purchases, drawing her into his new quest for bargains.

In the main bedroom she found herself looking at the enormous four-poster bed, its rich crimson drapes a perfect match for the curtains and the Turkish rug on the floor.

'Well, what do you think?'

A white bathrobe hung on the back of the door of the en-suite bathroom, slippers to match. It was his doing. His bachelor pad and he had taken great pains to make it comfortable. She felt like a child, afraid to say anything in case he thought she was making a joke out of it, and afraid to touch the ornaments and trimmings.

The bay window opened up more of the view for inspection and gave a new distance. From where she stood she could see the whole bay. Boats sailed past the lighthouse; seagulls rose and hovered above them, their wings gold in the sunset. Two trawlers steered towards the sea, leaving behind the lighthouse, the harbour walls, the faded shops, the narrow houses wedged between the public house and the church with its glinting spire.

He came and stood beside her. Nervous, excited, conscious of his eyes on her, she felt the same sort of anguish that she felt before the party. He was watching her. Embarrassed, she found it impossible to hold on to her composure.

'Look at me,' he said. 'Tell me what you're thinking.'

'I'm wondering why you asked me here.'

He put his arm around her. 'To get your approval. Now I'm wondering why you look so frightened. Are you afraid I'm going to lock you up? Keep you here for good?'

'Don't be silly. I'm not frightened.'

He lifted her hand to his lips and kissed it in a gracious, flattering gesture.

'I can't stay much longer,' she said. 'I'm expected home.'

'If I did lock you up here no one would find you.'

'I'd have to climb down the wall.'

'No creeper to hold on to.'

She didn't know what to say next, having decided that she wouldn't be led into something with him. In the end she didn't have a choice. There was no resisting him when he said, 'Cara, I'm totally besotted by you. I can't stop thinking about you. Don't you feel anything for me? What do I have to do to prove myself to you?'

She went to him, bold and uncaring, her arms outstretched in a ridiculous gesture, the sudden impact of her embrace making him stagger backwards.

'Hey,' he laughed, seizing her in an irresistible force. The glowing heat of his body searing her. He smelt of cinnamon and musk, and something else. Those intense seconds she forgot everything as he held her, turning her knees to jelly, a feeling of eternity in their embrace, the air throbbing with mystery and possibilities.

Eventually she drew back.

He pulled her to him, kissed her again.

'I want to . . .'

This time he kissed her with infinite tenderness, easing her towards the bed, removing her clothes slowly with tantalising kisses as he did so, then his own, leaving nothing but the sheets satiny against their skin. Side by side they lay, Guy stroking the smooth lines of her body, pulling her close. With agonising slow kisses he moved down her neck to her breasts. She groaned with pleasure as his tongue circled one nipple, then the other. He continued on downward exploring with soft, delicate kisses, flooding her with desperate desire. How long was it since she felt such an exquisite sensation, if she ever had? Guilty, she felt wicked, then wild as he rose above her. Wantonly she clung to him, losing track of where the sensations were coming from. When he thrust into her she tightened herself around him. They moved together, frantic, rough. Just before she came, she opened her eyes to see his glistening face rising over her. She slid her hands up his arms and pulled him towards her. They clung together, panting. He pushed into her one last time, and came with ferocity, shudders ripping through his body.

For a while they lay still, his arms around her, both of them quiet, her eyes half-closed, the scent of him washing over her. She fell asleep and when she opened her eyes the sun blazed through the gap in the curtains setting the fabric aflame, swathing his face in its orange light, casting the rest of the room in shadow, imprinting the moment in her memory forever. The sun was warm; the room cool from the open window.

He was looking at her, love in his eyes. She put her hand on his cheek, curious about him. What was it about this man that had made the sex between them so extraordinary? He was so different from her, yet he seemed to be able to read her like a book. Perhaps the study of women was part of this worldly-wisdom he exuded. She had no way of knowing. Reticent about the details of his life, he hadn't mentioned his dead wife a second time. He didn't talk about work much either. Too boring to discuss, he'd said, but she suspected that he was afraid to let her fully into his life. Perhaps he felt that there was a danger in letting her get to know him. What if she saw the flaws, found the faults and pitfalls? What if she found nothing but an empty shell?

After a while he stirred, pulled himself up, swung his body away and got out of bed. She watched the long lines of his lean body as he walked into the shadows, and thought how mysterious he was. He returned with a bottle of wine and two glasses. Carefully he uncorked the wine and poured. He leaned towards her to hand her a glass.

'Here's to you,' he said. 'You're wonderful.' She wanted to sing and dance, shout it to the rooftops, cry, die, the lightness in her head making her dizzy and the breath crushed out of her. He'd said she was wonderful and she was trying to see herself the way he saw her, growing increasingly nervous when she failed to do so. Yet she was happy.

14

'I'm having a bit of a fling,' Vanessa blurted out, busy varnishing her toenails bright red, her hair newly washed.

She wasn't the kind of girl who could keep personal things to herself. Her work was a different matter.

They were, all three of them, sunbathing, sprawled on a rug on the balcony of Vanessa's apartment, in their underwear, Lucy in her seat in the shady corner.

Suzanne said, with a touch of sarcasm, 'Bully for you.'

'Who is he?' Cara asked, not all that surprised. Vanessa was partial to the odd fling. 'Anyone we know?'

Vanessa nodded. 'The Indian boy in the gym.'

There was a collective sigh of disbelief. Suzanne sat up. Speechless, she looked at her. 'The teenager with the tangled hair?'

'Abdullah, the very one.'

'You're joking.'

'Cross my heart.'

Abdullah was the shy, heart-stoppingly young and sexy masseur with his ebony-coloured skin, his wildcat eyes, his black shiny hair and perfectly flexed muscles. The women swooned when he was around. His appointment book was full weeks in advance.

'Babysnatcher!' Cara laughed.

'Right enough. I caught him gazing at you from behind that window of his while he's doing his massages,' Suzanne said.

'Panting, his nose pressed to the glass no doubt,' Cara added. 'But he's so young.'

'It's disgusting,' mocked Suzanne.

Vanessa giggled. 'Jealous?'

'Of course I am. I always fancied him. But he's not what you normally go for.'

'Not normal, but it's very natural, believe me,' Vanessa sniggered.

'What's he like naked?' Suzanne asked in a hushed tone, not waiting for a reply, plunging in with, 'How many orgasms did you have?' her eyebrows raised mockingly.

'Hey! I'm not telling you every gory detail. He's good. That's all you need to know. I've no intention of letting the conversation turn into a carnal confession. I don't want to cause jealousy here,' she grinned.

'Oh, balls! What's the point of being with a beautiful male if you can't boast about his prowess in bed?' quipped Suzanne.

'I've no complaints,' Vanessa said smugly. 'He did all the work. All I had to do was lie there and think of England.'

'Where's your patriotism?' laughed Cara.

'Afterwards, I felt all slippery and wonderful, as if I'd been swallowed whole.'

Gob-smacked Suzanne said, 'Some people have all the luck.'

Cara said, 'What about Edward?'

'What about him?' snapped Vanessa.

'Well, you are seeing him, sort of.'

'Now for the lies and excuses,' said Suzanne, her sarcasm tinged with jealousy, having knowledge at first hand of the dangerous attraction Abdullah held for the women who flocked around him. It was in his handsome face.

'I don't know if I'll be seeing Abdullah again. It was only just the once.'

'It's never only once. Especially if he's as good as you say he is in bed,' Suzanne said, leaning on one elbow, excited about the whole thing. 'But just because he's good-looking doesn't mean he's any good for you.'

Vanessa gave a little laugh as she raised her head dramatically and looked Suzanne right between the eyes. 'I'll take that risk,' she said, her tone girlish and naïve.

'I'm telling you its dangerous. You'll go too far, get yourself into something that'll all amount to – nothing. Then you'll be devastated.'

'Rubbish!' Vanessa gave her a filthy look.

'You seem to be in a very condemning mood, Suzanne,' said Cara, her head bowed, thinking that these little arguments and misunderstandings that were happening between the three of them, not amounting to much, but threatening trouble.

'It was one night of passion,' Vanessa protested. 'What's the harm in that?'

Suzanne looked at her disapprovingly. 'You're so naïve, or else you're a good liar.'

'Do you think he might fall in love with you?' Cara asked.

'I don't know. That's a whole different ball game.' Vanessa sighed with pleasure at the thought.

'You're asking for trouble, Vanessa. 'You'll have to forget about him.' Her words gave Cara a queer feeling in her stomach.

Suzanne looked really concerned about her.

'You're getting fierce with your exaggerating.'

Cara was thinking of her own fling with Guy.

'I bet you're falling in love with him,' Suzanne accused.

'What would be the point of that?' Vanessa stretched her taut, tanned body and yawned. 'He'll be heading off back to India or somewhere hot before long. He hates the winters here.'

Cara left Vanessa's late. When she got home she sneaked in through the back door. All was quiet downstairs. Andy was in bed, awake.

'I was waiting for you,' he said, nuzzling her neck.

'I'm tired,' Cara said, but Andy in his determination to make love to her was taking no excuses.

She succumbed to him, to keep the peace, images of Guy rising up in Cara's subconscious, jostling each other for supremacy, distracting her. She thrust them out of her mind and concentrated on Andy with a zeal that startled him and brought him to a speedy climax.

'Who were you thinking of just then?' he asked, his voice full of suspicion.

Startled Cara looked at him. 'What do you mean?'

'Russell Crowe in *Gladiator*? You fancied him, didn't you?'

Cara sank back into her pillows with relief. 'I wasn't thinking of anyone,' she blustered

'Sorry. I shouldn't have said that. It hasn't been that good for such a long time. I suppose I get scared.'

Cara held her breath as she waited to hear what he was going to say next.

'I know after years of being together sex can get boring. If there's anything you want me to do that might spice things up, even if it's a bit kinky, I'm willing to try.'

Horrified, Cara said, 'Everything's fine the way it is,' squashing the conversation, the thought of attempting any kind of sexual adventures with Andy frightening the life out of her.

Gratified, he lay down and relaxed into a deep sleep. Cara buried her head in her pillow, tears soaking it at the cruelty of the world. Into the core of her everyday life had come this man, Guy McIntosh, with his handsome face and winning ways. She shouldn't see him ever again, but she knew she would, regardless of Vanessa's warning, and regardless of the turmoil and chaos he'd brought to her life. She needed him, that she truly believed. Without him her life was a shell of pretence. She was in at the deep end.

Cara kept herself busy, not a minute to spare, rushing around from one job to another.

'Hey!' Vanessa accosted her at the gym early the following Saturday morning. 'I want to talk to you.'

She'd been trying to pin Cara down for a chat, suspecting something was going on, but not knowing what. Cara was usually too busy, warding her off with a torrent of excuses.

'What about?'

'Nothing in particular. Stay and have a drink.'

'I can't. Andy's expecting me back,' Cara lied.

'Suzanne says she hasn't seen much of you either. She's wondering what's going on.'

'There's nothing going on.'

'Let's have a drink then. Just one before you go.'

'OK.'

Cara showered, lifting her head to the powerful jet, letting the water run down her body, delaying the conversation with Vanessa.

'How are you and Andy getting on?' Vanessa asked pointedly. 'You haven't said much about him lately.'

'We're OK,' Cara said, thinking of Guy. 'You're still seeing Abdullah?' She arched an eyebrow quizzically; thinking the best form of defence was attack.

Vanessa grinned. 'I tried to put him right out of my mind but I couldn't. Suzanne's right. A night of passionate sex like that and you're not able to let go, believe me.'

'Poor Suzanne, I don't think she's very happy at the moment.'

'She doesn't seem to be,' Vanessa agreed. 'Babies can be a handful.'

'So can husbands. I wouldn't fancy being married to Dick. He's too pernickety with his brand labels and correct ways.'

Cara finished her drink and left, escaping from Vanessa, avoiding one of the long leisurely chats they usually had in case she let anything slip about Guy.

Where was Guy? She hadn't heard from him. Did he have any idea of how much anxiety their night of passion was causing her? Did he care? It was true. A night of passion was difficult to forget. But Cara knew she couldn't risk it again because she had made her promises to Andy and she'd every intention of fulfilling them.

Cara was in Suzanne's house ten days later when Guy arrived unannounced. When he entered the room she shook from head to toe. She wanted to rush straight into his arms and might well have done had it not been for Suzanne and Dick's presence. Suzanne had been an unwitting accomplice in this secret and had helped Cara realise her passionate dream, but Cara wasn't about to pour out her heart to her.

Tongue-tied, she barely said hello to him. She couldn't help it and realised the failure in her words to express her new feeling. As soon as she could decently do so, she escaped.

Next morning there was a note on her desk. Isabella had written it down in her bold handwriting. 'Guy, he phone. Ring him.'

She phoned him, her hand over the mouthpiece furtively, and waited. His voice said: 'If you wish to leave a message for Guy McIntosh, please do so after the tone.'

Later he rang back and she arranged to meet him in Arklow on a pretext about his house. Full of guilt she hung up, and for the rest of the day she felt trapped in unreality, her surroundings unimportant. She couldn't bear the thought of deceiving Andy, but nothing was as important as her date with Guy, the time spent out of his company dragging. She kept looking at her watch. Mrs Moody, with her instinctive antennae at full alert, noticed.

'You're like a hen on a griddle. You off somewhere important?' she asked.

'I've got a property to show,' Cara told her.

By the time she reached Arklow it was getting dark. She parked by the harbour. The harbour was encompassed in shadows. Water slapped against the wall. A few lights flickered here and there, illuminating the wet pavement. On the quay two men stood talking, their faces ghostlike under the moonlight. The door of the hotel where Guy said he'd meet her was open, light flooding from it.

Inside it was crowded. People stared at her, questions in their eyes as to who she was going to meet. Squaring her shoulders, raising her head, she ordered a vodka and tonic, ignoring the inquisitive glances of the barman. She had a sense of being watched and took her drink to a corner, away from the men playing darts, hoping Guy would find her without any fuss.

There was a danger in pubs with glaring light. Yes, she'd avoid public places in future. What did it matter? She wasn't afraid of Andy. If caught, she'd deny it, she'd arch her eyebrows, stare at him blankly, say 'As if' calmly in a detached way, challenging him to dare think that she would dabble in anything as messy as an affair. He'd feel foolish. What did she care?

Still, it was alien to her to be acting like this. Trying to cover up the turmoil she was feeling inside, with the closed off look she'd been practising, she finished her drink. She wasn't good at this cloak and dagger stuff, this lying and cheating. Her nerves were jangling, her bones turning to jelly by the time he appeared.

There was an air of excitement about him, enhanced by an

element of danger that made her want to dance up to the bar to meet him. She stayed where she was.

'You were early,' he said, joining her.

'I'd never be late.'

He ordered vodka and tonic for her, and a draught beer for himself.

While they waited for the drinks he took her hand and squeezed it.

'Relax,' he said.

'We're being watched.'

He shrugged. 'Who cares? You don't have to be on your best behaviour here. You're not on show.'

The drinks arrived.

'Let's have a toast to being ourselves,' Guy said, lifting his glass.

'I wouldn't know who else to be,' Cara laughed, touching his glass with hers, taking a sip.

He leaned back, removed his tie, opened the top buttons of his shirt, and sat back to prove his point, oblivious of his surroundings. He chatted light-heartedly about the busy day he'd had, asked her about hers, no indication in his demeanour of their night of passion as if it had never happened. As soon as their drinks were finished they left.

They walked along the path of the hotel gardens. Without a word he guided her, his hand at the top of her arm, his manner brisk and proprietorial.

'I mustn't be too late home,' she cautioned him as they walked further.

'Don't think about home,' he said fiercely.

'I wish I didn't have to.'

They sat down on the little plateau in a clearing. The mist had blotted out the sea; the trees were blurred shadows. The air was heavy with the scent from the flowers. Guy took off his jacket and spread it out on the ground.

He took her in his arms, lowering her onto his jacket.

'I'm going to Cork next week. Come away with me,' he said.

'How can I? What excuse could I make?'

'It would only be for a few days.'

Cara was uncertain.

'I'll try. It's not going to be easy. I'm not used to taking time off without Andy being involved.'

'Well, you'd better get used to it.'

'I'll think of something.'

In the end it was easy. Cara told Andy and her father that she was going to a yoga convention in Youghal with a view to taking it up again.

15

P amela phoned Cara. 'I've invited Guy McIntosh to dinner
 on Saturday night,' she said to Cara in a voice rich with
anticipation.

'Oh,' Cara said, taken aback, not trusting her voice to say
anything further.

'I thought it was the least I could do to make him feel at
home. After all, he is a valued client. We'll invite Dick and
Suzanne too and Vanessa to make it into a cosy little dinner
party. Your father thinks it's a splendid idea.'

'I see,' said Cara, in a less than enthusiastic tone, wishing
that she'd never introduced her father to him.

An invitation to dinner seemed a bad idea to Cara, par-
ticularly as at family gatherings the uneasiness was obvious.
All their trivialities and differences of opinion and their fitful
feelings for each other would come to the fore. Cara suggested
this to Pamela, but Pamela, keyed up at the prospect of
meeting Guy, and not knowing how Cara felt about him,
was insensitive to the situation and not to be dissuaded. Heavy
hearted, Cara agreed to go, Andy in tow, the prospect of
having both Guy and Andy under the same roof for any
length of time too disturbing. The other guests were there
when they arrived.

Cara felt unreal, between two worlds. She'd gone through
the most amazing and unpredictable change that any human
being could go through. It was as if she was being snatched
away from her life with Andy and set on a new path. She

knew that Andy detected this in her. Perhaps it was in the new lightness of step, or the deeply reflective way she lowered her eyelids so that he wouldn't read the secret in her eyes.

Vanessa noticed the change in her too. Watching Cara's gold fingernails sparkling in the light, she was aware of her casting her charm on Guy McIntosh as if weaving a spell. With her hair looped on her head, and her plain black Stella McCartney dress she'd paid a fortune for, Vanessa thought how mysterious Cara was becoming. Her air of uncertainty made her seem younger and more beautiful too.

John, sipping his drink, looked at his daughter through his observant eyes in a puzzled way. She was different this evening, he realised, but he made no comment because he would no more criticise her than the man in the moon. Without a word he filled her glass. Andy and Guy circled each other, Guy looking directly at Andy, Andy looking away with sulky embarrassment.

Elsie peeped her head round the door, saw that all was well and, catching Cara's eye, she said, 'Ready?'

John put down his glass, Guy did the same, lingering at the open door to let Cara pass by. Cara was seated next to Andy, facing Guy, but it was Andy she kept her attention on as he unfolded his napkin with anticipation, saying, 'I'm starving.'

John carved. Elsie took her seat at the table. She'd been cooking all day, and exhausted, she sat at the end of the table, losing her nerve, fearing the meal might not be up to scratch.

Cara, tasting her soup, turned her attention to her father. She spoke little, asked her father questions, hoping for long drawn-out answers so that she wouldn't have to contribute to the conversation. She tactfully listened to his plans for dull meetings that she'd be glad to miss, already gone with Guy in her mind, sad at deceiving her father.

Andy was coming to the end of his complaint about his difficulty in getting his project off the ground.

Guy said, 'We found no difficulty in getting started.'

'It's easy for you. You're not working your way up from the bottom like me,' Andy challenged him. 'You can get anything you want, take anything you want. You only have to ask the IDA and organisations like that.'

'Now, what are you saying?' John asked him crossly.

'Money buys you your way in just like that.' Andy clicked his fingers in Guy's direction.

'We had something worthwhile to offer,' Dick said.

Cara closed her eyes and breathed in, slowly exhaling, cross with him, and overanxious.

'So have I,' Andy argued. 'But with me it's will they ever take this seriously? Will they look at this again? Whereas you canny foreigners can walk in, set up and put other people out of business.'

Conscious that Cara was looking at him, trying to get a message through to him with her eyes, he was unstoppable.

'How many companies have you formed this judgement from? You can't base it on one single one,' Guy asked.

Andy glared at him.

'There's the Bank of Scotland walking in here with their cheaper mortgage rates putting long established financial institutions out of business, and loads of others doing the same thing,' Andy whined on.

John, on the point of explosion, paused before he said smoothing, 'I can't have you casting aspersions on the national traits of the Scots. It's good to have healthy competition and a strong workforce. People who are going to turn up for work on time.'

Andy retaliated, 'I wouldn't mind getting up early in the morning to work in a nice comfortable job if I had one.' His face wore a careless expressionless that worried Cara.

'I have met many Scotsmen in my time,' Pamela said. 'Decent people they are too. Morally strict.'

'Really!' Elsie said, doubting the wisdom of Pamela's judgement on morals. 'The best part of the day is the morning time,' Elsie said, breaking into their conversation to avoid confrontation with Pamela. 'The birds are singing, the whole day stretching ahead.'

John laughed uneasily.

Raising her eyes, Cara glanced across the table at Guy briefly. He smiled at her. Blushing, she returned her eyes to her plate.

John, uncomfortable with this conversation, stood up and went round the table with the wine.

'Well, look at it from my point of view,' Andy swirled his drink in his glass, his nostrils flaring.

Cara wanted to run, or get very drunk. She spent so much of her time smoothing things over. She was wondering if it was worth bothering to do it this time. For Guy's sake she thought she'd better keep out of the argument for fear of exposing any sign of their intimacy.

Guy seemed to be taking her feeling into consideration too by overlooking Andy's offensive manner and casting her a reassuring glance.

'I'll get more wine,' John said, breaking away from the argument.

Pamela, eating her meal with gusto, changed the subject to redecorating, her third favourite topic after shopping and holidays.

'The house is that choked up with monstrosities, full of woodworm, no doubt. I'm going to start at the very top and work my way down. Fling out everything. We saw wonderful pieces of furniture in our travels,' she said. 'Didn't we, John?'

'Yes, indeed,' he agreed, not very interested.

'We have some nice pieces of our own,' Elsie said defensively, bewildered at the thought of having to dispose of the

Victorian furniture she'd brought with her from her own home. 'Haven't we, Cara?'

Cara looked at her with indifference, then realising she needed back-up, she said, 'Yes, we have, and I'm sure you'll want to keep some of them.'

'I'll leave things as they are in your bedroom, of course,' Pamela condescended.

'Suzanne could help you. She has a flair for it and a good eye.' Vanessa said, glad of the change in the conversation.

'Splendid,' Dick said. 'That'll keep her happy,' casting anything but a happy glance in Suzanne's direction.

Suzanne was busy keeping a close eye on Cara and Andy, feeling responsible for their disastrous marriage.

'Isn't that right, Suzanne?' Vanessa asked, her eyes on Guy. She was suspicious of him, thinking him to be a drifter, but his voice reminded her of Sean Connery. She closed her eyes and listened to it as he talked to John about fishing.

Cara feared she'd faint if this meal didn't end soon. Would they ever be alone, she wondered impatiently. Just the two of them without the tedium of this damned gathering. This time tomorrow she said to herself, we'll be off. Meantime, she'd better stay in the present if she wasn't to give the game away.

Finally, they were leaving, saying good night. Guy was standing attentively, opening the door for Cara, unable to kiss her, or make any kind of fuss of her.

'Don't worry about a thing, we can spare you for a few days,' her father said to her as she left.

'Thank you, Dad.' Cara kissed him goodbye.

Vanessa sprang quickly to her feet. 'I have to go too. Good night,' she said to everyone, giving them all a quick kiss on the cheek.

Cara lingered at the door, compelled to look at Guy one last time before she left. Their eyes locked, sealing a bargain.

'I think I behaved rather well, considering,' Andy said, on the way home.

'Considering what?' Cara was nettled.

'That they were all ganging up on me. Didn't you notice?'

'No.'

'Then, of course you wouldn't.'

'No, I suppose not.' Cara was too tired, suddenly, for words.

16

A way from everyday life it was like a dream, Guy and Cara under the spell of each other, the glorious countryside and good weather. Guy drove south to Cork fast, with assurance, the sunroof of his Mercedes coupé open, the wind blowing back his hair, his hand on her knee, intimate, relaxed. She glanced at him from time to time. He looked handsome and assured.

They stayed in an old-fashioned hotel, with dim corridors at the top of a dingy flight of stairs and doors of dark varnished wood. The wallpaper in their bedroom had a cabbage rose design and the big brass bed took up most of the space.

'No one would ever think of looking for us here,' Guy laughed, taking her in his arms.

Cara shivered with delight.

'Don't make fun of it, I like it here,' she said, looking through the long sash window at the clear sea glinting in the afternoon sun.

Before she had time to take off her jacket he kissed her hard, sliding her onto the bed, his hands fiddling with the zip of her trousers. Her body arched back; her arms entwined his neck. She was pulling him down to her. The bedspread smelled of detergent and mildew, the bed creaked as Guy pressed her into it. The knock on the door made them jump. They both sprang to their feet.

'Mrs Fuller thought you'd like a cup of tea,' a girl in a black dress and white apron said.

Cara blushed. Guy took the tray and closed the door.

'Room service,' he said pouring out the steaming tea, smiling at Cara's discomfort.

She drank hers, putting the cup carefully back on the saucer as she finished, her hand shaky.

'Come here,' he said. His smile brilliant, careless, as he took off his shirt and exposed his tanned taut chest, was the most natural thing in the world, his eyes on her mocking, defying her to resist him.

Silently, she went to him. He kissed her tantalisingly on the lips, undoing the zip of her jeans, pulling off her top.

'You're a beautiful woman,' he said, leading her to the bed, knowing she wanted him as much as he wanted her.

Peeling the rest of their clothes they lay down on the clean fresh sheet. Cara could feel the blood coursing through her as he caressed her body. She held herself still under his touch, felt his fingertips sliding up her back, stealing over her breasts, making small circles and arousing her.

'I want you,' he said, his voice hoarse, his hot breath on her skin.

His hands were up again to her neck, her shoulders, down her midriff. He pulled her on top of him, raising himself to meet her, his body solid beneath her.

With his hands on her hips he steadied her, pinning her there, neither one of them moving. Impaled like that their eyes locked, his not mocking anymore but consumed with passion. She stared at him as if seeing him for the first time as he thrust into her. As he continued the slow grind she gasped, her fingers digging into his sides. An involuntary scream rose in her throat. Pulling her down he devoured her with a kiss to staunch it.

'I doubt there's anyone around,' he laughed, when he finally released her.

True enough, the place sounded empty as they lay in one another's arms peacefully.

Later, they walked for miles along the strand, Cara's arm looped in his, and made love afterwards, their fear of making a noise forgotten.

They had coffee in the pub next door to the restaurant, sitting close together, something illicit about their happiness in each other giving rise to stares and speculation that they couldn't have cared less about.

Kinsale was a pleasant seaside town with steep narrow streets, the colourful awnings flapping in the breeze above the shops. The weather was beautiful. Cara walked beside Guy, buoyant as a bird. They ate lunch at a cafeteria, afterwards strolled along, holding hands, giggling, singing bits of songs while standing at the railings looking at the little boats, the dark gathering clouds on the horizon the only threat in the quivering air.

On the one wet day they had they browsed in the local bookshop, went up a lane to an art gallery and antique shop, drank tea, and ate hot buttered scones in a brightly painted tea shop nestling between two hills. They revelled in talking to one another, the flow of ideas and opinions never ceasing.

They drove all around, went to Blarney to kiss the Blarney Stone.

'It's strange to be back here,' Cara said, looking about to refresh her memory.

Nothing had changed. Out of the mist she picked out Blarney castle, set against rising hills, and a dark blue horizon.

'I remember climbing up those narrow stairs, the old caretaker cautioning me not to go to the top. He stank of whiskey. I didn't listen to him, climbed up to the roof of the tower. Elsie had no idea where I'd got to, the dear old thing was having an old-fashioned tea party with another guest and a titled old lady she'd stumbled upon. When she discovered what I'd done she was very angry. "Supposing you'd lost your nerve and fallen? How would I have faced your father?" she'd said. "You've cooked your goose now. We're going home, and not a word to your father or the fat'll really be in the fire."' Cara imitated her voice. 'It was probably the only time in her life she was really cross with me.'

'You haven't changed much. Still the adventurous spirit.' There was warmth and affection in Guy's voice as he laughed at the idea of Elsie too preoccupied with tea and titled ladies to keep an eye on her charge.

Guy wanted to know about her childhood. Cara talked of it, giving the impression that it was an exclusive, happy time, with her account of happy summers swimming and playing tennis, parties and friends, not the background of a child who'd lost her mother so young and who'd spent most of her time grieving for her. Hunched over, listened to her tell of those long ago summers, picturing them in his mind, he couldn't get enough of her stories.

Cara spoke of her past, but thought of the future. What would happen to them? Where would they go from here? Away from home, family and watchful friends, spending so much time together, their love blossomed. Waking each morning to find Guy lying beside her, Cara would snuggle into his warmth, listening to the chirping birds, watch the clouds sail by in the clear blue sky. Guy would stir, wake suddenly, surprised to find her there beside him, pull her to him, and continue the previous night's lovemaking that sleep had interrupted. It was the happiest time of her life.

'You look radiant,' he said.

'Its all the fresh air and exercise.'

'It's all the lovemaking.' His kiss was light and delicate, full of warmth and affection. She leaned comfortably into him.

They continued to make love whenever they could, rushing back from the sightseeing trips to be in each other's arms. Cara discovered more about her erogenous zones in those hot days and nights of passion, all sense of time lost.

'It's been lovely. I wish we could stay longer,' she said to Guy.

He shook his head. 'I have to get back. I must keep check of things. So do you.'

'We'll do it again.'

'And again.'

On their last evening together by the sea the sky was damson, the clouds menacing, the heavy atmosphere oppressive and foreboding. Cara's stomach was churning like the sea at having to return home. Guy drew her to him and slid his hands inside her top. She closed her eyes, hit by the sudden urge, pressing herself hard against him, wanting him there at that very moment, in broad daylight, in full view of anyone that might be passing, the desire making her hear beat fast, his salty kisses weakening her legs to a hollow sensation.

The sky darkened, the wind sprang up scattering petals of flowers, shaking the leaves of the trees. They returned to the hotel.

'That's the sad thing about love,' she said as they lay together. 'The price to be paid.'

'Well worth it,' Guy said, kissing the top of her head.

Back home Cara tried to return to normal life. She felt restless and disorientated, like a bird without wings. Her routine was the same as always, but she was different, and had been different since she met Guy. With a trembling excitement she waited for his call, hurrying off to meet him, leaving Suzanne perplexed and Vanessa to wonder if and when she would ever thaw out and tell her what was going on.

She walked the village streets in casual gear and trainers, her sunglasses on. Here, people lived cheek by jowl; immersed in each other's business. Walking fast, head averted, she only ever stopped to make quick purchases. She imagined as she left each shop, that all eyes were upon her.

On the Friday after she returned to work there was a party at Bradley and Thompson for the clients. Cara was late, held up by Guy who insisted on making love to her slowly throughout the afternoon. She hurried through the doors of the office to be greeted by the high-pitched noise of the party in full throttle. Mrs Moody, with an empty tray in her hands, looked cross.

'Where were you? her father said. 'I've been anxious about you. Your mobile was switched off.'

'I never have it on when I'm driving.' That wasn't a lie. 'I got held up in traffic.' Another lie.

'For two hours?'

'I went for a swim.'

'You're always swimming, or at the gym,' her father said, irritated. 'Who's looking after your office?'

'Half-day.' Cara smiled.

John shook his head. 'You're not keeping your eye on the ball.'

'I'm sorry you couldn't get me, Dad.'

'You're here now, that's all that counts. I have someone I want you to meet.'

John turned to some people, his hands clasped behind his back, his head inclined. Isabella interrupted going straight to John with a full tray of drinks.

'We hought to be paid hovertime for this,' said Isabella. Standing straight, she glanced coolly around her.

'It's good of you to do this, Isabella,' John said. 'These gentlemen will feel themselves honoured to be looked after by someone as lovely as you,' he said, surveying the beautiful creature in her thin scrap of a dress, flowers in her hair.

'This is Isabella, our receptionist,' he said, inclined his head, turning his eyes, without altering his smile, to the newcomers.

Isabella stepped forward with her tray of drinks.

As soon as she could get away Cara left, deceiving her father again. Since she got involved with Guy her code of conduct had altered. She made herself available for him, cancelled engagements to be with him, missed meetings, ignored friends and waited for his calls. Together they met and made love as often as they could, revealed their fantasies to one another and tried them out. They walked, talked. Andy complained that she was never home.

'We haven't actually seen each other for ages. We haven't made love since the night you went to the cinema with Suzanne. You're always home late.'

'I've had a lot of meetings lately,' she said, forcing herself to make eye contact with him.

'Are you seeing somebody else?' he asked, buttering his toast vigorously.

'What do you take me for?' she counterattacked. 'Haven't I got enough problems. Do I look like someone that needs to have her head examined into the bargain?'

She was leaving for work. He trailed her to the door, his face anxious.

'Cara, I'm sorry. I shouldn't have said that.'

'No, you shouldn't have.'

'I was worried about us, that's all.'

17

Guy phoned her office late one evening, saying, 'It's my birthday on Friday. I'll cook us a nice meal. Would you like that?'

'How lovely,' she said, delighted, but already guilt-ridden about Andy.

As soon as she put the phone down she began composing another excuse. She'd tell Andy she was staying at Rockmount for the night.

Guy was cooking when she arrived, still dressed in his suit from work, his tie loosened, surrounded by pots and pans, delicious smells emanating from them, and tiny jars of different coloured spices. The round table in the kitchen was set, red wine on it for the meal. A bottle of champagne rested in a silver bucket on the work counter. She put the red roses she'd bought beside it.

'I hope you like Thai food.' He was watching her, studying her face.

'I've never tried it but it smells delicious.'

He left the cooker and poured the champagne.

'This is a big celebration. I'm forty today.'

'Congratulations. I got you this.' She gave him the gift-wrapped parcel. He dried his hands on a towel before tearing it open to reveal a pale blue cashmere sweater she'd bought him in Brown Thomas.

'Thank you.' He kissed her, delighted as a child. 'You didn't have to get me anything.'

'I wanted to.'

'We're together, that's all I want for my birthday,' he said, removing his jacket and putting on the sweater.

'It suits you.'

There were no secrets in his eyes as he gazed at her and said, 'It's perfect, just like you.'

Self-conscious, she laughed to deflect him.

During the meal Guy said he was going to Edinburgh in a few days' time.

'I always take Ian on a trip this time of year.' He spoke rapidly to get it over with.

Immediately she felt the rejection and knew it was silly. She just couldn't bear the thought of him leaving. Didn't have the strength to be without him.

'Where to?'

'Vancouver. I have cousins there that I'm pretty close to. Ian's friends with their kids.' There was an edge to his voice. 'I should be looking forward to it, but I'm not.'

'How long will you be away?'

'About a month. It's important that I spend some quality time with Ian. He had a bad dose of flu last term and didn't get picked on the inter-schools cricket team, which depressed him, and he misses his mum, of course. He still finds it hard to accept it.' His voice trailed off.

Cara's mind was flooded with images of a little boy, his mother, a dark-haired beauty embracing him – turning to embrace her husband, Guy, her lover. She imagines Guy lying on a bed, his wife beside him, cradling their little boy.

'Tell me about your wife,' Cara said, suddenly wanting to know about this stranger, this woman he'd known most of his life.

'Hazel!' Guy examined his wineglass carefully, biding his time; the atmosphere suddenly charged, his past bursting upon them, a flood of memories threatening the space between them.

Cara put her hand on his arm, leaned towards him. 'You don't have to. I'm sorry, I shouldn't have asked.'

He resisted her touch. 'You have a right to know.'

Taking a deep breath he said, 'Hazel and I met when she was twenty and I was twenty-four. She was a trainee nurse, attractive, good fun. We married two years later, far too young. It seemed to be the thing to do. She wanted children, and I had a job as a sales rep, so there was nothing to stop us. When Ian came along we had no time to ourselves. It's hard to think back over those years, all the plans we made, all the things we were going to do. Life never works out the way you expect it to,' he said, a catch in his throat, his eyes hooded so Cara wouldn't see the pain in them.

She reached her hand out, took his, and said in a low contrite voice, 'I'm sorry, I shouldn't have asked you about her.'

He shrugged away her apology, and turned to her. Looking straight at her he said, 'It doesn't matter. I'm all right. I wasn't in very good shape for a long time after she died. I thought I'd never get over it. I couldn't imagine the future, having to manage without her. It was hard. I felt the weight of every one of those years, trying to cope with being a lone parent, Ian, only nine, missing his mother. But, extraordinary as it seems now, I've endured the loss, worked through the pain. I've learned to live through it, bringing up Ian on my own, getting the balance right between work and home life. Hazel's death brought us closer together. We knew we had to survive, so we pulled together.'

His eyes were far away, in another world. Cara wanted to bring him back and didn't know how.

'Most extraordinary of all,' he continued. 'I met you.' His eyes were sombre as he said, 'I didn't expect . . . I didn't dare hope . . . I hoped that one day I'd meet someone I could love. It was so lonely, but I never dreamt I'd find anyone like you . . . I knew after a certain time had elapsed that you were very important to me. We're akin, Cara, you and I. We see things in the same way, we think similarly, we're equal.'

Every muscle in her body was stiff with tension, as if the whole world had stopped still for a second. As if reading her thoughts, he put down his napkin, came to her, touched her face with his fingertip.

'Enough of this.' He wrapped his arms around her shoulders. She could hear him breathing, feel his eyes on her.

'Life goes on,' he whispered into her ear. 'It's my birthday. This is our night, just us here together celebrating, and I don't want to waste another minute of it. Let's go to bed and celebrate that we're alive and life is wonderful.'

'I'll be happy to,' Cara said, rising.

Guy took her in his arms, looking down at her as if she might disappear if he let her go. The sadness in his eyes dissipating as he kissed her.

Cara felt light-headed with happiness as he led her by the hand quickly through the empty rooms. They almost ran up the stairs.

In the bedroom they struggled out of their clothes and fell on the bed, Guy pulling her to him, kissing her in a frenzied way, unzipping her dress in a frantic attempt to do everything at once. They grasped one another in a deep embrace, twisting, grinding, as if they couldn't get enough of one another.

Cara stopped, leaned on one elbow, and said, 'Let's take it slowly, darling, we have all night.'

Hands shaking she reached up to him, drawing him down to her with tender kisses on his eyes, his lips, his neck, breathing in the raunchy, sweet smell of him. A deep shiver of anticipation ran up her spine, making her tremble as his tongue flicked her nipples. Trembling all over, surrendering to this blissful sensation as his fingertips moved ever downwards, caressing her skin with agonising slowness, moving between her legs.

Weightless, fluid in her overwhelming desire for him, Cara eagerly responded, wrapping her legs around him, her mind strung out with pleasure, her body taut, quivering like the bow of a violin, passion flowing out the very marrow of her bones.

He entered her, sending waves of pleasure coursing through her. In the release of his passion he called out her name, over and over again, flooding her with new sensations as he came. They fell back on the bed and lay panting, exhausted.

Cara woke up in the dark and lay listening to the waves pounding on the rocks, the wind howling, until Guy awoke. They toasted one another with champagne, sang 'Happy birthday' again, and made love once more.

'You've changed this house for me,' Guy said, looking around. 'Everything's different now, and do you know why?'

'Tell me.'

'Because you're part of my life.'

They made love again, and slept in one another's arms, their bodies damp with sweat. In his sleep he called out 'Hazel'.

When he woke up, he turned to her. Her throat tightened and she couldn't form words. She turned away.

'You look sad,' he said, touching her tangled hair, gathering her to him.

'That's what contentment does to me,' she answered, making light of it.

'I love you, Cara,' he said, sending a surge of joy through her, dispelling her doubts and fears.

Daylight streamed through the window. Hating the intrusion of anything that reminded her that there was a world outside, Cara got out of bed. She dressed standing in front of the mirror. Guy awoke and watched her while she did her hair.

'You look sexy.' He came up behind her removed the clip from her hair, letting it fall over her face.

They were both staring in the mirror, his arms around her shoulders. He began to massage the back of her neck, kneading the muscles gently. He leaned over her, silently taking possession of her, his eyes never leaving her reflection in the mirror. This was exciting, irresistible. She relaxed into him.

They made love again, time suddenly forgotten, Cara aware of a strange sense of their having grown closer to each other, more intimate, as though Guy's imminent departure pushed the boundaries of what they were doing.

'Is it wrong to be this happy,' she said, 'knowing that I'm committing a terrible sin.'

'How can it be a sin when it feels so right?' he said. 'I love you being here with me. It's where you should be.'

When she was leaving much later Guy held on to her, reluctant to let her go.

'If I don't leave now I never will,' she said.

'Maybe I won't let you,' he said. 'Maybe I'll keep you here forever.'

'Oh, Guy! You don't want me here all the time to turn into a piece of the furniture.'

He buried his face in her hair. 'You never would.'

She kissed him, breathing in the scent of him.

'I have to go.'

She gathered her coat and bag together. Guy walked her out to her car.

'We'll meet soon.'

'When? I want to see you before I go away.'

'I may not be able to come here tomorrow. I'll phone you.'

The next morning Cara was up out of bed before Andy awoke. She drank her coffee hurriedly and set off for work, glad to be in the safety of her car, her hands shaking with relief of avoiding a reprisal from Andy.

She phoned Guy, as promised.

'I'm staying home this evening just to be on the safe side.'

'What about tomorrow?'

'I'll try. I have to show a house at seven. The client can't get away during working hours.'

'Come afterwards.'

'It won't be before nine,' she said calculating the time the appointment would take.

She heard him sigh. 'I don't know if I can wait that long.'

Cara laughed. 'You'll just have to.'

Cara worked through the long stressful day. She was looking forward to another evening with Guy, not even scared that Andy might phone at the last minute, commanding her home on some pretext or other.

At lunch with Mark Downes, who was now permanently in the Arklow office, going over the details of the forthcoming auction, doubts surfaced in Cara's mind as she thought about Guy calling out his wife's name in his sleep. Even though he'd told her he loved her, reassured her in every way possible, she couldn't help thinking about it. 'In the blink of an eye' Shakespeare had said about the changes of love. Physically trembling, she toyed with her food, feeling suddenly insecure. Maybe she should hold off sleeping with him again for a while. Taunt him, play hard to get, make him wait. She knew that was impossible. She couldn't resist him and she knew it.

'What's up?' Mark asked, setting down his beer, his eyes curious.

'What do you mean?'

'You're not eating. You seem to be in another world.'

'Sorry, I'm tired, that's all.' Cara smiled at him, trying to hide her low her spirits. 'How many interested parties do you have for this house auction?' she asked, spearing a piece of cucumber with a fork, forcing herself to eat it.

'Just the two. That Mrs Marshall and the Fleming couple, and whoever else turns up.'

'You'll be doing it on your own, you know that.'

'You're joking!' Mark said. 'Single handed?'

Cara smiled regretfully at him. 'I've got an appointment at three o'clock at the office with Mr Mangan, the property developer who's interested in that tract of land we have for sale in Brittas Bay.'

'So you're dumping this on me at the last minute.' Mark suddenly looked like someone who'd lost his way.

'With your style and flair you'll have no problem. They'll be bidding against one another to beat the band.'

'Flatterer.'

Cara shook her head. 'Mrs Marshall's eating out of your hand already.'

'This isn't a joke, Cara.'

'Honestly, Mark, you're at the cutting-edge. You've got to stand on your own two feet from now on. You'll be doing the house auctions while I'll be concentrating on the bigger stuff.'

'I'll need somebody to hand round the leaflets, organise coffee, that kind of thing. I can't do it all on my own.'

'I'll phone Isabella, get her to come down and give you a hand.'

'Will she be free?' Mark asked, brightening at the mention of Isabella's name.

'She'll jump at an opportunity to get out of the office, especially as it's for you,' Cara said teasingly, as she gathered up her jacket and handbag and left, giving him no room for further argument.

It was eight o'clock that evening before she finished with her client. She raced him through the show house, desperate to get away, apologising profusely, glancing at her watch, offering to show him the house again the next day, seeing his bitter disappointment.

She drove to meet Guy like a maniac, knowing what she was doing was risky. She was tempting fate going back there so soon, but nothing was going to stop her, her intimacy with Guy was paramount. It was only a matter of hours before she would have to leave him again, the time they had left together so short before they parted.

Guy was at the front door to meet her, his face tense.

'You're trembling,' he said, taking her in his arms. 'I was worried about you.'

'I'll never get used to this. All the way here I was scared of getting caught. I kept wondering if Andy was following me, or having me followed.'

'Of course he isn't,' he protested, taking her coat. He'll be in the pub, lost to the world by now.'

She smiled at him to break the tension, but she wasn't so sure.

He kissed her. 'Come on,' he said, leading her inside. 'You're here now. We're safe here in our bolthole. It's amazing the tricks our imagination plays on us.'

'It's guilt.'

'I know. You got away from your client without much difficulty?' he asked.

'I felt wicked, rushing that poor man through the house. It wasn't really fair to him.'

The lights in the lounge were dimmed, the sound track from Tchaikovsky's *Romeo and Juliet* playing softly in the background. Guy poured her a glass of wine, handed it to her, bending over to kiss her on the lips before she took a sip.

'I'm glad you're here,' he said, kissing her again.

She put her glass down. They were in one another's arms, sinking down onto the rug, kissing hungrily, fumbling with each other's clothes, unable to wait. Cara was clinging to him drowning in exquisite pleasure.

Guy said, 'Let's go to bed, and make love slowly.'

Afterwards, he said, 'Don't you wish that life could be like this all the time? You and me together for good?'

'Yes I do, but it's a dream.'

'It doesn't have to be. Cara, I'm desperately in love with you. I want you to come and live here with me when I get back.' His eyes were on her, vulnerability in them that she'd never seen before.

Astonished, she sat bolt upright. 'Guy, how can I? What about Andy? I can't just walk out on him.'

'Why not? Is it because you haven't got the courage, or are you still in love with him?' he said impatiently.

Cara looked at him. 'I don't love Andy. You know that. We're not close emotionally or physically anymore, but we've been together a long time, we have a life together. I can't walk out on him just like that. I have responsibilities to him.'

'Can you look me in the eye and tell me honestly that you're happy with that set up?'

'No, but that's not the point.'

'It is the point. Let's face it. You're stuck in a rut. Doing your duty, nothing more. You're wasting valuable time that we should be spending together.'

'I know, and I'd love for us to be together, but I can't see an alternative. There isn't one.'

'I love you, Cara, and I want you in my life. That's my final word.'

Guy got out of bed.

Cara followed him.

'I'm flattered, but I don't intend to turn my life upside down. I'm trying to cope with it as it is. I can't just drop everything and come running to you. You'll have to give me time.'

'Not too long,' he warned, kissing her before she went for a shower.

She redid her make-up, brushed her hair and checked herself in the mirror, hoping that the creases would fall out of her black linen suit before she got home. She left, later than she'd intended, again, with Guy promising to phone her.

She tried to imagine how a life with Guy could be accomplished and couldn't imagine it. The more entangled they were becoming, the more hopeless the situation was getting. Guilt tugged at her heartstrings, the weight of her infidelity dragging her down as she thought about it. Her betrayal wouldn't be forgiven if Andy found out. But leaving him wasn't an option. Andy would never let her go. Yet how would it be possible to salvage her marriage after this?

18

Andy wasn't there when Cara got home. She showered, changed into her jeans and T-shirt, and watched television, unable to face the bedroom, dreading his return because she didn't want to have to talk to him; afraid her guilt would show in her face. She felt trapped, not wanting to have to sleep in their bed, the guilt and betrayal too much for her. There was no sign of him until she was about to go to bed. She heard his key in the lock, heard him in the hall. He came into the sitting room.

'I'm home.'

'Yes.' She kept her eyes on the telly.

'I stayed on for a game of darts with the lads.'

She heard the slur in his voice.

Noticing her resistance to his presence he said, 'I'm going to have a drink. Would you like a drink?'

'No thanks. I have a headache.'

'Then have a drink,' he insisted. 'It'll help you relax.'

He took a bottle of red wine from the cabinet and two glasses, put a full glass beside her.

He downed his drink quickly and poured himself another.

'Have that drink.'

'No, thanks, I'm tired. I'm going to bed.' She stood up and went to pass him.

He grabbed her arm.

She wrenched it away. 'I don't want one. I'm going to bed.'

He pinned her against the wall. 'You'll have a drink if I say so, Miss Prim and Proper.'

She tried to push him away from her but his strength held her. His eyes, dark and glassy, bored into her.

'Let me go,' she shouted.

'You're going nowhere until I say so.'

'Andy, what's got into you?'

'Tell me who you're sleeping with.'

'What!'

He grabbed her shoulders tighter, shook her. The room spun around her.

'You heard me. Who is he?'

'Let me go.' She struggled. He tightened his grip.

'You're crazy.' Her voice was shrill as she struggled to get free.

'Am I? Then where were you last night? Tell me that.'

'I stayed at Rockmount. I told you that that's where I'd be.'

He shook his head. 'No, you didn't stay at Rockmount. I phoned and you weren't there. So! Where were you?' His grip on her tightened more.

'Andy, stop this.'

'You were in Arklow with Guy McIntosh, weren't you?'

She stood still, looking at him, hardly breathing, and not knowing what to say. Andy was gazing down at her, casting himself in a superior role, his favourite judging one, enlarging the gulf between them by his interrogating manner, making her conscious of her part in the blame. Anyone other than she would have been better supplied with ready-made excuses. Would have said anything to get off the hook. She couldn't think of a lie.

'Leave me alone,' she said, shaking his hand off her arm.

She went to the sink and got herself a glass of water to give herself time to think. The glass rattled against her teeth as she took a sip.

'I think we should save the talking until later. You've been drinking.'

'Is that all you can say?'

'It's the only explanation for your accusation.'

He came to stand beside her. 'Really! So tell me that you didn't meet for lunch in the Arklow Bay Hotel yesterday?'

Cara spun around to face him. 'You're talking crap.'

'At one o'clock sharp yesterday you were hungry enough to eat a horse. Isn't that what you told him in your e-mail?'

Cara blanched. 'You read my e-mail.'

Andy laughed. 'Full marks. You see I'm not as stupid as you think I am. You slept with him, didn't you?'

Cara kept her head down.

'How could you?' he screamed at her. 'How could you do it to me? You got bored with me. I wasn't exciting enough for you anymore. You had to get it elsewhere. You're despicable, pathetic.' He was convulsed with fury, shaking like a leaf.

'Andy, listen. It wasn't like that. It wasn't planned. It just happened,' Cara said, trying to keep control of her voice.

Andy spat. 'What do you take me for? A fool obviously. God, you must have been having a great time behind my back. No wonder you kept running off, you lying deceitful whore. Where was your loyalty to me?'

Sweating, not at all his usual smart self, he ran around smashing bottles, and jars, spilling their contents onto the floor.

Frightened, Cara cowered in a corner, gaping at him open-mouthed. He came towards her, his face crimson, his fist bunched. He hit the side of her head. She fell back against the wall, her knees buckling, her arm raised to stave off the next blow. He caught the side of her face with his fist, not caring that the bruises would show.

She ducked from him, ran out of the room. He came out after her, dragged her up the stairs and threw her onto the bed like a doll. Ignoring her pleas to leave her alone, he stood over her, swaying, the zip of his flies grazing her cheek.

His voice was icy as he said, 'Take off your clothes, whore.'

'Please, Andy,' she whimpered, moving up the bed to get away from him.

'Shut it.' He grabbed her wrist and bent her towards him, tearing off her top, stripping off her jeans and pants together, flinging them aside.

He was on top of her, pushing her face into the pillows with his hand while he fumbled with his flies. She tried to pull free but, staked to the bed, her head turned sideways, she couldn't move. She stayed quiet so as not to anger him further, her anguish extreme.

A sharp stab of pain shot through her as he penetrated her.

'Stop!' she screamed.

He ignored her, ground into her, stripping away all sense and dignity from her. She stopped resisting and let him get on with it, having no alternative.

When it was over, he slumped down beside her without a word. She waited patiently without moving for him to fall asleep. As soon as he began to snore she crawled into the bathroom. Numb with shock, she locked the door and curled up into a ball on the mat. There she stayed, listening for any sound of him. When she was sure he was fast asleep, and wasn't going to wake up, she unlocked the door and crept into the spare bedroom. She lay in the hushed darkness her mind racing. How foolish she'd been to imagine that she wouldn't get caught. Now what was she going to do? Andy wouldn't stop at this. He'd never let her off the hook. Only next time it would be worse.

She finally fell asleep, and woke up to blinding daylight through the thin curtains. When she heard Andy's footstep on the stairs, the front door bang and the engine of his car starting, she got up, pulled the curtains back, looked up the road. There was his car heading off towards the horizon. Everywhere was quiet as a tomb, no one about.

In her bedroom she looked into the mirror of her dressing-table. There was a large purplish bruise over her left cheek. Her lip was cut. In the bathroom she bathed it in TCP, which stung like hell, went down to the kitchen and made a cup of tea which she barely touched. She didn't eat breakfast, just sat there without putting the radio or her stereo on like she usually did.

She could only bear silence. Everything felt out of place, even in her own kitchen. She waited, straining for the sound of Andy coming back. When he didn't arrive, she ran a bath and lay in it soaking the bruises that were spreading on her thighs and arms. She had a clear vision in her mind that she was at the edge, nowhere else to go.

Dressing in jeans and a jumper she took her jacket and a bottle of water and went to the beach. She walked along the edge of the shore with her shoes off. Her head ached with each step she took. The salt air stung her cut lip. She walked to the point, her jacket loose, her hair buffeted by the wind, the tops of her legs sore. The beach was enfolded in quiet, no one to be seen for miles, the receding tide leaving a trail of wet empty sand.

Cara walked along with her eyes on her footprints, trying to sort out the immediate future. Seating herself on a smooth rock she listened to the cries of the seagulls and the lapping of the waves against the shore. She felt as empty as the beach.

In that brutal state he was in the previous night Andy had been a stranger to her. But wasn't she a stranger to herself? Who was she anyhow? A woman who'd let a handsome man walk into her life, whom she went to late at night, in whose house she'd made love. She'd let him obsess her.

That first night of passion with Guy had initiated all the others, so that they gathered momentum and bore her away on a tide of lust. From then on a barrier had been drawn between Andy and her. Her actions had created isolation between them. But did she have to be humbled, punished for what she'd done, shamed in her own eyes by a violent jealous husband?

Now, in the clear light of day, she wondered how could she have let herself get so pre-occupied with another man when she was already married. Ashamed of herself, she realised that she should never have embarked on this adventure. The fact that Guy was handsome and assured was no excuse for her appalling behaviour. It had been a stupid mistake and would be used as a weapon against her.

Cara sat still for a while. Then she got up, walked. Suddenly the sun came out, drying the sand and sharpening the shadows of the sea birds hopping on it. In a sheltered spot, she took her jacket off and lay down on it. The sun warmed her and made her eyes ache. With her arms under her head, her body not moving, her mind flew away.

She wanted to run to Vanessa and Suzanne with her astonishing piece of news, wanted to tell them everything. But she was too tired. She would have preferred to sleep. Forever! That way she'd never have to face Andy again, or feel pain. How could she possibly live another day like the one she'd just been through. She'd rather be dead. But she wouldn't die. That would be the easy way out. No, she was doomed to live out her life with him.

When she finally got home Andy was in the kitchen, slouched in a chair, his hair dishevelled, his eyes red-rimmed, dark circles under them. He looked at her, not glad to see her.

She didn't speak.

He said, 'We've got to talk,' embarrassment changing his face, stretching his skin over his cheekbones.

Cara said nothing. She wanted to slip out of the house again, get into her car and disappear. Eventually, staring in front of him, he said he was sorry for hurting her. He said that the idea of her being with another man had driven him crazy with jealousy and assured her that it would never happen again. He said that it was the drink talking the previous night, not really him, and that she would have to promise not to tell anyone what had happened.

She stood staring at the floor while he talked. Finally, he looked at her, and when he saw that she was still frightened of him he stood up slowly and went to her.

'I didn't mean to hurt you,' he repeated, examining her cut lip.

She shivered and stayed silent.

'I don't want a scene. I just want reassurance that you'll never see him again.'

She looked away. He waited.

'We'll have to forget it ever happened. Will you do that?' His voice was brusque.

She didn't reply, but looked away, knowing that it would be impossible for her to ever forget this.

Suddenly, he slapped his hand down on the counter. She jumped back in fear.

'How can we get over it if you're on your dignity and not prepared to agree.'

Unyielding, she said, 'I'm not on my dignity, as you put it. I just haven't got your confidence in a future for us.'

He'd done her harm, plenty of harm, and he could do more. It was written all over his face the harm he could do to her. She knew she'd never see Guy again. Not after this. She darted a glance in his direction to try and gauge his mood.

'I won't be seeing him again,' she said finally.

He seemed to relax.

'Good,' he said. 'I want us to put this behind us. I'll get a job again soon and everything will be back to normal. I want it to be like it used to be. It will be, if you'll let it, Cara. We'll have a family. Whatever you want.' His tone was conciliatory, his understanding of her part of his strength, his breath reeking of alcohol.

Her heart ticked inside her ribcage like a bomb.

'I'm going to get a newspaper,' he said when she didn't speak.

He went out.

From the window she watched him walk up the road, his shoulders back, his face betraying not a flicker of the pain and turmoil they'd been through. He was less vulnerable than she was. He wouldn't let this row pierce his armour. He'll never learn his lesson, she thought. He'll always take advantage, always get the upper hand, and he'd never let her go either because he hadn't got the guts to step aside and let her get on with her life.

Then neither had she.

19

—————◆◆◆—————

Next day Cara went to Suzanne's for lunch. She put concealer on the bruises and shook her hair down over her eye, fretful that Suzanne would see the deep impression of his hand on her face. When she got there Suzanne was still in her bathrobe, her feet bare, her hair tumbling out of its clasp, Lucy in her arms.

'Come in.' Suzanne ushered Cara down the hall and into the kitchen, placing Lucy in her high-chair, pushing toys aside to make room for Cara to sit down.

'You'll have to excuse me. We both had a lie-in this morning.' She pulled the curtains fully. Her eyes, more familiar to the light, opened wide in surprise when she turned to Cara.

'What happened to your face?'

The bluish shadow on Cara's cheekbone looked suspiciously like someone had struck her, and her eyes had a feverish look.

Cara's eyelids wavered. 'I fell.'

'Like hell you did. Did Andy hit you?'

When Cara didn't answer Suzanne said, 'So, what's going on?' looking at her with cool appraisal, knowing that the truth was much more sordid than the excuse Cara was giving.

Cara looked away.

'Andy did that to you, didn't he?'

'Just a silly argument, a fuss about nothing.' Cara tried to keep her face expressionless, but tears were near the surface.

Suzanne saw them. 'He did that to you and you're saying it's nothing.'

'It was all my fault.'

Suzanne gaped at her in amazement. 'Cara, there's no excuse for that kind of brutality.'

Cara kept her head down.

'I knew things weren't good between you, but I didn't realise that they were this bad. You never said.'

'He'd been drinking. He lost his temper.'

'You're in trouble, deep trouble, Cara, you know that?'

Cara nodded.

'What are you going to do about it?'

'I don't know.'

'You'd better start thinking. You've been going along with fixed ideas about marriage, determined to make it work at all costs, gloriously blind to the fact that it doesn't always,' Suzanne said.

Cara looked desperate as she said, 'The honest truth is that I don't know what to do'.

'You could begin by telling me all about it, if you feel up to it.'

Cara shook her head slowly. 'I can't at the moment. Do you mind?'

Suzanne covered Cara's hand with hers. 'No, of course not, but I'm here, ready to listen, if you'll let me. You can't go on like this on your own.'

'Thanks, I appreciate that.'

The last thing Cara wanted to do was to confess her affair with Guy to Suzanne. Later Vanessa phoned her, displaying an uncomfortable interest in what was going on in Cara's life, saying that Suzanne was worried about her, asking too many questions. Cara was evasive, not wanting to talk to her about it.

'Come for supper. I'd like a chat with you.'

Cara was hesitant, not wanting Vanessa to see her in the condition she was in.

Vanessa was insistent. 'I've got this new recipe for lemon chicken. It's foolproof. Say you'll come.'

Cara succumbed.

Calm, composed, Vanessa said to Cara, 'You've got to tell me what happened,' moving around her kitchen busily preparing a Greek salad to accompany the chicken dish already in the oven.

Cara opened the bottle of wine, poured it out, and calmly, quietly told Vanessa her story, pausing only to take a gulp of wine. Vanessa interrupted occasionally to ask a question.

'You've got to leave him,' Vanessa said.

Cara interrupted. 'All day long I've been trying to work out how I could leave him and there just isn't any way to do it. I'd be risking my home, everything, and I can't do that at the moment. There's too much going on as it is.'

She took a discouraging article that had appeared in the Sunday newspaper about the complexities of her father's building site on the Quays from her handbag and showed it to Vanessa. The headline 'No permission will be granted' made it quite positive that her father's idea of ever being able to build on that site was absurd.

'I can't make things worse for him. He's invested everything he has in that site. He'll be very upset.'

'You're making excuses, Cara. You won't face your problem head on.'

Cara sighed. 'I can't. I have a duty. It's called marriage. Dad would die if he thought I'd walk away from it.'

'Duty! Spare me, Cara,' said an exasperated Vanessa. 'Your duty is to yourself. You've got to choose what's best for you and the kind of life you want to live. All this time you've helped Andy, carried him on your back, and how has he repaid you? By using you as a punch bag.'

Cara hung her head. 'I have made mistakes too.'

'You're too quick to blame yourself. Andy's a bully. You won't ever get anywhere with him. Surely you know that by now.'

Cara shivered, cold even though the apartment was warm. 'I don't know myself anymore,' she said.

Vanessa said, 'My father was a domineering, brutal bastard. He'd start his torture slowly, unobtrusively, maybe with just the rattle of his cup. His temper would build up over a period of days. My mother would wait, knowing what was coming. When he finally would lose it, usually over some trivial thing, she'd stand there quietly while the world broke over her head, scared to say a word. When he'd go out she'd sob for hours.' Vanessa took a deep breath to stop the tremor in her voice. 'I'd try to comfort her, make her a hot drink, brush her hair, talk to her, but it was no use. Long after she'd gone to bed I'd hear her crying, on and on into the night. I never knew what to do when he'd come back. He'd walk in, get into bed beside her. She wouldn't quarrel with him, and I'd lie awake, bewildered, isolated. I could never understand why she didn't stand up for herself. It was only when I'd grown up that I realised that she had no choice.'

'It must have been a nightmare for you.'

'I've tried to come to terms with it over the years by not thinking about it. And mostly it's all right, because Dad's simmered down now, and he's not bad to Mum. But, occasionally, it all comes back with sudden vividness, like a shock, when I'm alone, sometimes in the dead of night. Or when I see you like this. I remember myself as a girl, standing there, in my night-dress, exasperated with my mother. I try to face it again, like when I was young, go through it all, the feelings, everything. I never cried then. Now I'm so heavily armoured against the world that I won't let myself feel too much in case I wouldn't be able to pick myself up if I got hurt again.'

She leant back in her chair. 'Whereas you do have choices, Cara.'

'Have I? Your mother didn't have an affair?' Cara looked at her.

'No. There were no complications like that.'

'I did have an affair.' Cara's eyes were hooded

'You had an affair?' Vanessa shook her head in disbelief.

'Yes.'

Cara nodded.

'My God! Who with?'

'Guy McIntosh.'

'What!'

Cara squirmed. 'Don't look at me like that.'

'Jesus! I knew you fancied him. But an affair!'

'It was just a . . .' Cara couldn't say the word fling. 'It was nothing. Just a casual . . . fun.' Cara stopped, the lie choking her.

'Casual! Fun! Look at you. I've never seen you looking so damn miserable in my life.'

'Well, it was fun while it lasted,' Cara said, still trying to make light of the situation.

'Only not the laughing kind. Great sex, you mean?'

Cara nodded.

'I knew he fancied you. I should have guessed.'

Cara said nothing.

Still bewildered, Vanessa said, 'How did you think you were going to get away with it?'

'Andy was taken up with his computer, and with me being at work all day I thought he wouldn't notice,' Cara said defensively. 'I knew Guy wouldn't tell anyone.'

'Cara, you were mad thinking that. Andy's not a fool.'

'I got carried away. It was exciting. Guy made me feel beautiful and sexy and funny, and because I found him irresistible I couldn't stop myself.' She looked at Vanessa. 'I couldn't control it.'

Vanessa sighed. 'You fell in love with him.'

'Yes.'

'So, how did Andy find out?'

'He went through my e-mails.'

'He did what?'

'He read my e-mails. Knew exactly when and where I was meeting Guy.'

'The cute bastard. I knew he was no fool, but I wouldn't have given him that much credit.'

'I suppose I'd been behaving differently, avoiding him. God, look what I've turned out to be? A liar, a cheat. God, Vanessa! I hate myself.'

'So, you cheated on Andy. Now you see yourself as a victim who deserves nothing better than what you got, a good hiding, and who will have to spend the rest of your life in a miserable marriage.'

'What else can I do?'

Patiently Vanessa said, 'Cara, listen. You stayed dutiful to Andy, tried to be enthusiastic about his schemes. You kept your marriage going, and your home. So, you met Guy, and he made you feel alive again. He made up for what was lacking in your marriage. You went away with him. Andy got suspicious, and the whole thing exploded. He was violent towards you. I bet he listed out all your faults, things you did or said, right from the beginning, that he didn't like or that hurt him. I bet he blames you for the fact that he hasn't got a proper career too.'

Cara sat in silence. Vanessa was right. Andy had never seen her as a person, more an extension of himself.

'What about the fact that you pay the mortgage, take care of the finances?'

'That's what I'm supposed to do.'

'Why? So he becomes a dependant while you pander to him, serve him; cater for his every need. You spend your life looking after him.'

'I thought I was happy.'

'And is he any happier? You can hardly expect to put your marriage right now. You won't be content. Neither will Andy.'

Cara knew that, she didn't need to be told.

'Guy's not happy either, I'm sure.'

Cara swallowed. 'He is hurt because I can't get involved with him properly. Everything had to be hidden and secretive and that didn't suit him at all. He can't understand why I won't leave Andy for him.'

'Neither can I.'

'He's my husband, Vanessa. I can't discard him like an old pair of shoes.'

'Why not? You think that staying with him is preferable to being on your own for the rest of your life, do you? Or that you're such a terrible person that no one will ever want you again.'

'Something like that.'

'Cara, you're not making any attempt to justify yourself. All right, you had an affair. That doesn't give Andy the right to hit you. He harbours grudges, finds fault. He'll never let you off the hook. You're not going to go on suffering in silence like this. You can't.'

'I haven't got an alternative.'

Vanessa persisted. 'Staying in a marriage that's bad is wrong. You're missing out on your life. You're missing the excitement, the vitality that you could have with Guy.'

'That might not have lasted.'

'So what if it didn't. At least you would have had a bit of happiness for a while.'

'So what do you suggest?'

'Leave him,' cried Vanessa. 'Get a separation, then divorce him!'

'Divorce.' Cara spoke slowly, testing the word with trepidation.

'Yes, you can get one of those in this country now.'

Shaking her head, Cara said with strange reluctance. 'Of course I couldn't do that. On what grounds, for God's sake, a few bruises? That can't be legal or possible. Marriage is for life, according to the law.'

'Not any more. Not even in this Holy Catholic Ireland.'

'With Dad it is, and his word is law in our family.' Cara glanced away guiltily.

Vanessa refilled their glasses. 'Now you're rocking the boat, Cara. Leave your Dad out of it for the time being.'

'I can't do that, Nessa. His ideas may seem antiquated, but to him the marriage vows are very important. It would kill him if I separated from Andy, and I wouldn't want that. I owe everything to him.'

Vanessa smiled. 'You may owe him a lot but you're not twelve anymore. I keep telling you, you're a grown woman. It's your life, not his.'

'That's the worst part. I'm still a child inside, running after my Dad, always trying to please him.'

'You can't please your father all your life. The more you try to, the more he'll end up being disappointed.'

'He knows about Andy and me not getting on since I stayed at Rockmount when he and Pamela went on holiday. He expects me to sort it out.'

'He doesn't know that Andy hit you, or what a brute he is.'

'No, and even if he did, he'd still expect me to stay with him. He's very old-fashioned.'

'Well, I wish you luck,' Vanessa said, 'because you're going to need it, believe me, if you're hell bent on living with that madman. Such a waste! You're a wonderful person in your own right, Cara, and you deserve better.'

Cara considered this, 'God, I don't feel it,' she said, but her pale, bruised face brightened at the compliment.

'Your self-esteem is low, and who'd blame you. You're probably roaming around the house afraid to go to sleep in case Andy comes in drunk again, and in one of his moods.'

'Yes.'

'You're running true to form. Most women who stay in boring stultifying marriages are frightened of poverty and independence, especially if they're getting on and their marriages are well-off ones. Yours is different. You're financially independent and you're still young enough to start again.'

Cara sighed. 'Not that easy to get out of either.'

'Andy was different in the beginning. He was good fun.'

'But what about his occasional fits of jealousy? I remember how intense they were while they lasted, terrifying sometimes. You've got to face reality, Cara.' Vanessa put her hand on Cara's arm. 'You've got to deal with it; with Andy, with your pain. He's crazy, and the whole situation is intolerable.'

'I'm caught up in it. I can't see how I can break free of him. I'm too much of a coward.'

'No, you're not.'

'I have to try and retrieve things first, go to Relate, seek professional advice. Gosh, I don't even know how to go about it.'

'Too late for all that. It's gone too far. You're in danger. It's only a matter of time before there's another row. Next time it'll be worse. Andy will ruin your life if you let him. He'll take away your best years if you let him, and you'll never get them back.'

'He's done that already.'

'Don't discuss anything with him. You need the advice of a good solicitor. I'll introduce you to Roger Hamilton. He specialises in marriage breakdown.'

'Seems terribly final.'

'It is final, and if you get cold feet, think of the alternative. Being scared of him all the time, scared to death every time he walks into the house. Scared of him every day of your life for the rest of your life. What a nightmare! How can you continue to live with him again without thinking about what he did to you?' Vanessa was angry. 'Just think, if you get away from him now you'll be free to start a whole new life. Get married again, have kids, settle down, start all over again if you want to.'

'I can't even think like that.'

'You're a young attractive woman with a lifetime ahead of you,' Vanessa persisted.

Cara blinked back the tears. What if she really left him this time, for good? Faced the scorn, the ridicule. She got up shakily; thinking while she helped Vanessa stacked her dishwasher. If she did leave, where would she go? She didn't have any savings. She couldn't go cap in hand to her father. Vanessa would take her in. No, that wouldn't be fair to Vanessa. She had enough problems with her own family.

Vanessa made coffee.

'I don't want to see you suffer like this,' Vanessa said, reading her thoughts. 'You'll have to get out, rent a place, and get an injunction against Andy to keep him out if he comes after you.' She looked at Cara. 'There's nothing heroic about being stuck in a rotten marriage. Cara, you're welcome to come and sleep on my sofa. I'd love to have you.'

'I couldn't do that. What if you were entertaining? I'd be in the way.'

'I told you I'm off men at the moment.'

'What about Abdullah?'

He's OK for going to the cinema with, or having a laugh with. But it's not serious.'

'I'll think about it.'

'Don't take too long.'

20

When Cara got home from work the following evening there was no sign of Andy. Alone, she went through the kitchen to the living room, looking at her plants, her books in her bookcase. She went around touching ornaments and precious pieces of furniture. Even the word 'cottage' with secure, battened-down connotations wasn't stable anymore. She looked at the dining room suite, and the bookcase that would have to be dismantled if she were to leave.

Cara leaned against a chair in her need to hold on to something, looking out at her wild gooseberry bushes and trained vegetables. Everything reminded her of each milestone of her life with Andy. With heartbreaking surprise she was realising that the bond was broken, that, even though they'd been together a long time, they couldn't continue. All their ordinary life together, all the secrets they'd stored up, all they'd been through, all their plans and hopes, had come to nothing. She looked around, the deep cavity of loss soaking down into her with the realisation that her marriage was over. She was alone, splitting from her partner in life and, sadly, losing her precious home with its nest-like quality that she'd come to depend on. Yet all the precious things in her life were unimportant compared with the failure of her marriage.

She heard the front door click, heard Andy whistle nervously as he came in. She stood stock-still, her eyes closed, waiting sadly, the prospect of his company worrying.

'What's the matter? Are you ill?' There was something

concentrated about his question, at variance with his brusque demeanour. He waited for her answer, a great distance between them.

She lifted her eyes to him.

'No.'

He looked awful, as if he'd rather be anywhere else than with her, but was making the effort.

'Have you eaten?'

'No.'

'I'll make us something.' He went to the fridge, got out eggs.

'I don't want anything.'

She must be brave, determined, tell him she's leaving him. Gripping her chair, the cool words she'd rehearsed wouldn't come out. Lost in her despair, she thought she'd better tell her father first, the following Sunday, when she was expected at Rockmount for lunch. Yes, that's be the thing to do. Wait until Sunday. She hadn't been there for weeks, avoiding her family because of her own unhappiness. They didn't seem to notice; they were wrapped up in each other, their contentment in their own life and occupations, although aggravating sometimes, was a blessing in disguise. If she could catch Pamela on her own, test the waters with her first.

On Sunday, as she turned in through the gates of Rockmount, Cara knew exactly what the importances of the day would be there. Elsie would be organising the meal as though she planned for an army. Her father would be returning from his walk with Bouncer. She dreaded telling him, dreaded his anger. It would be evident in every word and gesture. What about Elsie's reaction? Elsie would feel sorry for her; it would get on her nerves. What about Pamela? Cara felt she might have an ally in her.

Elsie was in the kitchen, cooking a meal.

'I'll go and say hello to Pamela first,' Cara said, the delicious smells doing nothing for her appetite.

Pamela was stretched out on a sun bed on the terrace, in her swimsuit, a drink in one hand, a fashion magazine in the other. With her shiny blonde hair and golden tan she looked like a goddess.

'Come and have a drink, darling,' she said, sitting up to pour a glass of wine from the bottle in the cooler beside her.

'Thank you,' Cara said, no choice but to settle down beside her and sip her drink.

'Your good health,' she said, raising her glass.

'Yours too. Where's Dad?'

'In his study. What a bore work must be on a day like this but he will insist on doing it when he should be taking things easy. These evenings I even have to eat alone with Elsie, which for someone who looks forward to dinner with your Dad is awful. He gets absorbed in his work, doesn't like being disturbed. Has his supper on a tray in there.'

What a contrast it was to when they were newly wed and couldn't get enough of each other, Cara thought. Or even when they returned home from their holiday, all lovey-dovey. That was such a short time ago.

'Ah, well, if it keeps him happy,' she said.

There was a pause before Pamela said, 'He's decidedly unhappy at the moment. He's tired, irritable, which is out of character.' This was said in hushed tones.

Cara couldn't fail to notice the worry and frustration in Pamela.

'It's not as if he needs to work. He's got staff to do it for him.'

'I'll have a word with him,' Cara said. 'Not that it might do much good.'

'Thank you.' Pamela was relieved.

They sat in silence.

'How's Andy?' Pamela said finally. 'We haven't seen him for ages.'

'We're not getting on very well,' Cara began.

'I'm sorry to hear that.'

'In fact, we're on the verge of splitting up,' Cara rushed on, and felt her cheeks flame as she spoke.

'I can't pretend I'm surprised,' said Pamela, patting Cara's hand. 'Have you told your father?'

'I hinted at it. But you know what he's like about marriage. To him it's for life.'

'Some people aren't as lucky in love as he has been. You have to stand back and take a close look at your own situation, dispassionately. If it's as awful as you say, then you're better off out of it.'

'I've been blinded to his faults by loyalty all this time, living in a dream world, wanting everything to be right.'

'What about love? Do you still love him?'

Cara shook her head sadly. 'No. We're at rock bottom.'

Pamela swung round to face Cara, her swimsuit defying the force of gravity as she sat up. 'You're not going to let that stop you. Look at your face? Did he do that to you?'

'Yes. I can't bear the thoughts of going back.'

'He's still there?' she said, incredulously.

Cara nodded. 'Vanessa and Suzanne think that I should divorce him.'

'Oh!' Pamela said. 'What a good idea.'

Astonished, Cara gaped at her. 'You approve?'

'Of course. Vanessa couldn't have come up with a better idea. It's the only sensible solution. If it's over, it's over. Nothing to be done about it,' Pamela said brusquely. 'Clever girl, Vanessa. She knows her stuff.'

'Andy will never agree.'

'The chap's a damned idiot. Anyone can see that. There's nothing he can do about it if you've made up your mind.'

'He'll make life hell for me if I go through with it.'

'He couldn't make it any worse than it already is, could he?'

'I agree.'

'So what have you got to lose?'

'There's my self-respect, my home, Dad's good opinion of me.'

'You'll have to move out. You'll have to get a solicitor, take advice. I got out of a few scrapes in my time, I know what I'm talking about.' She took Cara's hand. 'You come and stay here. It'll be nice having company in the house.'

'Dad'll have a fit.'

'Leave your father to me.'

She squeezed Cara's hand tight.

'Thanks, Pamela, you're so kind, but I thought I might find somewhere on my own for a while. I need to sort myself out.'

'Of course, if that's what you want. But don't forget we're here for you. You have to stand up to the fellow you know, Cara. He doesn't work, doesn't earn a penny. He's an idiot.'

'Who's an idiot?' John strolled out onto the terrace, making them both jump.

'The gardener!' Pamela said, slipping on her sarong as she rose to greet him, giving him a kiss on the cheek, making him blush in front of Cara.

'You're such a prude,' she laughed breaking through his reserve with her sexy, worldly ways, hugging him.

He looked exhausted, his face pale, beads of sweat standing out on his forehead, in such contrast to his cool, glamorous wife.

Cara met his gaze and chickened out of telling him her news, deciding to leave it for a bit longer.

21

Cara managed to block out her depression with work. Any time she thought of Andy she found something worthwhile to do to occupy her; advertising schedules, interviews with clients, anything to make sure she hadn't time to think. The storm between Andy and her had abated, but it was only a temporary lull. Soon it would erupt again. He continued to behave like he'd been doing, sneaking around, listening to her telephone conversations.

He seemed to have lost interest in everything else; the air between them was fraught. Also, he seemed to have lost his direction. He was drifting, aimless. And he blamed Cara for not doing more to help him get a job. With her family connections he felt that she should be making more of an effort to get him something worthwhile. She was ruining his chances of making something of himself by her own ambition, and selfishness he told her. Couldn't she see that he was falling apart, he asked her. Cara could see it, but was powerless to stop it.

She was civil to him, too scared to fight with him, all the time telling herself that she would have to leave him soon, waiting for the best time to make her exit. At the same time she was wondering where she could go, scared of the prospect of leaving her own home.

On Thursday evening Vanessa called to the cottage.

'I couldn't get you on your mobile. Are you all right?'

Cara nodded.

'I got you this,' Vanessa said, handing her a gift-wrapped package.

It contained a brand new, top of the range, crimson lipstick, and nail varnish to match.

'Thought it might cheer you up.'

'That's so kind of you. Thank you so much,' Cara said, testing the crimson red on her lips.

'Suits you,' Vanessa said admiringly.

'I'd never have thought of this shade.'

'Guy sent this letter to my address,' she said, under her breath, handing her a letter. Cara recognised Guy's sprawling handwriting, and stuck it between the pages of her Nigella Lawson cookery book when she heard Andy coming into the kitchen. There was the faint sickening smell of whiskey off him. She made coffee. He looked at Vanessa, expecting trouble, having long since recognised her influence prevailing on his wife and thinking it harmful.

She sat demurely, as if she were up to something.

Andy eyed her warily as he said, 'What's news?'

'I just called to see how Cara was,' Vanessa said.

'We're all right,' Andy replied abruptly.

Surely she wouldn't say anything to antagonise him, Cara thought, her eyes on the coffee-pot, her head spinning. It would be all right. Vanessa had been prepared for a fight with Andy lots of times in the past, but Cara had always deflected her, defending his position as husband and the institution of marriage against her.

'I suppose it's time to hear your verdict on our marriage, my dear Vanessa,' Andy goaded her, seating himself deliberately between the two of them, making a stirring motion with his hand.

Vanessa's back arched. There was an uneasy silence. Andy looked from one to the other. This time she must have thought it better not to confront him directly about his destructive behaviour because she didn't answer him.

'She's told you her side of the story, I bet, but you haven't heard mine,' he said.

'I don't think I need to, the evidence speaks for itself,' Vanessa said, giving him a filthy look.

'The victim is innocent until proven guilty, M'lord,' he said.

'I don't think we should discuss it.'

Andy said vehemently, 'That's where you're wrong. I want you to hear what I have to say.'

'Go ahead then,' Vanessa nodded stiffly.

'I may have lost my temper, but contrary to what you might think, it's not the end of our marriage. We're happy, Cara and me, despite everything,' he added. 'I've said I'm sorry, and I'll do anything to make it up to her. I'll get a proper job. We'll have a family.'

'I don't think that'll be enough,' Vanessa said.

Andy swung round to face her full on.

'You can't go round beating people up and expect that getting a job will be enough to put things right,' she expanded.

Andy reared up. 'So what does Miss Mighty Mouth recommend I do "to put things right" as you say?'

'Sort out your drinking problem before it's too late.'

'So, it's all the fault of my drinking, is it?'

'In my opinion, yes.'

'Cara's behaviour has nothing to do with it?'

'It would appear that way to me.'

'Listen here,' he said, his face darkening as he was losing control of his temper.

Cara got between them. 'Stop this, Andy. You've been . . .' Cara's voice shook.

'I am not drunk, if that's what you're saying, neither am I staying to listen to the two of you bitching at me. I'm going out, and I will get drunk, just to prove you right. That should please the pair of you.' He stormed out the back door.

Vanessa said, 'You shouldn't stay here, Cara.'

Cara sighed. 'Not for much longer.'

'Listen, phone me if you need me, day or night. I'll leave my mobile switched on.'

As soon as Vanessa left Cara read her letter.

> *Dear Cara,*
>
> *I am sending this letter to Vanessa for safety reasons.*
>
> *I am desperate to hear from you. I tried to phone you but your mobile's off all the time. I want to talk to you, but I'm worried that there might be something wrong. I didn't leave a message at your office because I don't want to cause any trouble for you. I feel desolate without you, lost. I can't function properly. Phone me as soon as you can. Tell me that everything is the same between us, that there's nothing wrong.*
>
> *Guy*

Cara went to bed in the spare room, not wanting to confront Andy, not wanting to say anything that would anger him. It was after midnight when she heard the click of the key in the lock, and the stumbling on the stairs. He burst into her bedroom. His face was distorted with drink.

'You've made a fool of me in front of Vanessa.'

Cara clutched the duvet to her.

He moved towards her slowly, deliberately. She put her hands out to ward him off. Close up he reeked of whiskey, and perfume!

'I'm sorry, I didn't mean to.'

'Oh, you meant to all right. Got a kick out of calling me a drunk in front of your hot-shot lawyer friend?'

'No.'

'I suppose she's told you how to go about getting rid of me.'

He dragged her out of bed.

'No! Andy, please! We can talk about this sensibly.'

'Do you really think you'd get away with humiliating me in front of her?'

Before she knew what was happening she felt the sharp impact of his hand on her face. She reeled backwards, stunned, her head spinning.

He grabbed her by her hair, pulled her up to face him, madness in his eyes. 'Look at the state of you, and you have the nerve to criticise me.' Abruptly he let go of her hair. He laughed derisively in her face.

She staggered sideways, and fell, hitting her head against the wall. She tasted blood in her mouth as he knelt down on the floor, almost on top of her, breathing his whiskey breath on her face, an arm and leg pinning her down.

She leaned away from him.

'I'm warning you,' he slurred, gazing at her like someone demented, unable to stop himself, wanting control of her, not realising his own strength. 'If you ever attempt to criticise me again I'll kill you.'

She didn't move, just lay there, barely breathing, her heart beating wildly as she waited for the worst. Nothing happened. An endless amount of time seemed to pass.

Suddenly she disintegrated. 'Get it over with,' she cried out.

There was silence. His grip on her had relaxed. Slowly she twisted around to face him. He was asleep, his breathing deep and rhythmic, his mouth gaping open, his breath stinking.

She thought she'd suffocate if she didn't get away from him, and she was getting cramp in the leg that was trapped under him. If she made any noise he'd hit her again, just to shut her up. Gritting her teeth, she inched back, gradually pulling her leg out from under his and freeing her arm. She slithered away, rolled sideways. Slowly she pulled herself to her feet, took a tentative step forward, glanced down at his sleeping form, then another when he hadn't stirred.

She was at the door, out of the room, almost tripping on the stairs, hugging the wall to stop herself from falling. In the hall the phone was in her hand to call the police when it occurred to her that he might wake up before they arrived. The waiting! No! She couldn't wait.

She searched for her car keys on the hall table, feeling along it with her fingers because she was afraid to put a light on and couldn't see in the dark. Her handbag, that's where they were. Where had she left it? On the worktop in the kitchen: her money, credit cards, everything she would need was in it.

She crept to the kitchen, opened the door. Her eyes were growing used to the dark. She could see the shape of her bag on the counter. She grabbed it, fumbled for her keys, found them, stole back into the hall, grabbed her jacket, and unlocked the door. The key was jammed. Christ! A cold sweat broke out on her brow. Calm down, she told herself, twiddling the key. Got it. Head down, she scurried out into the night, leaving the front door ajar. She stumbled in the dark to her car, crying, shaking, no shoes on, the ground freezing.

Crouching in her seat, she switched on the engine, her hands shaking as she drove by the light of the moon until she reached the end of the lane.

She shouldn't have to let this happen to her, she thought, as she drove on. Why hadn't she left him sooner? Was it because she'd nowhere to go? Or was it because she still loved him? No, she didn't love him anymore. She hated him.

Vanessa answered on the second ring of her doorbell.

'I've done it,' Cara declared breathlessly, dropping her bag on the floor with a thump. 'I've left him,' she said, through bruised and bloodied lips, her eyes triumphant.

Vanessa hugged her. 'Good for you.'

She was examining Cara's face, taking her inside, locking the door, bolting it.

'I thought this would happen,' Vanessa said, bathing Cara's cuts in TCP.

'I should have made you leave with me there and then.'

'Did he rape you, too?'

Cara shook her head.

'He was too drunk. He fell asleep. I left before he came to.'

She didn't want any more questions. She didn't want to answer the questions that were brewing in her own mind. It was all too horrible, too brutal.

'You've really gone for good this time?' Vanessa said, when she heard the whole story.

'Yes. He'll go mad when he discovers it.'

Fear came into Cara's eyes, but also a chilling defiance as she jutted her chin. 'I'll be well away from him by then.'

'Where will you go?'

'As far away as I can go.'

'You can't just take off like that, with no plans.'

'I can't stay at Rockmount. Dad has no idea what's going on, and he has his own problems at the moment.'

'You can stay here with me until you sort yourself out.'

Cara looked at her. 'No. It wouldn't be fair to drag you any further into this mess. That's why I thought of going away and making a fresh start in another country.' Cara stopped abruptly, lost for words, hardly believing that this was happening to her, making up her mind suddenly, determined to go it alone, and not let anyone stand in her way.

'You can't do that. You'll have to face it head on, Cara.'

Cara looked desperate as she said, 'I can't,' and burst into tears.

Vanessa held her and let her cry her heart out, then poured them each a stiff brandy to help them sleep.

'Cara, you've always faced up to things. You're strong.'

Cara shook her head. 'I'm on my own.'

'No, you're not. You've got me here. Cheer up. It'll be great having you here,' Vanessa said, getting out the spare duvet and pillow from the hot press. 'And just think, no man to bother you.' She giggled like a schoolgirl.

Cara said, 'No more pain. No more fear.' Her shaking had stopped. She was beginning to get warm. 'I can do anything I want to,' she said calmly. 'I'll never commit myself to a man again.'

'Never say never,' Vanessa laughed, as she made up the bed in the spare room, happy to have Cara stay.

Cara remembered back to when things began to go wrong between Andy and her. He'd come home drunk, and she'd sleep in the spare room, pride and disgust alienating her, getting her off to a bad start. Andy would become cold and proud, too deeply sulking to make an effort to break the silence, her punishment for isolating herself. Those early rows had initiated all the others. Now, in this predicament, she would have to go to her father and tell him. He would be hostile, but at least it would be out in the open.

'He could have killed you in one of those tempers of his.'

'No, I don't think so. He'd never go that far.'

'You don't know that for sure, Cara, especially as he seemed to be getting more violent towards you all the time.'

Cara shivered, looked away deliberately to avoid meeting Vanessa's eyes.

'It's so strange. We went on for years, jogging along, conscious of things going wrong, but unable to get back to the way we'd been. Funny, I can barely remember the way it was, wanting to be with him all the time. But there must have been good times too.' She stopped, frowning with the effort of trying to recall them.

Vanessa waited for her to continue.

'I'd like to be able to remember them, but all I'll be left with is the memory of him hitting me. It was as if he couldn't stop himself from doing it.'

'Now he can't deny what he's done, Cara. You've got the power. You can go to the police, tell them.'

'I won't do that.'

'You have to. There's the phone. Go on, pick it up, make the call.'

'I can't do it.'

'You'll have to. I'm telling you, Andy's temper is rooted in his very existence. You can't separate him from it. When he began drinking heavily and got into trouble at work he denied it to himself, and so did you.'

'I think he managed to keep it hidden for a long time, you know.' Cara said. 'Do you know something, Vanessa. I have no idea who I am anymore.'

'You're Cara Thompson, thirty-one years old, and the world at your feet. There's so much living for you to do still, so much for you to see. Don't let Andy stop you.'

'First I have to face Dad. Oh, God! I'd rather fly off to the far side of the world than face him. He'll go bananas.'

'You'll be all right.'

'I've lost my nerve,' Cara said quietly.

'Only temporarily. Look, he certainly won't understand it, and he'll be heavy-handed with you because he's a domineering man in his own way, but he'll come round eventually. He's got a heart of gold.'

In the bedroom Cara undressed, and put on the pyjamas Vanessa lent her. She leaned sadly into the mirror as she brushed her hair. The room, through the mirror, was heaped with shadows, the cold bed in the corner awaiting her, her clothes lying untidily across it. Suddenly rousing herself, she began to fold them away, thinking of the trail of disorder she'd left behind her at the cottage.

In bed she lay thinking. So, she'd finally extricated herself from her terrible marriage. But she was scared of the consequences. How had this happened to her? This was something that happened to other women, not her.

22

The frantic ringing of the bell woke Cara up. Vanessa, half-asleep, stumbled from her couch almost collided with her on the landing.

'It's him,' Cara hissed, knowing at once that it was Andy.

He would have known that if she weren't at Rockmount she'd have gone to Vanessa's.

The doorbell rang again.

Cara stood terror-stricken.

'I'll have to answer it before he starts shouting and wakes up the whole place.' Vanessa opened the door, leaving the chain on.

He stepped forward as if he were going to attack her, his hand reaching up.

Vanessa took a step back.

'What do you want?'

There was an edge to his voice as he said, 'I want to talk to my wife. I know she's in there.'

'Go home, Andy. You'll wake the neighbours. This is no time to talk,' Vanessa said politely.

'Fuck the neighbours, get my wife.' He banged the door louder than ever. 'Cara, I know you're in there.'

Vanessa's voice was sharp with authority. 'If you don't go I'll call the police. They won't be long getting rid of you.'

Cara had never heard Vanessa use this tone before.

'I'll go when I've spoken to Cara.'

'She'll talk to you through her solicitor.'

His voice was dangerous as he said, 'If she doesn't come to the door at once I'll break it down. I mean it.'

Vanessa looked at Cara. Cara nodded, and went to the door, the chain the only barrier between them.

Seeing the pale and tragic picture he presented, loaded with self-pity, made her cringe.

He said, 'We need to talk.'

'There's no talking anymore.'

'Yes, there is. We can sort this out ourselves. We don't need an audience to air our grievances on.' He was looking past her at Vanessa who was standing behind her. 'Come home, Cara, and we'll sort it.'

'I'm not going back to the cottage.'

'Then we'll meet somewhere quiet where we can talk.'

'Andy, I'm not going to meet you. I've got nothing to say to you. Go home before you wake up the neighbours and cause a scene.'

Dumbfounded, 'You don't mean that? Sure you don't?' he said quietly, cowering like an animal that was being whipped.

'I do. You'd better leave before I call the police.'

Paralysed by her determination that he should leave, he stared at her.

'I can't believe you're doing this to me. You know you shouldn't play games with me, Cara,' he shouted at her.

'You heard her,' Vanessa said loudly.

'Bitch!' he burst out, pointing a finger at Vanessa. 'You keep out of it.'

The window above him opened.

'What's going on down there?' A man called out.

Andy flung himself from the door, an unforgiving look in his eyes. 'Hiding behind Vanessa's skirts. You won't get away with this. You'll have to face the music sometime. I'll be waiting for you. If you run off I'll find you, however long it takes.'

'Come on.' Vanessa took her arm, pulled her back, shut the door, Andy's voice subsiding as she did so.

Cara sat shivering while Vanessa made a pot of tea. She wrapped her hands around the cup, her heart hammering, and sat on the edge of her chair.

'Come on, make that call to the police. It's time to do it.' Vanessa put the phone in her hand.

'I can't.'

'Deal with it, Cara,' Vanessa insisted, pushing the phone at her.

'No.'

'Why won't you? Is it because you'll have to deal with reality if you make that call?'

Cara shook.

'Tonight you're all right, and tomorrow night. But all I can offer you is temporary safety, Cara,' Vanessa warned.

Cara knew that. She also knew that Andy would be more than a match for her in his waiting game.

In bed she lay staring up at the ceiling. She shut her eyes tight, going over the whole daunting story, every monotonous detail, her world passing before her in a series of events. Andy knew he had frightened her. Vanessa was right about that. Vanessa was right about most things.

Cara had to think of the next stage of her life. It should be easy. Yet it wasn't, and wouldn't be until she'd got rid of Andy for good. She wondered if Vanessa were right about Andy. How far would he go in a fit of temper? How would he react when he realised fully that their marriage was over? Must she be punished more; humbled further, shamed in her own eyes, made to pay for leaving him? She began to sob, not from remorse but from fear and bewilderment. Finally she fell into a deep, dreamless sleep. She could tell that Vanessa slept badly too when she saw her next morning briefly before she left for work.

Cara went to work too.

'What happened to you?' Mark asked when she saw her bruised face.

'I fell,' Cara said lamely, and slunk into her office to hide for the rest of the day.

All day Cara had a sense of being looked at, watched by Mark.

'Want to talk about it over a drink?' he asked her.

'No,' Cara said bluntly, without looking at him. She got on with her work, stayed late at the office. The longer she stayed at work, kept her head down, the more chance she had of getting Andy out of her mind.

Vanessa returned home with another letter from Guy. Cara tore it open. It read:

> Dear Cara,
> I'm going frantic with worry about you. Are you all right? I feel we're losing touch, not to mention valuable time together, and I can't stand it. I'm missing you like hell, can't sleep, and can't work. I have to see you. I have your photograph in front of me as I write. I keep looking at it like a lovesick puppy. I want to see you again soon. I want to talk to you, hear your voice and touch you. I want to believe that you're missing me too. It won't be long until we're together again, I feel sure of it. I'm due back in Dublin for a few days soon. I want to meet up with you. If you could phone me we could arrange a time and place that's suitable to meet. You'll get me at my office if you think my mobile is too risky,
> Guy

Cara read it out to Vanessa.

'The poor fellow's going out of his mind with worry, Cara. I think you should get in touch with him. Let him know the score,' Vanessa advised.

'I'm too ashamed to tell him what's been going on.'

'Don't you think he's entitled to know?'

Cara shrugged. 'I can't cope with it.'

Vanessa was going out with some of her pals.

'I won't ask you to join us. You probably want a bit of peace,' she said.

'On the contrary, I need action, the quiet is getting on my nerves. I can't sleep.'

'Come out with us then.'

Cara went with them but spent the time wondering if Andy would come back looking for her. She thought of Guy and replayed their love scenes over and over, realising at the same time, that she'd have to forget him and get on with her own life. She drank more than she intended, marvelling at the way it drained the pain and frustration of the day out of her.

Edward turned up, an eager expression on his face as he looked at Vanessa. At one point in the conversation he put his hand on her shoulder as he asked her something. She seemed to recoil at his touch. He talked on in his pleasant, rich voice, but every time he caught Vanessa's narrowed eyes he looked ill at ease. He left as soon as he could, with the excuse of a difficult day in the Dail next day. When they got back to Vanessa's apartment, Cara said, 'Edward left early.'

'He just came to ask me to a Dail dinner.'

'And you refused?'

'Dead right I did. The state of the nation is never for one moment off the menu at those events. It puts the wind up me when I'm stuck beside one of those guys going off at a tangent.'

'Edward didn't feel at ease tonight,' Cara said, feeling sorry for him.

'He'd have been all right if the conversation had turned to politics.' Vanessa spoke as if she were seeing things wrong with him on purpose.

'He seems to enjoy your friends. He's very tolerant of you, Vanessa. You treat him so badly.'

'Oh, we get on OK. He loves it,' Vanessa said, as if this excused her bad behaviour.

'Why do you bother with him if you're only going to be rude to him?' Cara asked. 'I thought you preferred the Greek god type.'

'Because I don't have to try so hard when I'm with him. I know everything about him, where he goes, what he does on his time off, and he knows everything about me. With the younger ones it's hard work and I don't get to know them long enough to find out anything about them. Anyway, he's always popping into the pub. I don't have to be civil to him every time, do I?'

Cara said, 'I don't know why he bothers. Mind you, the thought of being on my own for the rest of my life scares me. Maybe he feels the same way.'

'Why should you feel scared of being on your own?'

'Because I've never been alone before.'

Aghast, Vanessa said, 'Surely that's preferable to being Andy's punch bag? Cara, you need to see a solicitor. Shall I make an appointment for you?'

Cara knew she would have to see a solicitor. There was nothing to stop her, no sentiment to hold her back, yet making the appointment was the most difficult thing to do.

'No, not yet,' Cara said finally, 'I need time to think about it. I hate the idea of all that legal stuff.'

'Let me know when you're ready. By the way, I've warned Roger to keep the legal jargon to a minimum.'

'Do you think there'll be a quick solution to it all?'

Vanessa shook her head. 'It certainly wouldn't apply in your case. It would be only where both parties are in agreement and neither one has a claim on the other's assets. Then it's usually possible to achieve a quick result, approximately three months.'

'I can't see Andy being agreeable about anything.'

'Civilised and agreeable separation is rare. A case can drag on for years and years.'

'What about cost?'

'That depends on lots of things. How long it goes on, for one.'

'I'd better go and tell Dad, before I start all this.'

Alone, Cara thought of Edward, and wondered where his chosen path in politics would take him. She doubted that Vanessa would ever do the journey with him. Cara dreaded night time and sleep because her dreams were filled with rows with Andy and the angry bitter words she spoke to him in them, that she would never say to his face, would wake her up distressed, an awful way to have to face the day ahead.

When Cara arrived at Rockmount the house was quiet. Elsie was having her afternoon forty winks, Pamela probably in town shopping, her father out for a walk with Bouncer. She made herself a cup of tea and sat down in the kitchen to wait for his return, the safety and peace of it still intact, the ticking of the clock reminding her of childhood.

Bouncer was the first back, the sight of her making his tail wag, as she opened the back door, and bringing a smile to her father's face.

'Hello, darling,' he said, the sun falling on his stooped shoulders as he bent to kiss her cheek. 'What a nice surprise.'

'I was passing. Thought I'd call in for a chat.'

'Good.' He led the way to his study, Bouncer trailing behind them. 'How are you?'

There was something awkward about his posture as he took

his seat behind his strewn desk. He said flatly, 'I've sustained some heavy losses with the Quays site. It turned out to be a bad investment after all.' He looked flabby and defeated all of a sudden in spite of his smile, and in the light from the window behind him his hair looked whiter.

'Are things really that bad?' Cara asked, suspecting that they were.

He nodded his head. 'The bank manager is after me. He's getting impatient. Won't wait much longer.'

'I'm sorry,' was all Cara could think of to say, heartbroken for her father but knowing for certain that she couldn't come up with an alternative plan.

'The business should have been yours eventually, I know, and . . .' he stopped, his voice choked up, 'I can't keep losing money like this.' He took a deep breath. 'I've been doing a lot of soul-searching, considering everything, thinking about the future, and there's Pamela too. Should anything happen to me she'll have to be provided for. I'll have to let it go.'

Pamela wasn't the type of woman who'd be left on her own for too long, Cara thought, but said nothing.

'I'm afraid I may have to sell up.'

'Oh, no!'

He shook his head as if in disbelief. 'I never thought it would come to this either, but there you are. The house will have to be sold. It's a liability, mortgaged up to the hilt to finance the Quays project. The bank will take the lot if I don't move fast.' He looked around sadly as he spoke.

'I didn't realise things were that bad.'

'Of course not. How could you? I was sure we'd get full planning permission. I never dreamt the inspector would turn us down. Now selling is the only option if I'm to salvage something out of the mess. Take the bull by the horns and all that.'

He turned to look out the window.

Stunned, Cara remained silent, overcome with love for the man sitting there so vulnerable against this disaster that encircled the house, the agony of it etched into every line of his face. She stared at the garden, the white sunlight falling across the lawn, casting the rest of the garden in shadow. So this was why he'd been so quiet, almost turning his back on her when she approached, busy with the phone, or rushing off suddenly to some fabricated destination. He was cornered. There was no alternative.

He said eventually, 'I want to assure you that everything's under control, Cara. Things are never as bad as they seem at the time.'

'Under control! What will you do? Where will you live?'

Ever the businessman, he said, 'I'll have enough to buy a smaller house. There's the good will of the business. George has got some big wig sniffing around with plenty of money. We just have to wait and see what he comes up with.' He sighed, looked around him. 'I'm not destitute, Cara. We'll be all right when everything is sorted out.'

'What about Elsie? Where will she go?'

'She'll come with us, of course. That goes without saying. Pamela finds her quite useful.'

Cara tried to take it all in. Her family was moving on, and her livelihood was going too. She was being left to drift, directionless, after years of being a member of a team. She was at the edge of a precipice, about to fall into an abyss, no father or Elsie to reach out this time and grasp her before she plummeted to the depths of despair. They were leaving Rockmount. Everything it stood for was being wrenched from her. She felt nothing but emptiness all around her. Her dread of being alone resurfaced.

Her father was looking out the window again, ashamed to meet her gaze. The sun crept across the lawn, taking its warmth with it, casting them in its cool shadow. Cara felt cold suddenly.

Eventually he said, 'We're in good hands with George. He'll stave the creditors off for another while. He has a lot of common sense.' Observing her, seeing his failure through her eyes, and powerless to change his predicament, he said, 'Luckily, you've got your cottage, and you'll easily get a job, so it won't all have been for nothing.'

'Whatever you decide will be all right with me, Dad. You know that,' Cara said bravely.

He nodded, furrowing his brow, too choked up to speak. Eventually he said, just as she was leaving! 'How about you? You said you wanted to have a chat.' His kindly eyes looked into hers enquiringly.

Cara hesitated, looked at her watch, and said, 'Another time.'

'I'd better be off. I'm picking up Pamela at six.'

Cara didn't detain him.

In the hall Elsie stood with a quizzical smile, and coaxed Cara down to the kitchen for a cup of tea.

'I know it's a shock to you, but don't worry, my dear, we'll manage. We'll just have to pull together. After all, your father's an important man.' Lulled by the sense of security in her own resourcefulness, Elsie believed staunchly that being who they were was enough to see them through.

'It's hard to take in,' Cara said. 'Dad was so sure things would go his way.'

Elsie nodded. 'I know, and it's not going to be a bed of roses. But we'll plan carefully.' She tilted her chin. 'Cut our cloth according to our means.'

That old adage did nothing to reassure Cara.

'I don't think there's much time for planning,' Cara said, 'with everything's falling down around Dad. The banks are out for blood. He's like an old man.'

'He'll be fine as long as he takes things in his stride,' Elsie reassured her. 'I've got every faith in the Lord to see us through, and your father, of course.' With eyes full of pride she said, 'Luckily, I've got my savings in the bank. Come hail or shine, I'm untouchable. So, we'll manage,' she said brightly. 'And you'll manage too. You're young. You'll take it in your stride.'

Elsie took Cara's hand in her own worn one, in a gesture of confidence which also served to let Cara know that she was putting herself back in her old place in the family – in charge. Cara wasn't fooled. As she left Rockmount she could feel everything slipping away from her, no power over her father, Pamela and Elsie or their actions.

Shivering, she went down the steps. Pulling her jacket around her, she leaned against her car, willing the shaking to stop. She drove out of the gates, glad to escape the heavy weight of her father's misfortunes and facing the fact her own busy career was ending in disaster. She felt alone, at the mercy of her own fate in a hostile world.

She stopped on the way home to get some shopping, pondering over the frozen food section, trying to come to terms with the fact that her job was virtually gone and that what she was facing was an empty bank account.

Not wanting to face Vanessa yet, she drove to the beach, and walked along, thinking. The sky was overcast, the rain not far away. She stood looking at the sea rolling in, wave after meaningless wave, breaking on the shore, her eyes smarting from the salt.

'Dad's selling up,' Cara told Vanessa that evening.

'What!' Vanessa said, shocked. 'So quickly?'

'It seems everything went with the loss of the lousy planning permission. He has to sell before the bank moves in, and George has got a buyer. George saw it coming. Dad didn't have much of a say in any of it in the end.'

'Does that mean that your business in Arklow is gone too?' Vanessa asked anxiously.

'Unfortunately, yes. Lock, stock and barrel. With George negotiating for the best price he can get as speedily as possible. Even my company car has to go.'

'That's awful.'

'Dad's too cut up to deal with it. That's life at Rockmount as I know it gone down the plug hole, literally,'

'He'll survive. I know your father. He's a strong man, despite everything.'

'I'll have to get another job and soon. No home and now no job.'

'I can lend you some money if you're stuck.'

'I can't afford to pay it back. I'll clear out my desk in Arklow and start job hunting straight away.'

'Shouldn't be too difficult to get work in this property boom.'

Cara said, 'I'm considering a complete change.'

'Really? Do you have any particular career in mind?' Vanessa asked, surprised.

'I mean a change of location. I'd like a complete break.'

'Marbella? Cannes? How's your Spanish? French?'

Cara shook her head. 'Not good enough unfortunately. I was thinking more rural Ireland. Heart of the country.'

'Oh! That's a strange decision for a city girl like you.'

'I need to start all over again, make it on my own this time. It would be best to get right away from my family.'

'I agree.'

Vanessa went into the kitchen. Cara sank down into the sofa, her head in her hands, and stared gloomily at the telly, defeated at Vanessa's lack of enthusiasm. It wasn't that long ago since she'd felt the luckiest girl alive, bursting with energy and vitality, with a marriage and a partnership in a business. Now she was broke, her business and her marriage gone, along with her energy. She'd come to the end of the road, scared to go forward, scared to go back, not even as far as Rockmount to face her family.

She looked so stricken that Vanessa, who didn't like to see her down in the dumps, said, 'Come on, let's go for a drink. Take our minds off our problems. It'll do you good to get out.'

They walked through the now almost empty streets, past elegant Georgian houses on Fitzwilliam Square, most of them offices, to the pub, looking up and down in the noisy crowded bar, trying to find somewhere to sit. Cara suddenly noticed Edward in a corner, snuggling up to an attractive, leggy blonde.

Vanessa noticed him at the same time.

'Do you know her?' she said, eyeing Vanessa.

Vanessa snorted. 'No and I don't want to know. Next time I go into a pub I'll vet it first,' she said, flicking back her hair and swivelling her shoulders away from their direction.

'You're jealous!' Cara said, laughing, amazed at Vanessa's reaction.

'I am not.'

'Yes, you are,' Cara insisted.

Vanessa turned on her.

'How would you know what I am? You think you know me inside out, but you don't.'

Stung, Cara said, 'God, Nessa, I'm so–rry. I thought it must be the reason for your strange behaviour.'

'I'm not behaving strangely.'

'So–rry,' Cara said, shocked at Vanessa's reaction, realising too late how upset Vanessa really was at seeing Edward with another woman. 'We'll go if you want to.'

'No.' Vanessa stuck out her chin, brazening it out, elbowing her way through the crowd until they were enveloped in it.

23

The following Thursday Cara sat in her car in the suffocating heat. She removed her jacket. Her blouse was stuck to her back. The traffic was at a standstill. The streets were jammed, everyone rushing along, breathing in petrol fumes. She was returning to Vanessa's apartment after another stressful interview. Trying to sparkle and look sophisticated in this unnatural heat, at the same time answer relentless questions, felt impossible.

Nothing was going right for her. Camping out in Vanessa's was proving to be a nightmare, with Cara panic-stricken every time someone called to the door, obsessed with the thought that Andy might turn up. His behaviour had been so humiliating that night. Vanessa, wonderful friend as she was, made light of it, but Cara was embarrassed. She felt it wasn't fair to have her disturbed like that, in her own home, no more than it was fair to take up her time, and her spare bedroom, indefinitely.

She'd attended one interview after another, far and wide, but her efforts to find a suitable job were proving difficult. Bradley and Thompson had been her life. She'd helped build it up with her father to the exact business they'd wanted. Its sudden collapse had been a nightmare. Now she wanted a challenge, something to pitch herself into, and not necessarily in the city. She hated it.

The apartment was cool and silent. Cara locked the front door behind her, and dumped her briefcase in the hall. Glad to be alone she pulled off her shoes and made straight for the water cooler in the kitchen for a glass of water. She had a shower, wrapped herself in her dressing gown, and sat in front of her laptop, concentrating on the appointment section of the *Irish Times*, thinking she'd have to get something soon. The bills were mounting up; her car was due to go back to the leasing firm.

As she moved her mouse from appointment to appointment she saw an advertisement for a manager for an estate and letting agents in Bufferstown, County Wexford, a town close to Roslaire. The owner was a Mathew Arnold. That name rang a bell. This was the kind of business that would suit her and it was a good distance from Wicklow, and Andy.

Suddenly she became alive. She would look into it. She phoned Mathew Arnold and made an appointment for an interview with him for the following Monday afternoon, imagining him, from the sound of his voice, to be a tall old-maidish pernickety person with a bow tie. She felt he would be the type of self-absorbed man who would frequent art galleries and indulge himself in the best restaurants.

Cara was startled out of her reverie by Vanessa's key in the lock, and her cheery, 'Hello, there.'

'How are you?' Cara could see that Vanessa too was exhausted from the heat.

'It's impossible to concentrate on anything,' Vanessa said, wiping her brow with a damp towel, taking two bottles of Heineken from the fridge, and handing one to Cara. 'How did your job searching go?'

'Awful.'

'Weren't you supposed to be going to Rockmount this evening?'

'Couldn't face it.'

'I see.'

Cara was avoiding Rockmount, knowing from the phone

calls to Elsie that the house was on view and in turmoil, strangers coming and going, invading their privacy. Her father was preoccupied with his problems, Pamela organising everything, and Elsie, usually an extra pair of hands to help them cope with it all, was in a tizzy. Also, she was embarrassed at not having yet told her father about her situation with Andy.

'I've seen a job that I like.'

'Oh!'

'It's manager of an estate agents office in Wexford.'

'Wexford!'

'Yes.'

'You'll be moving out?' Vanessa asked surprised.

'If I get it. I've wasted so much time fooling around, going for interviews for awful jobs that I'd hate to work in that the idea of getting out of the city, away from it all appeals to me.'

'You won't know anyone in County Wexford.'

'I'll be free to make a fresh start.'

'Meet Mr Right this time.'

'If there is such a species,' Cara grunted cynically.

'I'll bet the place is crawling with young virile males.'

'You can come down to visit me regularly. You never know, in a while maybe we'll both be in living in Wexford.'

Vanessa laughed. 'I'd never leave the city. Not unless I was hunted down by a gorgeous looking man with great bodywork.'

When Vanessa arrived home the next evening she said, 'Guy phoned me at the office.'

'Oh!' Cara's eyes shot up.

'He's back here for a couple of days and he wants to see you. He'll be at his house in Arklow tomorrow evening. Will you go and see him?'

He had occupied Cara's thoughts since he left. She'd missed his phone calls, his love messages on her mobile. She'd missed him.

'I can't go there. If Andy finds out, it'll make things an awful lot worse.'

'Are you still in love with Guy?'

Cara looked at her. 'Yes,' she admitted, aching with longing for him, wondering how she'd managed without him. She'd shared more with Guy than any other human being.

'Then it's worth the risk, isn't it? You owe it to yourself to see him, and you couldn't be in deeper trouble than you are already in.'

There was no one at home in Arklow. Cara waited for him outside his house, looking at her watch every few minutes. She heard a car coming and turned to see Guy getting out of his car, walking quickly towards her, his face flushed, a sense of urgency in the set of his shoulders, as if he couldn't wait to be with her.

Exhilarated she went to him, her smile tentative.

'Cara, I thought I'd never get here. Were you waiting long?' he asked, his impatience to be with her showing in his face.

'Not very.'

'I got held up at a meeting. Not a damn thing I could do about it.'

He unlocked the door, opened it wide to let her pass. She walked ahead of him, stood in the middle of the sitting room, surveying it, unsure what to do next. Everything was the same as before, a log fire in the grate, fresh flowers, wine cooling in a silver bucket. He came to her, held her, looked into her eyes with a mixture of anxiety and relief.

'I'm so glad you're here. It seems so long since we've been together,' he said. 'I've missed you so much.'

She couldn't keep her eyes off him. Her life had been a vacuum without him. 'I've missed you too.'

He slipped off her coat, eased her into the sofa. He poured out the wine.

'How are you?' he asked, handing her a glass.

'I'm fine.' She lifted her face to him, her hair falling away as she did so. He noticed the raised scars that caught the lamplight, dark against her pale skin.

'What happened to you?' There was anguish in his voice as he gazed on the marks.

The prospect of sharing her burden, her unexplained pain, was too embarrassing to Cara.

'I fell,' she said flippantly.

Guy said, 'It was that husband of yours who did that to you, wasn't it?'

Cara bowed her head.

Clenching his fists he said, 'I remember his jealousy, but I didn't know it was that savage.'

Cara looked away. 'No one ever wins with Andy. I'd sound as if I'm stupid for letting him hit me, but I can't match his strength.'

'Why didn't you tell me? I'd have taken him on for you.'

He looked at her closely, meaningfully, met her gaze.

'I wasn't in touch with you.'

'Cara, you should have got in touch with me. I was mad to talk to you. Suzanne warned me against phoning you, so I guessed there was trouble with Andy. But I never thought it would be this bad,' he said looking at her scars.

Cara said, 'I thought I'd never get away from him, but I did.'

'Tell me what happened.'

'How can I tell you without making it sound ridiculous.'

'Try.'

'It seems unreal now,' she said, as she struggled to go back to the ugly scene.

'Andy read my e-mails. Found out that I had a date with you in Arklow. He'd phoned Rockmount to verify that I wasn't there.' She bit her lip, not wanting to give the details of the row that ensued. 'It all went wrong after that,' she said, remembering the harshness of his face, the tight grip on her bare arms as he held her down, the smell of his breath.

'I'd like to kill the bastard.'

'It was awful. Suddenly, without warning, the reality of what I'd been doing was brought home to me. There was nothing glamorous about a secret affair; it wasn't thrilling and exciting anymore. Overnight it was dangerous, threatening and distasteful. I was scared of Andy's wrath.'

Cara was struggling to say what was on her mind. Guy's look was wary. 'What happened then?' he insisted.

'I kept out of Andy's way, crying at the utter dreariness and desolation of our lives. After the first time he hit me he was so sorry, so contrite. I thought he'd never do it again. Then Vanessa and he had a row, and he attacked me again. As soon as he came into the room and I saw the state he was in I thought that I'd collapse. I ran away, moved in with Vanessa. I thought it would be great to get away from him at last. I thought I'd have freedom, adventure, and do the things I'd always wanted to do without having to endure his intolerable behaviour.' Frowning, Cara said with distaste, 'No man would understand what life is like for women who get beaten up and raped by their husbands. As it is, Andy's always in my thoughts, at the back of my head. At night I go over and over the scene, the things he did and said. I just can't get them out of my mind.'

'You poor darling, you've had a terrible time. You should have told me.'

Cara said, 'I didn't want you involved. It would only have made things worse.'

Grief-stricken, Guy held her hand, looking at her as if seeing someone completely different to the woman he'd known. She wasn't the strong dependable friend of Suzanne's he'd first met, or the busy city woman he'd come to know when he was buying his house.

'That first time I saw you at Suzanne's party you looked so beautiful and so vulnerable. I had this cockeyed notion that I could take care of you, and make you happy. Instead I made things worse with my reckless behaviour and demands.'

Obviously he was seeing her as she truly was. She could see the speculation in his eyes.

She despised herself for the tears. 'I'm all right,' she sniffed. 'I've got plenty of practical problems to keep my mind off him. Vanessa wants me to go for a judicial separation.'

Guy was thoughtful. 'I don't know about the machinations of the Irish law. But you have a case against him. It would stand up in court.' He stood up, walked around. 'Cara, you know that as well as I do. I want to protect you. You're all I've thought about since we parted. No matter what, we must be together now.'

Cara raised her head and looked at him.

'You don't want to be involved in this mess, Guy. It wouldn't do your reputation any good.'

'Don't be silly. I mean it, Cara.' He was watching her intently. 'You belong with me. I can't go on like this, watching you walk out the door away from me after we've made love. Besides, you need my protection now.'

She twisted to face him, a wild desire mixed with relief flowing through her veins, dormant for so long, suddenly coming to life, influencing events. She leaned forward, staring into his eyes, finding them as lonely as her own. She didn't move away when he took her face between his hands and kissed her slowly, drawing her into his embrace.

'Cara,' he said. 'I've been so miserable.'

'So have I,' she sighed.

'I did everything to try and stop missing you. Now I'm

sorry. I want to kill that husband of yours.' He lowered his eyes, masking the pain in them.

She buried her face in his chest. He stroked her hair, smoothing it off her wet face.

'Don't be sad.'

'I . . .'

He took her face between his hands and kissed her again.

'You're here now, that's all that matters.' He stroked her hair gently, then drew her down on the sofa, caressing the corners of her mouth with his lips, slowly tracing a line down the arch of her neck.

Shuddering, she reached for him, her need of him so strong that she wondered how she'd ever kept away. She lifted her face to him, letting him see the naked desire in her eyes. The expression on his face changed from one of anxiety to one of joy. They were kissing, drowning in each other, the only cure for all the pain they had both endured.

He took her hand, led her upstairs where they fell on the bed in a tangle of limbs, Guy caressing her body, making love to her as if he'd never get enough of her. In one violent shudder that erupted in a great deluge of pleasure Cara cried out his name joyously.

She woke up, the duvet had fallen off the bed, Guy sleeping peacefully beside her, his left arm flung out across her protectively.

'Hello there,' he said, waking up, moving closer.

They made love again.

'This is the best cure for all the pain we've been through,' he told her.

'I agree.'

'You're so beautiful. You've spoilt me for any other woman. You're perfect for me.'

'I'm glad.' She snuggled up to him.

'What am I to do if you don't come and stay with me forever? I can't be without you.'

'Don't say that.'

'Why not? It's the truth. I kept thinking you'd get in touch with me. I was mad with grief when you didn't. You were all I wanted,' he murmured. 'I never wanted anyone else since I met you, but I wondered if I'd ever see you again. I thought you might have gone off me.'

'Never.'

'I'm going back to Scotland tomorrow but I'll phone you. We mustn't lose touch with one another again.'

Cara promised to keep him informed about her situation.

24

O n Monday Vanessa phoned her before she left work.
'Meet me at Suzanne's as soon as you can.' The
phone went dead before Cara had a chance to ask what
was wrong.

Vanessa met her at the hall door, wringing her hands. 'I'm
glad you're here. Not a minute too soon.'

'What's the matter?'

'She's discovered Dick's having an affair. She's in a bad
state. The door's locked.'

Vanessa pounded on the door.

'Suzanne, let me in, please!'

Silence. Her pleas went unheard.

Looking at Cara, Vanessa said, 'We might have to get help.
What if she harms herself? I mean the state she was in when I
came round earlier, anything could happen.'

'Let me try. Suzanne, it's Cara, open up.' Cara rapped on
the door.

Slowly, the door opened. Suzanne stood there, rubbing her
forehead, finding it difficult to focus.

'It's all right,' Vanessa said, leading her back inside. 'We're
here now.'

'I'm so tired.' Suzanne said, staring blindly at nothing.

Vanessa gently led her to the couch and covered her with
a blanket.

Suzanne whimpered, 'I wish I were under the wheels
of a bus.'

'Have a little rest. You look exhausted.' Cara said, her heart going out to her.

She'd been so busy with her own problems that she'd forgotten all about Suzanne's.

Suzanne said, face averted. 'How could he do this to me?'

Her difficulty in comprehending what had happened made her look queasy, Her eyes half-closed, she said, 'He begged me not to leave him. Think of the scandal he said, think of my job, my reputation. I told him he should have thought of that before he started this affair, and in broad daylight too. It's crazy. How did he think he was going to get away with it?' Her eyes searched around wildly.

'Have you taken any pills, Suzanne?' Vanessa asked her, rummaging among the bottles on the dressing-table and finding nothing.

'He's worried about the scandal. "Think of my job," he kept saying. I should worry about his job. She works with him, you see.'

Vanessa held her hand, coaxing her to start at the beginning, spill the beans.

When she'd recovered a bit, she said, 'I had the day to myself on Thursday because Mum took Lucy for the whole day, so I decided to go into the city. At lunch I went to a little Italian restaurant in Duke Street, the one Dick took me to for our anniversary. I sat in a corner, self-conscious about being on my own. There was this blonde on her own at a window table, waiting for someone, glancing at her watch every few minutes. She caught my eye because she was so attractive. Dick arrived. I couldn't believe my eyes. My first reaction was how did he know I was here. I was getting to my feet to greet him when I saw him slip into the seat opposite her. She took his hand, smiled at him. I was rooted to the spot, staring at them.'

'Could have been a client, a colleague,' Cara said.

Suzanne shook her head. 'They looked too happy in each other's company for it to be a business meeting. They were talking and laughing together, staring into each other's eyes as they ate and drank. He whispered to her and she nodded her head. After that they seemed to rush through their meal. He got the bill, settled it in a great hurry and up they got and went out gaily, laughing and joking as if they couldn't wait to be alone.' Her voice broke.

Vanessa and Cara were dumbstruck.

'I know Dick's not perfect, but he's my man, and I loved him with his quirky way, prim and proper with his natty tailored suits and his two showers a day. He knew he only had to snap his fingers at me, and I would come running.' She heaved a great sigh. 'God, what am I going to do?'

'You didn't suspect anything?' Vanessa asked.

Suzanne said. 'There were always the little white lies that I caught him out in; saying he was at the office when he was on the golf course, that sort of thing. I let them go. That's what love's all about, isn't it? I did love him, you know. I'd have done anything for him. I looked after him well.'

'What happened when you confronted him?' Vanessa asked.

'I asked him to leave and he did, pretty quickly too. He ran out.' Suzanne sobbed. 'Didn't even put up an argument. I suppose it's all happened before, only I didn't know about it. It's like a play in which I'm acting the same part for a very long time, but I don't want that part anymore.'

'You'll have to talk to him, Suzanne, before you do anything drastic,' Cara said.

'He doesn't want to talk to me. He sees me as a stale and boring housewife since I had Lucy.'

'No he doesn't.'

'It's my own fault I turned myself into a boring old house-wife to please him. Then I became hostile towards him for what was happening to me. He spent so much time away that when he'd come home we'd hardly exchange a word.'

Fresh sobs broke out. Suzanne couldn't control them.

Cara said, 'He'll come back.'

'I don't think I want him.'

'You'll have to see him, even if only to talk to him,' Vanessa said. 'There's Lucy to consider. She'll bring you together, when you're ready. She belongs to both of you.'

'Maybe.'

Dick didn't return. It was awful to see Suzanne so sad, and so alone, every day harbouring the hope that he would one day appear, contrite, swing Lucy up in his arms, and beg Suzanne's forgiveness.

Cara drove along the coast road toward Roslaire, turning off for Bufferstown, a small seaside town, with a harbour flanked by an amusement arcade on one side, a fish and chip and ice cream shop on the other.

It was a typical holiday town; the sea swathed in a mist that also shrouded the far off hills like a protective blanket, making Cara realise that the summer was coming to an end. Farms were scattered around it, and Cara saw a factory or two in the distance. Strange that the town was called Bufferstown because it didn't seem a buffer to anything, except perhaps the sea. Yet, it was a fine town, as good as any other. In the centre she was confused, unsure which turn to take for Arnold's Estate Agents, so she parked and walked around.

There was a feeling of deadness about the rows of houses she passed, until she got to the corner where children were playing, their echoes flying back over their shoulders in the wind. Shops replaced the houses along busy Market Street. People waited at a bus queue, leaning against the railings of the church, which dominated the dull-coloured close together shops in a square of shops that had only their goods to distinguish them. On the opposite side of the square another queue was forming outside a pub called The Duck and Drake. Cara's watch indicated that they wouldn't have to wait much longer.

She went into the newsagents.

'Where's Bridge Street, please?' she asked the woman behind the counter.

'Next turn left. Are you looking for anyone in particular?'

'Mathew Arnold Estate Agents?'

'It's at the end, opposite Collins' fruit and veg shop. You can't miss it. Buying a house?' The woman's curiosity seemed to demand an answer.

'Something like that.' Cara thanked her, not seeing the need to be entirely explicit with a total stranger.

She found Bridge Street just as it began to rain and the drab house opposite Collins' greengrocers where huge baskets of fruit and buckets of fresh flowers overflowed into the street. Red geraniums swayed from hanging baskets.

Cara stood and looked at the dull façade of Arnold's Estate Agents, marked only by an ancient sign, written in faded gold lettering. She noted the cracks and fissures along the walls, and the rectangles of windows. This had been a sturdy house once, but its neglect had made it come down in the world. She thought that she was probably foolish to have come, and turned to go, reconsidered as she caught a glimpse of a woman standing at the door of the greengrocer's.

'They're open,' she called over to her, with a nod of encouragement.

The wrought-iron gate groaned to her touch. The tiny front garden was neglected. Cara walked up the path slowly and rang the doorbell. It jangled in the silence. Her arms were covered in gooseflesh as she waited, although the evening was warm.

A blonde girl in jeans and a white T-shirt dress came to the door. Her eyes, the same shade of blue as the wallpaper in the hall, were in bright contrast to her dull lacklustre hair. She had a ring in her nose.

'Yes?' She looked at Cara enquiringly.

'I have an appointment with Mr Arnold. My name is Cara Thompson.'

The girl stood back to let Cara squeeze by, then knocked at the second door off the hall, and opened it without waiting for an answer.

'Cara Thompson,' she said.

Mathew Arnold looked up reassuringly at Cara, standing very straight and very still in the doorway.

Getting quickly to his feet, he came to greet her, a small plump dishevelled man with thinning hair, completely different to what she'd imagined.

Clasping her hand firmly in his he said, 'How do you do,' smiling warmly. 'You're much younger than I thought.'

Cara was about to say her age but discarded any explanations. It had been years since she'd seen a place like it. She didn't realise places like this still existed. Her dreams of taking on the management of a thriving empire were suddenly blunted by this shabby shop with a fusty smell. No one seemed to have opened a window for years. Hardly the stuff of dreams.

'Take a seat, I'll be with you in a moment,' Mr Arnold said, and returned to his desk. His pen scratched across the page. The clock on his desk ticked.

While she waited Cara studied the room with its fine proportions and rounded French windows that overlooked a long narrow garden, overgrown, the flower beds full of weeds. In spite of the heavy furniture and heaped files that distracted the eye, it was a lovely room. Cara wondered how anyone could work in such untidiness.

'So,' Mathew began, pushing papers on his desk aside, drawing her CV towards him, 'you're looking for a change?'

'That's right.'

'You're well qualified for the job. With your background you probably ate and slept houses.'

'You could say that,' Cara laughed.

'Come, I'll show you everything. Where to start,' Mathew muttered to himself as he stood up again.

He showed her his books. She examined with care his list of assets. He owned the café premises, held the freehold of the pub, the hairdresser's, some shops, and several houses, all rented out. As he explained, he had bought at a time when property was cheap, with selective enthusiasm.

In the front room, going through his list of houses for sale, Cara became as enchanted as a child with a treasure. Though not all of them were beautiful properties, each one was a find. Some of them were out of town, every one practical. She knew she could sell or rent these houses, make them sound important and significant to whoever chose to look at them.

Mathew said, 'I've always sold houses to people for a living, but now unfortunately my health isn't the best.' He caught himself unawares as he spoke; his mouth drooped at the corners dejectedly as he said, 'Now I have to take a rest from it.'

'I'm sorry to hear that,' Cara said lamely, seeing most of his whole life behind him.

'I thought it would last one more generation, but my son isn't interested.'

Surprise lay under his words at the severance of old ties, and indignation that a job that was so admirable to him could seem so dreadfully boring to his son.

They went down to the basement where the account books were locked in a safe. He took them out and turned the dark stained pages, going over the figures with Cara. The letting side of the business brought in large fees, which Cara noted.

Mathew said, 'I've spent my life advising clients on property, how to invest in it, enjoy it, let it out, give it away if they so desired. As you can see it's a thriving business. We went through a bit of a slump in the eighties, but we pulled up again when TCG Tech came to town.'

Cara's life changed under her very eyes, the accounts putting a different perspective on the place. She could run this business on her own. She could even see the passers-by she was watching through the rain-washed window above her as potential clients. It would be exciting chatting them up with polite enquiries about their families, getting to know them that way.

'Come on, I'll give you a quick look at the upstairs.'

Stair carpet gave way to linoleum. Mathew led her to each of the three bedrooms, all similar, clean and polished, snow white bedspreads the only relief to the dark Victorian furniture. The vase of flowers someone had put on the windowsill made the bathroom, with its ancient cistern and old lavatory, less Spartan.

Mathew's face was intent as he said, 'These are the living quarters. I grew up here,' he said, his mouth tightening. 'This house is the only home I've ever known.'

Cara was watching him. She could imagine him always having lived in such a house.

'Of course it's Paul's if he wants it, but I think it might go to strangers. He never comes here now.' There was sadness in his voice.

Cara was lost for words. Finally she said, 'Where does he live?'

'The States. He's a film maker. I'm going to visit him for a couple of weeks, then, who knows where I'll go. I haven't seen much of the world. I'd like you to live here while I'm away, keep the place aired.'

'I'd be happy to,' Cara said, thinking that living accommodation would be a bonus and help her to save.

He took Cara for lunch, walking fast, his tie flying behind him, Cara pacing beside him across the square.

'It's not the Ritz, buts the food's good.'

The proprietor greeted them from his desk.

'We'll have a drink first,' Mathew said, leading her to a table by the window, ordering from the barman who brought a vodka and tonic for her, and a whiskey for him promptly.

A voice called out, 'Hello there, Mathew.'

Mathew greeted the middle-aged woman with a friendly wave.

An elderly man brushed past, enquired after his health.

'That's Bernard Breen, the vet. He's an important man in a farming community. He's just lost his mother. He's a client of mine.'

As he sat sipping his drink, he talked about the various people who'd purchased houses and land from him. Seeing his absorption in the lives of the townspeople, how enmeshed he was in their lives, Cara was impressed. She could see him homing in, taking his time with his prey, before selling or letting to them. Their emotions, frustrations and their intimate lives all known to him, oiled his business.

Yet Mathew was obviously a kind man whose clients came to him when they were in trouble. They respected him, probably put upon him because he was good-tempered. This strange relationship between Mathew and his clients touched her. In a world of chaos and misunderstandings and disappointments it was refreshing.

A vision of Bufferstown life was emerging from his impressive tales. This town was his empire, his pearl of great price. It reminded Cara of what her father had owned, what he had lost, and what she had lost in her expectation of wealth, mainly freedom to change things more easily in her life for the better. Still, she was prepared to start again and work for her own riches. Now it all seemed suddenly possible.

'Tell me about your son's films,' Cara asked to fill the silence that had fallen during the meal.

Mathew, politely, said, 'He makes nature films. I know very little about his world. I imagine it's all very interesting. He films in all weathers, loves the discomforts. It's a love affair between him and the camera. He's making his mark, I have to say. So, I thought, why hang on until I'm at the point of death to see him. Life is too short. I've made my money. I can afford to go where I like. My wife died, the years went by. I didn't remarry because I didn't want my peace violated. You might say my life has been unremarkable.'

He sat back in his chair, watching her.

'So what do you think? Are you interested in taking over as manager? I'll give you free rein.'

Cara looked at him. 'Very. But I need a few days to think about it. I'll phone you when I've made up my mind, if that's all right with you.'

'Fine.' Mathew leaned forward on his chair, put his glass down on the table.

Cara took her leave of him. She asked Vanessa when she returned to Dublin, 'Would you come and look it over for me? It's important to me, but I must warn you, it's a strange place.'

'I'd love to,' Vanessa said.

'Good. Tomorrow I'd better go and see Dad. I can't put it off any longer.'

————◆————

25

C ara pulled into the drive and sat looking at Rockmount, with its magnificent aspect, its sweeping view over Dublin Bay, and its classic charm. Her heart was heavy, not just because Rockmount would soon no longer be her family home, but because she had to tell her father she was moving to Wexford and why.

She sensed trouble as she entered the hall.

'I defy you to find any cobwebs anywhere,' Elsie was leading Pamela about, inviting her to inspect the polished furniture and gleaming windows.

'It's important that everything's neat and clean for the viewing this afternoon,' Pamela said.

It was the first time Cara had come face to face with Pamela since the house went up for sale. She looked wretched.

'Why your father felt the need to keep me in the dark about his business for so long I don't know,' she said, eyebrows raised in enquiry. 'I'm not a child. I can cope with whatever life throws at me.'

'He wasn't hiding anything, just putting a brake on to make things easier,' Cara said in defence of her father. 'He wanted to tell you but he felt so bad about it.'

Pamela tut-tutted. 'Him and his genteel ways. I keep telling him I'm not made of Dresden china.' She was stacking canvases against the wall. 'If I don't question him about his comings and goings, he thinks I don't care,' she said sadly. 'If I do, he thinks I'm interfering. I know it's all terribly difficult for him. If he'd have talked we'd have managed things better.'

'Where is he now?' Cara asked.

'Gone to the bank. He won't be back for a while. You know I was half-relieved to see him off this morning. He's not one to sit quietly while the world shatters around him. He's restless, on the go, all the time thinking of ways of retrieving as much as he possibly can from the mess. I don't blame him. I'd be the same.' Pamela walked around disarranging things. 'I don't know what he has in mind for us. I lie awake at night worrying.'

She was taking shoes out of the cloakroom, putting them back 'Where are my sandals?' she said, glancing around. 'The sooner it's all over and done with the better.' She rubbed her eyes as if to clear her vision and stared in front of her.

Cara could see that she was distressed beyond words and bewildered at the idea of having to sell up and move. Tragedy had struck the household, and wrought a great change upon them all, her in particular. This unfolding drama had quickened the tempo of their lives. Pamela was undertaking the supervising of the packing, her grief carrying her along. Usually with plenty to say, she became quiet suddenly, which was most unlike her.

Elsie wasn't saying much either, discriminatory in what she said for once, so as not to cause an argument, answering all Pamela's practical questions, such as who was coming to see the house and what time, trying to keep her feelings concealed.

Cara, sorry for Pamela, put her hand on her shoulder. 'Come out with me for lunch somewhere.'

'No, thank you, I have to stay here.'

'Elsie will show the people around.'

'No, dear, if you don't mind. I'm going to have a long soak in the tub.' She went upstairs to her room.

Elsie was polishing the hall mirror, her face red in its reflection. She said to Cara in a low voice, 'She has your poor father moithered with her endless questions and restlessness. When this? And when that? And after that what's happening? The poor man hasn't got all the answers. Between ourselves,' she whispered, 'she puts herself too much in other people's shoes. Makes the mistake of thinking things should be done the way she wants them done, instead of allowing others to have their way.'

When John returned he said to Cara, 'I'm sorry I wasn't here to greet you.'

'That's all right,' she said, giving him a hug.

'I'm going round in circles,' he said, rubbing his eyes as if to clear his vision.

She followed him into his study. 'You should have told Pamela everything sooner,' she said.

'You're right,' he said, forced to agree with her. 'I felt that I'd let her down by failing to provide adequately for her.'

Cara said, 'You should have had more confidence in her. She'll manage much better than you think.'

John stood aloof, gazing at the garden.

'Yes, I suppose honesty is the best policy in the long run. Now come and tell me your news on the job front.'

John shut his study door on Elsie, still polishing in the hall, singing the theme song from the film *Titanic* as if she were on a sinking ship.

John looked scornfully towards the door. 'I wish she'd stop that noise.'

'It's her way of keeping cheerful.'

'I'm sure, but it's getting on my nerves.'

'Dad, I've got a job.'

He sat down, and looked at her warily.

'It's manager of Mathew Arnold's business in Bufferstown.'

'Oh!' John said surprised and puzzled. 'I had dealings with

Mathew in the past. He's a shrewd man. Has a thriving business.'

'Yes, he has.'

'But why Wexford, Bufferstown of all places? What could possibly take you there?'

Cara gripped her hands together on her lap to stop herself fidgeting.

'I'm leaving Andy.' It was finally out.

She kept her eyes on the floor.

Astonished, her father said, 'But I thought you'd patched things up.'

'We haven't.'

He waited.

'Things have got worse recently.' Cara straightened up. 'Our marriage has hit rock bottom.'

'And you're not going to make an effort to resurrect it?'

Cara shook her head. 'It's over, Dad. I'm leaving Andy. For good this time.' Cara could hardly bear to look at him.

John stared at her. 'You can't mean that.' He looked uncomfortable in his chair.

Cara said sadly, 'There's no point. The situation's desperate.'

John sat back in his chair, his hands steepled. 'You have to stick with it, Cara. You don't have a choice. You took your marriage vows, for better or worse, 'til death and all that.'

'I'm going to see a solicitor about getting a separation.'

His eyes were sharp. 'Separation' he repeated incredulously, then, 'I see,' realising that it was a fait accompli.

He looked away. 'I was under the impression that there would have to be a very good reason for that.'

Defiantly Cara said, 'I believe I have grounds.'

'Based on what?' He waited, fidgeting with a paper knife.

She remained silent, not daring to tell him about the violence. He always disliked Andy. She could see it in his face.

'There was a period in my life when I saw no point in anything either, after your mother's death. My situation was desperate too. But I had no choice, I had to soldier on.'

'That was different.'

'Not that different. In fact, I wished at the time that I didn't have to wake up each morning.' After a moment he said, 'It went on for a long time.'

Cara looked at him.

'I had you to think of,' he said. 'You were mine, all that was left to me. You needed a home, and I was the only one who could provide it for you. I had no choice.' His lips were pursed, the lines on his face harsh, his eyebrows knit together with the effort of telling her this.

Cara thought of the deep silence that had surrounded him then, a stillness that removed him from her, as if he were on a small island and was untouchable.

There was a dragging silence as Cara said, 'There's something else you should know, Dad.'

John looked up sharply. 'Oh?'

'I had an affair. Andy found it, and he went wild.'

'I see,' he said, quietly seething, seeing everything differently.

Cara could tell by looking at him that he'd shifted the blame to her. 'And who is this . . . lover of yours?'

Her dignity crumbling she said, 'It doesn't matter.' She was trying to keep her answers evasive without being rude.

'It matters to me, Cara.' He was getting angry.

'No one you know,' she said, twisting the truth slightly. He didn't know Guy all that well.

'I have the right to know.' The words, laden with disapproval and threat, broke over her head.

'I don't think you do.'

John's face blanched. He sat still, holding back his anger. 'I'm waiting.'

It was horrible. Cara knew she was making her father angry but she also knew that to tell him it was Guy would be a disaster.

Her father said, 'Your mother was a beautiful woman. I thought I'd die if I didn't get her,' offering this statement to let her know that he understood what blinding passion was, even if he didn't condone her actions.

Cara looked at him, seeing his sudden sense of grief in that instant of recall.

Eventually he said, 'Are you still seeing this man?'

'No.' Coldness came over her, not towards her father, but because Cara realised suddenly that continuing with Guy would be an impossibility.

She wouldn't want the complication at this time, and he wouldn't want to be involved in her messy separation and ultimate divorce. It would tarnish his good name.

John eased back into his chair with relief. 'And you say you're going to see a lawyer about a separation?'

'Yes.'

'It's a costly business, the law. Where are you going to get the money from?'

Cara looked sharply at him. 'I have some savings.'

'Hardly enough, and I'm afraid I can't help you out this time.'

Suddenly Pamela appeared in the doorway. John turned to look at her. Cara could feel the tension between them.

'I could lend you the money,' she said, coming into the centre of the room. 'I have some money of my own.'

John rose from his chair, angry. 'No, Pamela,' he said. 'Your money has nothing to do with Cara. If she needs money, I'll organise it. No need for you to get involved.'

Cara looked from one to the other, too nervous to speak. Why was her father being bullying, browbeating Pamela all of a sudden?

Pamela stepped back, braced herself.

'You're no help to Cara with this interrogation you're conducting.'

'I'm entitled to know what she wants my money for.'

'You never questioned her motives in the past. In fact you cushioned her from every blow that came her way. Why stop now when she needs our help more than ever? I can help her out.'

Her eyes went to Cara. 'If you need a loan, come to me.' Her head tilted up, her look at her husband defiant, she said, 'I'll spend my own money how I want to.'

John stood open-mouthed, gripping the back of the chair.

'You can't afford this generosity, Pamela, at this time.'

'Why are you afraid to let me use my money? You think you might lose control? Is that it?' To Cara she said, 'The offer stands.'

Under his gaze she turned and left in a smooth whisper of silk.

'Thank you, Pamela,' Cara said humbly.

Her father was silent for a minute. 'Now look what you've done.' The sternness had left his voice, but the anger was still in his eyes.

He was suddenly shrunken, diminished, his face grey, his eyes impenetrable. Cara had never seen him this bad before. He looked ill.

Straightening up laboriously, and without another word, he followed Pamela, a child's terror in his tone as he called out to her. Cara heard his footsteps on the stair, heard him call her again and her voice answering him, before the sharp click of their bedroom door as it shut out the sound.

She knew she must tell Elsie before she left.

'I'm surprised you stuck him this long,' Elsie said. 'You're very brave to do it. It takes courage.'

'I don't feel very brave at this moment,' Cara said.

'So what if your father doesn't approve? It makes things harder, I'll grant you. Comes between you. That's just too bad. You know, it's amazing how much power you lose when you marry someone who tries to control your life. My advice to you is to do your own thing. Whatever you want to do. So you get out, create another space for yourself.'

'I'm doing that by moving to Wexford.'

Elsie nodded. 'It's good to get your own base. From there you can work out your own destiny. And if by chance you fancy a nice man like that Guy chap, you can go for it.' She looked at Cara with raised eyebrows.

Cara blushed.

'Call me a doddery old woman, if you like, but he's a fine fellow, with wonderful manner. He'll go far too. And he only had eyes for you.'

'Elsie!' Cara wanted to stop her, but she continued on determinedly.

'All I'm saying is that there couldn't be a better candidate.'

'He's gone back to Scotland, I think.'

They heard the clickety-clack of Pamela's high heels on the stairs and John's heavy step as he followed her.

Cara knew it was time to disappear.

She missed Guy. She saw him everywhere, in the street where he couldn't possibly be, in the pub drinking with friends, the same smile. She had to restrain herself from going to him, because it was someone completely different.

26

The following Saturday Cara and Vanessa went to the cottage to collect the remainder of her belongings. They got out of the car, and walked to the door, their shoes crunching on the gravel. Cara was afraid as soon as she opened it.

'What will we say if Andy suddenly returns?' she asked Vanessa who was already in the kitchen.

'He won't. I told you, he's in Cork, a darts match.'

Optimistic, and scared, Cara packed her clothes, heart pounding in spite of Vanessa's reassuring words. Grabbing only the bare essentials, they left, sneaking off like burglars. Before getting into the car, Cara stopped to take a last look around, a terrible sense of loss and failure in her at having to leave her beloved home. Looking back sadly, Cara realised that the cottage would never be home again to her. It would have to be sold because she would always see her marriage as the biggest failure of her life if she were to keep it on.

Suddenly, Andy appeared in front of them, from nowhere.

'What are you doing here?' he shouted, looking from her to Vanessa who started running to the car.

Recoiling, Cara said, 'I've taken my stuff because I won't be coming back here anymore.' There was accusation in her eyes as she looked at him.

'You can't go just like that. I won't let you go. You live here.'

'Not anymore I don't,' Cara said, walking away.

Andy followed her. 'I'll do anything you want.' He was desperate as he tried to detain her.

She managed to keep him at arm's length. 'This isn't a game. I'm seeing a solicitor, getting a separation, and a divorce eventually.'

'What?' Andy exploded.

'Of course, I'm not joking.'

Terror took hold of him.

'On what grounds?'

'Irretrievable breakdown, incompatibility.' She wasn't sure of the jargon.

'I'm not going to divorce you, Cara, and if you even bother to try I'll make life hell for you. I'll punish you, tell the world the way you deceived me.'

'Whatever you do, it won't make any difference. Our marriage is over,' Cara said in a reasonable voice.

'Come on, Cara,' Vanessa called, the engine of the car running.

'No, it isn't. You're hysterical, and you're unreasonable at the moment. It isn't over. We can work on it.' He raised his voice. 'I will not agree to a separation, certainly not a divorce. Never.'

Cara couldn't hide her fear.

Andy lowered his voice. 'I'm prepared to overlook your little sordid affair, start again, meet you halfway.'

She shook her head, looking at him hopelessly. 'It won't work. I'm serious about what I said. I know I capitulated in the past, but not anymore. Besides everything else, I'm tired of keeping everything going.'

'What a little provider you are,' Andy said with heavy sarcasm, 'but I know you. You'll be back before too long.' He was stooping over her like a greedy bird of prey. 'I'll be waiting.'

He would not give in any more than he'd ever understand

her determination. She continued walking away from him. He caught hold of her, pulled her to him, taking hold of her wrist, bending it towards him. She pulled free, her strength exaggerated.

'Let her go.' Vanessa took hold of her and led her away, Andy watching them. Cara hated that it was all finishing like this, the uncomfortable notion that he wouldn't be able to manage without her making her feel bad.

'You'll be back in no time,' he called after her. 'We're meant to be together.'

She didn't answer, but walked to the car uncertainly.

Vanessa drove off in silence.

There would be no going back, Cara knew that the division between them was now a monstrous gap, never to be filled.

Vanessa drove Cara to Bufferstown the next day. It was late when they arrived, the town quiet, a few people out for their Sunday evening stroll along the seafront.

Vanessa said, 'Nice place,' helping Cara haul in her bags, then inspecting each room, Mathew not back from his night-cap in the pub yet.

They unpacked, Vanessa singing at the top of her voice to make light of the situation. She put away Cara's grocery shopping that they did en route while Cara unpacked her clothes. When the job was done they sat down to a pepperoni pizza, exhausted.

'You'll be all right here. The neighbour opposite seems friendly,' Vanessa said, referring to the woman in the green-grocer's she'd seen watching them arrive.

'Nosy you mean.'

'Same thing.'

'Hopefully.'

'Be sure and give me a ring if there's anything you need,' she said when she was leaving.

'Yes, of course, but don't worry about me, I'll be fine,' Cara assured her, giving her a hug.

Cara waved her off, watching her drive away until she was out of sight.

'Alone at last,' she said aloud, the unexpected sound of her own voice in the silence making her jump.

She took a bath with a feeling of foreboding, leaving the door of the bedroom ajar, and went to bed. The bed was cold. The silence, punctuated by the mournful wailing of the foghorn, intensified her loneliness. The sea air through the top of the bedroom window was like a drug, making her eyes close. Before she went to sleep she heard Mathew's key turn in the lock, and was comforted by the sound of it.

The next morning she awoke to the cacophony of the dawn chorus. She opened the window, breathed in the sea air, gazing at the clear sky and the long stretch of sea front curving away to the horizon. She could hear the distant sound of waves breaking on the shore and the squawk of seagulls.

Cara felt strange as she made herself a breakfast of toast and marmalade, and chatted to Mathew when he made his appearance. When she heard the rattle of the door of the greengrocer's being opened she escaped to buy some fruit and make the owner's acquaintance.

It was a long narrow shop, the shelves on one side crowded with tins and jars of delicacies, baskets of fruit and vegetables on the other side. Cara stopped at the display of fruit, carefully choosing some ripe plums.

'Maulin' them won't make them taste any better,' said the woman from her stool behind the counter. 'They're fresh in this mornin'.'

Cara put the plums on the counter.

You're not from around here,' the woman said, eyeing Cara's smart clothes, giving her the once over, making her own judgements.

'No. I came to manage Mathew's place. I'm Cara Thompson.'

'I'm Margaret Collins, known locally as Mags. Where are you from?'

'Dublin.'

'Thought so. What part?'

'Suburbs.'

'I grew up in the city myself.'

'I guessed that from your accent.'

While Mags filled a bag with apples, oranges, pears that Cara had picked out, Cara noticed a photograph of Bertie Ahern and her together, both smiling happily.

'The opening of the new community centre,' the woman said, totting up on the till. 'That's two pounds, twenty pence, please,' she added. 'So, what brought you to Bufferstown?' she asked through a rasping cigarette cough.

'To earn a living.'

The woman looked perplexed. 'You left a good job in Dublin to come here?'

'Yes.'

'Failed romance, I'll bet.'

Cara shifted uncomfortably finding the woman's curiosity infuriating.

'Bufferstown's not known for it's healing powers, quite the opposite. Take Mathew, for instance, he didn't fare so well out of it, for a man who owns half the town. Pulling up sticks and leaving it in the hands of strangers is a sad way to end his career.'

'He'll be back,' Cara said.

Mags shook her head. 'I doubt it. He lost interest in the place after his son cleared off. Never got over his wife's death. She fell off the roof. Did he tell you that?'

'No.'

'What she was doing up there no one could ever fathom. There was no rational explanation given. I myself think she was cleaning the tiles, and said so to the police at the time. She was fanatical about cleanliness. Had a Brillo pad in the gate for finger marks. Accident it said at the inquest.'

'I'm sorry to hear that.' Cara felt alien to the town suddenly, and wary.

Mags subsided into a confidential tone. 'I hear his house could do with a bit of redecorating, antiquated, is it?'

Cara was vague as she said, 'Perhaps a little.'

Reluctant to continue this conversation, her dream of privacy shattering before her very eyes, she made to leave.

'Why Bufferstown? Do you have family connections here?'

'No,' Cara said. 'I just wanted a change. This is a good business town, I'm told.'

'It is, but it's a tightly knit community here, everyone minding everyone else's business. If you want my advice, don't get involved. Come to me if you need anything. Oh, there you are,' she said to the astonishingly attractive young man with an air of shyness who stood on the threshold.

'You're late. Out fishing again, I'll bet.' She turned to Cara. 'That's all he's good for. Up at the harbour with the lads.' She gave a laugh, flung her thick arms around him. 'This is my son, Brendan.'

Brendan flinched and moved away.

'The boat is the centre of his universe,' she continued. 'He's interested in nothing but fishing, in all weathers too. I tell him that one of these days he'll catch his death.' She laughed, turning to him saying, 'You could do with a shower before you start work. I don't want the place smelling like a fishmongers,' taking no notice of his embarrassment, killing his confidence altogether in front of Cara.

'I could do with a new set of balls too,' he muttered, humble, trying to manage a smile, the insults in front of customers the habit about his mother that he found the least acceptable.

Cara took her leave glad that Brendan's presence had

released her from engaging in further small talk, and went to work. Mathew helped her get acquainted with the business. Jane, his secretary, was also helpful. Her job was to arrange appointments for open views prior to auctions, give Cara weekly updates of listings, answer phones, change brochures. She'd worked there for the past four years and knew everything about the business. From the area, she knew everything there was to know about Bufferstown and everyone in the locality. She'd have the name of someone who'd be interested in a house for rent and would suggest a certain house or premises to them. She knew the language of the locals, know what to show them, what to withhold, what suited one, not the other.

'What's a bargain to one, is not to another. I rent for a year, at least, maybe longer if possible.'

Cara established a routine. Each morning she would jog along the empty wind-swept beach, past the fishing boats bobbing lazily in the harbour, swans gliding alongside them. At the end of the harbour she would stand to watch gulls swirling peevishly above the pale rocks, the smell of fish all pervasive, the place deserted at that hour of the morning. Hard to believe that in the next few hours it would be busy.

In the evening, after work, she went up to the flat, made supper, watched telly and went to bed. Mathew ate his meals at the hotel. A long-standing arrangement with the manager meant that it was cheaper to eat out than in, so he told Cara. He returned at bedtime, so didn't bother her much. When he left to go on his travels Cara wondered if Vanessa would come down to visit her, and hoped she would. Cara missed her friends, the touchiness of Suzanne, the tactile, often tactless Vanessa. She thought of her life ahead.

Her main fear was that she might bump into Andy sometime, somewhere. She would avoid all the places she knew he frequented so they wouldn't meet by accident.

On the following Thursday morning she encountered Brendan sweeping the pavement outside his shop.

'Hello.' He looked at her with a less uncertain air, leaning on his brush, welcoming the interruption.

She crossed the road.

'My mother's not here today,' he said. 'She's gone to a funeral in Wexford.' There was a smile on his face, a contrast to his misery of the last time they met, no longer servant today, but master.

'Are you settling in?' he asked.

'Getting there. It'll take me a while to get to know everyone.'

'Come out for a drink tonight. I'll introduce you to my friends; great crack some of them. You might like them.'

'Thanks, I'd love to.'

'Really?' he said, delighted. 'I'll meet you in the pub at eight o'clock.'

'OK. See you then.'

'Hello again.' Brendan said, that evening outside the pub. In jeans and brilliant white T-shirt; a contrast to his dull-navy overall of the morning, he looked dazzling as he politely led her to the bar, a smile dimpling his face.

Customers turned to stare at them, a total lack of inhibition in the dropped jaws. They would think that she was on a date. Cara smiled to herself. laughed at the stupidity of it.

Brendan introduced her to his pals, Paddy Meehan and Tommy McDade. They were friendly, accepting Cara into their little group, making her feel at home. Paddy, a garage-owner, promised to find Cara a reasonable, second-hand car.

27

———◆———

Cara was returning from a lunchtime walk alone when she heard someone calling her.

It was Guy sprinting towards her. He caught up with her, taking her in his arms, kissing her, his delight in seeing her flowing out of him.

Astonished she said, 'Where did you spring from?'

'I'm over for a meeting. I thought I'd surprise you. So here I am.' Instinctively his arms went round her waist recklessly, with the impulse of a child.

'Hey! It's broad daylight,' she said suddenly feeling crumpled, ungainly, that they were being looked at and she was making a fool of herself.

'If it's not convenient,' he began.

'Of course it's convenient,' she said, taking him inside, leading him upstairs. 'I live alone,' she said, proudly. 'I know it's over the shop but at least it's my own place.' She led him into the sitting room.

'Very comfortable too,' he said, impressed.

'Coffee?'

'Thanks.'

When she returned with the tray he was looking at photographs on the mantelpiece: her father and Pamela on their wedding day, Vanessa and her at Suzanne's wedding, Suzanne's happy face peering out between them.

'It's my favourite photo of the three of us,' she said.

'Happier times,' Guy said.

'How are Suzanne and Dick?'

'Doing their best. Dick realises what a fool he's been. He's desperately trying to make up to her for his indiscretion.'

'Not just for Lucy's sake, I hope. Does he still care for her?'

'Desperately,' Guy said. 'That's the strangest thing about it.'

Cara looked at her watch. 'I'm afraid I have to get back to work.'

Guy finished his coffee. 'I'll have to be going too. Will you come to Arklow this evening for dinner? I brought Ian over for a spot of fishing. I'd like you to meet him.'

Cara was shocked. Up until now it had just been the two of them, Ian rarely mentioned. What they did had been secret, their sense of secrets keeping them separate from people and the world at large. Now Ian was going to be in on it and the thought of meeting him was daunting to Cara.

'You will come, won't you?' Guy asked.

'Yes, I'll be there.'

Satisfied with that, he slipped away before Jane returned from her lunch break so Cara didn't have to introduce him. All afternoon she was nervous thinking of the evening ahead. There was no one in Bufferstown that she could tell. No one that she could talk to about it. After work she showered, changed into casual black trousers and a plain black top and drove to Arklow, trying to psych herself up for this meeting with Ian, the thought of it terrifying. She knew she would need to exercise great caution in dealing with him. Her life was messy enough without any further damaging events.

'I've made a curry,' Guy said, greeting her with a hug. 'The wine's cooling in the fridge. We're almost ready.'

Cara heard loud music thumping from upstairs.

'I can't stand it,' Guy laughed. 'It's Ian's favourite.'

A boy walked into the room, tall for his age, in crumpled black T-shirt, worn jeans and trainers, and stood gazing at Cara. The physical resemblance to his father was uncanny; the same dark good looks, and brooding eyes half-hidden by a fringe of dark hair, but his mouth was sulky.

'This is Ian, Cara. Ian, meet my friend, Cara.'

Self-conscious, Ian said, 'Hello' with a shy look.

'Are you enjoying your holiday?' Cara asked.

Ian's eyes moved to the floor as he said, 'It's all right.'

Guy said. 'Are you going to change for dinner?'

Ian shook his head. 'I don't need to.'

'Well, at least have a shower. You've been in those clothes all day. They're damp.'

Ian left the kitchen without a word and went upstairs; there was the sound of running water.

'Sorry about that,' Guy said embarrassed.

'He's clearly unimpressed,' Cara said. 'With this country,' she added.

'That's Ian,' Guy said lightly, stirring his Thai curry. 'Very little impresses him. He's been missing his pals.'

'I suppose it's not great fun for him being with adults all the time.'

'He'll have to get used to it.'

Suddenly Cara didn't see Guy in the singular anymore. She saw him as a family man, something she'd never really thought about before, bonded by blood to other people, specifically his son, a constant reminder of a past relationship, his wife still existing through Ian.

Ian was polite during dinner, saying 'yes, please' if he was asked if he wanted more. Cara asked him questions about his day. Ian kept his eyes on his plate every time Cara addressed him. His answers were brief, given in a monosyllabic tone, only giving the quickest of glances when he spoke. He was acutely shy; even Guy had to worm every word out of him.

This made Cara nervous. She shuffled her food around her plate 'Do you like it here at all?' Cara asked.

'It's no big deal. I much prefer holidays in Canada. Dad's promised to take me back.'

'Just because they make a big fuss of you there,' Guy said, turning to Cara. 'He gets a sympathetic ear from his Aunt Fiona.'

'I'm going to live in Canada one day.' Ian's eyes were defiantly on his father, letting him know that whatever his own plans were, he would have to be taken into account.

Names being mentioned like Auntie Fiona, Uncle Donald, personalities began to unfold with each remark made by Ian or Guy. All those years and all those lives that Guy had been so much part of were suddenly there; spreading out over a lifetime, reminding Cara of a previous life Guy had led independent of her. Though Guy smiled at her and was his usual affectionate caring self, Cara was decidedly uncomfortable and embarrassed. Ian, protective of his father, kept his manner to Cara chilly, the expression on his face clearly saying he's *my* father, and you're not getting him.

The strain stretched out for the duration of the meal, Cara guarding her tongue. As soon as it was over Ian went to his room. Things had been uncomplicated until then, the house with its lack of memories, and nobody but themselves to share it had given them liberty and a freedom to shut out the world. All of this Cara had taken for granted. Now she felt a painful discomfort in this family setting. A family she'd given very little thought to. Cara didn't relish the prospect of having to fight Ian for his father.

'He wants you all to himself.'

Guy looked at her. 'He's only a child,' Guy said in his need to defend Ian's manner. 'He's a bit self-absorbed like most teenagers, and he's a bit lost with no great sense of security since his mother died. He thinks I'm out of order wanting him to come and live here to finish his schooling.'

'You do?'

'Yes, Ian thinks I'm being unfair, and exploitative, purposely removing him from a life that he knows. He's jealous of me having any kind of life outside of him.'

'I know.'

'He thinks I owe him first consideration.'

Cara said, 'He's right. Whatever you do, he'll have be the main consideration, your obligations are to him first.'

'Yes, and that's the way it's been up until now. But he can't have it all his own way. I have a life too. One he'll have to learn to share.' His shoulders dropped as he looked at Cara.

Cara felt uncomfortable, not wanting to be caught up in the crossfire of this father and son emotional conflict.

Guy looked at her. 'I hadn't planned to say this Cara, not yet, but the time has come. I love you. I've never loved anyone the way I love you. I want to spend the rest of my life with you. I want us to be a family, have our own family.' He looked at her. 'In the not too distant future.'

Startled, she looked at him. She'd never thought of a family with Guy, never really having been free to consider it a possibility. Now that she was moving in that direction, freedom round the corner, she knew she would have to give it some thought.

'This house is a perfect family home, don't you think? A place we could all settle down in.'

'You already have a family.'

Guy said, 'I know, and I don't want to put any restrictions on you regarding Ian. You're young, Cara, too young to be Ian's Mum. I'm not asking you to fulfil that role. I'd like us to have babies of our own.'

'Guy, hold on a minute. I've too much on my mind to even

think about things like that. I can't take on anymore. I've no idea what's coming next.'

'I just want you to know how I feel. I never had much of a home life before, always on the road, always travelling, working to make something of myself. Hazel brought Ian up virtually on her own. She had a large family to help, I know, but to my shame I let her get on with it. I led a half-life, home at weekends and holidays. When she complained that she was unhappy I moved her to a big house in the suburbs because I thought it would make her happier.'

'And did it?'

He shook his head. 'It made me happier because it justified my dedication to my job.' His voice was sombre as he said, 'It only made things worse for her. I isolated her from her family and friends, both geographically and socially. She was upset about it.'

Images of his beautiful laughing bride in the photograph came back to Cara.

'I don't want to waste much more time without you. If you don't come and live with me I'll go mad.'

'Guy, slow down. This is all going too fast for me.'

'Is it such a crime to want you with me all the time, to want to protect you?'

Cara clasped her hands. 'I have to go through this separation first.'

'You can do that and still be with me.'

Her hands were shaking. 'No, it would make things more difficult, more complicated. Imagine it, you coming home from a hard day's work to find me in a distraught state from confronting a team of lawyers, or facing a court hearing. Things will get harder before they're sorted out, there'll be things we haven't even thought of.'

'We'll face it together. Stay in Edinburgh out of the way if we have to.'

'Trauma like that is bound to cause conflict. I'd still be married to someone else, socially unacceptable. I'd be an outcast you had to keep hidden. How could we think of having babies in that environment?'

'We'd weather it, marry when your divorce came through.'

Cara, thinking of the baby she'd lost, shook her head sadly; 'I may not be able to deliver on that score.'

'We could have fun trying. It'd be worth the risk.'

'Guy, this is not a good time to discuss the matter.'

'Why not?'

She lifted her eyes to his. 'I've been through all that before and it ended in heartbreak. I can't take that risk again.'

'Cara, it really matters to me that you're part of my life. We can't be apart. You know that as well as I do. I want to be seen with you, out and about, I want a relationship that's public, no more secrets, no more hiding in corners. You'll have to make up your mind one way or the other.'

Shocked Cara said, 'Don't give me an ultimatum, Guy. It would finish us.'

'I'm not, but why can't we get on with our lives, regardless of what's happening around us?'

'Things have changed,' Cara explained. 'Our relationship is not like it was before Andy found out. I'm going through a crisis and, until it's sorted, I can't make a decision. Besides there's my job, settling into it is taking up all my time.'

'You won't need it. I can keep you in comfort for the rest of your life.'

'You don't understand, do you? I want to make it on my own, if only to prove to myself that I can do it. You have to see that and understand it.'

Guy looked at her with a hurt closed-off expression, making her stomach knot up in a tight ball of sadness.

'I'd better go. We'll talk tomorrow when we're both calmer.'

'If that's the way you want it,' he said, letting her go, disappointment etched on his face.

At work next day Cara walked around her office in Bufferstown, unsettled, picking up files, putting them down again. She sat down at her desk, finding it difficult to concentrate, breaking out in a cold sweat thinking of Guy and of the no win situation she was in.

Guy was important to her. She didn't want to disappoint him, or let him down. She wanted to go out with him properly too, be part of his life too. But the slow process of her separation from Andy, her fight for what should be effortlessly and rightly hers was having significance in the other areas of her life, especially where Guy was concerned. She couldn't cope with his demands. She couldn't even think straight.

Did she want to be part of Guy's life? Or anybody's? After the trauma of life with Andy, could she surrender fully to another man? Could she trust another man? Was she prepared to lose her independence and put Guy first in her life? She was enjoying life on her own, and she knew she couldn't assume that Guy would put her first in his life. Surely Ian would take precedence before her if it came down to important decisions, or if supposing he were ill or in need of his father's undivided attention.

What about Ian? How would he take the idea of his father having another woman in his life permanently, a mother replacement? Since moving to Bufferstown Cara had been earning her own living. Now there was the prospect of buying the business, making it her own, to consider. Would Guy allow her to continue to be that independent woman? Or would she have to blend into his life as the second Mrs McIntosh? Would she have to do the cooking, washing, ironing for Ian and him? Would she have to drive to visit Ian at school, watch him play in his school's cup final, force him to change his socks and eat his vegetables? Would she have to clean up after him?

The sense of everything being lasting and forever, Ian calling her Mum maybe, was a frightening concept. If she and Guy did eventually marry, would he love her, honour her, cherish her until death? Or would he turn out to be another bastard?

She was hurt that Guy was pressuring her at a time like this when she'd enough pressure in her life. Just as she'd taken the first tentative step to freedom, he was pushing for more. Was she prepared to throw away her life, discard everything and everyone she knew as if it didn't count? Of course she wasn't. Her domestic skills had been put to the test with Andy. She wasn't having that kind of life again.

She was tired of being restricted by other people's desires and wishes: Andy dragging things out, never in agreement, Guy wanting to announce their love affair to all the world and have babies, Ian with his own agenda, wanting his father to himself, and who could blame him.

She sipped her umpteenth cup of coffee thoughtfully, half-heartedly reading through her mail, but wanting to see Guy again, and talk to him, reason with him. She loved him, loved spending time with him, but wished it could be in a more carefree way. She should phone him at his office, arrange to meet him. She lifted the phone. Put it down. What was the point of talking if they were only going to argue? He'd made his point clear.

That afternoon he phoned her, and asked to meet her. They met in a small hotel in Wooden Bridge.

'Well, have you thought about what I said?'

'I'm really sorry, Guy, for upsetting you,' Cara said with sincerity, hating herself for causing the hurt that was evident in his eyes. 'I feel that any sudden changes would only make things worse for Ian, and might be damaging for us all.'

'Maybe you don't think it worth making the effort,' Guy said quietly.

'That's ridiculous,' Cara said hotly. 'Don't you think I'd love to be with you if I was free, and things were less complicated? Ian needs time to adjust to this new situation with me. I need time to adjust to him, and everything else. My feelings for you are too important for me to do anything rash or stupid,' Cara said, getting worked up. 'I need time.'

Guy drew back. 'OK,' he said, subdued by the strain between them. 'We'll wait until the next crisis is over and then the one after that, and after that there'll be something else. Always something to get in the way.'

'What do you expect? You spring all this on me and expect my instant agreement.'

Guy flashed her an angry look. 'OK, I'll leave you to it. I'll ring you when I get back to Scotland. But you don't have to live on your own for the two years until your separation, you know, Cara.'

'I've never had time on my own before. I have to find my feet, by myself, and that may take a while. Who knows, maybe later on, when I've sorted out my life I'll think differently.'

The disappointment in Guy's face said it all. Cara's heart lurched as he said gruffly. 'If that's what you want. But I hope you realise that we're running the risk of losing one another.'

'I know that.'

He stood up, came to her, took her face in his hands. 'I think we're wasting time now, going around in circles.'

She looked at him unable to speak.

'Well,' he said at length, tight-lipped. 'I'd better get home. Ian will be waiting for me.'

Cara left, giving him a quick hug, an ache in the pit of

her stomach as she did so. Edgy and upset she decided to have a consultation with Vanessa to see if she thought it was ludicrous of Guy to insist that they should be together in a permanent situation.

28

Cara told Vanessa what had happened, explaining to her that Guy was a special man, that she'd fallen for him in a big way, but the appearance of his son and the shadow of his dead wife had made her insecure.

'I didn't feel at ease with Ian or he with me. From the minute he set eyes on me he was waging a silent battle for his father.'

'Battles are hard work and you haven't got that kind of fight left in you,' Vanessa said, her sympathy comforting. 'Why couldn't you just sleep with Guy from time to time, for the moment, without any strings? There's a lot to be said for that kind of relationship,' Vanessa said knowingly.

Cara shook her head, 'He won't have that, and I'm not really cut out for it either. He wants me to move in with him permanently.

'I suppose you can't blame him for being insecure. But why the sudden rush?'

'He's lonely. He's just turned forty, wants to settle down, have babies, for God's sake. Imagine him wanting us to have babies together.'

'What the man wants, the man wants, there's nothing you can do about it, and it's not as if you're twenty-five years of age still. Time's marching on for you too.'

'He wants it all; romance, excitement, stability, support, and he's picked the wrong one in me. I haven't got that much to give, not now, maybe not ever.'

'You can't end a love affair just because one wants more out of the relationship than the other is prepared to give. Things will change over time. You'll see things differently as a result.'

Cara shook her head, 'That's my point. I need time.'

'So you want the fun part, nothing serious?'

'It's not as cut and dried as that.'

'You sit there looking all sad and soulful, the romantic heroine, but not romantic heroine enough to make changes.'

Cara sniffed. 'I think I've done the right thing.'

'Only time will tell,' Vanessa said. 'If you really love each other you'll be together one day.'

Cara drove to Bufferstown, listening to Coldplay singing 'Trouble', thinking that that was all men were – trouble, with a capital T.

What did love really have to do with any of it? Love played tricks on you, love cornered you, narrowed your horizons, blinded you to everything and everyone around you. There was no pleasure in anything at the moment for Cara, not even the simple things like a chat and a cup of tea with a friend. Her chat with Vanessa hadn't made her feel any better. Vanessa, for once, was lacking in the support she needed. Then, affairs of the heart didn't mean as much to Vanessa, at least that's the image she portrayed. After all she'd been through Cara wanted her life back, and all Guy McIntosh wanted to do was tie her up in knots again.

On Saturday morning Cara slept late. Brendan knocked on her door around noon with a huge bouquet of flowers.

'They're beautiful,' Cara said, delighted. 'You're quite a romantic,' she teased him, arranging them in a vase of water.

Flattered, Brendan said, 'No one ever called me that before. Actually, I think I'm quite boring.'

'Never,' Cara said. 'Would you like a cup of coffee?'

'That'd be lovely, thanks.'

Brendan smiled appreciatively. He was suddenly uncomfortable, talking too much, acting out a role, describing the town, making it sound as if he owned it all, puffing himself up to look like a big man with a big future, instead of small town grocer.

'Take off your jacket if you like.'

'Thanks.' His movements were light and neat as he removed his jacket, and sat down comfortably at the table.

'Tell me about those beautiful flowers you buy. How do you know what to pick?'

Suddenly bright-eyed and eager to explain all the different species to her, Brendan was transformed from the awkward young man she'd encountered the first time she'd set foot in the shop into an enthusiastic horticultural expert.

Eventually he got to his feet. 'I'd better go and give Ma a dig out.'

At the door he said, 'By the way the Harvest Festival is in town.'

'I know.'

'Do you like Harvest Festival?'

Cara laughed. 'I've never been to one.'

'I'm judging the vegetable-growers competition. Would you like to come this evening?'

'I'd love to.'

'That's great.' Brendan did a little dance, stabbing the air.

Cara laughed with delight. Encouraged, Brendan danced to the door humming. 'I'll pick you up at seven,' he said, waltzing off.

Cara was happy, looking to a night out, a real date, the first since she arrived in Bufferstown. Brimming with energy she tidied up and went shopping. On the way to the supermarket a dress caught her eye in the window of Lydia's boutique. It was short with straps, in a shade of green that suited her, its light fabric perfect for the warm weather. On an impulse she bought it.

In the supermarket she went straight to the deli counter and bought cheese, delicious home-made bread and a bottle of wine, thinking that Brendan might fancy a snack later.

Jane was at the checkout.

'Who are you expecting?' she enquired, her eyes on Cara's basket.

Cara shrugged. 'Brendan asked me to the Festival.'

'Oh! he did, did he? I noticed he was getting quite friendly.'

Cara laughed. 'In a sudden fit of madness I said yes. What can you do when a gorgeous hunk asks you out? I could hardly tell him to get lost, could I?'

'On the contrary you'd have to ask him back for supper.'

'I thought we might feel a bit peckish afterwards,' Cara was winding her up, seeing that she was green with envy.

'He's only the best looking bloke in the town.' Jane sighed, throwing a bunch of bananas into her basket. 'I dropped enough hints to get him interested, but he never was. I assumed it was because he was so wrapped up in that mother of his.'

On the dot of seven Brendan appeared, in snow-white T-shirt and blue jeans, his teeth gleaming like china.

'Hi there.' He flashed her a dazzling smile.

They walked the short distance to the harbour in the twilight.

The harbour was alive with people oblivious to the noise and flashing lights of the Festival. It had turned it into a magical place, its daytime dowdiness camouflaged with bright lights that reflected on the water. Some sat on the wall, eating fish and chips or candyfloss or ice cream.

The Festival Queen sat on a gilt throne in the Harvest

tent, a crown of corn on her head, fruits of the harvest at her feet, symbolic of the year's bountiful crop. She smiled calmly as children ran riot around her, chasing each other around while tinny music thumped and loudspeakers called out numbers from the bingo hall. The air smelt of salt and vinegar.

Brendan joined the other judges at the vegetable-growers' stall while Cara walked among the stalls viewing autumn flowers and vegetables, bathed in the artificial lights.

They left when the winners were picked.

'You must love living in a place like this,' Cara said as they strolled through the throng.

'Yes, I do,' Brendan almost yelled above the rat-tat-tat from the firing range and the bleep of slot-machines. 'I love this time of year.'

He steered her along past the gilded sedate horses of the round-about to the big dipper where they queued among scantily clad teenagers, whispering together, their eyes on a group of boys, as they waited their turn.

Cara grasped the bar of the big dipper with both hands as it took off into the air. Brendan sat prim as a child, staring ahead bravely, his arm around her protective. Up into the darkening sky they flew, hurtling through space, heading for the stars, the wind rushing past their ears, the cold air slapping their faces, Cara's hair flying back as they went higher and higher.

At the top they sat suspended over the sea, the moon directly above them, and the town below them a toy town, a bracelet of lights around it.

Suddenly they were plunged towards earth. Cara, eyes tightly shut, screamed like a peacock in terror and triumph, and gripped the bar tighter as they took off again, the wind rushing into their lungs this time, making them giddy.

They finally alighted, Cara laughing, shaky on her legs,

clutching her wobbly stomach. Brendan took her hand impulsively to steady her, their giddiness and the artificial atmosphere giving them a new freedom with each other. They walked along by the row of bright caravans and stalls full of prizes. At the hoop stall Brendan ensnared a pink fuzzy teddy bear for Cara, 'I love you' written across its chest.

'Thank you,' she mouthed, taking it, twisting its ear affectionately, Brendan watching her curiously.

They walked along unconcerned. They got their fortunes from a slot machine,

'All your dreams will come true,' Cara's read.

Brendan crumpled his future up and threw it away. Cara laughed at his silliness.

He bought her an ice cream cone and led her to where the boats were, casting eerie shadows on the dark water, their halyards tinkling in the breeze.

He pointed out his plain blue fishing boat, the *Mermaid*, and told her about his passion for fishing, explaining the way he fished, how he'd acquired the skill for it from boyhood, often fishing at night alone for hours in the moonlight until he got the hang of it.

'I was too proud to let anyone see my first poor attempts at it,' he laughed.

'You know it's funny but I keep thinking that we've known each other ages, probably because your mother's always talking about you. It's Brendan this and Brendan that.'

'She's talked a lot about you too in the month you've been here. She's very fond of you.'

'Do you think she's doing a bit of matchmaking?'

'Trying to get rid of me, is she?' he asked.

They looked at each other and laughed at the very idea.

'Fancy a drink?'

'Yes,' she said, accepting because she wanted his company.

They walked to the pub, the Festival lights twinkling in the dark, and the noise receding. Cara stood beside the chattering groups, families and people just arrived for the festivities, all waiting to be served. Jane arrived with a group her friends. They stared at Cara and Brendan, their jaws dropped, all inhibitions gone with their curiosity. That they were already pairing them off was obvious from the expression on their faces. Cara sat quietly immune to their critical eyes as the conversation flowed.

'Come to the disco,' Jane said.

Brendan agreed instantly. As soon as they got there the girls swept him away, bouncing and swinging to Lucy Pearl 'Don't Mess Wi' My Man', Jane throwing Cara filthy looks every so often. Cara hung on as long as she could, deciding to go when the noise level and dancing couples reached a peak in her brain. She decided to go home as soon as Shania Twain's 'Don't Be Stupid, You Know I Love You' started.

Brendan insisted on leaving with her. There would be gossip, but Brendan, all inhibition gone, didn't seem to care.

'Cup of coffee?' she asked casually when they got back.

'Call me old-fashioned but I'd prefer tea.'

They sat at the kitchen table, talking.

'Why do you love fishing so much?' Cara asked.

'Keeps me out of trouble.'

'The world should be your oyster. You should be full of dreams.'

He let out a roar of laughter. 'I am. Ma thinks I'm still a child but believe me, I've got my own ambitions.'

He pieced together the story of his life for Cara: the horticultural college he left just before he qualified to help out his mother because of his father's illness, his dreams of growing his own exotic flowers one day, his fear of women, the result of his mother's domination.

'I think the poor woman destroyed me,' he said, smiling, his eyes were full of despair.

Cara didn't laugh.

'Why don't you retire her? She's had her day.'

'I couldn't,' he said, dismissing the idea. 'That would feel like a betrayal. We've worked together since I was a boy. She kept everything going after Dad died so I'd have something to inherit. I'm all she has now.'

Cara wasn't fooled by his loyal words. She saw his resentment in his eyes, and through his excuses not to get rid of her.

There was no need to explain her single status to him but she was dying to confide in him, tell him everything about herself; her disastrous marriage, her fear of the litigation she was confronting, but she couldn't bring herself to. 'I should go,' he said 'It's been a long day,' getting up to go, suddenly remembering the time.

They collided at the hall door as Cara went to open it.

'Sorry.' Brendan recoiled, blushing, hesitant.

'You're a grown man, Brendan, no need to be scared of women.'

Blushing, he said, 'You enjoyed yourself?'

'I had a lovely time, thank you,' she said, kissing him on the cheek.

'Maybe we could do it again.'

'I'd love to.'

He was gone, swinging off in the dark, whistling to himself.

29

'How did your date go?' Jane asked anxiously.

'Great.'

'He's a good laugh, Brendan, and you didn't look stupid or anything together.'

'That's reassuring,' Cara said sarcastically.

'No, I mean it. You look young for your age, and he looks older than he is. You just about get away with it.'

'Good, because I enjoy his company. I'm just having a laugh, you know, Jane.'

Jane quipped back. 'Mags won't like it. She can't bear to let him out of her sight.'

'Suits me fine. I'm not about to steal him.'

When Brendan sauntered into the office to invite Cara to lunch the next day, Jane leaned towards him, simpering, stretching out her arm to touch his. 'You won't get anywhere with her,' she said to him, pointing at Cara. 'She's hard as nails where men are concerned.'

He gave her one of his dazzling smiles. 'I like tough women,' he said.

Cara was beginning to settle down in Bufferstown. She couldn't believe that her life had changed so much. Her reputation was rising above all other estate agents in the locality, and made her a curiosity in the town. Working in an estate agent's that her father didn't own made no difference. Her adrenaline flowed as she searched for the right house for the right client. This was a business with potential, the incubation of her dreams to make it on her own.

Cara did Mathew Arnold's business justice, working all hours, out of the office most of the time, striving for normality. She was brimming with ideas as she sat at her desk each morning, going over her list of properties, concentrating deeply. Sharp, skilled at her job, her repertoire extensive and impressive, she was getting to know her clients, listening avidly to their requests, giving them advice. Soon she became recognised as the one to go to for a decent home or a good bargain.

At construction sites she visited she followed the builders around amid whistles from men up on the scaffolding. Impervious to their calls, she walked on, taking notes. She knew there was gossip and speculation about her, but she brushed it aside and got on with her life, buoyant in her belief in what she was doing.

By day she was a bundle of energy, at night a heap of exhaustion, often at a low ebb with a sick feeling of guilt and despair, her failed marriage making her sad, clear memories of Guy making her lonely. Sometimes she felt sorry for herself, sometimes she cried. Often she was angry at the way things had turned out. She didn't go to see her father because she was still embarrassed.

Here she was, on her own, no husband waiting at home after her long day's work, no parties or nights out. With all this freedom she'd never had before, so much time on her hands in the evenings, she didn't know what to do with herself. The only familiarity about her life now was her work. It, at least, gave a framework to her day.

Cara bought cream readymade curtains in Habitat to brighten up the place, and white bed linen and towels. Gradually Cara embraced her new life, feeling, for the first time in a long time, that she was doing the right thing, maybe starting something important. She was learning the way of life in Bufferstown, getting used to the different sounds; subdued noises like the rattle of the old pipes. All the time she listened for the phone, half-expecting Andy to have got her number, half-hoping to hear from Guy. It was difficult to sleep at night on her own. Sometimes she dropped into the shop for fresh vegetables and a tin of something for her supper. Mags gave her a remedy for sleeplessness; hot milk and cinnamon to be taken last thing before going to bed. Her chatter was always lively, interspersed with orders to Brendan to fetch and carry this or that. Often Cara went to the pub with Jane for a drink in the evening. Before going to bed she would stand at her bedroom window looking out at the sea, thinking of Guy wondering where he was, listening to the familiar and comforting sounds of the tide and the cry of the curlew. Despite everything, Cara was living her life, getting back to her old self.

On Saturday, the 21st October, she went to Dublin to the Irish Auctioneers and Valuers Institute in the Merrion Square Hotel for the annual general meeting to discuss such matters as policies and approve accounts. There were photographers there from various property sections of daily newspapers, architects. They all had dinner together, sharing stories, laughing, drinking.

Cara was chatting, enjoying herself when she glanced out of the window of the dining room and spotted Suzanne standing on the steps of the hotel looking distracted. Puzzled and surprised to see her, not knowing she was back home from her trip to Scotland to try and reconcile things with Dick, Cara wondered what she was doing here. Perhaps she'd decided to leave Dick after all. But why hadn't she told either Vanessa or herself? Cara watched her walk quickly off down the street. What was she doing out so late on her own? And why was she in such a hurry? Was she in some kind of trouble? Cara glanced around, saw that everyone was in deep conversation, and realised that this was her chance to slip away, catch up with Suzanne who, by now, was walking off quickly in the direction of Nassau Street. The heavy sweetness of her coffee made her feel queasy. She stood up to go.

'You're not leaving,' asked Frank, the architect she was sitting next to.

'I must go. Early start tomorrow.'

'What a shame,' Frank said, finishing his drink as Cara said her goodbyes. He escorted her to the door of the hotel, his manner flirtatious.

By the time she got free of him Suzanne was way down the street. Cara was in hot pursuit of her, almost running. She spied her disappearing round the corner and hastened after her, only to find that she was nowhere to be seen. Where could she have got?

At the traffic lights she took a deep breath and looked around, wondering where to turn. Then she spied a pub on the corner. Taking a chance she went in, scanning the noisy crowd. She couldn't see Suzanne anywhere. She was just about to leave when she caught sight of her at the far end of the bar. Pushing forward, she was suddenly halted in her tracks by the sight of a tall dark man at the bar who placed his arm possessively around Suzanne's shoulders and leaned forward to say something intimate into her ear. Although Cara couldn't see his face, there was no mistaking the fact that it was Guy. She would have known him anywhere. Suzanne said something to him and he nodded his head and laughed. Cara turned away, glancing briefly from the door, wondering what on earth Suzanne was up to.

Sickened to her stomach, she walked out of the pub in a stupor, what she'd just witnessed between Guy and Suzanne, making her shake violently. She could understand if they'd met for a casual drink. They were friends after all. And why hadn't she got in touch with Cara or Vanessa since she came home? Why all the secrecy? Why the look of pure joy on Suzanne's face when she turned to him?

So what if he was with Suzanne? What difference did it make to her? She'd refused to have him full time in her life. Guy McIntosh was fed up with her. He'd moved on. Slowly it dawned on her that they would never be together again. Never lie in bed and talk to each other long into the night like they'd always done. Hadn't she realised that a long time ago?

'Would you like to buy me out?' Mathew Arnold's voice was faint on the line from Tucson, Arizona.

'I'd love to,' Cara said. 'It's a wonderful idea, but chancy.'

'Not at all. It's a business you know very well, one you've been familiar with all your life, one that will always be in demand. People have got to live somewhere. You could make it worth ten times what you'd pay for it.'

'Whether I can raise the finance is the problem.'

'Let me know as soon as you can.' Mathew gave her his phone number.

The more she thought about it, the more Cara liked the idea of owning her own business, no other involvement this time. A new excitement struck through her as she bathed in a rose-scented bath and ate her supper leisurely thinking of Mathew's words. 'You could make it worth ten times what you paid for it.'

This thought she cultivated in her mind. It excited her. But what would she do for cash. She'd been saving recently while she bided her time in this sparse and lonely life of hers but that was nothing to what she'd require.

Her father's business had just been sold to a consortium, so there would be a certain amount due to her after the debts were settled. The cottage would be sold in due course, and she'd have her share in a reasonable space of time. That would take a load off her mind. Meantime she could use it to secure a loan.

'Wouldn't it be wonderful,' Vanessa said, when she came to stay for the promised weekend, catching on to Cara's enthusiasm. 'You'd be mad to miss this opportunity. Supposing you don't go for it, you'll always regret it.' Vanessa's enthusiasm overrode any disadvantages Cara thought she might have.

'So much depends on whether Mr Keene, the bank manager, will think it's a good proposition.'

'Why shouldn't he? You've got a good track record. You're making a name for yourself; you're strong, physically and mentally. You've always worked for a living.'

Cara phoned the bank to ask for a loan the morning after Vanessa departed, the first step, and no point in putting it off. Casting aside her fears, she went to see Mr Keene at the appointed time the following Wednesday, the effort nerve-racking. This was the difference between child's play and the real thing. His verdict would matter so much, and her father wasn't there to cushion the blow if he refused.

Her first stroke of luck was that Mr Keene was eager to hear her proposal. She would have to provide him with a five-year feasibility plan to be submitted soon, he told her. He would delay making any decision until he'd seen the figures and the premises first, but there was a possibility that he might be able to accommodate her. He pointed out, however, that Cara would be risking more than she had ever risked before in this undertaking. With that prevailing promise she set to work, furnishing Mr Keene with the information he'd requested immediately, determined not to miss this chance. She might never get it again.

From then on everything changed. As she explained to Vanessa afterwards, she peeped out from behind her shuttered world and used her own imagination for the first time. There was something else happening to her she realised. Relieved

from the constraints of her marriage, and of Guy, she found
that the world was still the same, and she felt ashamed of her
preoccupation with herself. Faltering along the way, she was
making the turning point.

30

C ara was working late at the computer in the front office downstairs when she heard footsteps crunch on the gravelly path outside. People coming home from the pub, she thought, as she went the window and looked out. The night was beautiful; the garden swathed in the light of a moon which hung out of a sky sprinkled with stars. Everywhere was quiet, the silence intense, the air humid, and no one in sight.

Just as she was settling down again, going through her files, she heard a muffled sound. In a panic she tiptoed to the hall, listening. When she heard nothing she went to her desk. She sat down, restless, trying to concentrate on the screen of her computer. She heard another sound. Quivering she went into the back room and snapped on the light. She saw Andy's dark bulk at the French door, the light brutal on his face as he opened it.

Startled, a scream rose in her throat. She choked it back as she tried to shut the door on him, ready to bolt it.

'Not tonight, sweetheart.' He wrenched it open, knocking her backwards.

Her heart turned over as he blundered in.

'I'll call the police.'

He laughed mirthlessly. 'For what?'

'Breaking and entering.'

'I'm not breaking and entering. The door was unlocked. So I'm paying you a social call. You're still my wife, you know. How are you anyway?' He smiled, coming towards her.

Cara took a step backwards, digging her nails into the palms of her hands to try and stop herself from trembling, unable to look at him without horror.

'I hope I didn't scare you,' he added. 'I was worried about you, afraid something had happened to you. You should have let me know you were all right.' He was looking around. 'Nice place. Nice to live in a place like this, no one to see what goes on, no one to give it a thought. Not like when you were in the city.'

'There's quite a big community here. Everybody interested in everybody else's business. Take the shop opposite. They hear everything.'

'I noticed it on the way in. It's all locked up. Not a sign of life anywhere.'

Cara stood quietly, her heart hammering loudly in her own ears, her unsteady breathing expressing the enormity of her distress. She hadn't come this far to be this frightened by him, yet she was terrified. He blocked her retreat. Her skin grew hot. She raised the palms of her hands to her face.

'How did you find me?' she said eventually.

He said, in a friendly voice, 'I had a letter from your bank enquiring about giving the house as security for a loan to buy Mathew Arnold Estate Agents. Thought I'd check it out, see for myself. You've no objections, have you?'

Her head pounded, insistent, like a drum beating out a rhythm of fear which swelled, taking her over, until it was part of her whole body, part of the hot night. Too late she'd stepped into a trap, as if she'd been blindfolded.

Teeth clenched, she said, 'What do you want to know?'

'Perhaps you could explain to me why you've decided to buy this place?' His tone was silken but there was an edge to his voice.

'It's a good business.' With a wave of her hand Cara indicated the premises.

He walked ahead of her into the front office, looked at its display of houses for sale.

'It's a tricky set-up, being in the sticks. Surely you could do better with a business in Dublin?'

'I couldn't have afforded anything in the city, certainly not a going concern like this one with plenty of room for expansion. Besides, I don't like the city anymore.' Cara was watching him closely. 'Everything's staked on this deal. I'm not running anymore. I found what I'm looking for.'

'And you've no regrets about leaving everything behind?'

'None.'

'What if it doesn't work out here?'

She moved away from him, glanced over her shoulder. 'It will.'

'Well, I was thinking,' he drawled, 'that if you're going to use the cottage as security I might as well be in on the deal.'

So that's why he was here. He wasn't letting her go if there was more money to be made out of her. He was her enemy. She felt it immediately he'd said the words.

'What do you want?'

'I expect there's room enough for both of us here.' His eyes challenged her.

When Cara didn't reply he said, 'I take that to be a no.' He seemed to grow taller as he spoke. She saw the warning signs. His face was red, his eyes jumpy. He had come to taunt her.

What had he anticipated, Cara wondered, that an understanding would be reached with some polite conversation and a deal struck for him?

'I just want a job, accommodation, and we'd share the profits of course, seeing as I'd be working flat out for you.'

'You can talk to my solicitor,' Cara said.

'Don't be like that. I just want some answers. Your bank people I talked to seemed so vague.'

'You talked to Mr Keene?'

'Oh, don't fret, he didn't give me any encouragement.' Cara flinched back from his gaze.

Impatience and anger penetrated him.

'What's wrong with you, Cara? Why can't you just come out with it and tell me what's in it for me?' He almost spat the words.

'This business has nothing to do with you.'

His face contorted in anger at her words.

Anxiety gripped her. Scared to death, Cara tried to breathe slowly but her stomach hurt. One glance at him was enough to tell her that all her hopes and dreams of freedom would fly like dust in the wind at his say so, the pulse of their lives in his hands. She ran her hand through her hair. Her head ached. What was going on in his head? She wondered. Every word they exchanged was wrong. Everything she said upset him. He was a complete nightmare to her.

'Well?' He was staring at her, his chin raised in an affected gesture, hostility and suspicion in his demeanour. 'Why don't you answer me. I could kill you with my bare hands,' he said, staring at her.

'Which is why you're here, I suppose,' she said, thinking that it would suit him if she met with some kind of an accident. He'd get everything without any effort.

He continued to stare at her in silence.

Into the vacuum crept panic. Panic and fear swept over her. Perspiration trickled down her spine. She forced herself to think.

'Let's have a cup of coffee, talk about it.' She tilted her chin to him, waiting for an answer.

'Fine. I've got all the time in the world.'

She made the coffee while he walked about calmly touching one object after another. It'll be all right she told herself, handing him the steaming cup, forcing herself to be civil to him.

At that precise moment her mobile phone rang. It crackled over her head, a miracle to distract him. She moved to answer it. Andy leaped and grabbed it from her, crushing her fingers as he did so.

'It's that sly Scottish bastard, isn't it?' His face was full of anger.

All she could see was his pale hand raised to hit her. She backed away. There was a bouncing thump, as he punched the side of her head. An explosion in her ear followed as a second blow thudded into her. She fell forward, sank to her knees like a stone, clutched a chair for support. It crashed to the floor. She gasped in fear and panic clasping the leg of the table. She winced. Her hands flew to head. A drop of blood fell on it.

'You talk about settlements and things, but all you can think about is getting rid of me so you can be with him,' he shouted.

He didn't care that she was a shivering mass on the floor. His darkening face swam before her out of focus eyes. She curled into herself, lay still, her hands on her head to staunch the pain and hide her humiliation and foolishness. The thought of her with Guy McIntosh was making him madder than ever. He could beat the living daylights out of her, punch her stupid, but it wouldn't remove his unbearable jealousy at the thought of another man having her.

'Can we talk about this?' she asked, shifting backwards. 'Work something out?'

'Of course we can,' he said, seeing the blood, helping her to her feet, another drop plopped onto to his hand.

He guided her to a chair, sat her down, grabbed a tea towel and wiped away the blood.

'There, all gone,' he said, running his hand through her hair, as if she were a child, a gesture of his she'd always disliked.

He filled the kettle. She watched him make another cup of coffee, dwelling on every move he made. He came and stood beside her, like a lost child, his hands dropping by his sides, his distress making him awkward.

'Would you like something to eat?' he asked.

Food was the last thing she wanted. The claustrophobic atmosphere in the kitchen, the heat, the accusation in his eyes made her want to retch.

'Why are you crying?'

When she didn't answer he said, 'I asked you why you're crying.'

She put her hand to her eyes, suddenly dizzy. 'I'm not crying.'

He put his arm around her shaking shoulders, propping her up.

She threw it off. Damn him. Just when she thought she was beginning to get on with her life he turns up. What did she have to do to get rid of him? The only way she would ward him off was to try and gratify his vanity, sit down calmly and say what he would like to hear. Have something to negotiate as insurance against trouble.

'Of course my intention was that you would benefit from this deal in the long run.' Calculation was in her flattery, asking herself what did I ever see in him.

The instinctive mistrust remained in his eyes. He was scrutinising her, judging her every detail.

'In what way?'

Cara brazened it out. In as steady a voice as she could muster she said, 'You'll get a really good settlement. Something worthwhile.'

He sat down, more sure of himself. The harshness and anger melted from his face like snow in rain. It was a very small victory for her, but something at least.

'I don't want a settlement. I want a share in the business.

You're a beautiful woman, Cara, but you're my wife, and I can't have you going off wherever and whenever you like. I love you the same way I always did.' He paced up and down in constant motion. 'Forever.'

She almost choked as she failed to stop the tears, seeing clearly, at that moment, the irreconcilable differences between them. He had never wanted to work. He wanted to go on as he had so far, carefully cultivating an image of himself as a man, deeply interested in a career. Whereas the truth was that he was a player of games, a nasty piece of work.

'I'm never getting back with you.' The words came out like a cry, as if she were playing a part in a play. Her whole body shook.

He said boisterously, 'Oh, come on. Aren't you overreacting?' as if he were glad to take his part.

'No, I mean it,' she said, suddenly feeling as if she'd re-entered that bleak world she'd just left.

He said, 'You're ill, confused. In a day or two you'll feel better. Go to bed. I'll stay down here, keep an eye on you.'

―――――◆◆◆―――――

31

C ara went upstairs, bolted the bedroom door and waited. When she heard him going to the loo she sneaked downstairs, out the French doors that were still unlocked, into the garden, and out between the hedges, afraid for her life. The moonlight was enough for her to see her way through the field behind the house. Fear and anger drove her along, the wet grass dragging at her trousers, slowing her steps.

She ran into the street that curved between houses to the seafront, her trainers slapping on the road that dipped and rose before her. When she heard footsteps ringing out metallically behind her she ran faster. A man and a woman were walking along, arm in arm, laughing. She slowed down. They turned to look at her, their voices dropping to whispers as she passed. Conscious that Andy might be following her she picked up speed and went like the wind her breath heaving in her chest, her speed fuelled by fear.

At the hotel her steps slowed and she walked unsteadily into it, disappearing out the back lounge door to the dark passage at the side of it. She stayed there, breathing heavily, her sense of relief short-lived, panic striking her with every footstep that came and went past the pub. She waited for what she considered a suitable interval to go back in, but just as she decided it was a safe bet she peeped in the window and saw Andy at the bar, his head bent. He was waiting for her, loitering over a pint, irritated, watching. Afraid, she moved back into the shadows. Eventually he finished his drink and left.

Panting with fear, she went to reception to ask them to make a phone call, barely able to speak. What an evening it had turned out to be she thought as, her hand shaking, she lifted the receiver to phone Brendan, the furtive nature of the call apparent, her anxiety growing worse as the telephone rang and rang in the empty silence, the receptionist's eyes on her.

There was no reply.

She tried again, let it ring, having no alternative that she could think of. If Mags answered it, what would she say? Just ask for Brendan.

Cara was leaning against the counter; the couple who'd just arrived at the desk waiting to book in, watching her, and the receptionist glancing at her impatiently. Humiliated, she turned the other way. Just as she was about to give up, she heard a squeaky 'Hello'.

'Hello, Mags. It's Cara,' she said with relief. 'Is Brendan there?'

'He's out fishing,' said the sleepy voice. 'What did you want him for? Anything important?'

She would not reveal that she was desperate. Quick, before her nerves failed her altogether, say something, she told herself.

'Not really.'

'Are you all right, Cara? You sound funny.' Mags voice was high-pitched now.

Any moment Andy might come dashing in the door not permitting her to give Mags any further information.

'Cara, are you still there?'

Feeling foolish Cara said, 'I've had a bit of an accident.' The tremor in her voice betrayed her. She wanted to beg Mags to get Brendan quickly, plead with her for help, but she couldn't. The receptionist was beside her, writing now, her eyes on Cara. She knew Cara and Cara knew that the gossip in the hotel was lively at the best of times.

'Oh, you poor thing, what happened? Are you hurt?'

'I'll tell you later. I'm at the hotel. Can you get in touch with Brendan.'

'I'll try his mobile. Wait there.'

The phone clicked. Cara tried to gather herself together and drag herself out into the lobby where voices were loud as people said good night to one another.

She sat down to wait for Brendan, her hand beating nervously against her thigh, thinking of Brendan and Mags, the cups of tea across her counter, the bits of gossip, Mags keeping her going when she was lonely. Life wasn't worth living if it was going to continue like this.

Brendan arrived in his waders.

'What happened to you?' he gasped, shocked at the sight of her.

He asked her again.

'I'll tell you later.' It was so much easier to stay silent, so much simpler not to have to think for the moment.

He led her out to his van, holding her. 'Cara, who did this to you?' he asked as he helped her to his van.

She moved away from him, defiant and doubtful, not wanting to tell him about the scene with Andy, pride holding her back. The heat of the van spread through her as he drove her home. Gradually her shaking subsided.

'You'll have to tell me. This has to be tackled,' he said, as soon as they were inside.

Calmly, directly she told him about finding Andy at the French doors and the row which had ensued, her eyes shut against the look of horror on his face.

'Why did he do it?'

'Because I left him.' Her hands twitched, plucking at a tear in her jeans, none of her normal behaviour.

Horror-stricken Brendan watched her weeping, hardly believing that this was the same girl who'd cheered up his life since she came to live opposite.

'Because he's crazy, that's why.' Cara evaded his eyes, chewing her lip, her arms across her chest protectively. 'I'm stupid. I didn't see it coming,' she said, her voice sank to an audible whisper. 'I should have. He's done this before. I thought it had ended.'

Brendan exploded in fury. He clenched his fists, his voice cracked like thunder. 'If I get my hands on him I'll break every bone in his body.'

'It has to end,' she cried.

'Ssh,' he said, putting his arm around her. 'This time he's done it for the last time. He's crossed the line, coming here like that. It'll never happen again.'

Cara's whole body shook with sobs.

'It's all right,' he said, holding her. 'You'll be all right. We'll make sure of that.'

He smoothed her hair, seeing fresh bruises illuminated by the light. He talked to her as one would talk to a small child and looked at her, shaking his head, baffled at how anyone would want to hurt this beautiful woman he was holding in his arms.

She moved back, not wanting to cry on his shoulder.

'I'd better get you something to drink,' he said.

He went out into the darkness. She heard him opening the shop. He came back with a half-full bottle of brandy.

'Mother keeps this for medicinal purposes,' he said winking at her.

She drank it quickly.

'You'll have to go to the police and tell them what he did to you.'

She shook her head. 'No.'

'Why?'

'I have my reasons. I don't want them questioning his motives.'

'It's no good keeping the details from them just because you're ashamed of the situation. They should know the truth. That husband of yours is a sick man and danger to society. He comes creeping in here, taking you unawares, and upsetting you like that. You've got to go to the cops. I know Tom Green, the local cop.'

Cara hesitated, weighting up this fact, shivers of alarm down her spine.

'You've got nothing to lose,' Brendan said, fearful of upsetting her further.

'I'm not so sure about that.' Cara sat there, assessing the consequences of a confession, shifting uncomfortably at the thought of having to give a detailed description of her own husband and of the events of the night. 'No, I'm not going to do it.'

'So, you're going to keep quiet and carry on, an obedient quiet little wife?'

She had to keep her dignity at all costs. Brendan wouldn't have any patience with this sort of thing, and why should he? She could see from his eyes that he saw her differently. Her cool sophisticated disguise had cracked before him. She was a doomed person in his lights, letting her life get wrecked by a crazy husband. This Cara was new to him, and he was finding it hard to apply these observations to her.

'Do you want to keep on trying with your marriage?'

'No,' she said in a terrible quaking fear.

'Then, you'll have to come to the police station with me. You're in danger, Cara.'

A transformation was taking place in her. She knew Brendan was right. She also knew that Andy had a passion to possess her, knew that he'd knock her into oblivion if she did anything else to anger him. He'd attacked her three times now. Each time he'd been less recognisable than the last. She never wanted to come face to face with him again. Though she found the idea of going to the police and giving a description of her own husband so that they could hunt him down like a common criminal, repellent, she agreed.

They were silent, Cara not wanting to talk, Brendan not knowing what to say.

Finally he said, 'You're an incredibly brave person, Cara, but you can't live here without some way of protecting yourself.'

'Such as?'

'Get an alarm system installed right away. Keep all doors locked, keep your eyes open and, if he does come back, and I've no doubt that he will, get me on my mobile straight away. I'll give you the number, and keep it on at all times from now on.'

Cara nodded.

'Now go to bed. I'll sleep on the sofa.'

Sergeant Green filed her complaint. He was sympathetic, and concerned, advising her that she could get a barring order against Andy, but that it would mean going to court. When Cara refused to take action as drastic as that he gave her his mobile number, telling her to phone him if Andy made another appearance or threatened her in any way. He promised her that he would have a patrol car round to her premises in a matter of minutes. But Cara was still scared.

She phoned Vanessa next day when she felt a bit better, and told her what had happened.

'He's cornered now,' Vanessa said. 'He can't go running around like a mad dog. That was his last ditch.'

'I'm not so sure,' Cara said.

'You've called his bluff,' Vanessa assured her. 'But, for

Christ's sake, don't ever try to take him on alone again if
he does come near the place.'

As it turned out, though, Andy did not return and so evaded
the police for the time being.

32

---◆---

It was stuffy in the Star of the Sea church in Sandymount at the Sunday Mass. Sandwiched between her father and Pamela, Cara kept her hat pulled down over her eye to hide her scar.

The priest's voice was soothing as he gave the final blessing. Pamela sang 'Faith of Our Fathers' with gusto, her face shining in the heat. John sang along tunelessly, his head bowed. Cara shut her eyes, trying to pray, believing, perhaps, that in some way, she was responsible for her own downfall and Andy's.

They poured out into the chilly wind, the church bells ringing, the organ music receding into the background. Parishioners who'd almost bowed to John in the past moved quickly away, or saluted brusquely because he was of no value to them anymore. He fingered his tie, his purposeful mood fragmenting as he was brushed aside.

Cara saw for the first time the embarrassment in him. How much better his life had been when he'd been a prominent businessman, owning so much, always busy, always in demand, with money and influence. He was a man apart then, someone people flocked to seeking advice and direction. Now he was being avoided.

Father Hayden, the parish priest, standing outside the church door, extended his hand to John who shook it heartily, trying to reach out and reclaim the prestige he'd lost. In that gesture Cara could see that he was a man who desperately needed deference. But she would not pity him. He still had his beautiful wife, who adored him, and a daughter and sister.

Pamela, not seeming to notice her husband's embarrass-ment, waved to this one, called out 'Hello' to that one, saying, 'What a relief that's over' as they drove back to Rockmount for a final Sunday lunch.

Cara helped Elsie with the cooking. After a walk with her father and Bouncer, she went into the garden where Pamela was staking a rose tree, chatting over her shoulder about trivial things, her high-heels digging into the lawn. 'I'm doing this so as to forget the awful business of moving,' she said.

It began to rain; the wind blew back Cara's hair.

Pamela let out a cry. 'What's this?' she said, flicking back Cara's hair again.

There was a pause.

'Nothing.' Cara shook her hair back over her forehead, her bruises making her look like a clown.

'So, he came back. What was it this time? A touch of jeal-ousy? His old insecurity back? Not that it was ever gone.'

Cara told her.

'Do you really think you can go on like this?' Pamela asked, her voice quivering with anger. 'Pretending it isn't happening. There's his bad moods, good moods. He'll come after you, with harmful intent, what are you going to do? Wait until he tears your body apart?'

'Please don't tell Dad.'

'Of course I won't, but get on to your solicitor about getting rid of that husband of yours quickly, before he kills you.'

Pamela and Cara made their way to the kitchen.

Elsie was reading in the kitchen, comfortable among her Sunday papers.

'Do you think you could make us some coffee, Elsie, while I put these in water?' Pamela asked, pointing to a few wind-blown roses, the last of the season.

Elsie stood up, her movements slow and forceful, a tired old lady suddenly, as if it was all too much for her, as if she couldn't stand Pamela a minute longer.

As soon as Pamela returned upstairs, Elsie said, 'She's a bit of a bully. Full of charm at the church. Such an exhibitionist.' She stopped. 'I won't sully my tongue with the word I'd like to use for her, especially not on the Sabbath.'

Cara laughed.

'My opinion counts for nothing with her, my wishes never considered. She always gets her way in the end. He's not forceful enough with her. He loves her too much to go against her. And it's getting worse. He can't wear what he likes, say what he likes anymore. She's a kind of addiction with him. I just hope it's not misguided.'

'It isn't. Pamela loves him too and she's stuck by him.'

Elsie nodded in reluctant assent.

'It's a shame so much has gone wrong. He's such a respectable man.' She sipped her coffee thoughtfully, looked at Cara over the rim of her cup. 'Mind you, what is respectability if you're unhappy? I myself don't give a fig what people say. Neither should he. It's a waste of time. When my husband died people interfered, told me what to do. Nobody thought about what I wanted. They all knew best. I was alone, torn in all directions. John finally got the better of me when you lost your mother, God rest her. I knew you'd be pushed and pulled from Billy to Jack, so I did exactly what I wanted to do and that was take care of you.'

'I am glad,' Cara said warmly.

'She has decided that I can't go it alone. So we're all moving together. I'd much prefer a place of my own.'

'That mightn't be a good idea, Elsie,' Cara said. 'You'd be lonely on your own.'

'I don't think so.'

*   *   *

On Monday morning Cara got up early and went across the road to see Mags and Brendan.

Before she had a chance to say 'hello' she saw Andy hovering at the entrance to the shop. Her hair stood on end with fright.

Brendan sprang to attention. He snapped his fingers, and jerked his head towards the back of the shop.

'Get in there. Don't move,' he said, intent on the man hovering at the door. Mags, all of a flutter, pulled her inside the counter, put a finger to her lips.

As Andy approached, Brendan tried not to stare. When he got to the counter Brendan leaned towards him in a confidential manner, all ears.

'Can I help you?' he asked politely.

'These plums,' Andy said, taking one. It was gone in two bites, juice running down his chin. Andy leaned on the counter, elbows propped, looking through the door.

'I was looking for Cara Thompson. She doesn't appear to be in.'

Brendan shrugged. 'I haven't seen her around today. Could be away. She comes and goes. What's she to you?'

'My wife,' Andy drawled.

'Oh!'

'I'll go and get a bite to eat and come back later.'

Brendan nodded. 'She could be back by then. That'll be seventy pence, please.'

Andy threw coins on the counter and left without a word. Brendan had a great desire to go after him as he strode off, purposeful. He overcame it by serving the next customer.

'What's the bastard up to now?' he mused as Cara waited, jammed against the wall wondering what to do, knowing that Andy wasn't going far, that he'd hang around waiting for his bait.

'Go,' Brendan said, 'I'll be watching out for you.'

Reluctantly she left the shop, crossed the street, stopped outside her door, unlocked it, took a step back, looked up and down, and went in.

Andy came from nowhere. He was behind her, pushing his way in after her. In desperation she turned to run out again. This was too much for him. In one swift movement he lurched towards her, grabbed her roughly and pressed her close to the wall.

'So you've got yourself another boyfriend,' he taunted her.

'No, I haven't.'

'I saw you at the Festival with your man opposite.' She struggled to get free.

He tightened his grip. 'You think you're smart but you won't get away from me this time.'

He was breathing deeply.

'Let me go,' she shrieked just as Brendan crashed through the door, advancing towards Andy possessed by a fearless anger, his hands poised to strike, nothing but retribution in his mind. He grabbed him, hoisting him off the ground, white with fury.

Their eyes locked in recognition.

'The new boyfriend,' Andy said, breathless in surprise.

'You keep your hands off her.' Brendan clutched him in a vice grip. Andy pushed him off.

The two men writhed around, Andy trying to fend Brendan off, Brendan grabbing him blindly again, delivering a blow into his jaw.

'Lay off her. Leave her alone,' he shouted.

The second blow thudded into Andy's face. Cara could hear the crack of splintering bone. Andy's face contorted with pain, then in one violent jerk he slumped forward, slithered down the wall, and sprawled on the floor, blood pumping from his nose. Brendan knelt over him, his fist flexed.

'Stop,' Cara shrieked.

Andy lay still.

'He's dead. You've killed him.'

''Course he's not dead.' Brendan looked at him dispassionately, longing to finish him off. 'It's hard to kill a bad thing. The punches bounced off him.' He shook him. 'Get up, you stupid git, stop playing silly games.'

Both watched mesmerised as Andy lay motionless, not a sound. Brendan lifted each eyelid. The eyes were vacant.

'Call an ambulance,' she said in a stunned tone as she knelt beside Andy, trying not to panic, more concerned now about Brendan's plight, if Andy was dead, than her own.

'OK.'

The sight of the ambulance tearing up the road, the paramedics clambering out, would haunt Cara for a long time to come. Andy, unconscious, was strapped to a stretcher and taken away, watched by a helpless Cara, tense with fear, a calm Brendan, Andy's blood on his clothes, and a group of anxious people who appeared from nowhere, demanding to know what had happened.

The siren sounded as the ambulance sped away.

It was all over in a matter of minutes. Brendan, his arm around her trying to stop her from shivering, led her back inside. Ashamed of her cowardice, Cara realised that she should have got rid of Andy a long time ago. She tried to pray for forgiveness, 'Oh, my God, I'm sorry for all my sins.' No more of the prayer would come to mind.

Cara went to the police station again to make a statement. She tried to brave it out, be decisive, not cowardly, as she gave an account of the events that led up to the fight to Sergeant Green.

She returned to work the next day, hoping it would stop her from thinking. Her hands shook as she sat in her office, unable to get Andy out of her head. Looking out onto the street, even the passers-by seemed threatening. Her head pounded, the pain made worse by the heaviness in the air. Weariness came over her, slowing her down.

'Want to talk about it?' Jane asked, bringing her a cup of tea.

'Later, when we're on our own.' Cara said, this brief exchange establishing her need for privacy.

She should talk, not skulk around, but she couldn't.

The gossip was flying around, the news filtering through that Cara Thompson's husband, a drunk, whom she'd run away from, had come after her. Repetition of the tale all over the town made it grotesque, everyone having his or her version of the story.

Customers gazed, commenting on the weather, anything to keep her talking, hoping she'd say something, their unasked questions begging for answers. What did they think of her? A foolish stupid girl, bringing trouble to their town?

She kept going, listing properties in different sections to them: for sale, short-term rents, long leases, easy to sell or rent properties, the topic never more than a breath away. It became a balancing act right up until closing time each day. By the end of the week she wanted to run and hide, the look of curiosity on people's faces wherever she went extending her fear further and increasing it.

Over a quiet drink after work, with Jane, Cara overhead two men discussing the poor gob shite who'd had his head bashed in by Brendan Collins. This choice piece of gossip culminated into a lump in her throat, her discomfort so great that she finished her drink without tasting it, shame catching in her throat like indigestion. Her blood ran cold as she left, the curious looks following her. She longed to disappear, get as far away as possible where no one knew her.

Jane followed her. 'Cara, I'm here for you. Talk to me. There's no point in repressing it.'

She should be able to talk her, talk to someone, but she wasn't.

She waited for darkness, so she could walk in obscurity, the rain and cold, the sky black, presaging a storm. As she passed the Collins' house she saw that the lights were on. She didn't go in.

Mags pursued her, hounding her for information, Brendan kept out of her way. She was unable to eat, or sleep, the memory of what happened burning into her brain. What had she done to Brendan? Would he be charged? What would happen next was the thought that prevailed. Would Andy recover and would he make finding her a quest?

Customers were waiting for her, full of curiosity wanted to see how she was faring. What Cara didn't realise was that they were genuinely interested in her, wanting to help her pick up the pieces. She had captured their hearts, this smiling, sophisticated friendly newcomer, so full of life, nothing too much trouble, her grasp of the place amazing, her devotion to her job impressive.

Sergeant Green phoned at last to tell Cara that Andy had made a full recovery and had been discharged from the hospital. There would be no charges against Brendan.

33

With a bit of persuasion from Brendan and Vanessa, Cara took a week's holiday and went to stay with her family in their new home in Monkstown, a small bungalow in a cul-de-sac, whose bay window was its main feature. The strain of moving house had told on them all. John and Elsie were affected by Pamela's restlessness as she paced around the place, arranging and rearranging furniture and ornaments, determined to do her share and prove she could manage to run a household without making a slave of Elsie.

Elsie was trying to justify her existence in this small house, exhausting herself cooking and polishing, even though there was far less to do. There was something important she wanted to tell Cara, in private, only they never seemed to be able to get a private moment, all of them huddled together in this bijou bungalow.

'What is it?' Cara asked, taking Elsie for a drive.

Elsie told her about the row she'd heard between Pamela and John.

'She wants to put me in a home.'

'What!'

'Somewhere out of town, where I won't know anyone, won't have my own things. I heard them rowing about it.'

'I can't believe it.'

Cara wondered if Elsie's imagination was playing tricks on her.

'It's terrible,' Elsie hissed.

'Dad wouldn't hear of such a thing.'

'Unless she gets the better of him.' She lowered her voice. 'She's a bully, you know.' She began to cry.

Upset by her tears, Cara grasped her wrinkled hand.

'Don't worry she won't do any such thing. I won't let her.'

She went to her father when they returned.

'No, of course not.' John was tight-lipped.

'Elsie has this notion that Pamela wants to get rid of her.'

'What nonsense!'

'Said she wants to put her in a home,' Cara said, looking at her father with concern.

'Pamela did mention something about that.'

'You wouldn't let her do it, Dad?' Cara looked warily at him.

'I forbade her to even think about it. I don't know what's got into her. It's all part of this restlessness that seems to have afflicted her since we moved. She thinks this house too small for the three of us. I think we'll be fine if we manage things carefully, give each other breathing space.'

Cara decided to tackle Pamela, quietly, when she got her alone. Find out exactly what her intentions were.

'You know I don't know what we're going to do with all the stuff we've left over from Rockmount.'

'Get rid of it. Give to charity. I'm sure Oxfam would be glad of the clothes. Can I have a word with you about Elsie? You weren't thinking of putting her in a home, were you?' She looked at her challengingly.

Pamela went pink. 'Not exactly. More of a home from home really.'

'Don't beat about the bush.'

'This friend of mine runs this marvellous place in Leixlip, magnificent grounds. She'd have her own private room, en suite.'

Cara said, furious, 'I'm warning you, Pamela. Don't even think about it.'

She took a deep breath to stop the tremor in her voice. 'Elsie was always there for me. You couldn't think of sending her away from her family.'

Pamela shrank back from her. 'It was only an idea, nothing settled.'

'She can't be abandoned now that she's old. I won't have it. I just won't have it.'

'Right. You've made your point. Your Dad was against it too.'

Cara said with a sense of relief, 'Good.'

'It's just that she's getting on my nerves with all of us cooped up together.'

'Why don't you get a job?' Cara suggested. 'Even a part-time one. That'd get you out of the house.'

'What a good idea.'

'Cara thinks I should get a job,' she said to John.

'Doing what?'

Pamela shrugged. 'Anything. As long as it pays of course.'

'I don't want you to.'

'Why?'

'It's not necessary for you to work. Your place is here with me. I can provide for you adequately.'

'How can you say that when you know that we could do with the cash?' Pamela was losing her temper.

John turned to his newspaper, refusing to discuss the matter further.

'Why won't you even talk to me about it?'

'I'll talk to you when you calm down.'

'I am calm,' she screeched, making him smile.

He laughed. 'If only you saw yourself when you're angry,' he said.

'All I said was that I wanted to get a job, and you retaliate with that rubbish about my place being here with you, as if you couldn't manage without me for five minutes. You managed on your own for years.'

John bashed his newspaper. 'It's so much easier to stand there accusing me of not letting you work, than actually making the decision and going about getting work.'

Pamela exploded. 'How dare you. I'm perfectly capable of . . .'

'There's the door,' John said, adapting to her humour, playing along with the idea. 'Go and get yourself a job, only don't make your potential employer nervous with that temper of yours.' A smile broke out on his face as he looked at her.

That remark made Pamela smile too.

'I'm serious, John,' she said, defiant but doubtful of her potential at the same time.

'So am I. You'll have no problem. A good-looking woman like you.'

'Only in your opinion.'

He smiled. Putting down his newspaper he rose, encircled her in his arms. 'In everyone's opinion.'

'Who, for instance?'

'Father Hayden for one. He's always calling to see you with some flimsy excuse or other.'

Pamela laughed. 'Priests don't count. Where women are concerned they have no judgement.'

'I don't agree with you.'

Flattered, calmer, she smoothed her hair and preened herself in the hall mirror before she went out. 'She doesn't realise how terrifying she can be,' he said to Cara good-humouredly. 'Scares me half to death sometimes.' Loyalty forbade him to speak further.

He sat reading to suppress the warning bells, which had been ringing in his head about Pamela and what she was about to do.

*   *   *

On Monday morning Cara at last kept the appointment Vanessa had made for her with Roger Hamilton having cancelled the two previous ones. His suite of offices overlooked the Halfpenny Bridge, people walking past. People walked in and out, lawyers, secretaries, clients, no words exchanged between them, purposeful looks on their faces. Telephones rang. She could hear the voice of the receptionist, polite and impersonal.

Cara straightened her back as a tall distinguished man with a commanding presence entered the reception area of Hamilton, King and Company, Solicitors. He was a good-looking man, older than she expected, about fifty years of age, she guessed.

'You must be Vanessa's friend, Cara,' he said cheerily. 'I'm Roger Hamilton. How do you do.'

He took Cara's extended hand, shaking it firmly, his dark eyes taking her in, leading her into his office.

Seated at his desk, tomes of law books stacked on shelves behind him, he said, 'I wanted to have a chat with you first to establish your reasons for wanting a separation. I also want to make sure that you are resolved on this course of action so that we can proceed without delay.'

'I am.'

Roger read from his file, 'Cara Thompson, The Cottage, Bramble Lane, Arklow, 31 years old, estate agent, no children, is seeking separation from her husband, Andrew Thompson, of same address.'

Cara nodded.

Professional to his fingertips, he said, 'Now if we could go through some points before we decide how best to proceed. When did things start to go wrong?'

'Andy never held down a job for very long,' Cara said.

'How long would each job last?'

'A few months. There was a sort of pattern to it.'

'Tell me about it.'

'He'd get off to a great start; he'd be full of enthusiasm for the company, the management, everything. Then, gradually things would start to go wrong.'

'Why was that, do you think?'

In a trembling voice Cara told him about Andy's various jobs, trying to explain why they didn't work out.

'He'd have a row with his boss, usually precipitated by Andy giving his views on the proper way to run the department, something like that. The jobs he got never seemed to be suitable. There was always something wrong; he didn't fit in, or he didn't agree with their way of doing things, or the staff were against him.'

'So he'd leave?'

Cara nodded. 'Or, more usually, he'd get fired.'

'He didn't contribute much to the household expenses?'

'Well, no.'

'So, you were the breadwinner?'

'Yes.'

'And the homemaker?'

'Yes.' Cara eyed him.

Roger looked at her perplexed. 'It strikes me that you've been treated abominably. Why did you put up with it for so long?'

'I always thought Andy would find a suitable job eventually, and stay in it. But he didn't. When he couldn't get the perfect job he decided to go it alone. He formed his own company selling software. I bought him a computer, and he seemed to be getting along fine, until the . . . violence.'

'What brought on this violence?'

'His drinking was getting worse because of his frustration with each job loss, and,' she lowered her eyes, 'and my behaviour, I suppose. I had a brief affair.' Cara felt her face burn as she looked at Roger, his eyebrows raised slightly in mild surprise.

'Andy found out and went wild.'

'He hit you?'

'Yes.'

'He'd never hit you before that?'

'No.'

'Is that the only time he's been violent?'

'No. He attacked me after that. That's when I left.'

'Conduct is very relevant to the case,' Roger said, jotting down notes. 'This affair you had is over I take it?'

'Yes,' Cara said. 'I never dreamt I would do such a thing, and I certainly never thought that I'd be taking this route.'

'I know it's a sad business,' Roger agreed. 'But think how much more tragic it would be if you were stuck in this marriage for the rest of your life.'

'I stuck it as long as I could.'

Roger looked at her sympathetically, then at his notes.

'Seems convincing enough to me,' he said, and moved on to the examination of their joint estate and listed the cottage, paid for by John Bradley, its maintenance paid for by Cara, and discussed the settlement each of them would be entitled to. 'There seems to be no obstacles to a smooth separation once we've gone through the pertinent legal technicality. Your income, earning capacity, property and other financial resources you are likely to have are taken into consideration with regard to the financial needs, obligations and responsibilities which each of the parties to the marriage has or is likely to have in the foreseeable future.'

The following evening Cara called to see Suzanne who'd phoned to say that she was just back from her stay in Scotland with Dick.

As she drew up to Suzanne's gate she saw Guy coming out of Suzanne's house.

She thought she was imagining it. But no, it was definitely Guy.

'Hi, Cara!' He was coming towards her.

They stared at one another in shocked silence, the air rushing to her head.

'Hello!' Her voice was strangled, as if she were choking. 'What are you doing here? I thought you were still in Scotland.'

'I'm here for a few days. I was just calling to see Suzanne. Trying to be of some help to her.'

They continued to stare at one another in mortified silence.

'How are you?'

'I'm fine thanks.'

'You're looking very well. Wonderful, in fact.'

'Thanks,' she said, embarrassed. 'And you? How are you?'

'OK.'

'Ian?'

'He's back in school of course.' His eyes were still riveted on her. 'Happy enough for the moment.'

Suddenly she said, 'I have to go,' looking at her watch.

'Oh! Would you like to have a drink with me? Could we go somewhere, just for half an hour?' He was watching her with that deep, penetrating look of his.

'I'd love to but I'm on my way to see Suzanne.'

'One drink. I've got to be somewhere this evening too, so I won't keep you.'

Cara wondered if Suzanne was the 'somewhere' he had to be. It was none of her business. Besides she secretly wanted to talk to him too.

They walked to the pub on the corner in awkward silence. The strangeness of the situation dawned on her while he got the drinks. When he returned and sat down opposite her she felt unnerved, his physical presence, after all this time, overwhelming. Here she was, with him at last, and she didn't know what to say. They were lost to one another, the intimacy between them gone; only embarrassment left.

She summoned all her will power to look straight at him. He was staring at her, a slow smile appearing on his face.

Bluntly she said, 'So, what did you want to talk to me about?' She raised her eyebrows quizzically

'Well, Suzanne, in fact.'

'Oh.'

'She's so unhappy. Worried about Lucy. The baby is teething. Crying all the time.'

'Suzanne's inexperienced, that's all. It's no fun for her. It's so strange that they split up. The last thing I expected was that she'd be dumped by Dick.'

'Dick didn't dump her,' Guy protested, defensive of Suzanne.

Cara froze. 'Maybe not technically, but he did have someone else for a while, and he did leave her.'

'I know, and he bitterly regrets that. That other relationship had no future. He hoped to get back with Suzanne, planned to meet up with her. When they did get together she made certain demands that he couldn't possibly meet.'

'Like?'

'Quitting his job. Getting a nine to five locally that wouldn't involve all the travelling. Rather than make promises he couldn't or wouldn't keep, he decided to be truthful and tell her there was no way.'

'So he's messed things up again.'

Guy shook his head. 'Dick is anxious to get back with her again, but she refuses to take his calls. He's very upset.' A strange feeling came over Cara as she watched Guy's face and listened to his version of the situation. She thought she knew him so well, knew everything about him, could read his mind like a book, saw his insecurities, his hopes, fears, doubts, dreams and longing. But he remained a mystery.

Dick would be upset if he knew that his wife had fallen for Guy.

'What's he planning to do?'

'I don't know. He hasn't confided in me, but I think that at this stage he'd do anything to get her back.'

Cara waited for him to tell her about his involvement with Suzanne but he didn't and, when he didn't, she said, 'The sad thing is that they're so good together. So right for one another.'

Guy leaned forward. 'I'm not qualified to judge other people. I've made my own mistakes.'

'Yes.' Cara said with righteous indignation, looking at her watch. 'Oh! I have to go.'

Guy's face fell.

'I'm meeting someone.'

She picked up her briefcase. Guy got to his feet, insisted on accompanying her back to her car and seeing her off, on his best behaviour.

Cara, desperate to break free, said, 'I'll see you again I'm sure.'

'I hope so,' he said, not suggesting another meeting.

Cara went off alone, thinking of Guy. Often she'd imagined meeting him again, in all sorts of places, in all sorts of circumstances. What should have been a shared delight had been a disappointment, and an embarrassment. There wouldn't be any point in telling Suzanne about their meeting, only upsetting things further. Guy would hardly discuss it with her either.

She called to see her the next evening. Suzanne was standing very still by the window, dust motes drifting through the slanted sunshine, Lucy in her arms, everything quiet until Cara broke the silence.

'Did your time together in Scotland do any good?'

Suzanne shook her head. 'I wanted him to come home, settle down in a different job that didn't involve so much travel. But he wouldn't hear of it. He loves his job, and he's needed in Scotland. Takes off all over the place from there. He's in Paris at the moment. Loves his trips abroad, does Dick.'

Cara imagined him going from hotel to restaurant for his evening meal, showered and scented, all smiles and affable, a mysterious smile on his face as he stepped along the exciting glamorous boulevards.

'So you'll be spending more time in Edinburgh, then?'

'I suppose so.' Her voice was full of uneasiness.' She looked across at her. 'Marriage is nothing if it's not compromise.'

Lucy began to whimper.

'She's in pain. It's her teeth. We didn't get much sleep last night, did we poppet?' Suzanne said, observing Lucy closely. Lucy, her fist in her mouth, was dribbling, began to sob.

'I hate when she's not well,' Suzanne sighed, propped Lucy against her shoulder, pacing up and down. 'I'll give her a bath. Calm her down.'

Not once was Guy's name mentioned. Cara knew it wouldn't be.

34

━━━◆━━━

'Good to see you,' Roger Hamilton said, shaking Cara's hand. 'Let's get down to it then,' pulling his notepad to him, reading what he had written.

'Have you heard from Andy's solicitor?' she asked.

'I spoke with him on the phone. Andy's decided that beside his share of the assets, he wants maintenance from you as well, and legal costs.'

Cara felt giddy, faint with the shock of his words. She put her head in her hands. 'Oh, my God! I don't believe it.'

Roger got out of his chair, came around the desk. 'Can I get you anything? Water? Coffee?'

Cara shook her head, her eyes on his polished shoes.

Roger watched her as, tears in her eyes, she said, 'He's determined to get his pound of flesh. He's determined to ruin my life with his greed. He got everything I ever had and now he wants more.' She put her hand briefly over her eyes. 'I didn't think he'd go this far. But I don't think that's fair, do you?'

There was a pause. Roger leaned towards her, and said, 'Fair doesn't enter into this sort of thing. It's what he wants and he's every intention of getting it if he can.'

Cara took a deep breath, closed her eyes for a second, as if to shut out his words. 'He's not such a fool, is he?'

'It's an extraordinary demand in the circumstances.'

'I'm on my own now. I've got to manage my life, keep myself. He won't give me the chance to get on my feet.'

'He never did.' Roger put his arm around her, held her firmly. 'I don't blame you for being upset.'

'What am I going to do?'

'We're going to have to come to some arrangement with him. The sooner the better if you don't want this case to drag on indefinitely.'

'I don't want to have to give him anymore. I don't want anything more to do with him. I want him out of my life for good.'

'I'm afraid that's not possible. There's a lot to be sorted out; the cottage, contents, investments, wills, pensions. We haven't even started yet. That's why I want to discuss everything and see what sort of deal we can come up with. Something we're all agreed on.'

'Andy hasn't got investments of any kind.' The idea made her laugh.

'But you have.' He leaned towards her. 'And he'll want his fair share as he sees it. We'll have to go through your assets, discuss everything, see what we can do.' Roger drew his notepad to him. 'I will have to furnish them with a statement of assets, then we can discuss them. There's your will, pension fund. There's money due from the sale of your father's business. You were a partner in that, so you'll get a certain amount. Your father hasn't discussed a figure with you?'

'Not yet, but that's nothing to do with Andy.'

'I'm afraid it is. Everything has to go into the melting pot.'

'Whatever about money from the business, I'm not keeping him as well. I have enough responsibility to keep myself. I'm my first priority from now on.'

'I acknowledge the injustice towards you in all of this. I agree that Andy is greedy and selfish and unfeeling. He's also obstinate and will fight for what he believes is his right to the last breath.'

Cara trembled, a feeling of defeat draining her. How could she expect to get away with anything from Andy?

Rising to his feet, Roger said authoritatively, 'We must be patient. It's going to be difficult.' He looked enormous towering over her as he spoke. 'I'm afraid we're going to have a fight on our hands. But we'll win out in the end.'

Cara stood up. She was suddenly very tired. Taking a deep breath she said, 'Let's hope so.'

She didn't believe Roger's words. Not that his opinions and beliefs lacked validity. It was the strength of Andy's determination that was forcing a situation whose outcome nobody seemed to want to face. She turned away, uncertain, telling herself that she'd bitten off more than she could chew.

Nerves jangled up after her interview with Roger Hamilton, and longing to have a chat with Vanessa, Cara sought her out at her office. Vanessa's office was quiet for once, dust covers on the computers, the others gone home, Vanessa conscientiously working while waiting for Cara. They went to The Four Seasons for a quiet drink.

'You must be determined to fight your corner, no matter what it takes,' Vanessa advised her when Cara had given her a progress report on the separation.

Cara took a swig from her bottle of Heineken. 'I haven't any option.'

'That's the spirit.'

'He's trying to out-manoeuvre you, deliberately removing everything he can from your grasp.' Hadn't he always done it only somehow she hadn't noticed. 'He'll try to worm every last cent out of you too. He's proved beyond doubt that's he a mean-minded explosive piece of shit.'

'It's pathetic the way he's got me cornered,' Cara said. 'Living in my cottage, biding his time, believing that I *owe* him.'

Vanessa leaned forward. 'It's nothing new. It's a game he's been playing for as long as I've known him. Leave him to Roger. He'll deal with him.'

'I'm not so sure.' Cara's shoulders fell.

'What are you not sure of?'

'That I'll ever be free of him. That whatever happens in the future, he'll have to be my first consideration, no matter where I am or what my circumstances are my obligations will be to him first.'

'Say it all to Roger.'

'Roger sees the whole situation as it is. This husband of mine has never been supportive.'

'He's never really been a husband, only a substitute for one. Your marriage was a joke.'

'Except that no one's laughing. Now he's become an enemy, and I've got to fight him if I'm not to be crushed by him. And another thing,' Cara said to Vanessa, 'I'm worried about the cottage. I'm sure it's in a terrible state. Most of my clothes and stuff are still there.' Between her teeth Cara said, 'I told him he'd no right to have his pals in there all the time.' Her sense of security felt threatened by Andy's wrongfulness.

'Go and get your things out when he's away at the darts championships in Cork next weekend. He'll be there.'

Cara nodded. 'You're right. He never misses them.'

Cara was angry, but at least now she had a purpose, a place to channel her anger, negotiating with Roger to fight Andy all the way until she got what she wanted. When the ties that bound her to her marriage were cut loose, hopefully she'd emerge a stronger calmer happier woman. Resolutely she left Vanessa; glad of this anger that buoyed her up all the way back to Wexford.

The cottage was in darkness, Andy's car gone. Cara inserted her key in the lock and entered the hall with the silent stealth of a burglar. She tiptoed into the sitting room, picking her way through the humps of furniture with the pinprick light from her torch. In the middle of the room she stood, letting her eyes adjust to the dark. Moving forward she went to her bookcase and began to pack her books. When she was packing her Louise Kennedy wine goblets she thought she heard a sound on the staircase. Was someone in the cottage after all? She stood still, holding her breath, listening.

Only the sigh of the wind broke the silence. Relieved, she continued packing, adding her Waterford glass candleholder. She sneaked upstairs to their bedroom, nerves tingling, moving as quickly as she dared without making noise, anxious to get away before Andy came back. The bedroom door was ajar. She knew immediately that something was amiss because of the peculiar smell of strong cheap perfume. She went softly forward, picking out two humped shapes on the bed: Andy, his arm flung across a blonde-headed girl, their faces close together. Startled, she stepped back into the gloom of the landing, anxiety in every single part of her body, her heart beating furiously, she ran back down the stairs.

'Stop.'

Cara swivelled around. The flash of the light being switched on made her blink. Andy came running down the stairs.

Shocked at the sight of her he shouted, 'What are you doing here?' He was breathing fire.

She got to the front door, opened it.

He slammed it in her face.

'Wait!' He grabbed her arm.

She gasped, 'Let me go.'

He dropped her hand abruptly. She pushed past him to get some space between them. He grabbed her, trouble vibrant in his bright red face.

'I asked you what you're doing here?'

'I came to get some of my things.'

'You have no right to break in.'

'And you've no right to have some tart in my house,' she screamed at him, pointing to the denim jacket thrown over the banisters, the pink shiny high heels strewn in the hall.

'Mine,' said a woman's voice.

Startled, Cara looked up to see Tracey, the barmaid from The Crowing Cock, coming down the stairs, her long hair tousled, her bosom burgeoning out of a skimpy top that showed off the stud in her belly-button, her legs barely covered by a short denim skirt that she was fastening.

'Hi, Cara,' she drawled insultingly, placing her multi-ringed hand possessively on the curve on Andy's arm.

'It's you,' Cara said, taken aback. 'Would it be rude to ask how long you intend to stay in my home?'

Tracey hesitated, casting a look at Andy in desperate confusion.

'This is my home. You're sleeping in my bed,' Cara said.

Tracey said with an insulting smile, the stud in her tongue glittering. 'I didn't ask your permission, did I?'

'You don't need to,' Andy said, turning to Cara. 'It's none of your business.'

'We'll see about that,' Cara scowled at him.

'You're the one who took off. You walked out on me. What was I supposed to do?'

'That's not the point!' Cara shrilled, shaking with rage.

'It's very much the point. If I'd wanted to be a monk I'd have joined a monastery. And don't start lecturing me on morality. You're the trail-blazer when it comes to doing the dirt. So don't get on your high horse with me. I'll have who I want here, when I want, and you won't stop me.'

'Fine.' Cara stopped. 'You'll be hearing from my solicitor.'

She swept out of the house, head high, cheeks blazing with fury.

She got in her car, fighting back her tears, slammed the door viciously.

Her head spinning she roared off.

She phoned Vanessa. 'It's all bad news I'm afraid.'

Cara told her how she found Andy and Tracey in bed together at the cottage.

'You must have been furious,' Vanessa said.

'Andy was furious. Tracey kept shooting him anxious glances expecting him to explode at any second.'

'You're weren't expecting anything less from the bastard.'

'No, but I'm torn in two. On the one hand I want to be rid of him, on the other I want a fair settlement.'

35

O ut of the blue Guy phoned her.
    'I hope you don't mind me ringing you.' His voice
was hesitant.

Cara hesitated. 'No, of course not.'

'Would you like to have dinner with me at the Strand
Hotel in Roslaire, just for a chat? I hear that their restaurant
is very good.'

Cara agreed to meet him and regretted it the instant she
put down the receiver. She stood looking at it, shaken by
the effect of the call. Getting over Guy, and the turmoil of
the relationship between them, why was she reliving every
detail of the pain that had lasted long after it was over? Why
should she want to endure that pain again? Shouldn't she
be protecting herself against it by keeping a wide space and
distance between them, at all costs, even if it meant breaking
the date? That's what she ought to do, even if it meant an all
out confrontation with him.

During the meal Guy watched her covertly; knowing it was
an effort for her to act normally, on tenterhooks underneath.

He rested his knife and fork, tense.

'Is everything all right, Cara?'

'Fine. Why do you ask?'

'You're not happy. Don't tell me you are, because it
wouldn't be true.'

'I'm trying.'

'Want to talk about it?'

She toyed with her food. 'We've been through all that.'

'I'd like to help, as a friend. Anything I can do?'

She looked at him, smiling. 'Nothing, honestly. I'm coping.'

'Yes, but I can see that you're suffering.'

'Let's not go on about it. It'll only spoil our meal.'

'Don't be silly. I'd rather know what's going on.'

She fiddled with the edge of her serviette.

'Why are you so nervous?' Guy asked.

He looked at her with such warmth and interest that her defences melted. She put down her knife and fork in a gesture of hopelessness and finality. 'I'm in a lot of trouble,' she said.

He leaned across the table eagerly. 'Tell me about it.'

Cara glanced about her. The dining room was nearly full. A waitress was standing nearby, waiting to take their empty plates.

'Not here.'

They finished their meal and left, pausing in the street before making their way along the path, and out on to the Strand where it was cool, her hair blowing back from her face. They went on for a while in silence. Coming to a bench, Guy said, 'Let's sit here.'

He sat sideways, his arm resting along the back of the seat.

'So, what is it? Tell me.'

'I'm trying to be reasonable, and that's difficult because Andy's doing what he wants at everyone else's expense, leaving me no choice but to get nasty.'

'What's happened so far?'

'We've submitted a full statement of assets. We can't do anything until the sale of the cottage is agreed and Andy is being very unreasonable about that.'

A child ran along the path, chased by its mother.

Cara watched enviously.

'I hate the complications, decisions, but the problems are mine and I have to sort them out.'

'You didn't realise it was going to be this difficult.'

'I thought I could deal with Andy.'

'But you can't.'

'I have to. I don't have a choice.'

'Can I be of any help?'

'No, thanks. I've got to deal with this myself, and I'm trying to buy the business, that's keeping me sane.'

'Problems there?'

'The usual sort when you're starting a business. Money is the main one. I haven't any.' She straightened her back. 'Andy's solicitor wouldn't let me give the cottage as a personal guarantee unless he gets a stake in the business.'

Shocked, Guy looked at her.

'That I refused, and Andy sought revenge, demanding maintenance, succession rights, anything he could think of.'

'So what do you feel he's entitled to?'

'A settlement, half of everything we own at present. My solicitor has to make a full financial disclosure.'

'I can't bear to think of you going through all of this and not being able to help you.'

Cara sighed. 'I'm angry, and exhausted, but it's there, inevitable, threatening. I know it all must sound pathetic to you but I'm getting through it.'

'What are you going to do about the business?'

She laughed. 'Don't worry, I'll think of something. I'll talk to Mathew Arnold, get him to wait a bit until I've got Andy out of my hair and I've organised the finance. At the moment there's no one to lend it to me. I wouldn't like to ask Dad. He's on a tight budget these days. All my friends are struggling like me.'

'I would lend it to you.'

Cara said stiffly. 'I couldn't possibly borrow from you.'

'Why not? It'd be better than waiting to see what happens with Andy. You deserve better. I think that man is bad. I'm afraid he'll do you more harm.'

'He's not a murderer if that's what you're thinking.'

'No, I wasn't thinking that. But he won't allow you to go. He'll try to contort you into what he wishes you to be security for him. To him you're a refuge from the big bad world and the trauma he's been through.'

'I'll get it sorted.'

'You've changed, Cara. In such a short space of time too.' He gazed at her, searching for signs of the Cara he'd known. 'I can't believe the transformation.'

Cara rolled her eyes. 'So much has happened. Suddenly, I've grown up. I dread it all, hate facing the difficulties, delay, decisions. But it's my problem, no one else's. The business is my excuse, my refuge. It takes up such an amount of time that while I'm working I don't think of Andy's next action.'

'You're a brave girl. Don't let them discourage you.' Guy said, putting his arm around her shoulders and giving her a hug.

Faltering, she tried to control her shaken breath. Her body felt hollow with longing for him. She ached to reach out and touch him. To hell with her self-protection, pride, the ways she portrayed herself to the world. She would have abandoned it all if he'd only take her in his arms. She longed to make love to him there and then. If the truth were told, she had wanted to for weeks but she knew not to make a fool of herself. Now she was too nervous to make a move herself because it mattered too much, and because a picture of him with Suzanne rose up before her.

They sat separated from one another in their own locked-up thoughts, neither one knowing what to say next.

'I saw you with Suzanne one night in a pub in the city,' Cara said suddenly.

She looked ahead at seagulls hovering round them. They both watched them.

'Why didn't you come and rescue me?'

Cara glanced up at him and was struck by the lack of expression on his face, as if he was determined not to convey any emotion.

'How could I do that? You didn't look as if you needed or wanted rescuing. I thought you were having an affair.'

He laughed. 'You never mentioned this the last time we met. A touch of the green-eyed monster?'

'No.' She sat stiffly, watching the seagulls circling.

'Sorry. I shouldn't have said that,' he apologised.

'It's OK.'

'How is Suzanne, anyway?'

'She's fine. Trying to make things work with Dick.'

They walked back to the car park of the hotel.

'We might see each other again soon?' Guy said, a question in his raised eyebrow.

'I hope so. Are you coming back to Ireland for good?' Cara asked.

'I'm not sure,' he said, looking away. 'It depends on a lot of things.'

'Thanks for dinner. I enjoyed it.'

Cara got into her car, and was gone like a bullet before temptation got the better of her and she went into his arms.

Next day she drove to Dublin to see Vanessa.

Vanessa appeared in the doorway of the pub, carrying her briefcase as if it held rocks instead of legal files. She dumped it next to the vacant chair beside Cara's and threw off her jacket, while Cara ordered two bottles of Heineken.

'I'm exhausted, and hot. I need a shower. I couldn't concentrate anymore so I left. How are you?'

'Restless, otherwise fine.'

'How was Guy?'

'Well.'

In a careful voice Vanessa asked, 'Do you still love him?'

Cara leaned back; knowing that question was coming. She closed her eyes so that she wouldn't have to meet Vanessa's gaze. 'I don't want to think about it,' she said finally.

'You're going to have to.'

Cara sighed. 'I knew you were going to tick me off.'

'What did you expect? You can't treat him like an ordinary person in your life. He's here for a while and if you go on seeing him, even on a casual basis, you'll have to make a decision about him.'

Cara put her hand over her eyes. 'Not now, Vanessa,' she said. 'I won't be able to think straight until things are sorted out with Andy, and I definitely won't resume anything with Guy.'

'I think you're mad to let him slip through your fingers like that.'

'Do you?'

Vanessa flung her hands out in frustration. 'If you wait until you're sorted out it'll be too late, Cara. Guy won't hang around while you're all preoccupied with your marriage problems. He'll be gone.'

That was Cara's cue to tell Vanessa about her suspicions regarding Guy and Suzanne, but she couldn't bring herself to.

'I've decided not to get involved with anyone for the present.' Cara bit her lip, finding it hard to keep the tears back. 'I've decided I'm in enough trouble without provoking anymore.' Cara looked away.

'You're not fit to make a decision like that. You're only half-functioning.' Vanessa sounded like a parent reprimanding a child.

Cara put up with it because she knew Vanessa meant well.

'Oh, yes I can. I'm going to get on with my life, live in Bufferstown, make something of myself.'

Vanessa said, 'I know you say all those things. But I'm not convinced that you'll be all right. Why don't you talk to someone, a therapist, who could help you sort yourself out?'

Cara glared at her. 'I'm not mad.'

'I'm not suggesting that for a moment. But you need someone to help you see things clearly.'

'It's all as clear as crystal to me.'

'No, Cara. You've closed yourself off from your feelings and emotions, thinking you're taking it all calmly in your stride. But beneath that calm surface you're simmering with emotions that need sorting out. They'll blow you apart if you don't address them. How will you ever get back to normal then?'

Cara glanced at her. 'Who do you propose I see?'

'I've got a choice of several really good psychologists that I could recommend.'

Cara had thought about it for a second. 'Thanks, but no thanks,' she said.

They finished their drinks and left. Cara felt drained after they parted, though her defence of her actions had been a small triumph, and had made her feel decisive, in charge of her own life, if only for a short time. Things were unsatisfactory, and far from sorted, she realised that. She also realised that Vanessa had barely stopped short of calling her a fool, but the implication was there.

She was tired of waiting for the phone calls from Roger, tired taking what came next in her stride, groping her way along while Andy and his solicitor prevaricated.

The sale of the cottage was in abeyance, as was the purchase of the business. It felt as if Cara's whole life was in abeyance. There would have to be an agreement between Andy and her over the sale of the cottage before it could be sold. At this point Cara was sure that, no matter what was agreed, Andy would get the lion's share. Part of her wanted to rush to Guy, fling herself at him, and tell him that he was the only one for her, but her pride forbade it. Also, how could she run to him when he had somebody else?

36

The lights of Bufferstown were more like a warning than a welcome. Cara walked through the front door with the same feeling of trepidation she had the first time, seeing again the whole scene, Andy, Brendan, the fight. She was forced to relive the episode again and again in her mind, the memory of it prevailing.

There was a loud knock at the door, a nonchalant whistling from Brendan, while he waited for her to answer.

'Hello, come in.'

'What's the fierce look for?' His charm and friendliness were the same as ever.

'Sorry. I just hate answering the door.'

'So you're back,' he said conversationally, looking at her bags, the teasing back in his voice. 'How are you?'

'I'm fine. Come in and have a glass of wine with me.'

Brendan sat with his glass of wine. He looked happy as he said with a mischievous smile, 'What did you get up to while you were up in the big smoke?'

She sat away from him, arms crossed. 'Nothing much. I'm afraid its pretty gloomy stuff.' Cara took a mouthful of wine.

'Want to talk about it?'

'I'm in trouble again.'

'What happened?'

'I went to the cottage to get some personal stuff,' she said.

'Was he there?'

'He's been there all right. Got a woman installed.'

'I bet he has. Can't imagine anyone as resourceful as him battling on his own if there was the chance of any kind of assistance from an attractive woman. He's a fool.'

'I left. He wouldn't let me take any of my things.'

'A fool obsessed with his wife. Put the whole thing behind you,' he advised. 'Let the solicitors fight it out between them.'

'Sorry, I shouldn't bore you with it all.'

'I'm happy to listen. I've got all night.'

Cara shook her head. 'It's made me more determined to fight my corner.'

'So you should be. Just as long as you don't get savaged by it all.'

'I won't.' Cara jutted out her chin.

Brendan laughed. 'You should be going out more.'

'I'm not in the mood.'

'You should really, though. Come clubbing with us,' he said, wiggling his bum. 'A bit of dirty dancing would do you good.'

'I'm not in the mood to go clubbing, getting groped under the strobe lights, by some loser even more desperate than me.'

'You'll be with me. You'll get in the mood once you hear the music.'

Putting his arm around her Brendan said, 'Come out with me and enjoy yourself. It's Christmastime. You're too lovely to stay in and brood. There's a nightclub in Wexford, legendary for its music and atmosphere. Would you like to come?'

He was doing his best to encourage her to get on with her life. But Cara was hurt by life and was suffering. What was more, she wanted to suffer. She wanted to dwell on her losses and mourn them. Brendan was too young to understand that, his world secure, everything ahead of him to look forward to, life to celebrate and anticipate. That was the difference between them in Cara's view. Their suffering was unequal, and that fact alone, apart from the ages, created a monstrous gap.

Cara's reaction to her life in crisis was to get up in the morning, go to work as usual and smile her way through the day. That wasn't difficult. She had a real affection for the Bufferstown community and her job. In the evenings she stayed in, refusing to face life head on, busying herself cooking, cleaning, listening to music.

There were phone calls between her father and herself. Painful, strained conversations with him, during which he tried, and failed, to keep the hurt and anger he still felt over the break-up of her marriage out of his voice. Cara's attitude towards him didn't help either of them. She made no pleas for understanding and no attempt at filling him in on the details of her separation. He didn't want them. He preferred to distance himself from these matters. Such things happened in other families, not his. Besides, he was still coming to terms with his new life. He was still with no comprehension of how he had got to where he was, or when his business had started to collapse, failing to understand why this tragedy should have happened to him because he'd thought he was untouchable. Cara was dreading Christmas. It was bound to be dismal in Monkstown.

On her nights alone Cara fantasised that Andy would evaporate into thin air with the sale of the cottage. That her father would arrive on her doorstep to inspect and congratulate her on her success at building a life of her own despite everything, and full of apologies for not having been more understanding towards her. Not once did she fantasise about Guy coming back into her life as a lover. That was over, gone for good, and she knew it.

There was plenty happening in her life for her to focus on. She had a busy week's work ahead, an early appointment with Mr Keene to discuss progress with the purchase of the business.

Roger phoned. 'I hear you went to the cottage,' he said, acting as though nothing surprised him.

Cara sighed. 'I went to the cottage, thinking he wasn't there. I wanted to get my stuff out of there before it got ruined,' she said defensively. 'Andy was there unfortunately. He lost his temper with me.'

Roger's voice had a reprimanding sound to it. 'I know. His solicitor said you provoked and upset him.'

Cara said with a look of triumph. 'He had no right to have another woman there, or to attack me.'

'Agreed. But it happened, and don't you go there again.'

'Don't worry, I won't.'

'I've got your welfare to consider. Keep away; let me handle things because it's caused more complications than it is worth.'

'Come to the night club,' Brendan said. 'It'll be a bit of craic. You can't shut the world out, Cara. You'll become a martyr and a right pain in the ass,' he argued.

'I've nothing to wear.'

'That's an excuse. You look great in your jeans.'

Finally Brendan persuaded her to go to Glitter the following Saturday night. Brendan, looking cool and smart in new Diesel jeans and a white French Connection T-shirt, ushered her through the leaping throng. After a couple of dances, Brendan bouncing around as good as the best of them, Cara squirming with embarrassment, she took a break and stood to one side, looking on the gyrating mass, listening to the out-of-tune music, not sorry to have said goodbye to her youth.

Eventually, back at her place, they ate a dawn breakfast of scrambled eggs and rashers cooked by Brendan, their conversation casual as they relaxed in the sitting room.

Brendan said finally, 'I'd better be going.'

In the eerie light they stood facing one another. Brendan's face was an outline, but Cara could make out the shadow of a question mark in his raised eyebrows.

'Sorry I wasn't better company,' she said.

He touched her face 'Not true. You're a good laugh.'

'I'm a wreck, and you know it.'

He leaned forward and gave her a kiss on the cheek.

Cara pulled back. 'I haven't anything to give anyone at the moment.'

'I like being with you. You're a caring woman, not a silly twit like some of the girls of my acquaintance. You're hurt at the moment. That's all. There's no shame in that.'

He leaned forward again and gave her a soft tentative kiss on the lips. 'I fancy you like mad,' he said. 'You know that.'

Disjointed thought ran through her head. She should relax, let him make love to her. He was holding her, his eyes looking into hers as he slowly put his arms around her, his gaze on her admiring. She was losing herself in his embrace, her head spinning, everything blurring. Knowing she was playing with fire. It was dangerous to tease a young man who was clearly smitten with her. Still, what harm was it, she thought, as Brendan sagged into the sofa, happily pulling her down with him.

He moved his hands over her body, kissing her at the same time, his young lithe body full of excited nervous clumsiness, so different from the self-assurance of Guy. Everything about him was different. Cara thought that she should throw caution to the wind, let herself go. It wasn't that it was anything important, all they were doing was having a good time. What harm would it do to dull the pain of recent times down? How could she face a future if she couldn't let go of the past and the pain that went with it?

Half-drunk, exhausted, vulnerable though she was, logic prevailed, taking precedence over sentiment. She wasn't prepared to throw caution to the wind, not even for Brendan who liked and wanted her as she was, and was prepared to have her on any terms, who would make love to her unconditionally, if she would only let him. Her defensiveness reappeared.

'Brendan,' she said, pulling back. 'Stop.'

'What's wrong? What's the matter?'

'Nothing. Nothing at all.' She was rising, straightening her clothes. 'I think you should get going before the town wakes up.'

'Who cares about the town?' he said.

'Your mother for one. She'll think I'm a bad influence.'

Brendan rose and, blushing like a schoolboy, said, 'Don't treat me like a child, Cara. I'm not interested in what my mother thinks.'

'I'm sorry.' She could feel herself blush to the roots of her hair. 'It was great. You're great.' She stopped.

'But!'

He looked up, his eyes questioning as he waited to be told the real reason why she stopped his advances.

'We had fun, that's all. I don't want it to go any further than that.'

'I'm not exactly looking for a permanent relationship,' he said.

'You mean a lot to me, Brendan. That's why I don't want to mess things up between us. I'm not good for you,' she said, following him.

She waited for him to yell. Instead he stood crumpled. 'I think I should leave.'

She reached out and touched his hand. He ignored her and walked towards the door. She followed him downstairs.

'When you do work out what it is you want, let me know.'
He slouched to the front door, disappearing through it.

Cara made her way slowly upstairs, sorry to have embarrassed him like that, realising how valuable a friend he was. How could she help it if she didn't feel for him what she felt for Guy? He didn't touch her the way that Guy had done. For her to make love to him while loving someone else would have been impossible. So she spent the rest of the weekend avoiding the pub so as not to bump into him.

The first Christmas out of Rockmount was charged with concealed anxiety, everyone trying their best to hide their sadness and to be happy. Cara, wishing that this normally magical day might be over soon, went for a long walk with her father and Bouncer, who for once was reluctant to go and leave the delicious smell of roast turkey behind him. The arrival of Vanessa the next morning to whisk Cara off to the races was a happy excuse to make her getaway, at least for the day.

Back to work after the Christmas break, the first thing Jane said to her was, 'What have you done to Brendan?'

'What do you mean?'

'I met him at the harbour last night with the lads. He's miserable.'

Her big mouth was open, waiting for Cara's reaction, no trace of her usual mocking smile.

'I don't know what you're talking about,' Cara said, opening her diary, checking her appointments for the day.

'You dumped him. So Tommy said.'

'Not exactly, and not that it's any of your business.'

'Don't pretend with me, Cara,' Jane flung at her. 'You've been flirting with him for a while now, playing games, going all gooey and helpless when it suits you. And suddenly it's hands off, don't touch me time.'

'I think you should get on with your work, it's what you're paid for, not meddling in my business.'

Jane wouldn't be stopped. Standing in front of Cara, arms akimbo, her tight skirt barely covering her thighs, she said, 'He wanted you. He'd have done anything for you. You knew that. You should have proceeded with caution. But, oh no, you went in feet first, no sensitivity at all, and then, when he had a go, you wiped the floor with him. How could you be so cruel? You've insulted the poor chap and hurt him badly.'

'That's a strong accusation,' Cara said, fuming.

Jane moved forward impatiently. 'You were the only woman he trusted himself with and you abused that position of trust.'

'I don't see it like that.'

'Because you don't want to. You thought you'd do a bit of cradle-snatching, but you suddenly didn't fancy him because he wasn't experienced enough.'

'How dare you. It wasn't like that. We were enjoying one another's company, having a good time that's all.'

'You were having a good time, tempting him, knowing he fancied you, thinking of no one but yourself.'

'I didn't want it to go any further.'

'You should have told him sooner. You had power over him, with your responsible job and your fancy clothes.'

'Jane, calm down, it didn't get anywhere. Brendan's a friend, that's all. I was honest with him on Saturday night.'

'Honesty isn't always the best policy when you leave it that late. It can be brutal.'

'He's young, his whole life stretching out before him. He wants a good time too, and I'm sure he'll find someone to have it with.'

Jane said, 'He's vulnerable, insecure. He needs someone caring and considerate.'

'Someone like you?'

'If I get the opportunity I'll teach him a thing or two.' Jane said, turning away.

'I bet you will,' Cara said and left the office to meet a client.

Crippled with remorse, she avoided the shop and Mags, and sought Brendan out at the harbour that evening as he was setting off for a fishing trip.

'I'm sorry if I gave the wrong impression. What I did was immature. I shouldn't have started anything.'

No response, Brendan stared ahead.

Cara took a deep breath. 'I'm trying to apologise. You're not making it easy for me.'

'If it makes you feel better, I'll accept your apology. I just hope you meet your perfect man one day.'

'Can we still be friends? Your friendship means a lot to me, Brendan.'

Brendan leaned forward and gently touched her arm. 'It's all right. I'll get over it.'

37

Cara was at her desk at eight o'clock sharp on Wednesday morning, a long day's work ahead, the thought of it pressing on her mind. She checked her diary for the week, wrote in notes to remind her of things to be done before Jane came in to interrupt with persistence of personal questions which she didn't feel like answering.

The stillness of the place alarmed her. A shadow fell across the frosted glass door of her office, filling her with a feeling of trepidation. There was Andy lurking in the doorway, looking the worse for wear, the after-effects of too much drink, and that dangerous look on his face that she'd come to know so well.

Her blood ran cold. She turned to flee, but he was beside her, making her stay.

'You stepped out of line,' he said, barging in, pushing her back down into her chair.

Cara was stuck to the chair.

'That solicitor of yours, giving you all sorts of fancy ideas,' he said.

He talked in a low voice, taunting her, announcing his list of disappointments, calling her a slag, swiping his hand across her desk and keeping his expression menacing. All the time he paced up and down unnervingly. She sat, her hands covering her head, her heart racing with fear, his coming back to Bufferstown the last thing she expected.

'You have a nerve getting your solicitor to advise me to accept the offer.'

'You shouldn't be here, there are rules of conduct to be adhered to. We have to deal with this in a professional manner.'

'I'll deal with it in any damn way I please.'

'There are rules of conduct.'

'I'll do what I like. I'm sick of solicitors and their legal jargon, going on and going on, costing a fortune every time they send their formal letters or open their mouths. What do they care about us? They couldn't give a flying fuck about us and our differences.'

'That's not true. They're doing their best.' Cara was crying. 'You're making things worse, every single day that you drag this out.'

Andy said, 'You're urging me to sell my home, commanding me to take the first price offered.'

'I want you to accept the offer. It's a good offer, the best one we're going to get. Anyway, I shouldn't be talking to you.'

With a shrug of his shoulders, a flicker of his eyes, which barely concealed his agitation, he said, 'I'm not selling my home.'

'But we've got to.'

'No. I don't have to accept the offer.'

'I refuse to be treated like this,' Cara said.

'Too bad. I'm sorry if you don't like what I'm saying but that's the way it is.'

Furious, Cara said, 'You're making things worse, putting extra pressure on me with your intolerable behaviour. I'll tell you something, you won't get away with it. I'll fight you every step of the way. I'm determined this time. See if I don't.'

'Lover boy given you a bit of a boost, has he?' Andy's clenched fist dug into the small of Cara's back.

She shuddered, she couldn't stand it, the place reverberating with his voice, taunting, teasing and humiliating.

'Please, Andy,' she began, hating herself for being helpless, her inability to fight back her greatest humiliation. 'Be reasonable.'

Without another word he walked away. The gate banged after him.

She should have been in control, but she was shaking, Andy's trespassing making her want to hide. The look of hatred on his face had made her ill. She detested him, wanted him to disappear, wished he were dead.

Jane arrived on the dot.

'What's happened to you?' she asked, seeing Cara's burning face and red eyes.

'Andy just paid me a visit.'

'What! Get on to the cops, now. That's harassment.'

She picked up the phone.

'I feel sick,' Cara said, her embarrassment increasing her discomfort, because Jane was determined to call the police.

A client arrived with his wife. Cara was trapped with them, ready to scream, her breath coming in short gasps. Panic-stricken, terrified, she stood there, unable to breathe, the weight of the four walls pressing down on her. Desperate to get away from them, she stood perspiring, her eyes stinging with tears.

'Are you all right?' the man asked.

Choking back tears, swallowing hard, she closed her eyes. Suddenly her legs gave way, and she stumbled to the nearest chair, gripped it as she sank down into a black abyss.

When she came to Jane was standing over her, gazing into her eyes, the light blinding.

'Drink,' she commanded, her face distorted in the glaring light.

Escorted by Jane, she went upstairs, and lay down on her bed.

Brendan was outside his shop later on.

'I heard you had a visitor.'

Cara said, 'Yes.'

Brendan clenched his fist, his face darkening with rage.

'He shouldn't be hanging around you, he's a stalker. Doesn't he realise that you're not married to him anymore?'

'He's not interested in me, only the cottage.'

'I'll give him a good hiding again if he comes back. He'd better watch his back.'

Cara stared at him, realising that nothing had really changed between them.

'Thanks, Brendan. I appreciate that.'

This would create the best gossip in the town, but Cara knew she'd have to stay and face whatever came her way, find the courage and stamina from somewhere.

There was no way in which she could negotiate with Andy alone, strike a bargain between them, without becoming compromised by him. As far as he was concerned she owed him, and he demanded and expected her to provide for his future. Her obligations were to him as he saw it. He was her duty, her responsibility. No matter how she tried to get away from him, he wouldn't let her. Would her commitment to him be for life? Would she have to support him always?

On impulse she drove to Dublin to see Roger next morning, leaving Jane in charge of the office. Sheila, his secretary, looked at Cara in surprise.

'I know I don't have an appointment, but I thought I'd pop in on the off-chance that he'd be available for a quick chat.'

'He's in court.' Sheila frowned at her watch. 'I'm expecting him in about ten minutes. Would you like to wait for him in his office? He has appointments at two thirty, but I'm sure he'll fit you in.'

Cara said 'Thanks', and went across to the reception area. She sat there leafing through a copy of *Hello* magazine, imagining Roger in court deliberating, enunciating each word in his cool authoritative tone. Cara wondered if he would be longer than Sheila anticipated.

He appeared suddenly.

'Cara, what a pleasure,' he said, shaking hands.

'I was passing,' she lied. 'Thought I'd drop in for a quick word.'

Trying to sound casual, knowing that this little chat would probably cost her an extra seventy or eighty pounds.

He took his seat behind his desk, businesslike.

'So what can I do for you?' His smile was diplomatic as he sat back in his chair, his direct gaze on her inviting her to get to the point.

'Andy is creating difficulties,' she said, telling him about her latest encounter with him.

'Yes, he's being most unreasonable. But that's what we expected. As far as he's concerned he's the injured party, so he sees his demands as justified. He's doesn't want to sell the cottage. It's his home for the past five years, he's in it still.'

'Does that give him the legal right to withhold the sale?' Cara asked.

'Only until both parties have reached an agreement.'

Cara smiled. 'He'll drag that out as long as he can.'

'Probably.' Roger cleared his throat. 'There's not much we can do if Andy keeps finding loopholes. Unfortunately, there's no rehearsal for this kind of case. This case is a precedent.'

Cara stood up. 'Andy is taking full advantage of this, isn't he?'

'Yes.'

'I can't bear the thought of not knowing what's going to happen.'

'House prices are rising. You'll get more for the cottage eventually,' Roger had assured her by way of consolation.

'I want to know where I stand.'

Roger leaned forward, looking at her intently. 'I can't guarantee that. This is a delicate situation and needs careful handling. That takes time.'

'I don't care how delicate it is, Andy will have to stop his nonsense. We'll have to put a time limit on him. I've got rights too, Roger. I'm tired of being manipulated by him. Tired of being dictated to by him. I've been letting him live in the cottage, managing myself on very little, now it's outright war. Handling it the way you feel it should be handled is getting us nowhere. He's still dictating terms through his solicitor. Put a deadline on the sale of the cottage.'

Roger said sharply, 'I'm not prepared to do that. If we rush things we'll only aggravate the situation.'

Cara rose, rubbed her hand across her eyes.

Roger, his voice in complete control, said, 'I can't push this to the limits, no amount of pressure can be brought to bear on this case, at this time. The situation's too delicate, and we don't want to antagonise Andy or his solicitors even further.'

'What am I supposed to do? Wait for ever?'

Roger rose, stepped towards her, stretched out his arm and touched her shoulder. 'If you bear with me, I'm sure we'll get the right result.'

'How do I know that? How do I know to trust you to do that?'

Roger said, taking another step towards her, 'I'm sorry you're not happy with the way I've handled this case so far, but I'm doing things the way I see fit. If you want me to continue acting for you you'll have to accept that.'

'Fine, but remember, I can't wait around for the rest of my life while Andy exploits me. I've had enough.'

Roger looked at her levelly. 'You'll have to exercise a certain amount of patience.'

Cara didn't look up at him. She took her bag, and, turning, almost ran out of his office.

So far Roger had done nothing to prevent Andy getting his own way. Cara was furious at his seeming ineptitude to deal with her case. What humiliated her most was his inability to make progress as she saw it. She felt a strange sense of homelessness as she went to see Vanessa, of not belonging anywhere. She seemed to have stepped out of her life and into a vortex, with no family ties. Since her family home was sold, everything had changed. Her father, though dispossessed of his professional status, was settling into his own niche and, in their own exasperated way, Pamela and Elsie were managing fine too. Their relationship with her, that she'd taken for granted, was remote now, leaving her feeling disoriented and struggling with her own identity. She belonged to nobody anymore, and felt alone, like when her mother died.

She was ashamed of the way she was handling the situation, wallowing in self-pity, losing control.

Vanessa was waiting for her.

She said, 'How did it go with Roger?'

Cara flung herself into the sofa. 'I lost my temper with him.'

Vanessa put down her customary pile of folders she was reading; marked the one she was on with a yellow stick. 'You did what?'

'I more or less told him to get the finger out. I've had enough of his shilly-shallying.'

Vanessa gaped at her. 'What did he say?'

'He said he couldn't do any more than he was doing at present. That it all takes times. I just feel I'm being manipulated.' Cara covered her face with her hands to ward off the lash of Vanessa's tongue.

She felt Vanessa's arms around her, felt the squeeze of sympathy.

'It's OK,' Vanessa said softly. 'The ball is in your court. It's your money, your shot. But you won't fight Andy on your own and you certainly don't want to expose yourself to his tactics without the shield of a good solicitor like Roger. You may not think it now, but he's the best in the business.'

'You're probably right.'

'I'm sure he has a plan of campaign and Andy can't hold off forever. The cottage is your main equity, so eventually things will take their course and it will have to be sold, the money divided.'

38

Cara was almost blinded by a huge bouquet of flowers behind which the smiling happy face of Brendan peeped out as she was finishing work the following evening.

'To cheer you up.'

Relief at seeing him standing there, the impulse to rush into his arms, and give him a hug, instead she said, 'Thank you,' in a subdued tone. 'I'm glad we're still friends.'

Brendan said, 'I felt foolish after that night, but I feel a lot better now.'

'I see.' Cara didn't follow a word of this. 'What's changed?'

Something had happened to bring a bright smile to his face, and make him stand taller, and look confident.

He looked at her. 'Let's call it enlightenment.'

Cara, relieved that no permanent damage had been caused by her, said, 'Do you think this enlightenment has a future?'

Brendan laughed at her.

'We've got off to a good start.'

'Jane?' she asked.

'How did you know?'

'Let's say the office is a brighter, happier place.'

The following day Jane came into to work in her minuscule skirt and high heels, the smell of perfume all pervasive, her dark roots died out of her hair. She was businesslike, acting as if she was the boss.

'There's a house for rent near the harbour. I want to check it out.'

'Who for?' Cara asked with interest.

Jane sat back, crossed her legs demurely. 'Me. I need to get away from home. My Mum has me stifled.' She fluffed up her hair, preened herself in the mirror.

'This is a bit sudden, isn't it?'

'Not really. I've been thinking about it for a long time.'

Cara put on her commanding tone, in her role as boss. 'It's a bit big for one. A whole house?'

Jane looked defiant. 'I've got savings. I can afford it.'

'Brendan wouldn't be involved?'

'Maybe.'

'You don't need to go that far to impress him, he's pretty taken with you already.'

'We need somewhere where we can be alone.'

'Are you thinking of moving in together?'

'I didn't expect this interrogation.'

Cara's voice was surprisingly gentle. 'Tell me it's none of my business if you like. But if you want my advice, take it slowly. Proceed with caution. Make him wait.'

'I've been after him for years, Cara, and now that I've got him I don't intend to waste any more time. Besides, I have to take the lead, get him away from that mother of his.'

Feeling a stab of pity for her, Cara said, 'I'm glad. For both of you.'

Jane was gone, rushing out the door, the key to a new life in her hands. Cara thought of her own life, all the nights she spent alone, and lonely, knowing she'd rather be on her own that have all the sneaking around with Andy, or living the lies and deceit with Guy, or the sharing of a place with Brendan.

It was four o'clock in the afternoon on the next Friday. Vanessa had told Cara on the phone to try and get away early, that she had something to tell her. Here they were languishing in the Westbury Hotel, amid hard-hitting businessmen discussing projects, and well-heeled ladies, with nothing to do but linger over their afternoon tea.

'Edward proposed,' Vanessa said, spooning strawberry jam and cream onto her shortbread.

Cara sighed. 'You dragged me all this way to tell me that? I thought you had real news.'

'I have.'

Cara looked at her.

'I've accepted.'

Dumbfounded, Cara said, 'What?'

Vanessa laughed. 'I've accepted Edward's proposal.'

Cara stared at her hardly believing her ears. Vanessa seemed happy, waving her arms excitedly as she told Cara where and when the proposal took place, how Edward had got down on one knee and begged her to marry him.

'I quite enjoyed it, actually,' she added with a grin.

'I bet you did.'

In the silence that followed they sipped their tea and ate tiny cakes with forks, Cara trying to digest the fact that Vanessa, after all her diatribes about marriage as a useless state, was about to take the plunge herself. Cara didn't dare ask what had happened to the blonde they'd seen Edward with. Vanessa had either conveniently forgotten all about her or didn't care.

'I know he's not perfect,' Vanessa said, finishing a mouthful of sponge cake, touching her lips delicately with a serviette, 'but he's the only man in the world I could tolerate in my life for more than six months. We've sort of got used to one another.'

'Is that good enough?'

'Good enough for me.' Vanessa eyed the passers-by, a faraway look in her eye, a sign that the subject was closed.

'Well that's all right then,' Cara said, thinking a wedding would probably never take place.

'You're acting as though it's a joke, Cara.'

'No, I'm not,' Cara denied, grinning.

'I want you to take it seriously. Look, Cara, Edward spells security,' she said, reading Cara's thoughts. 'And he loves me.'

'I know that.'

Cara couldn't voice what was not right about all this without seeming offensive. She didn't like the idea of Vanessa getting married just for the sake of it, as though marriage was nothing more than a day out, her posh friends staring at her, seeing right through her motives. She was worthy of better than that.

'Is that enough to see you through the lean times? If you're not in love with him? You've told me that you don't love him so many times.'

'What's love? Look, Cara, love dies and passion fades. All you're left with is what Edward and I have got already; an understanding, a tolerance of one another's irksome little habits. That's if you're lucky.' She thought for a moment. 'Anyway, it's my turn to have someone taking care of me for a change,' she said.

'Will that see you through a lifetime together?'

'It's more than a lot of people who get hitched have.'

Cara put down her cup. 'Why are you doing it, Nessa?' feeling enormous pity for her sitting there sipping her tea, for once not rushing off somewhere, letting the world go by. 'Surely it's not to prove something?'

Vanessa shook her head. 'I don't give a damn what people think, but you know I've had enough clubbing, chasing young men whose only interest is pumping up their biceps. I'm fed up with the whole single thing too. It gets a bit embarrassing after a while. Now I want stability and a quiet life. Edward

understands that. He's had his youth too. We're both ready
to settle down.'

'You're beginning to sound very middle-aged all of a
sudden.'

She looked at Cara, ready for an argument. 'I thought you'd
be pleased that I'm trying to make a life for myself. You don't
approve, do you?'

'I just want you to be happy.'

'There's nothing wrong with settling for security.'

'You make a good living. You have your own place. You
don't have to rely on a man to keep you. You despise women
who get married for that reason.'

In a low confidential tone, Vanessa said, 'Cara, I'm lonely
and I'm not ashamed to admit it, nor am I going to apologise
for it.' She looked defiantly at Cara.

'I'd like something better for you,' Cara said, and immediately added, 'Sorry I shouldn't have said that. I was thinking
more of the younger men you seem to prefer.'

'You get tired trying to keep up with them. I've tried out
different varieties, different ages, and realise that they are
from a different world, their lives so different to mine.'

Not wishing to provoke her any further Cara said, 'Did you
set a date?'

'A few months' time. We won't wait too long.'

'You won't have everything organised by then: invitations,
dress, cake etc.'

'Oh, bugger the formalities. The wedding will be a small,
private affair, somewhere quiet. I'm not having all that
parading up the aisle in a big dress and tiara. I'd look
stupid. I want a few relations, close friends, and I want you
and Suzanne to be my bridesmaids. Will you?'

'I'd love to.'

Suddenly Vanessa was talking about marriage as if it was
the greatest invention in the world.

'I've had my chance at it,' Cara said. 'Andy and I blew it.'

'You can have another one. You deserve it,' Vanessa sounded like a fairy godmother bestowing a great gift.

'I don't think so.'

'You don't have to sit moping around thinking of what might have been for the rest of your life, or blotting out the pain with some young stud who's happy to worship at your shrine and can't really hurt you.'

Edward arrived, and kissed Vanessa on the cheek, proud as a peacock. She touched his shoulder.

'Congratulations,' Cara said, shaking hands with him.

'Thank you. I feel like the cat that got the cream,' he said, his cheeks puffed out, his eyes glowing.

Elsie greeted Cara with a bright smile and a kiss.

'Where is everyone?' Cara asked.

'Pamela's at work, your father's resting. He'd not fully over the flu yet.'

Elsie was back to her natural self again, deciding his routine, in her sweet-natured, ruling-the-roost again way, guarding her beloved brother, presiding over his food, what he drank, and making sure he rested plenty and took things easy.

Her father had a contented, if bloated, look about him, lost in his newspaper, and the uneventful, contented life he'd always lived before Pamela came along. Cara listened to them discussing what they would have for dinner, all exasperation gone from Elsie's voice.

'What does the doctor think?'

'I'll be out walking in no time,' he said.

Bouncer at his feet picked up his ears.

Pamela came home from work. She looked slim in her new navy suit and crisp white top. Her hair was cut shorter and lightened with new blonde highlights. Her bid for freedom had obviously paid off, because there was a lightness in her step, that hemmed-in look was gone from her face.

'You look great,' Cara said.

'I feel as though I've been released from jail.'

John, taking no offence at this statement, was delighted to see her, enquiring about her day, advising her not to work too hard in her capacity as function organiser for a new hotel in the city.

'I'm enjoying it,' Pamela said to Cara. 'Meeting all sorts of interesting people.' She was full of chat about a forthcoming event.

'Any chance of a cup of tea, Elsie? I'm gasping.'

'I'm off duty, I'm afraid,' was Elsie's curt reply. 'But I was going to make one for Cara so you're in luck.'

Elsie was treating her with formality, as though she were a visitor, still not letting her guard down while she was around.

'I don't deserve this,' Pamela wailed to Cara and John when they were on their own, suddenly changing her tune. 'I work hard all day, and here I am collapsing, trying to keep the wolf from the door.'

'I never get it right with her,' Pamela said. 'I should hate her for her contempt for me, but I don't.'

'How you exaggerate,' John said. 'Elsie hasn't got a mean bone in her body, never mind having contempt for you. It's just her way.'

'I mustn't complain. She's marvellous company for John when I'm not here,' Pamela said to Cara with a wink that clearly stated that if Elsie weren't around, Pamela would be tied to John and the house.

'Vanessa and Edward are getting married,' Cara told them, still finding it hard to get used to the idea.

John looked up in amazement.

'That's wonderful news,' Pamela enthused.

'Yes, indeed,' said John, surprised. 'I hope it works out for them both. I didn't think marriage was on the cards for Vanessa.'

'Well, she likes him,' Cara said.

'I hope that's enough,' John looked concerned.

'She's liked him a long time, and more than she pretends to,' Pamela said wisely. 'I wish them every happiness.'

'So do I,' Cara said.

'They'll need it,' John said, giving Cara a sideways glance.

'When's the big day? I could organise it?' Pamela was full of enthusiasm once more. 'Will Bertie Ahern be there? I know Edward's friendly with him.'

'The wedding's going to be very private, but Vanessa's talking about a big engagement party very soon.'

'I'll go and give her a ring, see what I can do to help her arrange it, my hotel would be ideal. Practically next door to Leinster House.' Pamela rushed off to the phone, almost colliding with Elsie and her laden tea tray, saying, 'Not now,' to the bewildered Elsie.

'That's the thanks I get,' Elsie said. 'Always the same. Here one minute, gone the next.'

'Never mind,' said John. 'I'll have Pamela's cup,' smoothing things over as usual.

39

The engagement party was a formal affair, the men in stiff suits like a church congregation, an incongruous bunch with pumped up bodies, talking about politics and the law, and sipping champagne out of glasses the size of gold-fish bowls.

Vanessa was the central attraction in this arrangement of friends, elegant in a Louise Kennedy black silk cocktail dress, cut on the bias, her hair done in a forties roll. She was full of excitement, her fingers nervously tugging at the new string of pearls around her neck as she greeted everyone.

Her women colleagues surrounded her, loud, laughing, confident types. They too were finding it incredible that the prospect of marriage could do so much for Vanessa, who'd never had any regard for it in the past.

'Amazing,' Pamela said, looking at Vanessa, also finding it hard to believe that she could be so happy.

Edward, beside her, stuffed into a dinner jacket, his face red from champagne, was in a state of glorious contentment.

'She'll make the perfect wife,' said Pamela to him. 'You're a lucky man.'

'What took us so long, I really don't know,' he replied, his eyes feasting on his beautiful bride to be, and turning to Vanessa he said, 'no one could ever compete with you, my darling,' stretching to kiss her earlobe, his neck not quite long enough to reach her lips.

Vanessa beamed amid the laughter, loud voices, everyone

talking at once; She greeted more guests with kisses and hugs.

Suzanne appeared, looking slim and stunning in a strapless black dress that accentuated her golden tan, her blonde hair loose around her face.

'Suzanne!' Cara said, hastening towards her. 'How lovely to see you. I didn't expect you'd be here.'

'It's lovely to see you too. I wouldn't miss this for the world,' Suzanne grinned, kissing Cara's cheek. 'Isn't it great, you can't imagine how delighted I am for Vanessa.'

'Where's Dick?' Cara asked, looking around. 'Is he with you?'

'No, well, it's bad news I'm afraid. We're apart again.'

'No! I'm so sorry. He hasn't gone off with someone else?'

'Well, actually, no. Things aren't working out between us. What's more, I've come to my senses, and I actually find myself attracted to someone else. I must have been blind not to have noticed him before because he was right there under my nose all the time.'

Cara gazed at her.

'Who . . . ?'

'There you are, Suzanne,' someone said. 'I'm glad you could make it. How's Lucy? I'm dying to see her.'

'I love your dress,' one of the women said to Vanessa who had just joined them. 'Is Louise making the wedding dress too?'

'Yes, but I'm not having a conventional one. Something very simple.'

'You won't have to give up your job like I did,' said Suzanne.

'Her career is everything to her,' said May who stood ferociously proud and defensive of the daughter who'd fulfilled all her dreams, the plumes of her cocktail hat pitched high on her tiny head, making her look like a Sputnik. Vanessa's father had declined his invitation to the party, through lack of interest, because of the ban Vanessa had put on his boozing.

'Life's improved for women since my time,' May added. 'They've got it all; washing machines, dishwashers, micro-waves, no need for them to give up work.'

'And when the babies start arriving there are epidurals, breast implants, false nails,' a woman in the circle added.

'No need to hang around when there's a row with credit cards and mobile phones,' said another.

'Not to mention vibrators,' Vanessa sniggered to Cara under her breath.

'Anyone seen Samantha?' a big rugby-type butted in, part-ing the giggling group.

'She couldn't come. She fell and broke her ankle when she was at a meeting in London last week. Poor thing's in plaster.'

'Crikey, how did she manage that?'

'Sliding down the leg of a barrister,' someone quipped.

Everyone laughed unsympathetically.

'What does the woman who has everything want for a wedding present?' asked a perplexed Suzanne.

'A fireman,' Zoe, Vanessa's sister shot back behind her hand. 'I reckon she'll need a good hose down once in a while,' she added, giving Edward a scathing glance.

May, shocked at the turn the conversation was taking, said to Cara, 'Look at them knocking back the champagne as if it's going out of fashion. I wish it were Zoe who was getting married instead of Vanessa,' she said. 'She really could do with a husband.'

Zoe, chest bulging out of her pink satin trouser suit, her caramel make-up plastered on, squinted spitefully at her mother through her spiky false eyelashes. 'Don't start,' she hissed.

Her mother bit her lip. 'A child needs stability,' she insisted. 'You could do with someone like Edward.'

'Oh, for God's sake, not another bleedin' lecture,' Zoe said, 'I'd rather have sex with a gorilla than that balding retard. If there's one thing I hate it's a man who's losing his hair.'

'Zoe!' her mother hissed. 'It's common to pass personal remarks like that in public, especially about Edward. He's been so good to our family. You in particular.'

'Oh, yea!' Zoe said, shoving her angry red face into her mother's. 'If he hadn't frightened the bejasus out of my Joe with his threats I might be married now.' She clambered off in her platforms, alerting the others to the fracas, and setting May's feathers fluttering frantically as she trembled in mortification.

May said to Cara in a tragic voice, blinking back tears, the other women straining to hear her words, 'She's got more ex-boyfriends than she has shoes. She doesn't seem to be able to keep up a relationship.'

'She's young,' Cara soothed. 'She'll get sense.'

Cara recognised Edward's brother James, the best man, staring at her, trying to place her.

'You're Cara,' he said finally, his fishy eyes roaming her face, delighted with himself for remembering her name.

'That's right,' Cara replied.

'Amazing, isn't it, how Eddie got Vanessa to agree to walk down the aisle with him,' he said, shaking his head, the noise and laughter swirling around him. 'She was so dead against marriage.'

'Perhaps she realised that she really was in love with him after all,' Cara said politely.

James's laughter rang out. 'I've no such illusions,' he said. 'It's a good career move, that's what it is. He's got all the right connections.' He was looking around at the world of privilege, their behaviour loud and disorderly. 'And money.'

'Love can be logical too, you know.'

He shook his fat head. 'No, wealth is the link that forged them together. She's got the golden key to his heart now.'

'So, they can pool their riches then.'

'Let's hope they have a pre-wedding contract.'

'Let's hope ordinary things like having a baby or two won't get in the way.'

'It won't,' James said emphatically. 'They both burn the midnight oil, Edward with his political functions and golf at the weekends, Vanessa preparing cases. They won't see one another long enough to make babies. Besides, Edward's consumed by his job, kids would only get in the way. And, let's face it, Vanessa's getting on a bit.'

Cara turned away from him, desperate to lose herself in the crowd. A sudden interested expression on his perspiring fat face stopped her.

'You got spliced too some years ago, I seem to recall.'

'Yes.'

'I remember thinking at the time what a waste of a lovely girl.'

Cara squirmed, and carefully examined the range of delicacies, truffles, hors-d'oeuvres, enough food for an army at the table nearby. Not to be put off, James, looking slightly baffled, mused, 'I don't see him anywhere? Is he still around?'

Cara looked at the waitresses who were serving champagne, guests drinking it with triumph. She savoured a lonely moment while talk flowed effortlessly around her, her appetite blunted by her dislike of this obnoxious man. Why did she have to stand there and trade insults with a moron like him? She wanted to say, 'Fuck off, you cruel bastard' but for Vanessa's sake she restricted herself to, 'Get lost,' and this time walked away from him, her face red with rage.

She kept her eyes studiously on the plump woman stuffing a wedge of something into her mouth, her eyes greedily on the exhaustive supply on her plate. She wished she could leave but she couldn't go just yet, Vanessa might need her, and she hoped Vanessa would need her for a long time to come. Despite James's predictions, with a husband, and possibly a child or two, she and Cara would still enjoy their time alone together. Cara valued the pleasure they took in each other's company, talking and arguing, Vanessa's astute mind weighing up the situation, or sharply focusing on some aspect of a problem. Occasionally they sat there saying nothing at all. Cara admired Vanessa greatly. She always met whatever challenge came her way and, though her job meant that her days merged into one another, she always had time for her friend.

People were talking about politics and things that Cara had no interest in. Glasses were being refilled. Cara wondered how Vanessa would fare out in marriage. She believed she had the stamina to hold onto her marriage while continuing with her practice, and still giving as generously to less fortunate women as she had been doing. Finally she was getting away, smiling graciously to this one and that, walking towards the foyer.

A shadow fell across her.

'Hello, there.'

She turned to see Guy, looking tanned and perfect. Shock turned her legs to jelly as he came towards her with a delighted smile. Pulling herself together with all the effort she could muster, she said in a shaky voice, 'Hello, Guy.'

'You all right?' His expression was one of mild amusement at her discomfort.

'I'm fine, thanks. Vanessa didn't say you were coming.'

'I'm here to congratulate the happy couple. I wasn't sure I'd make it though. Would you like a drink?'

'No thanks, I was just leaving.'

Guy sighed deeply. 'Pity because I wanted to talk to you.'

'Oh, what about?'

He steered her to one side.

'Would you like to value my house for me?'

Startled, she looked at him.

'You're selling up?'

'Yes.'

'*Why?*' Why were her legs trembling? What was wrong with her? It was as though the ground had opened up and a great yawning gap was there in its place.

'I'm moving back to Scotland for good.'

'Why?' seemed to be the only word that would come out of her mouth.

'Ian doesn't want to live here, and there's no other earthly reason for keeping it on.'

'Call me at work tomorrow, you have my number,' Cara said, taking her leave.

'Fine,' Guy smiled. I'll be here for the next few days.'

Suzanne appeared. 'Guy, you made it.'

'Suzanne!' It was obvious from the expression on his face that Guy was thrilled to see her.

She was taking his arm, leading him towards the party, enchanting him with some anecdote. She wasn't the only one. Cara noticed that all eyes were on Guy. Had there ever been any hope that she'd hold the attention of a man so attractive to women?

Pamela put a hand on her arm. 'Nice to see Suzanne happy at last. She told me she was seeing someone, has been for a while now. Quite taken with her, isn't he?'

Cara ordered a taxi to Vanessa's apartment where she was staying the night. So, it was Guy Suzanne was with after all. That would also explain why he was spending so much time in Scotland, not just because of Ian, and why Suzanne had stayed on in Edinburgh, inviting Guy to cosy little lunches alone at her house, no doubt. No wonder Suzanne hadn't bothered to keep in touch. How much things had changed she thought, how much she'd let slip through her fingers.

Next morning over coffee Vanessa said, her mind on the previous night, 'They all seemed to enjoy themselves.'

'Enormously. It was a great party.'

'I'm not fooled, though. They came to gasp and marvel.'

'You gave them something to gasp and marvel at. You looked stunning.'

'Thanks. I phoned Suzanne, asked her to pop round for coffee, but she's frantically busy with Lucy, and having to spend time with the parents. She sees so little of them.'

'She's probably with Guy.'

Vanessa looked up.

'I think there's something going on between Guy and Suzanne, Nessa. I deliberately never told you, but I saw the pair of them one night very intimate in a pub in town, and last night they only had eyes for each other.'

'So, they're good friends. Why shouldn't Suzanne have a drink in a pub with him?'

'Suzanne was supposed to be in Edinburgh at the time. She hadn't even phoned us to tell us she was back home.' Cara looked pleadingly at Vanessa. 'If you know anything,' she paused to take a deep breath, 'I'd rather you told me – the worst.'

'As far as I'm concerned Suzanne's running round after Dick, trying to keep track of him, and perhaps leaning on Guy for strength. Dick is such a piss artist and you know how Suzanne gathers the troops round her when she's feeling fragile.'

'Yes.'

'And Guy's good at rescuing damsels in distress.'

'Don't I know.'

'I don't think there's any more to it than that. I certainly haven't heard that there's anything serious going on there.'

'Guy's selling up, moving back to Scotland for good.'

'Why?'

'He says its because Ian doesn't want to live here, so he's going to relocate to there.'

'It makes sense that he should be close to his son.'

'And Suzanne.'

'Oh, come on, Cara, don't overreact. Guy's just getting on with his life. Anyway, you strung him along for ages, then dropped him.'

'I didn't string him along. The timing was wrong, that's all.'

'When is the timing every right? You were in the midst of a full-blown passionate affair with him, and you suddenly shied away at the first sign of a commitment, remember?'

Cara stared at her. 'How could I commit to him? I was still married to Andy? It was getting dangerous, in fact.'

'Well, whatever the reason was, strictly speaking you're not in the competition anymore.'

Silence prevailed.

'Listen, Cara, maybe he's playing a little game with you, making you jealous, making you realise that there are other women who'd love to go out with him, to see what your reaction would be. Maybe you reacted exactly as he wanted you to. You were bowled over by him last night, desperate to get him back, I saw the green-eyed monster shining in your eyes when Suzanne sidled up to him with her wide tragic eyes and her broken heart. He's probably having lunch with her at this very minute thinking that more of the same treatment will bring you on your hands and knees crawling to him, begging him to have you back.'

Cara bit her lip anxiously. 'He's vulnerable, Vanessa, since his wife died. I hope Suzanne doesn't mess him up.'

'She won't. Suzanne nearly had a breakdown over Dick's

philandering, remember? She needs someone stable around her.'

Maybe Suzanne really wanted him, had harboured a secret desire for him all along, what if something serious really was going on? Cara was genuinely worried and nothing Vanessa had said allayed her fear.

40

Jane was at her desk chatting to Brendan, playing with her hair, dangling her shoe; the romantic sparks flying between them. He was looking at her as much as to say, dump the work for the rest of the day and meet me down at the harbour. Now that they'd found that they were right for one another, they were beginning to get annoying, their flirting evolving into seriousness. Jane wasn't interested in her work; she was far too interested in the business of bewitching Brendan.

'There's a time and place,' Cara said, looking from one to the other.

'See you later,' Brendan said and left, giving Cara the briefest of glances.

Next day Cara drew up outside Guy's house, turned off the engine, and sat looking at the magnificent views, the mist coming in slowly over the sea, the rain reduced to drizzle. Full of anguish, her insides churning, she got out and walked to the door, the puddles making her shoes squelch on the soft surface of the new tarmac driveway.

Guy looked bashful when he opened it. There was a briskness to him; an exactness in his perfectly fitted suit, as if he'd got ready with the greatest of care, the smell of after-shave pervading the air around him.

Guy said, 'Your things are in my wardrobe. Would you like to get them?'

'Thanks.'

Cara went upstairs, noting the highly polished surfaces, the flowers in vases strategically placed, and was impressed.

In Guy's bedroom the sun from the bay window high-lighted the bed, reminding Cara of their incredible love-making. This was the room where she'd broken all her own rules, and her marriage vows. This was where they'd spoken quietly together, each one confiding to the other their secrets, illicit longings, fulfilled each other's lustful dreams, shared their hopes, both of them knowing the heartbreaking and pointless predicament they were in.

Cara wondered if he'd shared this bed with Suzanne, and couldn't imagine it. All she could see was the bleak loneliness of the room. The magic it had held for her gone with the removal of her suits and the closing of the door.

Guy was waiting with hot coffee in the kitchen. 'It's a wrench. It's difficult, I never thought I'd have to do it,' he said. 'I really loved it here. I hate leaving it. All I've done here seems pointless.' He stood gazing out the window. 'I thought Ian would come over here for the occasional weekend, perhaps finish his education here. But he's adamant about staying in Scotland with his pals. Can't say as I blame him.'

'It's a fine house, good proportions. You'll make a nice profit,' Cara said, looking at it from a business perspective.

Guy sighed with exasperation. 'Yes, that's a small conso-lation, but hardly the point,' he said crossly.

'I didn't mean to be unsympathetic.'

Guy immediately said, 'Sorry, that was an insensitive remark.'

He was struggling, she could see how hard it was going to be for him to part with the home he'd put so much time and thought into, and he now felt compelled to part with. His grief for the loss of so many things that he'd loved about the house, and the country he'd adopted as his own, was barely concealed beneath his calm surface.

Cara wanted to let him know that she understood his plight but couldn't say so without getting personal, and this was a strict business arrangement, one she was finding almost impossible. She braced herself, moving back marginally, picking up her tape measure, her notebook, wishing she could vanish.

'I shouldn't burden you. It's not easy to explain all the complications and problems,' he said.

There was a pause, both lost in their own thoughts.

'It never is. I came here one night when you were away. I sat looking at the house.'

'Why did you come?'

'I was lonely.'

He leaned closer. 'I should have given you a key.'

Cara shook her head. 'That would have made me lonelier.'

He gazed at her steadily. She faltered, and turned away. He leaned towards her.

'Cara,' he said softly.

She took a deep breath to steady her breathing, her body empty and hollow with longing for him to take her in his arms again, her eagerness to abandon her pride making her turn to him, all her self-protection meaningless,

This was her moment.

She felt herself blushing under his gaze. Overwrought, ready to burst into tears, she turned to him.

'I don't have to rush off,' she said.

The phone rang.

'Excuse me, a moment.' Guy went to answer it.

'Hello,' he said sharply, overflowing with impatience at the interruption. 'Suzanne,' he continued, shooting Cara a confused, anxious glance, before hastening to say into the mouthpiece that he was on his way. He replaced the receiver. Their eyes locked.

'I'm afraid I have to go out,' he said, looking at his watch.

Cara's started to say something, but her throat seemed to seize up and she stood, transfixed, welded to the spot.

There was a defensive look in his eyes as he said, 'I'm sorry to rush off like this.'

She followed him to the front door.

'Right, I'll see you.' Cara left quickly.

She gave a little wave and drove off.

The drive home was a nightmare. Cara gripped the wheel of her car with shaking hands, gazing ahead, trying to concentrate on the road, a knot of anguish in her stomach. What a fool she'd made of herself. Vanessa was wrong. Suzanne hadn't just been meeting Guy occasionally. She wasn't just his friend's sad wife, with whom he had the occasional drink to console her. She was his woman. They'd been seeing each other not as friends, but as lovers. Suzanne had been thrilled to see him at Vanessa's engagement party. And he only had eyes for her. A hot wave of embarrassment swept over Cara at the thought of Suzanne and Guy in bed together.

She felt stupid. It was her own fault, she chastised herself. She'd let him slip through her fingers, as Vanessa had so rightly said. Not that she had meant to. First of all she'd been terrified that Andy would find out about their affair, so she was trying to be cautious, then when Andy did find out, Cara wasted time waiting for his temper to cool down while she procrastinated about the right time to leave. When Guy proposed marriage, his passion for her unquestionable, she'd put him off again by shoving her problems in his face and telling him she needed to find herself.

The truth was she was scared of a full-blown commitment, Guy wanting more than she was prepared to give him. Vanessa had been correct on that score and Cara could see that now. Never once had she reckoned on Suzanne stealing a march on her. Suzanne, clever, shrewd, conniving, sneaky, her marriage to Dick doomed by then, fully aware of Guy's situation and taking advantage of Guy's vulnerability, had grabbed him on the rebound, wheedling her way into his heart with her concern and sympathy. So, Cara concluded, while Dick was off pissing round the world Suzanne had helped him pick up the pieces after Cara, and now they were very much in love.

Her heart lurched as she drove on, brushing away the tears, breathing hard, and knowing she'd never see Guy again, certainly as a lover. Her heart ached at the thought of the love they'd had for one another. She was recalling precious moments they'd had together, their easy friendship, their chats long into the small hours of the morning. She thought of Guy cooking in his kitchen on the night of his birthday, fully togged out in his good suit. She thought of his strength as he made mad, passionate love to her. She remembered his face, suddenly serious, as he told her that he loved her, and her heart almost burst open.

She lay in her bath, eyes closed, picturing Suzanne and Guy together. She felt her face crumple like a baby's at the incredulity of it. It was sordid, that's what it was. Dismay, anger, indignation struck her, and finally self-pity. Why had this happened? What had she done to deserve it? In her mind Guy seemed unreal, his actions not living up to the man she'd come to believe him to be.

She got out of the bath, dried herself, brushed her hair, and got into bed tired, having run the whole gamut of human emotions.

Roger Hamilton phoned Cara and said he would like to see her without delay, that there had been some new developments he wanted to discuss with her. When she arrived at his chambers the following morning Roger was animated, smiling as he took her into his office.

'It's good news,' he said. 'The inevitable has happened, what I was expecting. Andy has found someone else. A wealthy New Zealander.' He rushed on. 'And he's gone off to New Zealand with her to seek her fortune.'

'Oh!' Cara said, trying to take in this new, sudden development.

'The pressure's off. He's agreed to sell the cottage, he wants his share sent out to him in New Zealand.'

'Where did he meet her?' Cara asked in wonderment.

'That has no relevance to the case but apparently at an international darts competition in Wales. It's good news for us, he's after something much more profitable this time.' Roger smiled his professional smile.

Cara's smile was tremulous. 'I can't believe it.'

'It's true. You're being cast aside like yesterday's news. You're finally going to be free of him.'

Cara gave herself a little shake. 'Are you sure it will last?'

'Not to be too delicate about the matter, it will last until her money runs out, if his track record is anything to go by,' Roger said. 'I don't know exactly how much this woman is worth, but it's a fair amount by all accounts.'

'You don't think he's acting hastily,' Cara asked still cautiously, 'that he'll change his mind?'

Roger shook his head. 'That doesn't concern us. If this woman has enough money to prop him up for a long time to come, and she seems willing to, it will give us the time we need to sell the cottage, and put the judicial separation in place. Then we can proceed with the divorce. What Andy does with his life will not concern you, my dear. You'll be enjoying your freedom too much.'

Cara's eyes slithered away from his face. She shut them for a second. 'I see,' she gulped with relief, concentrating hard, trying to digest everything she'd heard.

Finally, her beloved home that had been violated by Andy

was now coming on the market. Cara was horror-stricken suddenly by the thought that she was losing it.

'If only I could buy it back,' she said.

'Best thing to do is to let it go,' Roger said, matter-of-factly. 'You suffered enough in it, you don't want to live in it again.'

Cara reflected. 'You're right. I did suffer in it.' She was blinking back the tears, the victim once more, outraged at the thought of Andy walking off into the sunset with some rich bitch, leaving such devastation behind him.

'I should be getting compensation from him for what I went through there,' she said indignantly. 'Not having to pay to get rid of him.'

'That's not the way things work unfortunately,' Roger said solicitously.

Finally, Cara lurched out of the office with relief at the staggering news, down the stairs and out the door in the direction of Vanessa's office to relay this amazing piece of information. All thought of anything other than the fact that she was on her way to freedom was temporarily forgotten.

Vanessa looked her in the eye. 'That's the best news I've heard in a long time,' she said, hugging her. 'You're on your own again.'

'Yes,' Cara said in a shaky voice.

Practical as ever she said, 'What's the next step? Where to?'

'I've no idea. I can't think further than this moment.'

Cara told her about the phone call from Suzanne at Guy's house.

Vanessa narrowed her eyes. 'I don't believe it. Not for a moment do I think that Suzanne would use Guy to get over her grief. But there's only one sure way to find out.'

'What's that?'

'Ask her. Look, Cara, now that you can progress with your

life, make plans, do what you want to do, don't go missing any more opportunities. As long as you're sure of what you want in life there's no reason why you shouldn't go after it.'

Suddenly Cara did know what she had to do next. Before she gave herself time to change her mind she was out the door of Vanessa's office, calling 'I'll phone you' over her shoulder, and back into her car, taking off at speed to Suzanne's for a confrontation.

Suzanne's car was in the driveway, Suzanne home. Cara sat gazing at the house, trying to calm herself enough to pluck up the courage to go and ring the bell. A mother passed by pushing a buggy with a sleeping child in it. Cara shifted in her seat. She waited another few minutes to make sure Lucy was tucked up for the night.

Eventually she went and tapped on the door. Suzanne opened it, her eyes wide with pleasure as she said, smiling, 'I'm so glad to see you. Come in. I've just got Lucy off to asleep. I don't want to wake her,' she said in a low voice. 'And if I move her she'll waken.'

Lucy was sleeping in her pram, her body curled, her arm stretched out, legs drawn up. The living room was untidy, clothes and toys strewn everywhere, carelessness Suzanne's trademark.

'So, will you be going back to Scotland soon?' Cara asked, the sleeping Lucy a disadvantage to any kind of confrontation.

'Hold on a second.'

Suzanne pushed the pram into the front room.

Returning, closing the door softly, she said, 'I shall have to come to a decision soon. I want to work. It's such a little thing to ask. Dick doesn't approve, he can be so cruel at times, but it's all right for him, he can slip off on a business trip to quell his restlessness whenever the notion takes him. It's so lonely for me. I need the companionship,' she said, dissatisfaction written all over her face. 'I'm striving to free myself from the shackles of house and baby twenty-four hours a day. I've applied for a job here, where I'd prefer to be. It's the first step.'

'Reasonable enough, I would have thought.'

'I'm hoping Dick will see sense and agree to come back and live here. The awful thing is the thought of leaving Lucy in a crèche,' she said, a shadow of dread in her eyes.

'What about your parents? Couldn't they help out?'

'Not every day. Neither of them are up to it, and besides they have their own lives to get on with.'

Suzanne was acting as if there was nothing untoward. She'd always been a tactful person, but now she was being tactful in such a way as to be completely cruel.

'But what about Guy?' Cara almost whispered. 'How will he take it that you're not going back to Scotland?'

'Guy? What has Guy to do with anything?'

Cara licked her lips. 'Well . . . at first I had no idea . . . what I mean is I didn't know you and he were . . .' She couldn't finish it. She swallowed.

'Cara, what are you trying to say?'

'I thought you and Guy . . . I saw you in the pub together when you were meant to be in Scotland, and Pamela said something to make me think . . . The other evening you phoned him when I was there, taking details of the house. He was rushing off to have dinner with you.'

Suzanne burst out laughing. 'Cara, you've got it all wrong. He was meeting Dick to try and persuade him to take over his job here, so that I could stay in Ireland, and not have to go traipsing off to Edinburgh again. I phoned him to tell him that Dick's flight was on schedule.'

'But what about that evening you were together in the pub?'

Suzanne laughed. 'Guy phoned one evening and asked

me if I'd like to meet him for a drink. He was depressed. He's been marvellous ever since Dick did the dirt, protective, helpful, so I went along to cheer him up, but that's all there was to it.'

'I thought you two were having a fling.'

'Oh! You thought you'd caught us out?' Suzanne laughed.

'Yes,' Cara said sheepishly. 'Pamela more or less confirmed it by saying that you were seeing somebody, and she thought it was Guy too.'

'I was seeing someone in Edinburgh. Not serious, just a bit of diversion, to make Dick jealous. It didn't work so it didn't last long. Listen, Cara. You loved him, and he loved you. I saw how he was with you. He adored you, worshipped you. When you shook him off and didn't want to know anymore he took it very badly. In Edinburgh I found him sobbing one night at his house. He was heartbroken. He thought you'd be back together again after the storm with Andy had blown over. He waited, hoped. It didn't happen. He blamed himself for rushing things. He'd stopped going out, so I made him accompany me to a few places, just to get him to function again. Gradually he began to calm down.'

There was silence.

'He's not in love with me, Cara. It's you he's in love with, has been for a long time now. Surely, you know that.'

'I . . . Oh, God.' Cara stood there, her hand to her head.

'What is it? I've upset you. I'm sorry if I've spoken out of turn, but honestly, everything I've told you is true. I swear it. He's always talking about you. Why, only today he mentioned that you'd been round, and how he couldn't bear to have you just as a friend, after what he'd had with you in the past.'

Cara's head was churning. She went hot, then cold.

'He indicated nothing of that to me.'

'He thinks it's all over for good, that there's no point. You told him you had to sort yourself out before you could get involved with anyone again.'

Cara nodded. 'I didn't reckon on getting things sorted out with Andy so soon,' Cara said, telling Suzanne the news.

'That's terrific.'

'Neither did I reckon on how much I'd miss Guy,' Cara said sadly.

'Why don't you phone him and tell him your news?'

Cara shrugged. 'Too late. He's off to pastures new. I'm very firmly in the past tense.'

'He's not gone anywhere. He's in bed with a chill.'

'Since when?'

'Since that night he met Dick for dinner. He was cold and shivery, then went home early. Listen, why don't you go and see him, sort things out?'

'I don't know if I can look at him again, I'm so embarrassed. Anyway, he wouldn't want to see me if he's feeling rotten.'

'Don't be silly. Go for it, Cara! Before it's too late, and he is gone for good,' Suzanne said enthusiastically. 'Guy is a handsome wonderful man and there are women out there only dying to get their hands on him. So if you still want him, you'd better do something about it,' almost pushing Cara out the door.

Back in Bufferstown Cara ran a bath. She lay in the hot water, easing out the knots in her muscles, turning on the hot tap with her toes when it started to cool. Lying back, she looked down the length of her body, thinking of Suzanne's reassuring words, and wondering what she should do.

The next evening she drove to Arklow filled with apprehension. What would she say when he answered the door? That she was just passing, that her car broke down, that she'd come to enquire after his health, since she'd heard he hadn't been well?

She was scared as she rang the bell, felt herself shiver when she heard his quickened step.

'Oh, it's you.' Guy was dressed in the blue sweater that she'd given him for his birthday.

His hair was springy and wet as if he'd stepped out of the shower.

'Hello,' Cara's voice was quiet as they gazed at one another.

It was bizarre, standing in his doorway, hoping to be asked in.

'I heard you weren't well. I came to see if there was anything I could do,' she said lamely, her heart hammering.

'I would never have thought of you in a nurse's role,' he said, leaning against the jamb of the door, his eyes glinting with mockery.

'I haven't come to offer my services. Just call it an act of mercy,' Cara said in an attempt at flippancy. 'Can I come in?'

He stepped back. 'Yes, of course, it's just that I wasn't expecting visitors.'

The smell of after-shave and shampoo lingered as he led her through the hall.

A small table lamp and the log fire transformed the place into a cheerful cosy room. Guy moved the coloured throw draped over the sofa.

'Here, sit down.'

Cara sat into the hollow he'd left, felt the warmth where he'd been sitting. He poured out two vodkas, added the correct amount of tonic. He took a large swallow of his drink, put it down, and sat quietly, but awkwardly, his eyes on her puzzled.

'How are you anyway?' she asked eventually, for something to say.

'So you detoured this way to enquire about my health,' he said sarcastically, not making things easy for her.

'No. I came specially.'

Cara sipped slowly, feeling slightly intoxicated after the first few sips, and nervous of saying anything wrong.

Guy was looking at her critically, his eye sliding over her face, resting on the curve of her neck.

'I thought you'd gone back to Edinburgh,' she said.

'I would have been, except for this damn chill I caught. I'm anxious to get back. The work won't wait.'

Cara shivered at his words. 'Of course not,' she said.

'I'm all set. The furniture removers will be here as soon as the place is sold.'

'I'm moving on too,' Cara said. 'Andy has agreed to the sale of the house. He's off to pastures new.'

'So I hear from Suzanne.'

'Oh!'

Their eyes met.

'It's great news,' Guy said. 'Gives you the opportunity to do the things you want to do, buy the business, build it up, if that's what you're after.'

'Yes, it is.'

'That'll keep you busy. Suzanne also said that you thought that she and I were lovers.'

Cara felt herself blush to the roots of her hair.

'You were so lovey-dovey anytime I saw you together.'

He gazed at her. 'I wanted it to look as if I was happy, having a good time, so I made straight for her so I wouldn't look pathetic and sad every time I encountered you.'

Cara couldn't resist a laugh. 'You could never look pathetic, even if you tried.'

'Believe me, I was in a bad state after you turned me down. And I was furious with you for rejecting me.'

'I didn't reject you.'

'Oh, yes you did, just at the peak of our relationship when everything was going for us, you put every obstacle in the way of us making a go of things.'

'Everything was not going for us. I was married, with a husband, if you remember rightly,' Cara's voice was rising. 'Then there was Ian. He wasn't exactly pleased to meet me. In fact he couldn't wait to see the back of me.'

Guy was on his feet. 'Don't blame it on Ian, Cara. You cold-shouldered him. You kept glancing at the door, dying to get away.'

Cara rose to her feet too, indignant. 'What did you expect me to do? The boy didn't want me around. He saw me as some kind of threat.'

'It wasn't just that. The thought of having to take him on board was repulsive to you. It was written all over your face that you weren't prepared to make the effort.'

Cara looked at him defiantly. 'I had enough on my plate, things to get out of my system.'

'So you went off to find yourself, and instead lost yourself in that young boy from the bog, what's his name? Your neighbour, Brendan.'

'Brendan! How did you know about him?'

'I went to Bufferstown to see you, to beg your forgiveness for being so trying as to force you to make a decision you obviously weren't ready for. Mathew Arnold's was closed. Your neighbour, the greengrocer, told me you were gone off to a nightclub with her son, and wouldn't be back until all hours. She said that you had been seeing a lot of each other lately.'

'Mags! She never mentioned that you'd called,' Cara said, amazed that Mags could keep something like that to herself.

'I asked her not to. I said it wasn't important, but of course it was. I'd wanted to tell you that I was prepared to give you time to get over your marriage, get to know Ian, but thought that it was pointless. Then at Vanessa's engagement party you were cool and distant. I was upset, but I wasn't going to show it.'

Cara couldn't believe her ears. The words he'd just spoken were the very ones she'd have given anything to hear only a short while ago.

'Brendan wasn't important, not in that way. We're friends, that's all.'

'Well, it doesn't matter now. I'm going away, and you'll have all the time you need to get over your marriage, and get a new life going for yourself.'

There was silence. Cara said, 'I must go.'

Guy put his hand out to her as she was leaving.

'Can't we forget everything for a little while. Concentrate on just the two of us. Make love? We made beautiful love together you and I.' His voice was teasing as he smiled slightly. 'I really want to make love to you again.'

He was talking as if what they'd just been through had been a tiff, a lover's quarrel, no lasting harm done, nothing said irrevocably, no bitterness that they couldn't overcome with a bit of sex.

Cara could feel his eyes burn through her. She pulled back from his grasp.

'If you think that an hour of recreational sex would take our minds off our problems and make us feel better, you're mistaken.'

'It's not like that. I'm jealous of your new found freedom, I want you before another man gets his hands on you.'

'There's no one else.'

'There will be.'

Cara shook her head. 'No one that's going to deprive me of my freedom when I get it. I don't want a life abiding by someone else's rules and regulations, never being able to do anything without considering another person. Andy was a bully who did everything to stop my progress. We lived our lives in a sheltered little world, dominated by him. Any step out of line upset him. I only realise now the effect it had on my life.'

'Nothing like the effect you'll have on my life if you keep turning me down.' Guy was shrugging off her refusal. Cara marvelled at his tenacity.

'I can't switch my feelings on like a tap.' Cara was struggling and he knew it. 'It has to be for real.'

He wasn't smiling anymore as he looked straight at her.

'My feelings are real. I've told you already how I feel about having you in my life permanently.'

Cara said. 'I've taken a big step forward in my life. I've left everything permanent behind.'

Guy gave a sharp intake of breath, hesitated for a second, then said, 'That's just how you feel at this minute.'

Cara could feel the bulk of him, the warmth of his body through the fine wool of his jumper. She smelt the smell that had pervaded her senses long after he'd gone from her life. She stood there not moving.

'Time's too precious to waste talking seriously like this. Come back to Edinburgh with me. What do you say?'

'We should have talked seriously a long time ago, Guy, and saved ourselves a lot of heartache. I can't be rushed into anything right now. I have to get back to work. I've missed enough time as it is.'

He dropped his arms to his sides in a helpless gesture and stepped back from her. 'Time is a precious commodity, Cara, and I don't have it to waste. If you go now, you go for good.'

Cara left, opening the front door herself, letting it swing back almost in his face.

41

Three months later Cara was settling back into a routine, working, walking in the evenings, the exercise keeping her healthy and focused. She made a point of going up to Dublin early on Saturdays to shop and have lunch with Vanessa, or Suzanne, or both of them, if Suzanne could organise a babysitter. She was helping Vanessa choose her wedding and going-away outfits, and compile her wedding-gift list. Arranging the wedding was turning out to be quite a task, the numbers invited growing rapidly despite Vanessa's protestations that this was to be a small affair, with no frills and fuss.

The week before the wedding, on her way back to Bufferstown, she detoured via Arklow and drove up the rutted lane to Guy's house. The blinds were drawn, the house dull and empty. Cara got out of her car and stood on a bank covered with spiky grass overlooking the beach. A man was exercising a dog, walking rapidly, muffled up against the wind. The creaking sound of the trees in the wind and the glitter of the sun on the water made the loneliness of the scene unbearable. Unable to lift her spirits, she drove away, gripping the steering wheel, wondering why the sadness had taken her by surprise and was such a shock to her system. She continued her journey thinking of the long months stretching ahead, wondering where Guy was at that moment and what he was doing.

She drove faster, swerving to avoid a truck on a narrow

bend and, shaken, slowed down, a rude sign from the truck driver a warning.

'I'm so nervous,' said Vanessa in a tremulous voice, ravishing in her blue silk beaded wedding dress, her face half-hidden by her insanely fantastic Philip Treacy trilby.

'Don't be, you look beautiful,' Cara said.

'Fabulous,' Suzanne agreed.

'What about this hat?' Vanessa agitatedly adjusted it with clumsy anxiety.

'It's perfect,' Cara said. 'Edward's going to love it.'

'I wouldn't be surprised if he doesn't show up. I've been so horrible to him lately. Get him on his mobile, Cara, please. See if he's on his way to the church.'

'I'm sure he's there already,' Cara soothed. 'He's hardly going to miss his own wedding.'

Vanessa sighed. 'Yes, I suppose we have to go through with it now.'

'It'll be all right,' Suzanne said, taking Vanessa's hand reassuringly.

'I do love him you know,' she said as if to reassure herself.

'We know,' they said in unison.

'Now come on, you're late,' said Cara.

The little blue church on the hill was bathed in sunshine. Inside, the first few rows of seats were full with familiar faces of relatives and friends, their anxiety dissipating at the sight of Vanessa at the entrance. A hush descended as the organ struck up with the wedding march. Edward turned towards the door, a joyful expression on his face as she came to meet him, followed by Cara and Suzanne. Proudly he took his place beside her, his eyes shining as he smiled at her.

They took their marriage vows before an altar decked with narcissi, arum lilies, and freesias, their heads held high. Hearing Vanessa, who swore that she hated the very idea of the marriage, repeat her vows in a strong confident tone, Cara marvelled at the quirkiness of human nature.

'You may kiss the bride,' the priest said.

Edward leaned forward to do so with a tender kiss that brought a sob from May in the front row. Vanessa's father, next to her, shrank back behind his wife.

Vanessa and Edward were triumphant as they came down the aisle to the fanfare of organ music, Cara and Suzanne following. May, watery-eyed on the arm of Reggie, Edward's father, smiled bewilderedly at the guests.

'Such a lovely bride,' Suzanne said to May.

'Isn't she?' May was triumphant, as if she'd given birth to Vanessa especially for this occasion.

Edward turned to Vanessa and gave her a kiss as the camera clicked. As soon as the photographs were taken he whisked her into the waiting Rolls-Royce. Vanessa's father, watching the white-ribboned car move off into the Saturday traffic, slapped Cara jauntily on the bottom, and said, 'Not long 'til opening time.'

He was ushered away by a blushing self-conscious May. Cara was left with Edward's brother, James, the best man, who stood in total silence, the awkwardness between them painful.

Making a big effort she said to him, 'Great to see them so happy,' her genuine delight for her friend showing in her smile.

'I'll give it a month before they're at each other's throats,' he said, and with a roar of laughter he was gone, off to spread his bonhomie among the throng.

Guests gathered in the foyer of the hotel and stood around eyeing one another. Edward's mother, Maud, who approved of Vanessa because she was a career woman, was expensively dressed in a designer outfit, her smile not reaching her calculating eyes. She was being treated like a queen by

Reggie, her husband, who was summing up the guests with grey gimlet eyes over the tops of his glasses.

Cara circulated, looking from one happy face to another as champagne was served. Dick arrived, to Cara's surprise, a meeker, milder man, attentive to Suzanne, anxious to make a good impression on her, so different from Andy, who couldn't have cared less about anything in the end.

Cara looked around, wondering if Guy would appear out of the blue, but there was no sign of him.

In the dining room the tables were magnificently laid, a rose in front of each place setting. Beef, salmon and salads in pale smooth sauces were served. There was a different type of wine for each course. What a chance it must have been for Pamela and Edward to pore over wine lists, showing off their skills, Cara thought, enjoying every mouthful of the meal, her eyes on the greedy Maud eating with gusto, her heavily ringed fingers glittering in the sunlight.

Under cover of eating and conversation, James, with eyelids lowered, was contemplating Zoe from head to toe. Vanessa ate nervously, turning to talk to Edward almost between each bite. Watching her, Cara wondered if she could go through a wedding like this ever again and knew she never could.

As soon as the meal was over, Vanessa's father stood up. With his thumbs in his waistcoat armholes, he started with, 'Well, here we are.' He took a deep breath. 'Thank you all for coming, and thanks to all the people who helped to make this day possible.'

There was a pause, all eyes on him, Vanessa's anxious.

'No one could accuse me of being soft,' he continued.

'You're right,' Zoe muttered under her breath.

'But a day like this makes me go soft to the core.' Tears stinging his eyes, he stared at Vanessa, who appeared unperturbed, though her alert eyes were fixed determinedly on him.

'Now we're in for it,' Vanessa's cousin Lavinia, who lived in London, whispered to Cara. 'He's in the Trade Union.'

'It's a shock,' he went on, his eyes on the end of the room, as he leaned slightly forward, 'to see me daughter, Vanessa, wed.'

Cara felt her toes curling, thinking of the forty guests who were waiting to hear what he was going to say next.

He cleared his throat. 'Across the gap of years I've come to truly value Vanessa. She's given me courage, and taught me most of what I now know about life today. That we should love one another and depend on one another, because our lives are inter-linked; that arguin' and fightin' gets you nowhere and that living in separate compartments makes you lonely.' Pointing upward, he said, 'I thank the Good Lord for this day,' and with a mixture of modesty and nonchalance he raised his glass of water, 'Vanessa, I salute you, and your good husband, Edward, who's welcome to the fold.'

Instantly the guests were on their feet, emotions roused as they toasted the bridal pair, and their future.

Tense and rigid Vanessa sat dutifully, her eyes studiously lowered, a slight frown on her brow as she tried to ease away the imminent tears. An astonished May looked at her husband as he sat down, tongue-tied once more, but well satisfied with the world, having neatly laid all the ghosts of his past to rest, in his opinion.

'Well, of all the hypocrites,' Zoe hissed.

'Shh', said Cara, not wanting the moment to be spoilt. About to explain the motive of Vanessa's father as a worthy one, she leaned towards her, but Zoe, suddenly looking up, saw James trying to catch her eye and gazed back, everything else forgotten.

Edward stood up and addressed his father-in-law first, 'My wife and I want to thank you, Mick, for your kind wishes.

Today, I'm the luckiest man in the world.' He looked lovingly at his wife.

Vanessa, her face radiant, slipped her hand into his as he came to his last words.

James, next, began by saying, 'One of the traditional rewards of the best man is being allowed to kiss the bridesmaids. Nothing would give me more pleasure.'

Cara and Suzanne bowed their heads.

He continued, 'Vanessa and Edward remind me of the story of the princess and the frog,' he continued. 'Unfortunately, though, no amount of kissing will turn steady Eddie here into a prince.'

'You've got that bit right,' said Zoe, goading him on.

To May's disgust everyone laughed.

Would the speeches ever end? Cara wondered. Vanessa, in the midst of laughter, was still tense, until the conversation flowed again, bouncing back and forth like a ball, anticipated answers given to expected questions.

The wedding cake was cut, the meal coming to an end, Maude and Reggie busy eyeing up everyone, assessing their importance in terms of their background. Zoe cornered James, leaning towards him as though she were offering herself to him, her breasts, like two baby watermelons, bursting out of her dress.

'She frightens me,' Vanessa said to Cara in a tranquil tone, but her eyes were troubled.

Zoe, hearing this, said to Cara, 'I'm sick of my relatives, Dad's boring speech, Vanessa with her old-fashioned ideas.'

Suzanne went off with Dick to mingle.

'Come over to the bar and have a proper drink,' Vanessa's father said to Cara. 'Vodka, gin?'

Vanessa had charged Cara to try and keep him away from the bar.

'No thanks, I won't have a drink,' she said.

'I think I'll have a small whiskey meself,' he wheezed in the haze of smoke from his cigar. 'This atmosphere's not good for me condition,' he moaned, edging her towards the bar.

May, with her enthusiasm for disaster, heard this. If anyone were to spoil the wedding it would be he. Placing herself between him and the bar she said, 'Atmosphere won't be the word for it if Vanessa catches you.' This form of attack was a success, usually.

He ignored his wife. To Cara he said, 'It's me ticker. I don't suppose working down the docks did it any good. You got up every morning, your innards tender from all that heavy lifting.'

'Lifting the glass to your lips was what made your stomach tender,' Vanessa said, not unkindly as she joined them, the words of his speech still tangible between them.

He was gone, knowing when he was licked, waving to someone in the distance.

'Come on,' Vanessa said, escaping to a corner of the lounge, flopping into a couch, 'I don't want any trouble,' she said, exasperated.

'He'll behave himself,' Cara said. 'And that speech!'

'I know.' Vanessa's eyes widened in amazement at the thought of it. 'I would never have dared to hope for such a wonderful day as this has been. I'm not worthy of this much happiness.'

'Of course you are.' Cara had a lump in her throat.

Edward appeared. He stood smiling and blinking at Vanessa as if he still couldn't believe his luck at having her as his wife. 'Come on, we've got a plane to catch,' he said, leading her away.

'Time's dragging on,' said James, looking at his watch. He murmured to Suzanne. 'They're behind schedule.'

Suzanne said, 'I'll go and see what's keeping them.'

Suddenly, the staircase filled with light. Vanessa and Edward appeared dressed in casual clothes. Vanessa, laughing, threw her bouquet to Cara.

To Cara's bewilderment she caught it and clutched the magnificent creamy lilies tenderly to her bosom, overwhelmed by a tremendous sense of loneliness to see the bride and groom go.

'You can't take her away,' she said to Edward. 'Let her stay, come back for her later.'

'What a strange notion,' he laughed.

They were leaving for the airport, taking the brightness and happiness of the day with them.

Vanessa hugged Cara and said in a muffled voice, 'Thank you for all your help.'

Cara, her arms around her, said, almost weeping, 'I'd do anything for you, you know that.'

'And I for you,' Vanessa said.

'I'm going to miss you.' Cara kept her head down, choked with misery.

'One last look,' May said, catching her daughter's hand.

As Vanessa turned to her she saw her father edging off, nudging his way through the throng, and called him to come and say goodbye. May held on to Vanessa, cherishing her to the last. Edward was, by now, desperate to escape.

'Here I am,' Vanessa said, reluctantly letting go of her mother, following him to his BMW coupé. She waved, calling optimistic assurances to her mother, and was gone.

May, wiping her eyes, said, 'I don't know how she could have had second thoughts about Edward. He's such a catch.' All the fuss of the day had exhausted her.

Everyone was asking where the honeymoon destination was, but Edward's intention to keep the honeymoon a surprise for Vanessa had worked. James was the only one who knew and he was sworn to secrecy. Guests returned to the bar to go over the day's events and have one last drink.

42

John was waiting up to let Cara in, as she didn't have a key. Seeing her sad face he put his arm around her and drew her inside.

'I know you think me a ridiculous romantic, but this is not the time for being melancholy. Vanessa's not giving up her life. She's happy.'

'It's not that. It's everything,' Cara said, her tears brimming.

His arms were around her as he led her into the sitting room.

He kept his arm around her while she sobbed. Indulgently he listened as she said, 'My own life is such a mess, Dad.'

Eventually he said, 'Cara, I know you're not happy, and I'm afraid I'm partly to blame.'

She dried her eyes, and looked at him.

John looked directly at her. 'I'm afraid that I've interfered wrongly in your affairs.'

'What do you mean, Dad?' she looked at him, puzzled.

Bashful he said, 'I asked Guy to leave you alone.'

'You what?' Cara said, loud enough to cast a net of anxiety over Pamela who came rushing into the room.

'I did what I could to get Guy to go back to Scotland. I knew how unhappy you were, and I thought it would help you.' He held up his hands, examined them, a hopeless expression on his face as he floundered, having gone farther than he'd intended.

'What did you say to him?'

'I told him he was making you miserable, that it would be better if he left you alone altogether.'

Horrified, Cara felt her ribs straining apart, and the veins in her legs swell at the shock of this news.

'How did you know it was Guy?'

'I stumbled upon the two of you one evening in The Arklow Bay Hotel restaurant. There was no doubt in my mind then,' he said. 'I felt him to be untrustworthy after that, and better off out of your life.'

'What did you say to him?'

'I explained the situation to him as I saw it. I told him that your marriage was not something to be trifled with.' His voice dropped. He rubbed his thumb across his cheek, perturbed. 'I couldn't stand by and watch you ruin your life.'

Cara couldn't believe her ears.

'You shouldn't have interfered,' she said and stopped, seeing his stricken face.

Her father, in trying to compensate for his new helpless inefficient state, had taken on the burden of her suffering, and was fast becoming a burden in himself.

Cara locked her hands tightly together to stop herself from shouting.

'Well, I hope you're satisfied, because he really is gone this time,' she said.

'No,' he groaned, covering his eyes with the palms of his hands, 'I'm not satisfied at all.' He kept his eyes on his feet. 'The whole thing's . . .'

'A nightmare,' Cara finished for him.

'I see now it was the wrong thing to do.'

Pamela, hearing the raised voices came into the room and gazed with apprehension from one to the other. Holding out her hand to John and smiling, she said, 'It's very late, come to bed.'

She glanced at Cara. 'You'll be all right, won't you?'

'I'm OK,' Cara answered in a wobbly voice.

Pamela took John's arm and led him to their bedroom.

Cara stumbled to the spare bedroom, her head bent, her arms folded across her chest, her nerves shot to pieces. She could hear her father's voice in the next room gently explaining something to Pamela, his voice droning on. What precisely he was saying Cara had no idea.

Her father was so vague these days, she thought, undressing and flopping into bed, where she lay feeling uneasy and depressed, her body weighed under the duvet and her despair. She tossed and turned, listening to her father reeling off something, probably all the reasons for his actions, and Pamela's replies, breathless with incredulity. To think that I always believed that I could never live up to his standards, she thought.

The house had gone quiet, the clock ticked. It was strange to be in this house, lying there, under this roof, with her family whose opinions mattered less now that Cara was an independent woman. Sitting up suddenly, she said aloud, 'Now, I don't have to.' With that thought she fell into a deep sleep.

She awoke next morning to the sound of the church bell ringing, its sound echoing as if from a great depth. A cold harsh light seeped through the window. Sunday morning was quiet in the Bradley household, nobody up early. Cara would have liked to get up and away. She wasn't comfortable being there, but she was afraid of disturbing the others. Outside there were footsteps on the path, a few early morning Mass-goers. She must have slept because the next thing she knew Elsie was coming into her room, carrying a cup of tea. Voiceless, gesturing towards the kitchen she left. When Cara heard her father moving around she slid from her bed and got dressed.

'Cara!' Pamela called out to her.

Cara went to her. She was sitting in bed curled up, a cup of tea in her hand, the steam of it rising to her face, the room untidy, her clothes strewn everywhere.

'Can I have a word with you before you go?'

'Yes, of course.'

'Things aren't as bad as you might think,' she said, putting down her cup, slipping on her dressing gown. 'Don't be cross with your father.'

'Fathers aren't allowed to interfere like that,' Cara said.

'He did what he thought was best.'

'There was no reason in the world for him to take such a step, Pamela.'

Pamela wound an arm through Cara's. 'It's not his fault, darling. He thought he was doing it for your benefit. He wanted me to tell him everything I knew about your marriage and I wouldn't. He thought there was hope for its salvation.'

'Don't make excuses for him,' Cara said reproachfully.

'I should have told him what I knew,' Pamela insisted on holding herself responsible, her apologies repeated so often that Cara had to touch her hand and beg her to stop.

Pamela, in a reckless moment said, 'I think you should phone Guy, have a word with him.'

'It's far too late for that.' Overwrought, Cara was trying to keep her composure. 'I'm not going to be a parasite, chasing him around.'

Pamela looked at her, considering. 'You really should get in touch with him. I know you wouldn't regret it. I am trying to think of some sensible thing you could say to him.'

'He won't want to talk to me. He's gone and that's all there is to it.'

'Absence sharpens our perception, makes us see things more clearly.'

Cara shook her head. 'No point in discussing it.'

Not to be outwitted, Pamela said, 'You could always leave

him in peace once you knew that for sure. But, honestly, I think you should talk to him. It will at least settle things once and for all and stop you churning up inside.'

Cara thought of Guy, far away where she couldn't reach him, let him know how upset she was. She was thinking of what she could say to him, a temporary comfort, because she knew that she could never reach him, that no amount of pleading with him would change things. He would reject her.

'He wouldn't want to know,' she said to Pamela.

'Well, if that happens you won't have any more worries about him, and you can get on with the rest of your life.'

Cara was thoughtful.

Pamela said Elsie would have breakfast ready. 'I love Sunday mornings, don't you, the exquisite luxury of lying in a hot bath, breakfast handed to you, no work to think of.'

Cara met her father going down the corridor, puffing.

A stern line of apprehension curved his mouth as he said, 'Good morning, darling. Did you sleep?'

'Yes thanks, Dad.'

He led her into the lounge where he began to walk up and down as if waiting for a train.

'I hope you're not too angry with me,' he said with a certain amount of concern.

Cara, still feeling indignation and self-pity from the previous night, judged from the sight of his face that he didn't really understand the harm his interference could have done. He was driven by fear of gossip and could only see the opinions of others and judge situations by the old-fashioned 'standards' he'd been brought up with.

'No,' she said, turning away.

'Good, it's over then. Let's forget all about it, shall we?'

No matter how hard he tried, he couldn't put himself in her shoes, but could only be himself.

He followed her into the hall, looked at his reflection in the mirror and straightened his tie. Cara looked at him. He was just a man watching life go by, watching himself growing old. It was nothing irrevocable, no harm done, nothing to prevent them from carrying on as normal.

'I'm off to Mass,' he said. 'See you ladies later.'

'I'll be gone, Dad. I'm going to call in on Suzanne on the way back to Bufferstown.' Cara was determined not to hang around for more deliberations over her love life from either of them.

John's face crumpled. 'I'll say goodbye then. See you soon, and take care of yourself.'

Cara kissed him lightly on the cheek and went to the kitchen, where she dutifully answered all Elsie's questions about the wedding as she tried to eat, repelled at the amount of food on her plate.

'Suzanne's got a part-time job in a finance company, starting tomorrow. I'm calling in on my way home to wish her luck,' she said.

Elsie said, 'These married women are never satisfied with their lot. They take up one thing after another, never stick at anything,' Elsie said pointedly.

'She's bored and lonely at home all day with only Lucy for company,' Cara said defensively.

'Like the rest of us,' Pamela said, coming into the kitchen and dropping down in the chair next to Cara. 'The gilded cage is not for some.'

Elsie's lips twitched as she began to answer back, but seeing the uselessness of it, refrained. Instead she gathered up Cara's plate and knife and fork in tremendous haste and turned up the volume of the radio.

*   *   *

A tall, shapeless girl with straight black hair opened Suzanne's hall door, her big bulk was swathed in loose-fitting clothes.

'Who you want?' she asked in a foreign accent, her lips disappearing into the fold of flesh around her mouth as she spoke, her brown eyes sweeping Cara's face with a wary distrustful look.

'Is Suzanne in?'

'I get her,' she said, turning away.

'It's Cara,' Suzanne said, coming into the hall. 'Don't leave her standing on the door step, Juliette.'

The girl drew back.

'Cara, this is Juliette, from Brittany. Juliette, meet my friend, Cara.'

'How do you do,' Cara said, extending her hand.

'Very well,' Juliette bowed her head as she shook hands with Cara and went off.

'Haven't I done well,' Suzanne said in a low tone as they went into the kitchen. 'Getting Dick to agree to employ her was a nightmare. He wanted a leggy blonde from Sweden.'

Dick, Lucy on his knee, heard her.

'Show Cara your new teeth?' he said, lifting Lucy up.

Lucy smiled and dribbled, her eyes goggling at Cara.

'Isn't she beautiful?' Dick said proudly.

'She certainly is,' Cara said, taking Lucy's hand, seeing one of the strangest glimpses of Dick she'd ever seen, the proud parent.

She forgot for a moment that he was a man of ambition, a ruthless go-getter, and saw him only as a doting Dad.

'I'm being obscenely teased,' he said to Cara. 'Just as you arrived she was telling me that I should go to Mass,' he said, bouncing Lucy up and down.

Suzanne said with a smile, 'I'm trying to save your soul,' her face shining with tolerance.

Dick looked at his wife, his eyes penetrating.

'I can't say I believe in God, so there's nothing to save.'

'You'll regret those words some day,' Suzanne answered, swatting a fly that hovered over Lucy.

Dick said, with a smile, 'I really don't give a toss, Suzanne.' To Cara he said, 'Saint Suzanne! Imagine it,' and laughed cruelly. 'I'd rather go and get the Sunday papers instead. Read about some atrocities. Will you excuse me, darling,' he said to Lucy, lifting her into her pram. She bawled. He gave her her bottle and, raising his hand in farewell, left.

'He'll go to the pub to read the newspapers,' Suzanne explained to Cara.

'At least he's back home.'

Suzanne sighed. 'It's never over with Dick. He wants adventure, but he wants his marriage as a refuge from it too.'

'And you're happy with that?'

Suzanne looked at her. 'I want security, for Lucy and me. He adores her, now she's getting interesting.'

'I could see that.'

'And he's letting me go out to work.'

'You're happy with that.'

'Happier. I'm still working on him.'

Lucy was falling asleep in her pram in the corner. Suzanne cautiously tiptoed round the kitchen, making coffee.

'It's easier for men to dissipate their frustration by slipping off down to the pub, with not a care about a child's vaccination or what's for dinner,' she added.

'He'll be here for a while, will he?'

'He has a conference in Edinburgh next week, then he's home for good.'

'Oh!'

'He's finally decided to take up Guy's position as managing director.' Suzanne puffed out her chest proudly.

Cara said, 'That's great news.'

'Of course he'll be on six months' trial. But Guy will show him the ropes.'

Cara stared, not fully comprehending the suggestion behind this piece of information.

'Guy's coming back?'

'Just for a week or so, staying here, I'm not sure when though.'

Cara's eyes were fixed on Suzanne's, as if only in hers could she see any hope at all of solving her problem. 'Suzanne, I'm in a hell of a predicament.'

'What is it?'

'Dad has interfered terribly.' Cara relayed her story to Suzanne and finished by saying 'and I thought he was selling up and leaving because of Ian.'

Surprised Suzanne said, 'No wonder Guy was wretched, with both you and your father putting him off, and Ian to consider as well.' She was thoughtful as she said, 'I suppose from your father's point of view that it was the obvious thing to do. No malice intended. He must have done it in the hope of saving your marriage.'

They looked at one another.

'He'd do anything to preserve the status quo,' Cara said. 'He hates nothing more than a broken home and, of course, he had hoped for something better of me.'

'He probably thought it was a bit of a fling, nothing serious in the vaguest sense. He was trying to save you from yourself.'

'I hero-worshipped Dad from a child, you know. He's gone down in my estimation.' Cara's jaws ached with tension, feeling the injustice of the situation more keenly than ever.

'No harm in that. You made something of him that he never was.'

'And what am I to do now?'

Suzanne was thoughtful.

Cara looked at her, trying to see a true reflection of her thoughts.

'Get in touch with Guy.'

'That's what Pamela advised.'

'It's the only thing to do, set your mind at ease. I wonder how Vanessa and Edward are getting on.'

They contemplated in silence their separate thoughts of Vanessa and Edward, both lonely for her.

'Strange to think of her married,' Cara said.

'She had no choice. Edward forced the issue with his now or never attitude.'

'I didn't realise that.'

'Oh, yes. There was someone else chasing him and Vanessa, being crazy about him, had to make a quick decision.'

This amused Cara. 'She didn't tell me that,' she said laughing.

'She thought you had enough problems of your own, so she unburdened herself to me instead.'

'Hmm. I think we came across the competition once when the two of us were out together.'

'Well, it worked whoever she was. It got Vanessa going.'

'It certainly did.'

'Lucky for us we like Edward,' said Suzanne, 'or we might have had serious disintegration of this little group of ours. That would never do.'

'Never,' Cara agreed.

43

Bufferstown was Cara's escape route once more. But back among the town's inhabitants she felt restless and aimless and couldn't settle down. After her day's work she walked alone every evening with the air of the recently bereaved, drifting along, thinking that perhaps she ought to get in touch with Guy. Not through a phone call though, e-mail, or a text message would do. Yes, e-mail with a simple message would be best. Coming to this momentous conclusion, and actually composing a message, she was finding the idea irresistible.

Maybe she'd send him a postcard. One evening, she lingered at the harbour looking at postcards on a stand outside the sweet shop. Mick, the shopkeeper, a bent man with a moustache, looked frozen as he served the last whipped ice cream cone and rolled down the shutters on jars of coloured sweets and amber, green and white striped sticks of rock, folded in cellophane, flashing gold lettering. His face was florid as he unhooked the newspaper stand and took it inside.

'Nice evening for a walk,' he said as she paid him for the postcard. Peg, his wife, seated in her little glass cage at the far side of the shop, counting piles of silver, waved to her.

The tide was in and slapped against the wall. Numbers rasped out from the bingo hall and wafted across in the wind with the smell of chips. Cara strolled past the new café on the corner where a sprinkling of people sat at tables outside. The olive-skinned Spanish waiter was trying to take an order from a woman with closed lips. Unable to understand what she was saying, he leaned towards her, with the correct amount of deference, but with petulant eyes.

Cara had a cappuccino and sipped it. The seafront was quiet, the distant buildings now dark shapes. The sun appeared suddenly. Some cyclists passed by, their bicycle wheels sparkling in the evening sunshine, a few strollers walked by. These people were no strangers to Cara, the knowledge of them all in her very existence. The life of Bufferstown pumped through her veins now, flowed into all areas of her life and controlled it to a certain extent. There would be no point in chopping and changing. She was settled.

There and then she took courage and wrote the postcard and tore it up. In the pub next evening, Brendan and his pals were all together.

'What have you been up to?' Brendan asked.

Cara told him about Vanessa's wedding, feeling very alone, but trying to keep up the morale. The pub seemed to be at its worst, full of people enjoying themselves, deeply rooted in their own lives, Brendan no exception. The decision to get in touch with Guy intruded on her thoughts and seemed the crucial point of her life. There was no turning back from that, no longer any room in her heart for weakness or indecision. She purchased another postcard and returned home quickly with a sensation that if she didn't rewrite it her life would be ruined.

She wrote:

> We need to talk.
> Cara.

So there it was, the card that would re-establish contact. Cara looked at it, the dull coloured sea, the harbour, a sheltering arm around Bufferstown. Would she send it? Yes, it would have to go. Perhaps her father had done her a favour after all, she reflected, as she posted the card. It had taken an atrocity to shake her into action. She thought of her father now sitting in the lounge with his book and his glass of whiskey, reading in the lamplight, Pamela's arrival in the room a signal that it was bedtime, the simplicity of his new life more appealing than he'd ever dreamed of.

A week later, one evening as Cara was going to buy something for supper, she saw a lovely girl with long black hair come out of Brendan's shop and hurrying along the pavement, her step light. Brendan stood at the counter packing cardboard boxes for delivery, jovial and anticipatory, all ready for a chat.

Mags called Cara into the back where she was making tea.

'Have a cup,' she said, pouring her out a scalding cup of tea.

'He's falling for that fragile Smith girl from that new housing estate.'

'The Meadows,' Cara supplied.

'Newly married too,' Mags hissed through compressed lips. 'She has a stud in her tongue and one in her belly button. Ugh! She's in and out every minute and hour of the day. It's a worse distraction than the fishing. He's like a hen on a griddle every time he sees her, as transparent as water, that fella.'

Brendan joined them, his face pink, knowing his mother was talking about him, violet shadows under his eyes from lack of sleep.

'Look at the two of you, like a couple of oul' wans behind twitching curtains.'

Mags said to him, 'Don't you go filling your mind with romantic thoughts, you've got deliveries to do.'

'You amaze me,' he said, perching himself on a crate. 'Nothing but grumbles out of you.'

Mags clicked her tongue. 'I've seen enough of her for one day.'

'As a matter of fact it's none of your business,' Brendan said, taking a bite of an apple. 'She was here about her car.'

'Oh?'

'I'm thinking of buying it. It's a Range Rover in good condition.'

Mags sat on her stool, and spread out her large feet in carpet slippers. Cara went and picked out some vegetables, took coins from her purse and paid Brendan, looking at his innocent face, thinking how much she'd hate to be in Jane's shoes.

'You're being a bad boy,' she said, thinking that Jane had rushed things. She should have taken more care not to let him deviate like that. Then, on the other hand, maybe that's the way he was.

He grinned at her. 'Mum's making mischief. There's nothing to it. It's turned nippy,' he said, rubbing his hands.

Taking her purchases quickly Cara made her escape.

Outside the sky had darkened. Cara let herself into her front door desperate for her own physical comforts; a hot bath, a nice supper, a glass of wine, and the book she was reading. The phone was ringing.

'Hello,' she said.

'Cara! It's Guy.'

'Guy! Hello.'

'You wanted to talk to me?'

'Yes . . .' Cara hesitated, not knowing where to begin.

'I'm in Wexford. Can I take you to dinner tonight? Would that make it easier for you?'

For an instant Cara's voice failed her.

'Eh . . . Yes, that would be lovely.'

'I took the liberty of booking the new Italian restaurant, Caprice. Dick says it's good.'

'So I've heard.'

'Shall we meet there at eight?'

'Fine.'

She wore her new black mini dress she bought in a Karen Millen sale, turning sides to check that her tummy didn't show. Pleased with the effect, she ran a hand through her hair, deciding to let it hang loose, thinking of her rendezvous with Guy with a mixture of excitement and dread. Having told him that they needed to talk, she wondered now if she'd done the right thing and what she would say to him. She would tell him, of course, straight out what had started this whole business off, not put a tooth in it as Elsie would say.

It was only fifteen minutes drive to the restaurant in Roslaire. Guy was waiting. He looked different. Casually dressed in jeans and a pullover, he seemed more at ease than she did and less concerned than usual with the image he presented. But then it hadn't been he who'd run the risk of making a fool of himself.

'Cara!' he greeted her with warmth, putting his arm around her. 'I meant to phone you earlier today, but the time flew with meetings going on and on.'

'Oh, you're here on business.'

'And to see you. What will you have to drink?' he asked, leading her into the bar.

'A glass of white wine, please.'

The drink seemed to take the edge off some of her awkwardness. That and the extensive menu they pored over provided Cara with a certain amount of confidence.

They gave their order and were shown into the restaurant, made intimate with dim lighting.

'How have you been keeping?'

She managed to look directly at him. 'I'm fine.' She went on looking at him. His eyes dark and glittering with amusement, he said, 'Still loving the job?'

'Yes, but to be honest it's a bit lonely, especially with not having Vanessa at the other end of the phone. How are you?'

He nodded his head. 'Good.' He was quiet.

'How's Ian?'

'He's enjoying being back at school. He's with a nice group of kids this year, made friends already. It's lonely without him though,' he said reflectively. 'I don't like living alone.'

'Yes, I suppose it stands to reason you must be lonely.'

'I thought that was all over when I met you.' He looked at her. 'I miss you, Cara, and the way things were when we were seeing each other all the time, before all the trouble.'

He was making it easier for her, Cara thought as she cut into her calamari and took a forkful to lift to her mouth. Her hand shook a little, so instead she rested her fork on her plate and took a gulp of wine to fortify her nerves.

'Dad told me he asked you to keep away from me.'

'Yes. Yes.' His knuckles whitened round the glass he was holding.

He was staring at her. 'He didn't like the fact that I was seeing you while you were still married to someone else. He made it known what he expected of me. I didn't blame him.'

Embarrassed, Cara blushed, 'It's the sort of interference which makes things worse than they really are sometimes.'

'He made me realise that my presence in your life was only causing you further pain. That I was doing you no good.'

'He gets funny ideas. No one would want to listen to him. Believe me, I know, I speak from experience. He's prone to summing up a situation before it's fully clear to him.'

Guy looked doubtful. 'You mustn't blame him entirely. He had your interest at heart and, believe me, Cara, if you'd really wanted me in your life he wouldn't have put me off.'

'Oh!'

Guy shook his head. 'He didn't sway my decision. If you'd given me the least encouragement I'd have stayed around. But you wanted to get on with your life and I couldn't change your mind on that.'

'Perhaps I was a bit hasty.' Cara paused and looked up at him. 'Perhaps I should have fought harder for the good things. What you and I had together was good. I realise that now.'

Remorse at the thought of having to live her life without him made her eyes fill with tears, much to her disgust.

'You'd made your decision and you had to work through it. I went away unhappily,' Guy said. 'You gave me nothing to hope for.'

As if in some way she might compensate for this she said, 'That's why I got in touch with you.' Before her courage deserted her she rushed on, 'Oh, Guy, don't you see? I don't want to lose you.'

Surprised at her sudden outburst, Guy put down his knife and fork; 'I don't want to lose you either, Cara.' He was frowning, his face in confusion, the words he was saying not corresponding with the look of in his eyes.

Cara went rigid. 'What's the matter?' she asked, alarmed.

Guy shook his head. 'I couldn't ask you to give up your lifestyle for me, now that you're getting there, making it on your own. I tried that once before, and I'm not going to make that mistake again. You have to follow your dream.'

'I'm sure we could work something out. It wouldn't have to be conventional; it could be anything we like. I know there are things I want to do, like making a go of Mathew's business, buy it, perhaps, and that's where it all gets mixed up. It's just something I feel I have to do.' She laughed, embarrassed.

'I don't want to get in your way, or do anything that will necessarily cause you pain.' His hand went up in a nervous gesture.

Guy continued eating at a loss for a solution. Cara sipped her wine and looked out the window towards the harbour. The ferry was waiting patiently for all its passengers to board. Cara was thinking of Vanessa and Edward, probably on the other side of the world, and Suzanne and Dick, starting all over again, trying to make a go of their marriage. She thought of her father and Pamela, learning to live with his retirement, and Elsie, battling it out with them. She thought of Ian, happy again, and she thought of her lost marriage, Andy, and the time that seemed to have been wasted trying to save it, Andy definitely on the other side of the world, chasing another dream.

'There are worse things that could happen to me than you getting in the way,' Cara said.

'What would be the worst thing?'

'That you would never come back into my life. It's only a two-hour journey from the airport to Bufferstown and I could go to Edinburgh some weekends.'

'That arrangement would give us a chance to see how we get on together, wouldn't it? We could try it, by all means, but don't you think that we'd want to spend a bit of time together first? he said. 'You know, Cara, it's very important to learn what day to day living together would be like.'

'Yes, I know it is,' Cara frowned.

'Relax. It's not marriage I'm proposing.'

Marriage had become typified by a memory of drunkenness and fights, and Andy walking out, Cara awaiting his return, anticipating something dangerous or violent to happen.

'Could you take your holidays and come to stay in Edinburgh for a bit?'

'I suppose I could.'

They smiled at one another in agreement for once.

As they left the restaurant the sun was setting in ribbons of crimson. The sky was dark and colourless. Guy drew close to her, suggesting complicity.

'We could start the holiday now if you like. I'm staying at the Strand Hotel tonight.'

Cara looked at his face, full of love, and wondered how she ever believed that she could have lived without him. She could almost hear Vanessa whisper in her ear. 'If you want him, go and get him back. He's the only one who bowled you over.'

He caught Cara's eye and grinned at her, holding her in his gaze.

What else could she do but agree. She reached up, her arms clasping him.

'Guy!'

He raised her chin, the coolness of his fingers sensuous on her face. His eyes on her were flecked with gold. How beautiful he is, she thought, drunk with lust for him. Maybe she would pine for home when she was in Edinburgh, knowing no one there, unable to find her way around, but what the hell, she'd give it a try.

'Too much worrying about the future is unproductive,' Guy said, as if reading her thoughts.

She said, 'I love you, Guy.'

He held her so tight that no answer was necessary.

'I've made you smell of perfume,' she laughed, sniffing his jacket.

Live a little, Vanessa had said. With a jolt Cara realised that she'd only been existing without him.

What a life before them; a life of loving, confiding, consoling and adventure, she thought, walking beside him, holding his hand. This is it, she said to the lightly falling rain as they made their way to the hotel.